Without a word, Refit squeezed the trigger. The shotgun *ba-loomed* in the confined space. The double-ought pattern caught the mercenary dead center in the chest.

He staggered back, arms jerking from the impact, his pistol flying away. He bounced off the hangar wall behind him. Miraculously, he remained standing.

The first thing Refit noticed was the lack of blood.

Bent over from the force of the pellets, the merc straightened, revealing a tattered shirt with no body armor underneath. His stomach and chest were pocked with deep holes centered in bunches of pulpy-looking flesh. The man stretched his arms at his sides and grunted. "Hurts like hell, but you can't kill me."

The puckers in his flesh suddenly spat out the double-ought buckshot. Still perfectly round, they went bouncing across the pavement.

Refit fired again, but the hammer fell on an empty chamber.

Other TSR® Books

F.R.E.E.Lancers
Mel Odom

Dragons Can Only Rust
Chrys Cymri

Dragon Reforged
Chrys Cymri

Winged Magic
Mary H. Herbert

Runes of Autumn
Larry and Robert Elmore
(available July 1996)

Trail of Darkness
Darlene D. Bolesny
(available September 1996)

F.R.E.E. Fall

Mel Odom

F.R.E.E.Fall

Random House and its affiliate companies have worldwide distribution rights in the book trade for English language products of TSR, Inc.

Distributed to the book and hobby trade in the United Kingdom by TSR Ltd.

Distributed to the toy and hobby trade by regional distributors.

Cover art by Robh Ruppel.

First Printing: May 1996
Printed in the United States of America.
Library of Congress Catalog Card Number: 95-62206
ISBN: 0-7869-0493-3

8255XXX1501

9 8 7 6 5 4 3 2 1

TSR, Inc.
201 Sheridan Springs Rd.
Lake Geneva, WI 53147
U. S. A.

TSR Ltd.
120 Church End, Cherry Hinton
Cambridge CB1 3LB
United Kingdom

DEDICATION

This book is dedicated to two of the hardest working editors in the business.

Marlys Heeszel, whose warmth, perserverance and wit kept things together. And who shares an interest in those mysterious zombies popping up in New Orleans. Thanks, Marlys, and no more 360s on the ice!

Brian Thomsen, who invited me into this world of flawed heroes and dark intrigues. The best of the heroes seem to dwell the longest in the shadows. Looking forward to your next opus.

And to Brett Skogen, a classy guy who plays every ace on the line.

And finally, to the King, Elvis Presley, whose music kept me going into the small hours of every morning, and reminded me that you have to follow your dreams. I'm here, man, TCB.

1

Chicago, Illinois	***10:13 a.m. CST***
Great Lakes Authority (GLA)	***1613 Greenwich Mean***
87.7 degrees W Longitude	***March 28, 2024***
41.8 degrees N Latitude	***Friday***

Assignment: Charon's Crossing
Tactical Ops: Protection & Transportation of VIP
Status: Code Green

"You're the one they call Download, aren't you?"

With ease, Jefferson Scott navigated the gap between the double-parked delivery van and the street-cleaning droid working the gutter. There wasn't enough distance between the front bumper of the Alfa Romeo CLS Quadrifoglio he drove and the bright red fire panic station on the corner to put another coat of paint. The Daley-Shintai Plaza went by in a blur. People nearby scattered, and the old man minding the newschip stand put his hands over his eyes.

Scott pulled the two-seater high performance sports car back into the street, dropping the right two wheels off the curb and neatly cutting off a baby blue Oldsmobile Aerotech Romana.

The Olds screeched to a stop, and the driver laid on the horn in frightened indignation. The cleaning drone came to an automatic stop when it sensed the presence of the sedan.

Other cars on West Randolph Street had pulled over, giving way to the Quadrifoglio. Scott kept his attention loosely on his driving, remembering that the Chicago River was coming up; traffic at this time of the morning could be a pain.

"Yeah," he said to his passenger, "I'm Scott." He was of medium build and rangy, with short-cropped dark brown hair and watery hazel eyes that he'd noticed in an earlier inspection in the mirror were bloodshot all to hell.

At the intersection of Randolph and Franklin, he tapped the accelerator and laid on the horn. Traffic froze all around him, and he whizzed through against the red light.

His passenger, Patrick Cornell, was affiliated with Fiscal Development, Inc. out of the Middle Atlantic Alliance. Cornell was a dapper little guy in an expensive blue pin-stripe Armani that could have been traded in on a good used car with low mileage. Nothing as fancy as the Quadrifoglio, true, but Scott figured he could have gotten a three-year old Philigenco Aquino no problem.

At the moment, Download knew cars like nobody's business.

"Pay attention to how she handles," a gruff voice whispered in his ear. "This is a high-spirited lady you're grinding now, cowboy, not some no-clue shrew working off a feel-good stretch. You gotta coax and command all at the same time to get the best ride out of her."

Traffic along Randolph leading over the Chicago River was totally whacked. Stalled cars choked the road in the westbound lane. A bright green Channel 28 Instant News helicopter hovered over the area, the minicam waldo under its belly scanning the cars.

"There's been a wreck," Cornell said. He sat scrunched up in his seat, arms sucking like tentacles into the plush leather interior of the sports car.

"I see it," Download said. At least a dozen cars up, a flatbed-mounted float advertising Uncle Chou's Soy-PorkTubes and the Chicago White Sox had collided with a garbage truck. The guy who'd been dressed up in the weenie costume was wandering drunkenly through the gathering crowd while a mounted traffic cop tried to pursue.

"Double-clutch and downshift," the whisper said in Download's mind, "and stay off of the damn brake while you do it."

Download went with his reflexes, double-clutching and downshifting, keeping the rpms high. When he hit the accelerator again, the four-wheel-drive, four-wheel steering of the Italian sports car pulled it on-line and it shot south on North Wacker Drive.

"Is there any reason we're in such a hurry?" Cornell asked.

"We're late, hombre," Download growled in a voice that wasn't quite his own.

Cornell looked at him, eyes wide as the car's speed accelerated yet again. "Are you all right? You sound different."

"I'm just jim-dandy," Download replied. He looked away from the street just long enough to give the corporate executive the winning smile that had crossed hundreds of finish lines all over the world. It wasn't Scott's smile, though, and it felt oddly out of place on his face.

"Damn Yankee sissy-boy," the voice said in his mind.

Download agreed with the opinion, though he knew if he was in his own right mind—or at least *alone* in his own right mind—he'd probably be a little tense himself. But he wasn't alone. Dwayne "Bighouse" Ryerson was riding shotgun inside his head. In his time, Big, as he was called by all his friends, had been one of the best Grand Prix drivers around. For the time, his skills were all Download's.

That was all courtesy of the Download device, created by Dr. Andrew J. Rhand, FREELancers' one-man Research & Development brain trust. The device was actually in two pieces. One part was back at the FREELancers' base where it could digitize various skills from unique individuals who possessed them, so they could later be used by Jefferson Scott.

The other part of the device rode Scott's right shoulder like some mechanical insect leeched into his flesh through the regulation FREELancers-gray jumpsuit with crimson piping. Steel-sheathed fiber-optic cables were wired directly into the right side of his brain through implant modules.

Somehow, though even Dr. Rhand didn't know the means, a number of the people whose skills had been loaded onto the disks had managed to find a home in Scott's mind. So many phantom afterimages were in there now Scott had lost count, and there wasn't a day that some of them didn't try to intrude on his thoughts. But Big was a favorite of his, a huge man with a good nature and a Texas-sized smile.

"I read about you," Cornell said as they screeched into the westbound lane of Madison. "You're not a metable, are you?"

"No," Download replied. They shot across the Chicago River. If he could catch the traffic just right at the on-ramps at John F. Kennedy Expressway, he figured they could still make O'Hare Airport on time.

Metables were a whole new breed, and many of the FREE-Lancers were metable. Scientists who'd done research on the subject of metability were convinced metables had been there all along. Mathematical and musical prodigies displaying amazing abilities were referred to as Savants, and those metabilities were the most common denominator. Many metables, the scientists argued, had existed in the past but lacked the means to express their Savantism. If a prodigal child was born into a backward community where musical instruments were unavailable, or the community had a limited system of counting, no one ever would have known.

But music and math weren't the only areas in which metabilities had flourished. With the increasing growth and speed in science and technology in the last century, many other metabilities had surfaced. A number were rooted in physical manifestations involving what had been known as extrasensory perception. Others were due to slight cellular changes involving molecular energy exchanges and metabolic efficiency.

"Why couldn't we have met Ms. Underhill at her office?"

"Lee is a busy lady," Download said. "She's just getting back from a business meeting down in New Orleans."

"About opening a branch office in the Ohio-Lower Mississippi Basin Cooperative, like the media has been hinting about?" Though obviously terrified, Cornell showed definite signs of interest.

Download remembered then that Fiscal Development, Inc. dealt in investments. "I'm afraid I'm not at liberty to say."

The media had been full of speculation lately, and a lot of it had centered around the possibility of a public release of stock to fund the branch office. At the same time, the Ohio-Lower Mississippi Basin Cooperative had been trying to get its act together and devise a cohesive government, something it hadn't had since the United States fragmented in 2011.

However, god only knew how many of the voodoo stories coming out of the Gulf were true. *ScreamBytes*, the largest-selling New Age magazine of its kind, had reported sightings of the dead crawling from their crypts and graves. Sociologists were just beginning to study the rudimentary communities the dead were setting up in the sewers under the major cities.

Download kept his foot hard on the accelerator as they roared across the Chicago River.

"Perhaps I could make it worth your while to tell me what you do know," Cornell said. He put his arm against the window as the Quadrifoglio screamed around a corner.

"Whatever you do," Download said, "you must be involved in a lot of money. Lee doesn't put up with jerks unless they can pay for the privilege of pissing her off." The on-ramp for the John F. Kennedy Expressway was in front of him.

An eighteen-wheeler carrying perishables sped toward the on-ramp. Black smoke peeled back from the twin stacks.

Download raced for the on-ramp, slipping out into the oncoming traffic lane to get the necessary room to maneuver. "Just take it easy, son," Big whispered inside his mind. The noise of the big truck's diesel engine rattled inside the sports car, muted by the acoustic defenses till it sounded as if it were miles away instead of only feet. "You're gonna make this run like a big dog shaking off water."

"You can't make that!" Cornell cried, putting his hands on the dash in front of him and bracing himself in the seat.

Download grinned, though he knew the expression wasn't his own. When the skill transfers took and didn't bring much psychological baggage with them, it was easy to enjoy the feeling of confidence granted by the software.

"Can too," Big chuckled in the back of his mind.

The cel phone mounted on the dash rang, and Download picked it up. He was passing the eighteen-wheeler now, drawing almost bumper to bumper. "Scott," he said.

"We've got a Metable Condition Red squeal from the Chicago special unit," Matrix said. "They're asking for assistance."

Of all the people in the FREELancers operation, Download felt Matrix was almost as screwed up by what life had handed her as he was. At one time, the former Irene Domino had had a husband, two children, a mortgage, and a full-time job as homemaker. Pressures created by the children and her husband's job situation caused her Savant abilities to surface, creating an alternate personality.

Blackouts started, robbing her first of minutes, then hours, and finally whole chunks of time. Later, no one could really say when she'd started beating her teenagers at video games, but police detectives had little trouble locating all the automatic tellers she'd rewired and stolen money from.

Her defense counsel argued that the second personality had created itself as an answer to the personal and economic pressures Irene was having, then went out and committed the crimes. The jury didn't see it that way.

Irene Domino was given two years in a medium-security women's prison. Only a few months into her sentence, her husband divorced her and took custody of the children, leaving her with a court order to stay away from them. In the writ, Irene was referred to as an unstable personality who might harm herself and her children.

Lee Won Underhill had learned of the Savant through sources of her own, but if the woman's abilities with computers hadn't been phenomenal, the FREElancers' director never would have gone to the prison and offered her a job with the agency. That had been years ago, and now Irene Domino was Matrix. She hadn't gotten any closer to reclaiming her family, but that was by choice. Despite all the counseling she'd undergone, and the training she'd had on computers, both legitimate and in prison, her Savant side still lurked in her mind. Any time a programming problem reached out and attracted her too much, her human self was submerged and the Savant took over, determined to conquer whatever challenge was before it.

"Who's catching?" Download asked. The on-ramp was seventy yards away and closing.

"Refit and the Tandems," Matrix replied. "The Tandems are already busy farther north. Refit's on a special op and can't come off. You're the closest agent we have in the area."

Part of the special agreement the FREELancers had with Mayor Hubbard and the city of Chicago was to handle any and all metable problems that cropped up. The primary reason for their involvement was because FREELancers was the largest collection of metables in the GLA, and the theory was to fight fire with fire. But a close second was the fact that Underhill wanted first shot at recruitment.

Even though the FREELancers agents put a good face on being metable, they still were not largely accepted by the general populace.

"I'm going to be late," Download said. "I'm pushing the clock now."

"The metable is a thirteen-year-old boy," Matrix said. Her voice was softer, yet more strained. "I've done some checking into his background since I got the call. There's a history of abuse. His stepfather. I haven't gotten all the details." She hesitated for a moment. "Please, Jefferson."

Big was already nudging Download's mind. "You can't turn down a woman's honest request for help, old son."

Download knew it. Despite everything—all the years of substance abuse and the phantoms that crowded the shadowed areas of his mind—there was a big piece of him that was all too human. "Call the Dragon Lady," he told Matrix, "after you give me the address." He downshifted and tapped the brake, shedding speed like a DuckTool Sewer Scavenger shedding slime. The eighteen-wheeler roared ahead, its rear bumper missing the front of the Quadrifoglio by inches. Cornell seemed to experience an epiphany of religious conviction as they slewed in front of an armored car with Japanese markings.

A line of red script pulsed across the windshield, replacing the speedometer readings. THIS UNIT HAS BEEN TARGETED BY MISSILE-CAPABLE WEAPONS. RECOMMEND EVASIVE ACTION AT ONCE.

The Quadrifoglio's power plant screamed as Download pinned the accelerator to the floor. In a heartbeat, the Japanese courier was a memory. One hand on the wheel, he reached under the seat and pulled out the magnetic cherry, rolled down the window, and stuck it on top of the car.

After all, now he was on official business.

* * * * *

Outside Melaka City, Melaka ***11:24 p.m. Local Mean***
Indonesia ***1624 Greenwich Mean***
102.3 degrees E Longitude ***March 29, 2024***
2.4 degrees N Latitude ***Friday***

"We've found another entrance, sir."

Colonel Will Tabor stepped out of the armored Land Rover and moved swiftly into the protective cover provided by his men. "Keep it here and running," he told the driver.

"Yes, sir," the man replied, offering a respectful salute from the brim of his sweat-stained hat.

"You're sure it's another entrance to the catacombs?" Tabor asked as he joined the smaller man at the side of the street.

"Positive."

Tabor glanced up and down the street. Melaka City, under martial law as it was, didn't have much in the way of nightlife. But he knew the underground, which objected to the way he'd stepped into leadership of the country, plotted against him continuously.

The skyline was dark, unbroken by the street lights that stood at silent attention above many of the single-story structures. The onion domes of the Islamic mosques looked like mushrooms scattered throughout the city. Occasionally, some of them were lit up by the three-unit helo patrol Tabor had ordered maintained around the urban area. The streets sloped gently toward the coastline, and the wind blowing in from the west carried the strong smell of fish from the docks.

"I thought exploration of the catacombs below this mosque was finished six weeks ago," Tabor said. He was a big man, standing six-feet-five and going three hundred pounds, which would have surprised anyone just looking at him because he was so proportionately built. He had deep coppery hair that hung in ringlets almost to his shoulders and a thick walrus mustache. His face was pale, the freckles covering it burned dark into the skin. He had cerulean blue eyes, but the right one was covered by a bionic goggle screwed directly into his face. His hawkish gaze missed nothing. He was dressed in a Banana Republic vest over a khaki shirt with the sleeves rolled up to midforearm and khaki jodhpurs tucked into calf-high military boots. A radio in a pseudo-leather harness rode his left shoulder; its ear/throat hook-up dangled around his neck.

"Nine weeks ago," Chee Kim Fook said. He looked incredibly small beside the colonel. Thin and wizened, with a shaved head and almost twice Tabor's thirty-eight years of age, Fook wore a cheap summer suit that had once been white but was now gray from wear and the tropical heat. He cleaned his wire-rimmed spectacles with a monogrammed handkerchief. "But during cleanup only a few hours ago, another branch of the tunnels was discovered."

Tabor's heart sped up in anticipation as he walked through the side door of the mosque. He crossed himself as he passed through the foyer. Melaka was a land filled with religion. The Islamic beliefs were the most widely practiced, but stood alongside Buddhism, Confucianism, Christianity, Hinduism, and animism, which was practiced by the interior tribes.

The interior of the mosque was marginally lit by candles. "Does anyone else know about this?" Tabor asked. The Melakan underground had developed a number of deep-throats within his organization, not because his men were selling him out, but because they were so confident of their hold on the nation that they weren't careful whom they spoke in front of.

"No," Fook answered.

Tabor took a penflash from inside his vest and switched it on while Fook took a battery-powered lantern from a niche against the door leading to the children's praying room, where the first entrance to the catacombs beneath the mosque had been located.

A thin carpet rendered in mandarin orange and patterned with huge flowers covered the floor. The room was small, and there was no furniture. Often upon walking through smaller mosques like this one, Tabor had seen the children laboring over the Koran, learning to read the Arabic language.

Two of Tabor's sec-force stood beside a rectangular opening in the back wall. The crisp lines of their sky-blue uniforms held a film of plaster dust. The edges of the opening looked as if they'd been hacked out of the underpinning of the wall with a hand axe.

Tabor shined the penflash into the opening. A narrow set of stairs corkscrewed down into darkness, as if they were sinking under the weight of the low, uneven ceiling that followed them. Battery-powered torches were spaced along the outside of the wall. Their light was erratic, some of the batteries nearly dead.

"I want new batteries installed in these units, Wallsey," Tabor told the sec-sergeant beside him.

The sergeant nodded. "Yes, sir." He turned and spoke quickly over his hand-held radio.

Tabor had no worries that the assignment would not be swiftly carried out. Pete Wallsey had been with him during the Mideastern Sand Wars when Iraq had overrun their position with the horn-plated Wyrm Kings that had tossed tanks and MAP units aside like a child's toys. A lot of experienced men had died in that battle before Tabor had been able to set off the low-yield tactical nuke that had wiped out the nest the Iraqi bio-war department had designed.

Playing the penflash beam over the interior of the narrow corridor, Tabor followed it down. Fook was a shadow at his heels.

The corridor had been constructed of like-shaped stones and carefully mortared into place. It held a finished look, but showed splotchy stains where water had seeped through into the lower chambers. It had taken almost two days with gasoline-powered pumps to clear three of the lower rooms that had been below the current water table. As close as it was to the Strait of Malacca and Indian Ocean, the country had a lot of groundwater, though much of it wasn't usable, contaminated as it was by the sea salt that washed up through the various tributaries.

A feeling of vertigo swirled through Tabor with a brief, electric intensity. The stone steps were narrow and shallow, making it hard to find a comfortable pace that wasn't jarring or too widely spaced.

Ten feet up from the bottom of the winding stairs, a new hole had been broken through the inside wall of the curve. Broken rock littered the steps. Three sec-men labored over two five-gallon buckets connected to a single pole, filling them by hand. Over their lower faces, they wore filter masks, already stained dark with accumulated powder.

"A new torch was being hung," Fook said, handing Tabor a mask. "The man doing it thought he heard a hollow space on the other side of the wall."

"I thought all the walls had been thoroughly checked." Tabor slipped the mask over his head, the strap catching briefly on the bionic goggle over his reconstructed eye. Fast as he was, the Wyrm King had been chained lightning on the attack. One of its legs, hard with a chitinous outer coating and equipped with a daggerlike horned projection, had removed the eye and wrecked the orbital.

The wound and the period of time after had been a turning point for Tabor. Even hiring out to fight other people's wars held little in the way of recompense. Replacing the eye had been arduous and expensive, and the government he'd worked for had given him only a medal with a pretty ribbon attached and a few cluckings of sympathy. Then they'd gone in to see what they could reap from the prize Tabor and his unit had delivered to them. That's why, when Melaka had come along with all its promise, he'd struck fast . . . and for himself.

"They were," Fook said. "The man who found this one was lucky. You'll see when you take a look at the wall."

The sec-men stepped back at Tabor's approach.

The colonel ran the beam around the opening. The wall

separating the newly discovered chamber from the corridor was easily three times as thick as any of the walls they'd gone through so far. Long white scratches marred the surface of the rock left in place around it.

There wasn't enough room for a walkway. The opening began barely two feet above the stone stairway and was only little more than that wide.

Tabor dropped to one knee and examined the opening. The rectangular hole shot straight back for over two feet. Crawling through was going to be a major exertion. He rubbed his hand over the rock surface, instantly coating his fingers with dust. Even with the mask on, he could taste the sour smell of the stones and the centuries that had passed since the tunnel had been walled up.

The darkness at the other end of the opening swallowed up the penflash's beam.

"This section is older than the catacombs we found here earlier," Tabor said.

"Yes." Fook knelt on the steps above him, also peering into the hole.

"Who's in there?"

"Zeiter and Robbins."

"Anyone else been in there?" Keeping the area secure was a primary concern. There was much still to be learned, and the scrolls sometimes weren't large enough to be readily noticed.

"No," Fook said.

Tabor unbuckled his gunbelt and slid it off. His jacket and uniform blouse were next, leaving him stripped down to his undershirt. The humidity had already drenched him with perspiration. "What about Margo?" He shined the penflash into the hole and shoved his arm inside.

"I have already requested her presence." Fook hesitated. "She was less than cooperative. She took great care in elaborating the point that she'd just finished a forty-two hour shift inspecting the items we'd discovered in the other chambers."

Forcing himself into the hole, Tabor found the fit almost impossible. He made himself relax, fighting against the claustrophobia that threatened to overwhelm him. "Did you tell her this branch of the catacombs appears to be even older than the ones we've previously been through?"

"She had the nerve to ask me if I was sure," Fook said. "I replied that I am not in the habit of making such mistakes in chronology, at which she made unforgivable references regarding my ancestry and personal hygiene practices."

Tabor refused to acknowledge the man's toadying and whining. At this point in the Melakan occupation, the talents Margo Peele brought with her were much more valuable than Fook's insights.

Although it didn't appear to do so, the shaft through the wall narrowed. Tabor locked his toes against the steps and leveraged as much muscle into the effort of getting through as he could. The perspiration coating his skin helped, making him slippery. Then he was able to grip the forward lip of the tunnel and pull even harder.

He breathed out, collapsing his lungs to make his chest smaller, fighting the urge to take a deep breath. Arms trembling with the effort, he pulled as hard as he could. The undershirt tore, and he felt his skin rip against the rough surface of the stone. If he got stuck, there was still a way out. He just didn't like being defeated at anything.

Abruptly, the restriction gave way, and he got his right shoulder through. He put the penflash in his mouth, biting through the filter mask to hold it, and grabbed the lip of the opening with both hands.

The room was maybe eight feet in height. It was hard to tell with the flat black of the pooled water covering the floor. The raw odor of trapped spoilage assaulted his nose, bringing up a retch reflex that he swallowed back with difficulty.

The walls were of uneven stone and spun around in an oval cylinder almost ten feet across. An artificed stone door was to the right, pushed inward and barely visible to the penflash's beam. A stone walkway climbed up out of the water and disappeared. Wet footprints tracked the worn surface of the second tunnel.

Tabor took the penflash from his mouth, then yelled. "Robbins!"

The answer came from a distance away, echoing hollowly and

letting the colonel know that the voice was coming from an even bigger room. "Yes, sir."

"How deep is this water, Corporal?" Tabor asked, playing the penflash over the liquid surface.

"About a foot, sir," Robbins yelled back. "You want to mind your step; the bottom is bloody slick."

Tabor pushed out of the tunnel and dropped into the water, which didn't come up much past midcalf. His boots were watertight. "Where's Zeiter?" He directed the penflash's beam against the cobwebbed ceiling so the light would be reflected over the whole room.

"With me, Colonel. We've set up a sec-post here. There're more tunnels branching off the main chamber, but they're all locked. Figured we'd wait on you before we started kicking doors in."

Fook climbed through the tunnel next, bringing Tabor's gunbelt and radio. He grimaced, the expression hidden by the filter mask except for the squinted eyes.

Tabor reached to the side of his head and pressed the button by his bionic eye. The operation had successfully given him back 20/20 vision through the damaged optic nerve, and the cybernetic orb also had thermal and magnification utilities built into it.

He punched up the thermal function and scanned the water, but nothing carried a heat signature. Going back to normal vision, he took the gunbelt and radio from Fook and strapped them into place.

Images on the wall caught his eye. They were almost hidden by the accumulation of dust and dead bacteria growth.

Tabor slipped his Gerber Mark VII fighting knife from the top of his left boot and used it to scratch at the inch-thick conglomeration. The extinct mass flaked away easily and dropped onto the water. Spores erupted in minute specks.

Tabor drew back and held his breath till the spores settled into the water. Some of what they'd uncovered in the various catacombs was still undecipherable, and much of it was dangerous. Biological agents had been among the discoveries.

"Something lived down here at one time," Tabor said.

"Otherwise that bacteria never would have grown." He played the beam over massive layers of webbing, searching for movement, but there was none. Evidently the spiders that had built the webs had also died out.

Wadding up a handkerchief, Tabor used it to wipe off a layer of buildup from the images on the walls. Rather than being done in the same cuneiform style as many of the other writings they'd discovered, large sections here were pictographs.

"For the love of god," Fook whispered hoarsely.

Tabor knew what he was talking about. The drawing in the lower right corner of the cleaned area naturally drew the eye.

Leading up to it were ornate drawings of a man wearing robes of royalty. The artwork was stiff and angular rather than loose and flowing. The man stood in front of a vertical sarcophagus covered with symbols. Once, the drawing had possessed color. During the passage of centuries and possibly thousands of years, the color had leached out of the stone or was drawn farther into it.

In the pictographs, the man was paying obeisance in front of the sarcophagus, his forehead to the floor, palms flat on either side of his face. In the next drawing, the sarcophagus lid was open and a nightmare being had emerged, all disjointed and drawn in heavy black, the head misshapen and too large for its body.

The next pictograph showed the nightmare-thing holding the robed man with two multijointed arms, offset by two other arms that were eviscerating the man, pulling the intestines out in knotted gobs.

Then the sound of a man's frightened death screams ricocheted through the chamber.

2

Chicago, Illinois | *10:33 a.m. CST*
Great Lakes Authority (GLA) | *1633 Greenwich Mean*
87.7 degrees W Longitude | *March 28, 2024*
41.8 degrees N Latitude | *Friday*

Assignment: Electra
Tactical Ops: Apprehension, Use Necessary Force
Status: Code Red

Seated behind the wheel of a Ford Econoline van that had last seen a coat of paint and exterior bodywork years ago, Refit watched the street crowds roving the West Side neighborhood. Most of the businesses in the area were sole proprietorships barely hanging on to economic life: hole-in-the-wall restaurants, pawn shops, a used-electronics outlet, secondhand clothing stores, and a closed laundry.

Halfway down the block, a man on a ladder was painting over a sign that had said "Two Guys From Sacramento." The new sign would read "Two Guys From Trinidad" even though there was only one restaurant owner. During a brief coffee run an hour ago, Refit had talked briefly with Feroze, the new proprietor, who *was* from Trinidad while the two guys from Sacramento had lived in Bakersfield.

The cuisine was also going to change, the restaurateur explained. People in the area weren't bean sprout and avocado eaters as the previous management had thought; they actually wanted hot and spicy Trinidad dishes. Feroze was convinced he'd make it big.

The waitress who'd filled Refit's thermos, a black woman in her midthirties named Augusta, wasn't convinced. She'd worked at the location when it had been "Two Guys From Greece," "Two Guys From Hong Kong," and "Two Guys From Ho Chi Minh City." Feroze had hired her, impressed with the way his prospective clientele all seemed to know her. She had an affinity for memorizing menus, she said, even when they were in foreign languages. Refit knew it was a Savant ability.

Augusta was also familiar with the face in the picture Refit showed her. The waitress recognized Jeannine Hartley from the street, not as the runaway daughter of GLA congressional representative Harris Hartley, who was presently expecting appointment to the GLA's ambassadorial steering committee after the unexpected death of Ethan Weisenthal. The waitress had confirmed Refit's intel that the Hartley girl was staying in the run-down apartment building across the street at the end of the block.

Refit had been watching the building for almost three hours since turning it up from street sources. It was boring work and allowed too much time for inner reflection. He kept the radio on, listening to a Golden Oldies channel where Elvis was changing addresses to Heartbreak Hotel and feeling lonely. The music was almost twice his age, but it keyed into the big man's tattered and savage soul.

A cluster of young men and women wearing black leather and chains caught Refit's attention. He reached into the passenger seat and caught up a small pair of United Weapons binoculars. Peering through them intently, he zeroed in on the razored mop of blond hair on the person at the lead of the street gang, then adjusted the magnification.

Jeannine Hartley's features were filled with hard lines. A twisted and scarred cyborged hand was tattooed on her right cheek in neon green and yellow, outlined in thick maroon lines. It was new. None of the pictures Refit had seen showed the tattoo, nor was there any mention of it in the text files he'd been given.

She was tall and thin, with only a hint of femininity beneath the leathers. From the way her clothes hung, Refit guessed she was carrying a pistol tucked in the front of her pants under the deliberately bloodstained tee shirt.

"Damn," Refit said as he dropped the binocs back into the passenger seat.

The tattoo announced that she belonged to the Cybered Shadows, an Asian street gang that had followed the Japanese into FREEAmerica. They were loosely affiliated with the Yakuza.

Jeannine Hartley for damn sure wasn't acting as if she were with the group against her will. If anything, she was leading it. Her father had been adamant about the fact that she'd been kidnapped when he'd talked to Underhill a few days ago, though he hadn't been able to explain the lack of a ransom demand. The congressman had appeared very distraught.

Looking at the girl now, Refit no longer had any illusions about the assignment being any kind of save. It was a salvage job, pure and simple. He also had the feeling the congressman was definitely thinking more of his appointment than his daughter. Jeannine Hartley was nineteen years old and was apparently determined to jump into the grave with both feet, her eyes locked firmly on her objective.

At the end of the block, Jeannine slid a passcard through the sec-lock on the doorway leading to the flight of stairs going to the upper floor apartments. The lower floor had once housed a vid theater, but it was closed now. Plywood sheets had been nailed over the windows of the ticket office and had gang markings spraypainted on them.

Jeannine led the way through the door.

Refit tagged the Burris transceiver on his trench coat collar. The sat-link put him through to the FREELancers Base.

"Matrix."

"Electra just went red," Refit said.

"You have visual confirmation?" Matrix asked.

"Yep. I'm on my way to see about bringing her in." Reaching under the seat, Refit slid out a plastic crate and took out two pairs of disposable plastic handcuffs.

"I'll call Underhill and let her know."

"Tell her I think we got snowed by the congressman," Refit said. "His daughter's with a gang called the Cybered Shadows, and she's there of her own free will."

"Anything else?"

"Give me ten minutes, then call the Chicago PD and ask for Detective Amos Haddonfield. When you get him, tell him I need an interface with the gangbangers unit and that he's going to be rolling into a hot zone." Refit gave her the location and ended the connection. Personally, he didn't think the FREE-Lancers administrator had been taken in by the lie. She'd known how things stood and assigned him anyway. Vaguely, it pissed the big man off, but these days he was willing to admit it didn't take much.

He opened the door and got out. At present, he was close to his natural height of six feet four inches. His face, like the rest of him, was scarred and tinted an unhealthy corpselike gray. His chestnut hair was short, wiry, and patchy due to the burn scars that marred his features. He was built broad and strong, partially due to his original genetics and partially from a long career as a steelworker.

That had been before the bomb planted by a faction of Temporary People lashing out at the steel mill's pro-union policy. Kent Mertz spearheaded the Temporary People and their anti-union tactics, which included out-and-out terrorism. The bomb had been intended for union officials visiting the mill. It had successfully eliminated all of them and most of the workers on the late shift. Charles Henry Magastowkawicz was one of the few survivors.

Upon seeing that he was burned over ninety percent of his body, the surgeons attending him had chopped his ruined legs off and expected him to die before morning. During the weeks that followed, he'd come to find out that he was a metable. Although his body couldn't repair the damage that had been done to it, doctors found he was the perfect donor accepter, with an immunosuppressive gene like none they'd ever seen. As a result, he could take massive transplants of tissue without risking rejection. Feeling that Charles Henry had died that night, and some *thing* had shambled out of the wreckage of the mill and the man, he took on the name Refit.

Crosshatches of scars, as thick as caterpillars, showed every seam of where his body had been stuck back together with mismatched parts. It was just meat, there for him to use and abuse as he needed. There was plenty more where that came from. For years he thought he'd dealt with that. Then Risa DeSpain, an EMT who had helped him on an earlier FREELancers assignment, had shown interest in him and had spent patient months pursuing contact through the agency. So far he'd avoided her, but he couldn't avoid the part of him that still longed for a normal life.

He walked to the side of the van and slid the door open. Without windows around the sides or in back, no one could see in. The rear of the van was stripped down to bare metal. A couple of steel rings had been welded to support struts on the ceiling, and bolted into the floor behind the two forward seats was a locked metal box. Refit operated the numerical combination lock and pulled the lid open.

He wore a long trench coat over his FREELancers jumpsuit, so the only thing that showed were brief patches of light gray pants tucked into hand-tooled cowboy boots. He added a fedora, then turned down the brim to help mask his features.

With the Cybered Shadows in the picture, going heeled was a matter of course. He took a Detonics .45 from the box and dropped it into the pocket of the trench coat, followed by a handful of extra magazines. The rounds were Para-bullets, gel capsules primed to explode on contact and induce unconsciousness with a minimum of physical injury. He added an aerosol can of OC.

After he locked the weapons box and the van, he turned toward the closed theater. Some of the letters remained on the marquee, announcing: LI E GIR S! NUD ! XAVER A HOLLNDE IN "CO-EDS GET ING DOWN ON T E FARM!"

The apartment building rose four stories above the abandoned theater. Refit didn't think he'd have any trouble finding the Cybered Shadows. He slipped a PassMaster card through the sec-lock slot and listened while the alternate programming did its biz, shunting through the simple binary systems. Without the FREELancers ID he carried, having the PassMaster would have guaranteed him ten years in a state penal institution.

The smell of piss and spoiled food burned the inside of Refit's nose as soon as he stepped into the foyer. Garbage bags had tumbled down the stairs, spilling a cornucopia of soy-coffee grounds, fast-food wrappers, and wadded diapers. At one time the shattered window at the first landing had been held together with gray duct tape, but chunks of it were missing now. A piece of cardboard had been taped over the outside.

Refit went up the stairs, past the wall of graffiti where children had left Crayon hieroglyphics that had been painted over in neon spray by the Cybered Shadows to mark their territory. Shards of light bulbs remained in the sockets overhead.

He stopped at the first apartment at the second floor landing and knocked on the door. No one answered, and he repeated it.

"Nobody lives there," a male voice told him.

Refit turned.

The speaker was a small Hispanic man standing in the open door of an apartment across the narrow hall. The remains of a Berliner Defense sec-droid pod that looked as if it had been ripped from a wall or ceiling, judging from the plaster chunks that still clung to it, sat only a short distance from the door on a crooked section of matted carpet. The weapon pod had been stripped from it.

"I'm looking for somebody," Refit said. "Maybe you can help."

"Mister," the man said, taking a pack of cigarettes from under one sleeve of his white tee shirt, "nobody around here knows nobody else's business." Still working one-handed, he shook out a cigarette and lipped it without taking his eyes from the FREELancers agent or revealing what was in his other hand. "Not if they know what's good for them. You know what I mean?"

"I'm looking for the Shadows."

"You a po-liceman?"

"No."

The man smiled, but it was cold and sterile, an expression shaped just for looks. "Good thing. Last po-liceman come around here looking for the Shadows got taken away in body bags from the alley out back."

"I'm not going out that way," Refit said.

"You must have a truck to carry your *cojones* around, homes."

"Just deep pockets," the FREELancers agent replied.

The man gave a dry chuckle. "I guess so. The Shadows, you'll find them on the top floor. Keep most of it to themselves. They're being led by some blond bitch now that's got no sense of humor at all. She's the one did for the cop."

Refit started up the next flight of stairs. "They keep a watchdog out?"

"Most times. I got a tip, homes. They see you, you might as well get down to it, man. You look like nine miles of bad road. They gonna know this ain't no social call."

"Never been accused of being a buttercup," Refit said. The man's laughter followed him up the stairs. He shoved his hand into his trench coat pocket and wrapped it around the Detonics .45.

More levels of debris and depression were stacked on top of each other. Seeing it, going back in his mind to the life he'd known as a child in Gary, Indiana sparked the anger that always accompanied him. No matter what the situation, he always felt its weight inside his chest.

When he'd joined the FREELancers, it was because he'd felt there was nowhere else to go. His unemployment was running out, and the insurance was structured so that it wasn't paying for all of his medical bills. Despite their curiosity about his condition, the doctors were still interested in getting paid. George Anthony Underhill, then head of the FREELancers, had recruited him and made the bills go away.

But somewhere along the way, a piece of Refit—an original piece of Charles Henry—had wanted to believe that belonging to an organization like the FREELancers could make a difference. Instead, his experiences had jaded him.

Going after Jeannine Hartley in the present circumstances was a real bender.

A little girl no more than two years old was playing outside a closed door halfway down the fifth floor hallway. She wore a diaper and nothing else. Her brown hair was down to her shoulders, and her eyes were still wide and innocent as she gazed up at him. She'd been chewing on a headless Barbie, but froze as he approached.

At the end of the hall, two leather-clad gangers wearing Cybered Shadows tattoos stopped leaning on the wall in front of the last door and glared at him.

Refit kept watch on them as he knelt and picked up the child. She started crying as soon as he had her. He turned, shielding her with his body in case the gangers attacked. They couldn't hurt him. He was wearing borrowed meat, but they didn't know that.

He knocked on the door. Strangely, the child didn't try to fight against him or yell very loud. She just curled up into a ball and whimpered, tears running down her florid cheeks.

The woman who answered the door was emaciated and outfitted with a bionic arm that looked as if it had quit functioning some time ago. Locked across the woman's stomach, the arm was stainless steel and ended in a purely functional three-fingered hand that had closed in on itself.

"She bothering you?" the woman asked, running her hand through her green-tinted hair in an attempt to smooth it into place. Her eyes were bleary, as if she'd just gotten up. She reached out and took the child in her one arm in a practiced maneuver. The little girl stayed in the compact ball but stopped crying. "Jeez, I'm sorry. Usually she just stays in the apartment, you know."

"I was just worried about the kid. Thought maybe she couldn't get back inside."

Some of the anxiety left the woman, and she hugged the child to her more tightly. "Well, thanks. Not many people around here would care." She licked her lips. "You looking for anybody special? I know some of the girls who work here.

Maybe I could point you in the right direction."

"I'm okay. Thanks."

"You look like a nice guy," the woman said. "If the girl you're here to see is busy, maybe you could drop by . . . see me instead."

Refit didn't know what to say. The offer surprised him.

"I know you're a nice guy," the woman said. "You could have hurt my kid. You didn't. That counts a lot in my book." She locked eyes with him. "You don't even have to pay me. Unless you want to, I mean. And the arm? It doesn't get in the way really."

"Thanks." It was the kindest thing Refit could think to say. He stepped away from the door.

The Cybered Shadows gangers had multiplied to five while he was talking. Two of them had baseball bats, and another had a length of tow chain. One of the two holding knives was a female.

Since they knew he was coming, Refit took the direct approach, cutting out anxiety as the middleman. He tagged the Burris transceiver, opening the channel to Matrix. "The PD?" he asked.

"Already en route. I've pulled your stats on-line through a direct satellite feed. Whatever happens to you, I'll be the next person to know." Matrix was also downloading audiovisual feeds from the apartment building for later use if necessary. Having his stats meant she'd know his medical condition at all times. Surgeons stood by at the FREELancers headquarters, but transplants were tricky.

"You got an ETA on the PD?" Refit asked.

"Ten, fifteen minutes. With the traffic, it's hard to estimate."

"Let me know."

"I will." Matrix sounded distant and cold, and Refit knew the Savant state was barely being held at bay as the cybernetics expert plied her talent. "Be careful."

Refit jammed his hands in the pockets of the trench coat and fisted the Detonics and the OC canister. He put on a smile. "Piece of cake. Just gonna work on a little aggression therapy."

3

O'Hare International Airport | *10:41 a.m. CST*
Great Lakes Authority (GLA) | *1641 Greenwich Mean*
87.7 degrees W Longitude | *March 28, 2024*
41.8 degrees N Latitude | *Friday*

Assignment: Oracle
Tactical Ops: Information Compilation
Status: Code Green

"Ms. Underhill." The speaker was a tall, gangly man with arms and legs much too long for his narrow body. Dressed in a conservatively cut dark blue suit that looked as if it had been fitted when he'd had a little more mass, he stood holding a card with his name on it, instead of hers, for security reasons. He had a thick mop of unruly red hair that he swept back out of his face, nearly knocking off his glasses.

Underhill didn't like his having called out her name so loudly in the airport terminal. Luckily, his voice didn't carry far, and the crowd was fairly extensive. She walked over to meet him, extending her hand and smiling. "Mr. Gregory."

"I'm on time," Gregory said, pointing at the Russian-made chron on his wrist.

"Yes." Underhill released his hand. At five feet in height, she barely reached Gregory's shoulder. Her glossy black hair was held up in a French braid. Dangling gold earrings held small garnets worked into the strands. Her burnished butter complexion, a result of American and Vietnamese ancestry, made her volcanic blue eyes more noticeable. She wore a white spandex skirt that ended just above her knees, white hose and heels, a white blouse buttoned at the neck, and a loose-fitting blood-red business blazer that reached her hips and was big enough to conceal the Beretta .380 in a jackass holster under her left arm. She carried a red purse and a carry-on bag.

"Your secretary mentioned that punctuality was important," Gregory said.

"It is. Walk with me, please." Underhill strode down the aisle toward the metal detectors. "You can dispose of the sign."

"Yes. I suppose I should." He laughed nervously as he wadded the sign into fourths and darted across the aisle to shove it into an incinerator slot on the wall. He jogged back to her side, accidently jostling an airline hostess pulling her bag behind her. He mumbled an apology and shoved his glasses more firmly up on his nose with a forefinger. "The university didn't say exactly what it was you wanted."

Gregory was actually Dr. Gideon Gregory, an archeologist with the University of Chicago. In his midthirties, the professor had been participating in digs all around the world since he was eighteen.

Underhill glanced at the professor and noticed for the first time that he had a nice smile. In spite of his gawkiness, he also appeared to be quite at ease with himself. "Tell me, Dr. Gregory, do you drink?"

"When in Rome," Gregory said. "Actually, there aren't many places I can think of where I haven't had the odd occasion to imbibe the local pressing."

"Wine, then."

"Yes." Gregory touched her elbow briefly and indicated the small bar along the runway. It was a touristy place with a big-screen holo in the back behind the bar and small round tables, each surrounded by four chairs and decorated with a plastic vase of paper flowers and a cocktail menu.

Underhill let herself be led, then allowed herself to be seated by the professor.

He sat on the other side of the table, his folded knees almost level with the surface. "Do you have a preference?"

"White. They have a good New Orleans here." Gregory went to the bar, and Underhill used the time to check in with Matrix over the cel phone. Time wasn't of the essence yet, but the deal was about to be laid on the table. She wanted to be ready.

"Matrix."

Underhill could hear computer keys clacking in the background. "Download and Cornell aren't here." They were supposed to meet her at the airport, but a call to the waiting limousine revealed that neither had made it.

In terse sentences, Matrix explained about the call from the Chicago police department.

"We could have taken a bye on this one," Underhill said. She didn't like anyone countermanding her instructions for any reason. She was like her father that way, and she knew it.

"I've been listening to the reports coming over the police bands," Matrix said. "The boy has already demonstrated an ability to generate projectiles made of ice."

"Snowballs?" Underhill said.

"More like spikes," Matrix said. "And he can shoot them with incredible force. He's put a number of them through doors and walls."

"Is there a source?"

"If you mean, does he have to stand next to a sink or a water fountain to create the spikes," Matrix replied, "the answer is no. One specialist on the metable enforcement team has ventured he might be using the moisture in the air."

"Or his body," Underhill said. The concept fascinated her. She and her father had pioneered the integration of metables into the espionage field, much to the chagrin of their colleagues.

The FREELancers' roots had begun back in the ashes of the Second World War. The US government through its Orion Foundation, recognizing a need for specialists in the field of warfare who could react quickly and decisively against great odds, created the Ganymede Bureau, the Titan Team of counter-terrorists, and Oberon, which was to be a top-secret strike force operating outside normal parameters.

George Anthony Underhill was chosen to head up Oberon in the 1990s, despite his youth. He'd taken a radical approach to putting his team together and didn't hold himself to just the military resources. He recruited free agents, people who normally were loners by nature, and added more training to the knowledge and skills they'd already acquired on their own. The concept was controversial, but the results were spectacular.

Then, in 1999, when a rescue attempt went awry and cost the lives of the people the Oberon team was assigned to save, Underhill's career and the future of the Oberon branch were sacrificed on the altar of politics. At that time, the division of the various states into their own alliances was just beginning. The federal government, already in disfavor with the public, wasn't willing to risk any more bad publicity.

But Orion wasn't willing to totally let Underhill and his group go. Underhill, working shrewdly and carrying the knowledge of where a number of bodies were buried, had the Oberon branch split off from the Orion group. By 2002, he succeeded, and Oberon became solely Underhill's under a brand new name: FREE. It stood for Fast Reaction Experimental Espionage, and Underhill began recruiting more metables than ever.

Whenever Orion needed a black ops mission run, they called for George Anthony Underhill and FREE. Impossible was just part of the job description.

Later the same year, Underhill recruited Dr. Andrew J. Rhand, and together they pushed the team to the cutting edge of technology and found even more powerful metables to enlist. Two years later, Underhill discovered the daughter he'd never known existed.

Lee Won Underhill had pushed herself to the top of the heap in the black market in Ho Chi Minh City. Finding her had taken some work, and she hadn't come cheaply. But when the dust finally settled between the estranged father and daughter, Lee Won Underhill took over the second chair at FREE. Things only got better.

But that wasn't the case with the rest of the world. The states continued to get more restless and irritated about the power and corruption of the federal government. Then, in 2011, Jim Bob Culpepper ran for election for Texas governor on a campaign promise to repudiate all the NAFTA agreements and to keep "Mexicans in Mexico." After he was elected, he began building his wall.

The structure was twelve feet high and ran the length of the Rio Grande. Utilizing the Texas National Guard, Culpepper topped the wall with barbed wire, put in mine fields, and built guard towers.

The nation was shocked. Some condemned Culpepper for what he'd done, but others said he'd set the new standard for speaking out against the federal government. The Justice Department started moving against the wall, demanding that it be torn down. Culpepper didn't hesitate to reciprocate, using military power as well as the solid right hook of the Texas electoral college.

President Humbolt, desperately seeking reelection, chose to do nothing. Texas had a lot of electoral votes. The wall stood. A Texas filibuster was already in progress at the Senate when a second wall went up in Arizona and didn't stop till it hit the fifteen-foot mark.

With Texas and Arizona shut off, California started getting hit with an influx of illegal aliens like the state had never seen before. New Mexico joined the Californians in wall-building.

A weak economy further served to split the country into haves and have-nots. With no relief and no agreement in sight, the country fragmented, and the once-great United States were no more.

Once on their own, it didn't take the states long to realize that alliances needed to be made with other regions that shared common needs. Basing the structure on the works of Jeremy Rifkin's *The End of Work* and *Global Paradox* by John Nesbitt, the states formed alliances.

The first alliance was the Great Lakes Authority, consisting of the heavy industry states: Minnesota, Wisconsin, Illinois, Indiana, Michigan, and Ohio. Iowa and Missouri successfully petitioned later to join.

In short order, the other alliances emerged: the Middle Atlantic Alliance, Ohio-Lower Mississippi Basin Cooperative, Mega-state of Greater Massachusetts, South Atlantic States Directive, and the Rocky Mountain Alliance. Before the Pacific Coast could get its act together, a nuclear disaster turned most of it into a wasteland. Burdened by environmental problems as well as by being radioactive, no one wanted those states around. Texas became its own alliance.

Cut free of the federal government and knowing a whole new field of opportunities had arisen in the developing political climate, the Underhills cut a deal with Chicago Mayor Dorothy Hubbard to move FREE to Chicago in exchange for political favors and stability. Hubbard had already proven herself to be an extremely savvy politician.

The federal government hadn't been happy about losing FREE, especially once they learned that Underhill was taking the organization totally independent, putting its skills on the market for causes he and his daughter deemed deserving. The name was changed from FREE to FREELancers as they went public in the media and advertised their services to domestic as well as international interests. They were years into the making of an overnight success. But it was coming.

"Download is at the site?" Underhill asked.

"Just arrived," Matrix said.

"Keep me posted."

"I will. In the meantime, Agent Prime and Scratchbuilt are in place as your backup as you requested."

The FREELancers administrator glanced up at Professor Gregory as he paid for the drinks and returned to the table. "I want Cornell out of there as soon as possible." She had gone to a lot of trouble to put the deal together properly. There had been, and still were, a number of variables.

"I'll relay the message."

"If you have to," Underhill said as the archeology professor sat across from her again, "pull Refit off his assignment and get him to bring Cornell here."

"At the moment it seems he has found his target."

Excitement flared in Underhill. Getting Jeannine Hartley

back had seemed a long shot when she'd agreed to the assignment three days ago. "What's the situation?"

"Code Red. He's just engaged a ganger group called the Cybered Shadows."

"When you get the particulars," Underhill said, "I'll need them." She broke the connection and put the cel phone away.

"Business?" Gregory asked, holding out her wineglass.

Underhill took it. "Yes, but back to ours."

"Ah, yes. Where were we?"

"Melaka."

The archeologist's brow wrinkled. "Melaka?"

"You were on a dig there last year. During the summer," Underhill prompted.

"With Dr. Henshaw," Gregory said, leaning forward with interest gleaming in his eyes. "Actually, he's the one you should be talking with. He knows far more about Melaka than I do. But I get the feeling you already knew that."

"Melaka . . ." Underhill prodded.

Gregory nodded. "Melaka, or Malacca, however you choose your spelling. The former seems to be in favor at the moment. It first came to historical prominence in 1402. Paramesvara, previously a prince in Sumatra, murdered the ruler of Tumasik—Singapore, as we call it now—and fled up the Malay Peninsula. Besides being a killer, he was also an industrious guy. Malacca, as it was known then, was only a small village of fishermen and pirates. Situated on coastal waters as it was, the career choices were understandable."

Underhill nodded. "Paramesvara recruited more pirates, then traders and other Malays. The traders and Malays were there to settle and cause the village to grow. Then Paramesvara opened negotiations in China with the Ming Dynasty."

Gregory raised his eyebrows, then lifted his glass in a silent toast. "You know some of the history. Good. I love addressing an able pupil. Anyway, with the Ming Dynasty deal in his pocket, Paramesvara had a lock on the trade routes in the area. Malacca grew even larger and faster. But all good things come to an end."

"Paramesvara died."

"By natural means, surprisingly, given all that he did to further himself." Gregory sipped his wine. "After that, rule fell into the hands of the Muslims in 1445 when Muzaffar Shah declared himself sultan and announced Islam as the official religion. Buddhists and Hindus in the area had halted the earlier run put on by Arab and Indian Muslims. After that, the Europeans arrived, trashing everything as they usually did."

Underhill didn't comment on the bitterness she heard in the archeologist's voice.

"As usual, they were brought by the chase and lust for wealth. This time the spice trade. But they didn't mind raping and looting and pillaging along the way. If you need any of this in detail, let me know."

"No, this is fine."

"The Portuguese were first, but were quickly followed by the British and Dutch. Spices were more in demand at that time than Levis are today in Russia. The three countries took turns claiming and holding Malacca. The British East India Company first gave the region the name Malaya. In a matter of years, they combined Penang, Malacca, and Singapore into a single territory known as the Straits Settlements. Which is why the strait there is known as the Strait of Malacca."

"In due time, that region was also declared to be a colony," Underhill said.

"Of course. You see how these things work, right?" Gregory went on, warming to his subject. "The Chinese had been a presence for a long time, but after 1850, tin deposits were discovered in the Straits Settlements and fortunes were on the line for the mining companies that sprang up. Chinese investors had more ready cash and fronted the money to develop the mines, then brought over Chinese immigrant laborers to work them, changing the ethnic mix and setting up some of the problems that followed later. To add napalm icing to an already packed cake of dynamite, the local Malay rulers began demanding more money from the mines."

In some ways, the situation sounded a lot like what had happened to the US, Underhill thought. But she already knew that history was doomed to repeat itself.

"In 1874, the British signed the Treaty of Pangkor, recognizing the strongest sultan's claim to the western peninsula. In reality, Abdullah was only a straw boss for the British. In 1896, the Federated Malay States were formed, adding four more territories. Then a 1909 treaty between Great Britain and Thailand brought even more territories into the fold. Under British control, of course."

"There were those tin mines to consider," Underhill said.

"And the rubber plantations that followed," Gregory agreed. "World War I showed the world that it couldn't live without rubber products. The Chinese became a powerhouse, though, and owned many businesses and controlled most of the money. They got into a spitting war with the Brits that got broken up by World War II and the Japanese invasion."

"Communism was also spreading on the peninsula at that time," Underhill commented. Most of the material she'd covered already, and remembered. But she wanted to get Gregory talking and relaxed.

"Right, and it was the Communist-organized guerilla groups that were the most effective against the Japanese. By the time the Brits got back after the war, politics had changed. Ultimately, the British had to help dig the Communists out, then ended up granting the area its independence and more or less walking away."

"Then the Malay countries began fighting among themselves."

"In earnest," Gregory agreed. "When there is no outside force to fear, disparate people often find the sources of those same fears inside each other."

"Words to live by."

"Riots broke out, then wars. Only it wasn't over just the tin mines and rubber plantations anymore. There was also usually a bumper crop of drugs run through Malaysia."

"There's no place without crime," Underhill said.

"True." The archeologist contemplated his empty glass as if he didn't know how it had gotten there. "Gradually everything quieted down. The 1980s produced concern over government corruption; then, in the 1990s when the British released Hong Kong back to the Chinese, things got interesting again."

"Lord Esmond Castlereigh," Underhill said.

"The very man. As you know, he owned family lands around Malacca. With the immigration coming from Hong Kong, he spent time and money and recruited from the best of those people. He was, of course, concerned about the Chinese using Hong Kong as a stepping-stone to taking over Malaysia. By 1999, though, business interests and successes in Malacca were phenomenal and growing geometrically.

"Castlereigh got a number of Savants for his investment" Gregory said. "However with success came an increased tax burden. By 2010, Malacca was supporting itself, as well as doing the lion's share for the other twelve Malay states. When FREEAmerica came into being in 2011, the people there were quick to jump on the bandwagon and declare themselves independent too. They took back the name Melaka."

"That's when the Arab countries started trying to reappropriate their lands," Underhill said.

"Right. The Brits followed, as well as the Portuguese, Japanese, and Chinese, all of them following corporate pressures. There were even small armed-force invasions that failed to make inroads into the country. Suddenly, Melaka had a military spending deficit it hadn't counted on, and a very poorly trained army to go up against experienced corporate raiders hitting its development companies and taking away the project research they were doing." Gregory looked up at her. "You know about Colonel Tabor? About how the bastard was invited in to the country to protect it, then virtually took it over six months ago?"

Underhill nodded. Tabor was a subject she was well versed on. "You were part of Henshaw's dig last year, weren't you?"

"Yeah," Gregory said. "I thought I'd landed a gig in the Ukraine, pursuing a line of inquiry I've been developing for five years. But that went bust because the government decided that letting foreigners in—even if they were doctorate material just wanting to nose around in a little local history—wasn't a good idea."

"Tell me about the catacombs," Underhill suggested.

The archeologist stopped toying with his glass. "That wasn't released to the media."

"No," the FREELancers administrator agreed. "It wasn't."

"Where did you get your information?"

"I'm paying you for *your* time."

Gregory rubbed a palm across his lower jaw. "We found one of them," he admitted. "Henshaw was working on a hypothesis he'd developed regarding a religious cult of some type that was in the area about the second century B.C."

"At the same time the Dead Sea Scrolls were written," Underhill said.

"That's what he was thinking. The Dead Sea Scrolls were discovered in 1947 and were about a religious community."

"The Essene Jews."

"Right. During some of his studies, Henshaw found an unsubstantiated document in Assyria claiming that the Essene Jews had met with another group who called themselves—loosely translated from Hebrew—Guardians of the Scarab. According to the document, the Guardians were interested in looking at the scrolls the Jews had written up."

"Why?"

Gregory shrugged. "I asked the same question. Henshaw said there was no definite reason given. There are only allusions to a bargaining for learning."

"The Guardians had scrolls of their own?" Underhill asked.

"I suppose. There was mention of a trade, but nothing was said of what came of it."

"How did the Guardians learn of the Essene Jews?"

"That was one of the questions Dr. Henshaw hoped to have answered." The archeologist gazed at her in contemplation. "Actually, I thought he might be the victim of a hoax. The last two digs he'd been on were pretty much fruitless, and his chief benefactor, who funded the biggest chunk of his excursions, died last year."

"How did Henshaw find the catacomb?"

"Through a census report left by one of the chief toadies of Paramesvara. One of the development corps workers came across some papers in one of the buildings they were tearing down to put up another structure. That was four years ago. The papers were all put in a box and placed in storage. Almost a year and a half ago, the storage facility was emptied, and the contents were auctioned off. A book dealer bought the papers, thinking he might turn a profit on a rare manuscript. From what Frank told me, this guy tried selling them for an outrageous amount to investors, but didn't find any buyers. Since the papers were written in an offshoot of Arabic, and as such were very hard to translate, not many people were interested. We're living in times of instant gratification. Hard to shake that."

Underhill glanced at her chron. At most she had another ten minutes with the archeologist. "But someone bought them."

Gregory nodded. "A fellow archeologist from London here on holiday. He recognized a few of the words. Arabic's not a big fave of his. Tiring stuff and very hard on the eyes. And that's not taking into consideration all the wrinkles with this language derivation. Thinking Frank might find something useful in the papers, he bundled them up and sent them as a present Christmas last."

"Have you seen them?"

"No." The archeologist smiled. "But I assume you have. At this point, I'd be disappointed if you hadn't."

"I've got a copy," Underhill told him. "Translated."

Gregory leaned back in his chair. "Amazing. Does Frank know?"

"Not until you tell him."

"And I will."

"Yes." Underhill had known that going in.

"He's going to be pissed."

The FREELancers administrator nodded. "For a while. But right now he's locked out of Melaka with no idea when he's going to be able to get back in-country. I'm working on a deal with some people. In a few weeks, maybe I'll be able to make that happen for him."

"If anyone could," Gregory said, "I believe it would be you. However, even then that country's going to be a war zone for some time to come. With all the new tech coming out of Melaka, and so many countries showing interest in it, the countryside's going to be a hotbed of industrial espionage." He scratched his chin as he regarded her. "But you're overlooking

Colonel Tabor and his bully boys."

"No," Underhill said, "I'm not. If my agency buys into this, Tabor's going to have to go."

"You make it sound easy."

Underhill leaned forward, resting her weight on her elbows on the table. She smiled slightly. "I hope not, because I'm planning on charging a lot of money to accomplish it."

* * * * *

O'Hare International Airport	***10:47 a.m. CST***
Great Lakes Authority (GLA)	***1647 Greenwich Mean***
87.7 degrees W Longitude	***March 28, 2024***
41.8 degrees N Latitude	***Friday***

Paul Derembang had difficulty controlling himself when he spotted Lee Won Underhill in the small airport bar. He was of mixed emotions, and had been since he'd identified the FREE-Lancers administrator's plane arriving at O'Hare.

He crossed the airport corridor and walked into the newsstand across from the bar. No one paid him any attention, but then he wasn't dressed in a nice off-the-rack suit the way he would have in the old days. Wearing khaki shorts with more pockets than he'd ever know what to do with, a neon-pink tank top with pictographs of iguanas doing every sex act Derembang could imagine—as well as a few he couldn't—black socks that reached his knobby knees, white tennis shoes he'd purchased from a sidewalk sale while across the street observing the FREELancers headquarters, a floppy hat, and round-lensed black sunglasses, he looked like a sixty-eight year old retiree. His skin was burned coppery from a constant exposure to tropical suns while working the rubber plantations when a teen, and despite all the time he'd spent inside since, the coloring had never left him. His hair though, once a rich black, had turned a powdery gray in the last twenty years. He didn't look at all like the ex-prime minister of Melaka. For over forty years he'd been active in Malaysian politics, and his face was known—better shaven—by a number of political heads abroad.

It was his first time as an assassin.

A nearby rack of books contained popular novels and corporate autobiographies in both English and Japanese. He stepped in front of the rack and followed it around till he was able to look across the corridor at Underhill, while still remaining partially hidden.

The pistol was heavy in his jacket pocket.

His throat felt dry at the prospect of what he was about to do. He turned the rack, anything to stay in motion, because he was afraid he'd go totally still and look terribly out of place amid all the hustle and bustle of the airport.

Reluctantly, he touched the pistol in his pocket. He'd gone to great lengths to procure the information about Lee Won Underhill weeks ago when he'd learned of her probable involvement in his country's current problems. He'd been in Chicago for six days now, and his sources inside the corporate world—which were wooing him, thinking he might yet again have the kind of political pull he'd had in the old days with Castlereigh—had let him know Underhill had been out of the GLA for much of that time.

Taking a deep breath and reminding himself that there was truly no other way to get the attention of those he sought, Derembang dropped his hand into his pocket and fisted the Model IX Pulser he'd bought from a zealous night clerk at the hotel where he was staying.

No one paid attention to him as he crossed the intervening distance, his breath tight in his chest. He wondered if Underhill would be armed. He hadn't really thought about that before now. Once, ten years ago, he'd been shot by a sniper seeking to kill Castlereigh. The bullet had broken his collarbone. Sometimes, when the weather was bad, his shoulder joint troubled him. Now he couldn't remember the pain of actually being shot. He wondered vaguely if it would hurt.

Underhill was still talking animatedly to her companion.

People continued passing by him, not even looking his way. Twenty feet out from the bar, Derembang pulled the Pulser out of his pocket and started bringing it level.

4

Chicago, Illinois | *10:49 a.m. CST*
Great Lakes Authority (GLA) | *1649 Greenwich Mean*
87.7 degrees W Longitude | *March 28, 2024*
41.8 degrees N Latitude | *Friday*

Assignment: Charon's Crossing, cont.
Tactical Ops: Protection & Transportation of VIP
Status: Code Yellow, Postponed

Download steered the Quadrifoglio through the tangle of emergency vehicles just off Pulaski Road and nosed in behind a fire truck butted up against the curb in front of the apartment building. When he parked, the passenger side door was almost flush with the rear of the fire truck.

He yanked the keys from the ignition and grabbed his pocket protector of computer chips for the Octopus from the thin drawer under his seat and wondered if he had anything among them that would be applicable for the present situation. The kit usually demanded a wide range of skills, from sniping to trauma aid. But most of them centered around violence, not talking to a frightened child with incredible powers. He opened the kit and gave Cornell a quick glance. "Stay inside the car. No matter what happens." He grabbed the stainless steel protective visored helmet he wore to keep the brain taps covered while in action and broke it down into two sections, folding them so they fit into the pockets of his jumpsuit.

"I really don't think this is the place—" The Fiscal Development man shut up with a startled yelp as Download used the remote control to the car to button it up. The window slid up quickly enough to trap the man's tie, and tightly enough that he wasn't going to get it loose without ripping the material.

The locks were also engaged so that Cornell couldn't open the door. With its armored hide and bulletproof glass, the Quadrifoglio was more than a sports car: it was a rolling juggernaut.

"What the hell are you doing here?" a yellow-slickered fireman demanded. He carried an axe in his gloved hands. Soot streaked his pale features and made his blue eyes stand out even more strongly. "You can't leave that vehicle there."

Download fisted the stainless steel necklace he wore and pulled his FREELancers ID up, holding it between thumb and forefinger so the fireman could read it. "Who's in charge here and where will I find him?"

"Chief Muldoon." The fireman hooked a thumb over his shoulder at the crowd of firemen standing around another fireman in a red helmet. CHIEF was printed across the front in shiny silver letters.

"What about the boy?" Download asked.

"He's still in there," the fireman said. "Got his mom's boyfriend in there with him."

"Is the boyfriend holding him hostage?"

"No. That crazy bastard went back in after the kid, though. Stood around out here making tough-guy noises while we were getting the other people out of the building. When the cops started asking him questions about why the boy went off, his mom said it was because the boyfriend was administering a lesson in discipline." The fireman drew a line across his knuckles. "Guy must have been administering it pretty damn thoroughly because he'd busted up both hands doing it. Blood on his shirt and pants weren't his either."

"What kind of shape is the kid in?" Download asked. He found a chip in the kit that looked promising: Lesley Wright, VICAP behavior specialist. He wasn't sure what VICAP was, though a tag lower down gave the information that it was linked with the Federal Bureau of Investigation, but behavior specialist was a step in the right direction.

"He's hurt." The fireman reached up to the fire truck and took the metal equipment case another man handed him. "It's hard to tell with all that snow covering him."

"Snow?"

"Or ice." The fireman nodded. "Only saw him for a minute or two from a distance, and I was helping a smoke-inhalation victim down the stairs. This kid's throwing ice spears, man. Never seen anything like it in my life."

Download nodded and headed for the fire chief's gathering.

The apartment building was a blunt stone finger stretching eight stories high, dwarfed by two corps buildings on the other side of the street. Urban renewal was creeping into the community again, forcing the neighborhoods out. Flames licked out of the top two stories, twisting and turning like live things seeking escape.

The police, a joint effort between the Chicago PD and their Cicero PD community counterparts, had succeeded in roping off the immediate area with sawhorses and bright yellow tape. Over a hundred civilians had already crowded into the street, held at bay by the police and the barrier markers. The media people were just starting to arrive in their vans, the long whip antennas needed for live broadcast extending into the air.

Download put the chip kit away in his back pocket, then shoved home the one he'd selected. The Octopus seized the programming voraciously, chewing it down in big bytes. Once the prelim run was finished, the FREELancers agent tripped the Unzip utility and the archived files flooded into his mind. The world opened wide between steps, and he dropped down through it as blue lightnings filled his vision.

He staggered, just a slight misstep that most people wouldn't have noticed. When his vision refocused, Big Ryerson was gone. In his place was Lesley Wright of the FBI's Violent Crimes Apprehensions Program. As behavioral specialist, she was responsible for profiling serial killers and rapists. Download knew that as well as he knew she preferred an English muffin with cream cheese for breakfast. He didn't know how that was going to help him talk to the boy but it was the best he had to work with.

"Guess it really worked," Wright said inside Download's mind. "I'm here. But I'm not supposed to be."

The FREELancers agent knew how she looked, because he had the disturbing sensation of having brushed her hair just a few moments ago in preparation for slipping on the headset that would record her skills. She was a big, green-eyed blonde with short-cropped hair and a birthmark staining her right cheek that she was saving up to have removed. Surprisingly, considering her job classification, she was in her early twenties.

"You're not here," Download said. "I am."

"What are you talking about?"

"Raise your hand," Download suggested, easing his control over his body. He hated using new disks. There was always an adjustment period as both parties got used to each other.

His left hand came up, and he held it curiously in front of his own face.

"Wow," Wright said.

Download took his hand back, edging her out of his nervous system. The fire chief was looking at him now. He fished out his ID again.

The ring of firemen opened before him.

"Is it always like that?" Wright asked.

"No," Download said. "Leave me alone for a few minutes so I can get some work done." He felt the chief's eyes on his face and suddenly felt self-conscious about the blemish on his cheek. Even though he was aware of bringing up his hand in an obviously practiced move to put his first two fingers against his temple so he could hide the birthmark that didn't exist, he couldn't resist the compulsion. Taking on the skill donor's insecurities and physical problems was one of the drawbacks to the Download machine.

"Something I can do for you, Mr. Scott?" Chief Muldoon asked.

"I need to get into the building. If I could borrow some gear, I'd appreciate it."

The chief hesitated. He was a short, broad man with a craggy face and a gold front tooth. "You going in for the boy?"

Download nodded.

"There's no way we're going to save the top half of this building," the chief said, "but my team inside reports that three or four other residents are trapped up there with him."

"Who started the fire?" Wright asked.

Download repeated the question aloud.

The chief hesitated. "Not for official release?"

Download shook his head, then accepted the suit and air tank one of the firemen handed him.

"We believe it was the boy."

"Why?" Wright asked.

"There have been small fires in the apartment building before. Going back three months. Mrs. Stokes and her son moved in four months ago." The chief pushed his helmet back, and flakes of black soot shook free. "The building super was already pegging the kid for it and demanded yesterday that he and his mother move out at the end of the month."

"Short notice." Download stepped into the fireproof uniform and pulled it up over his body. One of the other firemen helped him with the air tank.

"Yeah, well, I can't say that I blame him. Now it appears that it was too late."

Download cinched everything up, then took the helmet with accompanying Plexiglas faceshield. "What's the boy's name?"

"Robby Hatch."

Matrix whispered in Download's ear over the com-link she was maintaining from FREELancers Base. "Robert Eugene Hatch. His mother's name is Fern Stokes. That's her third—no fourth—married name. He's thirteen years old. Today's his birthday."

"Damn," Download said, gazing back up at the blazing building. "What about the boyfriend?"

"He's inside," the chief answered, looking at Download curiously.

Suddenly conscious that his bad side was showing to the chief, Download partially turned away and put his hand to his forehead again. He didn't fight the gesture because it would have taken too much thought, and he was working to assimilate the information.

"The guy sounds like a jerk," Wright said. She made him start stroking the side of his face, letting him know without words that motion helped provide a better cover for the birthmark.

"Curtis Duvall," Matrix replied, answering his real question. "I ran him through Criminal Records at the police department. He's loosely connected with Family Hastings."

"Who're they?" Download asked.

"I don't know the guy's name," the chief said. "Maybe one of the police officers got it."

Download nodded, which made keeping his hand over the imaginary birthmark even harder.

"Jeez," Wright complained. "It's getting crowded in here."

"Family Hastings," Matrix said over the staccato sound of her keyboard, "is an organized crime family here in the GLA. They're usually involved in white-collar crime, nothing too nasty. Duvall's file contains references to ties with Serle Hastings. I'm cross-referencing it now, but the file on Hastings is huge."

"Definitely not a nice guy," Download said, adjusting the weight of the air tank across his shoulders.

Matrix and the fire chief agreed. Lesley Wright took a pass on the observation, miffed that she wasn't really privy to the information being passed around. Download got the feeling that she hated being left out of the loop. Her professional career was riddled with insecurities, he sensed, and that had given her the edge she carried with her. Most of it stemmed from the birthmark and from her youth. She was experienced at her job. Some of the memories that tagged along with the borrowed reflexes let Download know she'd IDed over twelve serial assailants connected with murders as well as sex crimes.

"Get your friend to tell me more about the boy," Wright said. "A lot of pattern pyromaniacs have similar histories of torturing family pets, then killing them, usually in very controlled deaths, and setting small fires."

Download turned away from the firemen. "What's your radio frequency?" he asked the chief.

The man gave it. "That place is a death trap. We're going to lose the top three stories for sure. Maybe more if we can't contain the fire. If it gets to the gas main, it's going to be real chancy in there. The utility people have already shut the gas down, but there's still some residual buildup along the lines."

"I'll keep that in mind." Download glanced back at the Quadrifoglio and spotted Cornell plastered against the window staring out, working to peer around his captured tie.

"See if you can arrange a radio link with the mother," Wright suggested. "If you're determined to walk us into that building and face this kid, we're going to need to know more about him."

Download relayed the message.

The chief rattled off orders to one of his men. When the guy dashed off, he turned back to the FREELancers agent. "Do you need a handset?"

"Matrix?" Download said.

"Give me the frequency," she replied. "I can work a connect through the sat-com we're accessing."

"No," Download said, "just the frequency." Smoke blotted out most of the sky overhead in twisting coils interspersed with bright tongues of orange flames. When the chief gave him the call numbers, Download walked toward the building and fit the oxygen mask over his lower face. The Burris transceiver he was wearing had an auxiliary jack that buttoned him into the mask's built-in radio.

"Okay," Matrix said as he pushed his way into the main entrance of the apartment building, "you're on-line with the fire department on Tach Two."

Two firemen carrying an unconscious woman between them emerged from the elevator. "Keep this shaft free," one man said gruffly. "There're more people to be brought down."

"Where's it going?" Download asked.

"Six."

The FREELancers agent stepped into the cage, and the doors closed automatically. A smoke cloud coiled restlessly against the illumination coming through ice-cube-tray-shaped covers against the ceiling. The emergency exit hatch had been removed, but the elevator shaft was filled with more smoke than was in the cage. He shifted to Tach Two on the Burris. "Chief Muldoon, this is Scott. Where's the boy?"

Another voice came over the frequency. "Seventh floor."

"How is he?"

"Man, he's totally spazzed. Won't let anyone near him. One of those ice shards nearly took off Kempke's head when he tried to get him out of there."

Download swayed as the cage rocketed upward. He was sweating inside the suit, and breathing was laborious. The elevator cage stopped unevenly at the sixth floor, and Download stepped out into a smothering darkness that swirled around him. He pushed at the smoke with one hand, but succeeded only in swirling it around.

"Where are those damn files your friend promised?" Wright demanded.

It felt as if she were peering over Download's shoulder. He slid to one side of the narrow hallway as another fireman ran by him, carrying a small child draped over his shoulders. The boy's clothes were covered with smoke, but the respirator strapped over his face held a light dusting of mist that signaled he was breathing.

"Here," Matrix replied.

"What have you got?" Wright asked. But it was Jefferson Scott's lips she was using.

Download found the emergency exit and pushed through. Fire had eaten into the ceiling from the floor above. The hallway was narrow, the trapped smoke nearly occluding all vision. He felt the FBI agent's thoughts moving among his own. His thinking took distinct curves in the way his mind put things together.

"School files. Some of his daycare records," Matrix said.

"How did you get school files?"

"I hacked into the system once I had the boy's name."

Download knew Matrix had stepped over some of the boundaries Underhill had established. Taking risks with alliance laws like that was only to be done at the FREELancers administrator's discretion, and only for profit.

"She can't do that," Wright said.

"Go with it," Download said. "Be glad you have it."

"What?" Matrix asked.

"Talking to myself," Download said truthfully. He concentrated on climbing up the steps, feeling his way along the handrail, while Wright took over his speech center.

"Give me the elementary files first," Wright said. "Any signs of cruelty to the other children? Taunting? Pushing or shoving?"

"None."

"What about social skills?"

"Robby consistently receives low marks. The notes on his report cards indicate a need for more class involvement," Matrix said. "By second grade, he'd already been held back once and put into special-ed classes."

Download reached the seventh floor landing and took over again. "Can you get a fix on me in the building through the sat-com?" Each full-time FREELancers agent had a homing device planted in the base of his or her skull.

"I've got you on-screen now," Matrix replied. "Also, I've sent a heligyro out for you and the FDI rep. Maybe we can make up some of the time you're losing to make the delivery at O'Hare."

Download pushed his way through the emergency exit door. The hallway looked like a section of hell come to life. The next words out of his mouth were Wright's: "Do you have any notes from the SED counselor?"

"Antisocial. Insecure. Very internally driven."

"Anything about sexual abuse?"

"Nothing here."

A six-foot-long icy spear, at least six inches across at the base, was thrust into the wall. With the smoke so thick, Download didn't see it until he'd almost walked into it. He took off a glove and touched it, still not believing. It was cold, almost cold enough to burn his skin.

"Damn," Wright said inside his skull.

Download put his glove back on. "Can you scan this floor?"

"Done," Matrix replied.

"How many individual signatures can you ID?"

"I'm overlapping your com signature with your heat signature," Matrix answered, "so I can factor you out."

Download went forward, amazed at how dark it was. He tried to memorize the path back, how many doors he'd passed so far, but it was hard with Lesley Wright playing Ping-Pong inside his head while keeping track of all the conversations.

The Burris transceiver burped for attention. He switched it over.

"Mr. Scott," Chief Muldoon said, "we've got the boy's mother."

"Put her on," Wright said.

Download waded through patches of fire that had left burnt, curling twists of thin, threadbare carpet in their wake.

"Hello?" The woman's voice sound choked and emotional.

"What's her name?" Wright asked in Download's mind.

"Stokes." The FREELancers agent was surprised he remembered it, and irritated that the FBI agent hadn't. But then, he was actually accessing her skills, not her memory. It got very confusing when he thought about it, so he didn't.

"Mrs. Stokes," Wright said with Download's voice. "We're just trying to help Robby, okay? I've got just a few questions."

"Do you see him?" she asked.

"Not yet."

"Oh, god, please find my baby." The woman started crying hysterically.

"I will," Download promised. He had to squelch a moment of panic when he walked into a wall he hadn't even seen. His mind whirled, desperately trying to assure him he remembered the way back to the door. There were more ice spears along the way, some of them driven entirely through the walls and doors. The Burris tweaked in his ear. "Hold on, I'll be right back." He shifted channels. "Yeah."

"Four," Matrix said. "Yours, two others that are alive, and one that the spectro-haze utility says is already cooling internally."

"Where?"

"Farther down. You're headed in the right direction."

"Go to Tach Two and stay with me. Break in if you need to." Download stumbled. Caught off-balance by the air tank strapped across his shoulders, he couldn't recover and went down and forward. In a heartbeat, he was face to faceplate with the burned remains of an old man.

"Jeez Louise," Wright said.

The features were puckered tight from the heat that had sucked the moisture from them and turned them dark. Broiled in the orbitals, the eyes were a bubbling, black-jellied goo.

Download pushed himself up, determined to find the boy and wondering whose the other bio-signature was. He made the change back to Tach Two and let Wright know she could continue with her questions.

"Do you remember when they put Robby in SED at the school?" Wright asked.

"Yes. We tried everything. Learning was just so hard for him. They told me he was having trouble focusing on things."

"What about his clothing?" the FBI agent asked.

Download found a fire extinguisher on the wall and pulled it free. He was surprised it hadn't ruptured, because it was carrying a lot of heat. The hallway had become choked with flames. He pulled the pin and squirted out a large plume of white spray that shot through the smoke.

"What?" the mother asked.

"Did they have any trouble with his clothing?" Wright asked. "Did he change it often enough?"

"They talked to me about his coat," Fern Stokes said. "He had this ratty-looking 49ers jacket that must have been twenty years old. He wore it all the time, even in the summer. They wanted him to leave it at home, but I couldn't get him to do that. He even wore it to bed at night."

"Did he have problems with bed-wetting or uncontrollable bowel movements?"

"What the hell does that have to do with getting my son out of there?" the woman demanded hysterically.

"Mrs. Stokes," Wright said patiently, "once we find Robby,

we're going to need his help in getting him out of the building. The other firemen said he's not willing to come, and with the power he's demonstrated, it would be hard to force him. If he stays up here he'll die. We need to know as much about him as we can in order to help him."

Download stepped over another ice spear that was nearly melted. He loosed another cloud of spray and briefly cleared the way again. A glance over his shoulder showed that he wouldn't be going back the way he'd come.

"You're almost on top of him," Matrix said softly. "He's still alive. Both of them are."

"Please find him," Fern Stokes said.

"Tell me about Robby," Wright told her.

"He had some problems," the mother said. "Every kid does."

"Bed-wetting?"

"And the other. Sometimes I'd have to go to school and take him fresh clothes."

Part of the ceiling ahead of Download had collapsed into the hallway. Flames ran hungry tongues over the exposed wood and crumbled plaster. A swirling inferno moved through the hole in the room above. The fire extinguisher had exhausted itself. He used the empty container to bat the debris out of his way, sending hot coals and sparks shooting in all directions. He didn't see how anything human could survive in the furnace that the floor had become.

"Did they ever talk to you about bruises?" Wright asked.

"Robby was a clumsy kid," Fern Stokes said. "When he was little, he was always picking up bruises."

"Did you see him fall?"

"I was working at a diner. Waitressing. My husband watched him."

"What was your husband's name?"

"Robby was in second grade. That was a long time ago." Her voice sounded plaintive.

"Please, Mrs. Stokes."

As he listened to the conversation, Download felt his stomach getting queasy. The heat pressed in against him as he walked through a curtain of flame with his arms wrapped over his faceplate. He kept his chin tucked in to make sure none of the fire reached through.

"Nathan," Fern Stokes said. "Nathan Everson."

"Could you spell it?"

As the woman did, Download stepped through a clearing in the smoke that had been made by a pair of windows near the end of the hallway. He halted, trying to make sense of the doors through the confusion of smoke and half-seen surroundings.

"To your right," Matrix said. "That body mass is smallest. I've redefined the parameters of the search."

Download went to his right. He was sweating heavily under the suit now, felt his clothing sticking to him. "I need a B-sheet run on Everson, Nathan," Wright said through Download's mouth.

"Did you find him?" Fern Stokes asked.

An explosion sounded at the end of the hall, and the concussive wave slammed into Download from the side, bowling him over. He caught himself on his hands and had to drop the fire extinguisher. Within a few inches of the floor, he discovered there was a ceiling to the smoke. It drifted maybe as much as eight inches above the surface. Then he saw the boy, watching him with dead eyes.

* * * * *

Chicago, Illinois	*10:54 a.m. CST*
Great Lakes Authority (GLA)	*1654 Greenwich Mean*
87.7 degrees W Longitude	*March 28, 2024*
41.8 degrees N Latitude	*Friday*

Paul Derembang heard quick footsteps behind him, but he thought the person was too far away to be of any concern to him. He was vastly surprised when a hand dropped over his and covered the Pulser as he started squeezing the trigger.

The hand pushed his arm down, keeping the trigger from connecting and sending a laser beam on a path of destruction, and a well-modulated voice said gently, "No. That's not an answer you would have taken anywhere along your career." A dark-skinned man with dark hair and handsome features that might have been Malaysian stood at his side. He was dressed in an electric-blue suit and dove-gray turtleneck. "Nor does the Koran teach the ways of violence."

Derembang tried to yank the pistol back up, but the grip on his arm proved too much for him to resist. Aware that they were attracting attention from the airport crowd, he tried to step away. The grip was maintained, holding him easily.

The stranger stepped closer, taking the distance away. "Let me have the gun. Quickly, before someone sees."

Heart thudding inside his chest, Melaka's ex-prime minister looked deep into the smoky gray hazel eyes of the man who held him. "Who are you?"

"A friend."

Derembang started to object; then a feeling of warmth covered him, and he surrendered the weapon. "Do I know you?"

The smile was white and honest and compelling. "Not yet." The man plucked the pistol from Derembang's fingers and made it disappear into his jacket pocket.

"Are you going to turn me in to the authorities?"

The man laughed in obvious delight. "Oh, no. How could I be a friend and do that?" He clapped Melaka's ousted prime minister on the shoulder. "I'm here to help you."

"You knew what I was about to do?" Derembang asked. He allowed himself to be steered along, back to the terminals. A small cleaning droid whisked along the floor like a fat, sleek silver mouse, avoiding him with its internal radar.

Taking a final glance back in the direction of the bar, he saw Lee Won Underhill still talking animatedly to her male friend. She'd obviously never even been aware of his presence.

"You mean by appearing to try to kill Underhill?" The man nodded. "How could I not know, and yet be here in time to stop you?"

Derembang felt confused. "If you knew, why didn't you try to stop me earlier?"

"Because," the man replied, "if I hadn't waited till the proper moment, you might have wondered later if you'd have gone through with it. Or if you'd have given up."

"That was important to know?"

"Not for me, my friend," the stranger said warmly. "It was important for you. You need to know that the good that was once in you still remains. Because what you have ahead of you is going to demand every bit of that and more."

Derembang felt the regard of that smoky gray gaze. He felt strengthened by it. "I wouldn't have aimed to kill her."

"I know."

"I was only going to attack her and appear to be trying to kill her. If I was arrested, or shot dead, more attention would be directed to Melaka. The GLA has resources it could use that would prove helpful to my country, if the leaders could just be made aware of Melaka's plight. All other resources have been exhausted, and my country remains virtually enslaved."

The stranger threw his arm around Derembang's shoulders. "*Our* country, Mr. Prime Minister."

Derembang looked at the other man, wondering why suddenly he felt so at ease. "You are from Melaka?"

"It is my country," the other man said. "And I believe in it."

The statement made the older man so sad he thought he might cry. His heart grated like broken pieces of pottery inside his thin chest. "I have failed my country," he stated, "my people, and myself."

"No, my friend," the stranger said. "You've been betrayed. These things happen. You and I, we're going to make them unhappen."

The lines of movement had stagnated in the gate areas. A number of people talked with each other, unaware or uncaring that a civil war was going on while they went about their lives. Some of them flipped through disk-scanners for the latest news, but even those wouldn't take much notice.

"You are aware of the mercenary colonel, Tabor?" the Melakan prime minister asked.

"Yes."

"He has Melaka under martial law."

"Only for now. The wheel turns, my friend. Buddha teaches us that."

"I thought you were Islamic."

The stranger looked at him curiously. "Did I say that?"

"No."

"I thought not."

The crowd continued to flow around them. Derembang glanced back often, but he didn't see any sign of airport security following them. "Fiscal Development, Incorporated intends to hire the FREELancers Agency to collect on the overdue loans we took out."

"Yes."

"I didn't want that to happen. We have troubles enough."

A twinkle was in the stranger's eyes as he looked at Derembang and smiled. "Let's just take it one trouble at a time, my friend. And at present, the mad colonel remains by far the largest problem." He ushered the older man into one of the gates on the west side of the terminal.

The electronic tote boards announcing arrivals and departures pulsed in reds and blues. Beside them, powered by a multimedia chip source, ads ran for vacation spots.

"We're going somewhere?" Derembang asked.

Two tickets appeared in the stranger's hand as if by magic, as smoothly as he'd made the gun vanish. "Singapore. From there, we'll find transportation back into Melaka."

"To what end?" Derembang asked. The rush of jet engines almost drowned out his words.

"To find the underground resistance," the stranger said.

"Are you aware that they almost put a price on my head?" Derembang asked in disbelief. "I was one of the chief proponents of the loans that crippled us to Fiscal Development and assisted in recruiting Colonel Tabor."

"Yes," the stranger replied agreeably. "And at that time, you were acting in the best interests of Melaka. Just as you were only a few moments ago."

"They will not trust me."

"Then we'll make them." The stranger looked him over from head to foot. "But we're going to have to make some changes in your attire."

A voice inside Derembang's mind sounded very far away, protesting against the ease of accomplishment the stranger was talking about. Melaka was facing total devastation, while holding the potential of phenomenal success. "Who *are* you?"

"My name?" The stranger gave the tickets to a flight attendant who hurried them toward the waiting plane. Only minutes remained before it was to take off.

"Yes." This time Derembang focused, not willing to be deterred. Events were happening too fast, making things confusing. He wanted to be clearheaded.

"Mat Kilau."

Derembang halted at the entrance to the tunnel leading down to the big jet. He recognized the name. Mat Kilau was a national hero. In 1891, when the tribal chiefs had declared open rebellion against the British resident being forced on them after the murder of a British subject, a young hero had come forward to lead them, only one among many, but the best remembered. His name was Mat Kilau. No one had known who he was before the rebellion, nor had any known where he was or what had happened to him after the fighting had ceased. The rebellion had gone on to become called the Pahang War, and to be symbolized as the beginning of the struggle for Malay independence. Although many of the rebels were killed, and others surrendered or were later tracked down by the British military and punished, myths and legends had sprung up about Mat Kilau.

Some said he'd never died, that he was an eternal warrior awaiting his country's greatest need and would return.

Pahang, Derembang knew, was almost two hundred miles from Melaka. But no one had ever ascertained where Mat Kilau had come from, though all involved had claimed him as their own. And during those turbulent years that had shaped Malaysia, the warrior could have possibly wound up anywhere when the rebels had been broken and scattered before the British army.

But that had been over a hundred years ago. On the whole, Derembang had to admit this Mat Kilau was looking very well for a dead man, or one almost one hundred fifty years old.

5

Chicago, Illinois *10:49 a.m. CST*
Great Lakes Authority (GLA) *1649 Greenwich Mean*
87.7 degrees W Longitude *March 28, 2024*
41.8 degrees N Latitude *Friday*

Assignment: Charon's Crossing, cont.
Tactical Ops: Protection & Transportation of VIP
Status: Code Yellow, Postponed

Robby Hatch was in the doorway to a room that looked like a maintenance area. The boy was slim and pallid, red-faced from struggling to breathe through all the smoke. He wore a tee shirt with a Captain Ares picture on it and black jeans with patched-over knees. His blond hair was cropped short and had flecks of soot shot all through it. He lay on his stomach, his face turned to one side. His hands covered his face, but they were coated with ice.

The Burris transceiver crackled in Download's ear. "Scott," Chief Muldoon said. "You'd better damn well haul ass out of there. The top of that building is about to come down."

"I found the boy, Chief," Download said.

"Can you get to him?"

"I don't know."

Robby Hatch looked at Download, then started trying weakly to push himself away.

Another explosion sounded at the other end of the building. This time mortar and brick came hurtling along with the noise and flash of light shuddering through the smoke.

Download stayed low and crawled forward, his eyes locked on the small boy. If Robby Hatch topped five feet and went eighty pounds, it would have surprised him.

"If he doesn't give you a choice," Muldoon said, "then you don't have one. Are you reading me?"

"Yeah," Download said. His voice hurt from the smoke. Even with the mask on, traces of it were creeping in.

"Everson," Matrix said, "Nathan. I've got it. How much do you want?"

"Are there criminal records?" Wright asked.

"Yes."

"Search for child abuse, rape, incest, anything along those lines." Wright turned herself away from Download's voice and spoke into his mind. "Not wanting to take off the coat, the inability to control his bodily functions, the bruises, those all indicate sexual abuse. Schools can't do anything about it, though, unless there's definite proof."

Download looked at the small boy in front of him, imagining him much smaller, unable to defend himself. "Damn," he said as his stomach clenched into knots. "He was how old in second grade? Nine? Ten?"

"Eight," Wright said softly. "He was eight years old."

Part of the anger and revulsion he was feeling was his own, Download knew, but some of it came from the borrowed skills. "Eight years old. How could anyone . . . ?" He left the rest unsaid. It was too horrible to put into words. Everything he'd seen over the years, everything he'd heard of, none of it prepared him for dealing with it face-to-face. How the hell was he supposed to get Robby Hatch to trust him in the minutes, perhaps only seconds, they had left before the building came down around them?

The boy's eyes were bloodshot and tearing, but filled with fear as he dragged himself back into the maintenance room.

"I've got only one reference point," Matrix said. "Four years ago, Nathan Everson was brought up on statutory rape charges. He was accused of raping his girlfriend's fourteen-year-old daughter. Everson plea-bargained down to contributing to the delinquency of a minor. The DA felt there were some serious concerns about the daughter's compliance and willingness that could jeopardize a conviction if the case went to court. Everson also agreed to seek psychiatric help. At the time he was already seeing a counselor."

"The son of a bitch," Wright said. "It's all about control issues for him. He takes these kids, does whatever he wants with them after they get to trusting him, then makes them feel guilty afterward. Like they were as much to blame as him. Maybe more, because he'll tell them he couldn't help himself, and it's their fault for acting like they wanted him to do that to them. At that age, kids seek attention. They're just nudging past that veil that makes them think the world is totally there for their own amusement, and they're wanting reassurance. It makes them really vulnerable."

"Robby," Download called.

"Stay away—" A coughing fit broke up the boy's words. "From me."

Closer now, Download could see that it wasn't just Robby Hatch's hands that were coated with ice. The boy's whole body was, giving him a shiny, angular coat that looked like a sugar glaze.

"Think about it, Scott," Wright said in his mind. "This boy's been abused by at least one man—"

"Probably Curtis Duvall as well," Matrix said. "I found mention of some charges brought by the school administration against Duvall just a little more than a month ago. His mother changed school districts with Robby and stopped the process."

"Maybe it hasn't been sexual," Wright said, and Download knew he was talking out loud as well. He didn't worry about how it sounded to Matrix. No one believed him about the voices anyway. "But it was definitely a form of physical abuse. His mother didn't protect him either. In the first case, if she did know, she probably denied it to herself. In this second case, she took Duvall's side of things. There's no reason for this boy to trust you."

Download stopped moving closer. "Robby," he said, "it's okay. I'm just trying to help."

"Stay away," the boy croaked. He threw a hand out. There was a crackle of blue electricity; then an ice spear leaped from his fingers.

Download rolled to one side, and the shaft of ice plowed into the carpet with enough force to rip the material away. It was engulfed, hissing, in the flames behind him.

The boy pushed himself against the side of the wall, sitting up with his back to it, his hands clasped over his nose and mouth.

Download stared at the picture of Captain Ares on the boy's shirt. The agent wore his usual white tights, with red boots, gloves, cape, ram's-headed cowl, and stylized A on his chest. In the picture, the Captain was bending an iron bar in his gloved hands. Underneath was a saying Download recognized: THE CAPTAIN SAYS A HEALTHY MIND IN A HEALTHY BODY WILL TAKE YOU ANYWHERE YOU WANT TO GO.

Download stood up and started stripping the protective suit off, dropping it at his feet. The heat slammed into him, followed immediately by his first suffocating breath of smoke.

"What are you doing?" Wright asked.

"Trying to give him a reason to trust me," Download replied. He reached into a pocket of the jumpsuit and took out the trademark collapsible helmet. He put it on, working hard not to start coughing from the smoke. Tears ran freely from his eyes. He raised his voice. "*Robby.*"

The boy looked up from his hands. "You're Download!"

There was such a tone of hero worship in the boy's voice that Download felt embarrassed.

"Don't be," Wright said. "You've earned it."

For a moment, Download wondered if Wright's words came out of his subconscious and he was actually telling himself that he'd earned the right to be called a hero. Suddenly, he felt on thin ice again. He wasn't a hero. If Robby Hatch knew everything he'd done—spending half his adult life incarcerated in jail cells or as a patient in mental institutions as a result of the chokehold drugs and alcohol had held him in for so long—the boy never would have listened to him.

"He doesn't know that," Wright said. "You're his only chance. Get it together, Scott. Do it now, dammit!"

Download forced himself to take a step. How he saw himself at the moment didn't matter as much as how the boy saw him. "C'mon, Robby. Time to go."

"No," Robby said, pushing himself harder against the wall. He held up a hand. "Please don't make me hurt you. I don't want to hurt you."

"That's up to you," Download said. "I'm not going to dodge again." He wished he had a pistol loaded with Para-bullets. Underhill's legal staff could deal with the civil suit fallout.

"Keep him talking," the FBI agent said. "The more he interacts with you, the harder it's going to be for him to hurt you."

Download took another step forward. He held his empty hands out in front of him. "Robby, I only want to help. The Captain sent me here."

"Careful," Wright advised. "If he starts thinking you're lying, it's all over."

More of the roof came down behind Download. He made himself not look, almost choked up with the smoke, his lungs burning as if he'd inhaled live coals.

"Where's Captain Ares?" Robby asked. He didn't lower his hand.

The Captain was the most publicly accepted hero of the FREELancers. Summer Davison, the public relations director, had negotiated deals to put the Captain's face on everything from tee shirts to coffee mugs to lunch boxes to underwear. Everyone knew who Captain Ares was and that he stood for moral ideas.

Personally, Download often couldn't handle the Pollyanna attitude Captain Ares had and liked the thought of the Captain's face being plastered on someone's underwear.

"He couldn't be here," Download said, "so they sent me."

"Go away."

"The building's coming down, Robby." Download made his voice soft, but it was hard with all the smoke he was inhaling and with the sound of the fire all around him.

"You need to get out of the building," Matrix said. "The spectro is showing the infrastructure is coming apart."

Download held out his hand to Robby. "Come on, partner."

"No," the boy said. "I don't want to live anymore."

"Help me here," Download told Wright.

"Can't," the FBI agent responded. "I sucked as a daughter. Didn't know it until it was too late and living out on my own. My first marriage? Down the tubes in less than six months."

"Christ," Download said. "And you're a top psych profiler for the FBI?"

"Serial killers and rapists are generally loners," Wright said. "Loners I can understand."

"This kid's a loner."

"He hasn't killed anyone."

Download thought about that, the time inside his mind passing in nanoseconds. He scanned the room Robby had crawled into. Shelves contained cleaning chemicals, and crates lined the opposite wall. An electric-powered hot water tank was farther back in the corner, almost obscured by smoke.

"The fire started here," Wright said.

"You're sure?" Download asked.

"I worked closely with the forensics people recovering evidence. Sure I'm sure."

Download took another step.

"Don't," Wright said. "You're going to make him hurt you."

"I'm going to put him against the wall," the FREELancers agent said. "If he's got it in him to hurt somebody, we're both going to find out." He kept his hands out away from his body, then spoke where Robby could hear him. "I'm not leaving without you, Robby."

"You can't make me go."

"Control issues, remember?" Wright said. "This kid's trying to take control back."

"I'm not going to make you go," Download said. "I'm going to stay here with you. If that's what you want to do."

"Jefferson," Matrix said, "you've got to get him out of there."

But Download knew he could do it. When he'd submitted

to the Download surgery and changed his life, he'd been hoping to change inside. The problem was, his antisocial and self-destructive tendencies had gone with him. Death looked easier a lot of times than trying to put in another day.

Three feet from Robby, he stopped and leaned against the doorway. "I'm not going to let you die by yourself, kid," he said.

"Take a look around the room," Wright said.

Download folded his arms over his chest and scanned the room. "You figure this is going to fix everything, Robby?"

The boy didn't answer.

A coughing attack seized Download, and he had no choice but to give in to it.

"You need to get out," Robby said. "You're going to die."

"So are you."

"I want to."

"Maybe I do too."

Robby looked at him doubtfully. "Why would you want to die? You're a hero. One of the FREELancers."

"Doesn't mean my life has been a bowl of cherries."

"You can't even imagine what I've been through." The boy had a coughing jag of his own.

"Go over to the wall," Wright said.

"I'm busy here," Download objected.

"Do it."

Reluctantly, Download did. Time was running out. If Wright had something that would help, he didn't have time to argue with her about it. "I know about Nathan Everson, Robby."

"What do you know about him?"

"I know that you were abused by him." Download watched his vision change, focusing on spots on the wall that looked like shadows that had been burned onto the surface. The deep scarring of the shadows tracked up the wall, following the line of pipes that pumped heated water back to the various apartments. He didn't know what he was looking for, but he had the feeling that Lesley Wright did.

"How do you know?"

Download broke off the scan and turned back to face the boy. "I do."

The boy broke the eye contact. "My mom didn't believe me."

"She didn't know," Download replied. "That doesn't excuse her, but she's a person. People make mistakes."

"She's my mom," Robby said in a tight voice near the edge of breaking down. "She wasn't supposed to let that happen to me."

"Chill with that," Wright said. "You're going to push him over the edge. He doesn't need to deal with that now."

"He's trying to deal with it," Download said, knowing from personal experience as he watched the boy. He'd pushed himself to destruction, trying to accept the things in his life that he couldn't control. "That's what this is all about."

"I don't know. I think you're making a mistake about that, but I'm certain he didn't start the fire."

"Why?"

"Whole system's too sophisticated. Whoever put this together has experience in arson. Chemicals were used to start the initial blaze. The hot water tank itself was used as the initial flash point, judging from the burn marks I saw on top of it."

Download got the idea. "So when the hot water tank hit a certain temperature . . ."

"The chemicals ignited. But it doesn't stop there. Whoever prepped the trigger also used a line of chemicals along one of those pipes to lead the fire out into the crawlspace above the ceiling where the insulation is. The stuff that's been used in there is substandard. The insulation should have been replaced thirty years ago. Once the flash point was reached, the insulation caught on fire and the blaze spread throughout the building."

"And whoever set the fire had to have known that."

"You bet your ass."

"So it wasn't Robby."

"No way. He couldn't even have gotten information to do that over internet blackboard sources. This was professional. The person who did it probably even selected the time the fire would start by monitoring the heating cycles of the hot water tank."

Download considered that, time freezing as he worked it out mentally. One thing about the Octopus, when he was using a skill disk, it allowed him faster time with thought processes than anyone he'd known. The down side was that if he didn't know any more than anyone else, he spent more time being confused by it if he sped up the processes.

"I was in group," he said, "there was a firebug in there with us. He was an alcoholic, just like the rest of us, but the state was having him treated for pyromania, too. I remember that most fire-setters like to watch the burn."

"They do," Wright replied.

"So chances are, our guy is living here?"

"To time the cycles of the hot water tank and do the other prelim stuff," Wright answered, "I'd think so. And it's also logical to think of the perp as a male. The last stat I saw on fire-setting, eighty-two percent were men and boys."

"He'd also need to know when Robby would be around to be blamed," Download went on. "Points to one guy that I know of."

"Curtis Duvall," Wright said excitedly. She took over his voice and tagged the Burris transceiver. "Matrix, get me some background on Duvall. I want to know where he lived, if there were any fires at those locations."

"I'm checking."

"Also, any office buildings where he might have operated a business that had a fire after he left it."

Download looked at Robby trying to gain control over the coughing fits that were leaving him exhausted. The boy looked paler than ever, and the icy coating surrounding him looked thinner. "How long have you been able to do that?"

The boy shrugged. "A few weeks. Nothing like this, though."

"What brought this on?"

Robby looked defensive. "I don't know."

"It happened when Duvall was hitting you, didn't it?"

"Maybe."

"How long has he been hitting you?"

Lifting his shoulders, the boy let them drop again. "I don't know."

The flames were out in the hall just in front of the door now.

The heat inside the room had increased at least ten degrees, taking it to well over a hundred.

"Does your mom know?" Download asked.

"She says he's just disciplining me," Robby said. "I've always been a bad kid. She's told me before that if it wasn't for me, the other guys would have stayed."

The boy's words, delivered with self-loathing and certainty, damn near broke Jefferson Scott's heart. They hit a resonance within him that he thought he'd kept buried deep enough that he couldn't reach it anymore, first with drugs and alcohol, then with apathy. Instead, it rang loud and true.

"She's wrong," Download said with a thick voice. "She was just taking her disappointments out on you. I don't know why. Maybe she doesn't either. She'd have to talk to someone professional to find out." He paused. "You haven't been setting those fires either."

Robby looked at him in disbelief. "No. But Mom doesn't believe me."

"Maybe she doesn't want to believe you," Download said, "but I do."

Shaking his head, Robby howled, "It's too late!"

"No, it's not. We get out of here, we can work on setting things straight for you." The commitment was past his lips before Download knew it, and it sent a fierce stab of fear through him. Hell, he had enough problems of his own without borrowing someone else's—especially in areas he knew nothing about.

"You mean that?" Robby looked up at him, hope in his eyes for the first time.

Download took a deep breath. "Yeah, Robby, I mean that." He was willing to promise the boy anything at the moment to get him out of the building.

"If he senses you're lying to him," Wright said, "you're screwed."

"Have you taken a look at that fire outside?" Download asked. "We may all be screwed anyway."

"I've gotten a positive match," Matrix said. "Five buildings where Duvall has lived or worked in the last six years have burned down."

"Do a cross-reference," Wright suggested. "You said Duvall was connected with the Hastings Family. How many of those buildings did they have holdings in?"

"I'm checking."

Download focused on Robby Hatch. "Are you ready to leave, or are we both going to stay here and burn?"

"I don't want to go," the boy answered, huddling in on himself. "But I'm afraid to stay."

"Me too," Download admitted. He stretched out a hand toward the boy. "Let's see if we can make it, though."

"You're going to be there?" Robby kept his hands to himself.

"Yeah," Download said. "I'll be there."

Matrix came back on to the frequency. "I got a positive answer on three of the buildings. They were owned by Hastings Family holding companies. I'm still tracking the other two, but from the moves the records are making, it looks as if they'll end up as Hastings assets as well. The building you're in now is owned by one of their fronts."

"It was arson," Wright said. "And those are only the ones we can tie to Duvall. There could be other cases where Duvall started up a courtship with someone in a building to get the necessary research done on it, then burned those as well. With a little work, Duvall can be charged for them."

Robby reached his hand out, and the FREELancers agent took it. The boy's fingers felt brittle and cold and sticklike with the icy overcoating. The flames whirled and whipped out in the hallway. The smoke was converging on the broken windows and siphoning through.

"You know who started this fire, don't you?" Download asked.

"No." The answer came too quickly, too strongly voiced.

"I know it was Duvall," Download told the boy.

Denial formed fresh and hard in Robby's eyes. "He didn't do it. I did."

For a moment, Download was thrown by the sudden admission. He covered by selecting a chip from his collection of borrowed skills that he hoped would get them out of the building. Lou Henriksen was a Hollywood stunt man that specialized in action-adventure vids.

"Not him," Wright insisted. "He's protecting his mother."

"Robby," Download said as softly as he could over the roar of the fire, "did you see the dead man out in the hall?"

Reluctantly, the boy nodded.

Download squeezed his hand gently. "Do you want to tell his family that you killed him?"

"No." Robby squeezed his eyes tight. In response to the internal pressures that Download knew the boy was feeling, the icy shell around Robby hardened. "It was an accident."

"No," Download said. "It wasn't. This fire was deliberately set, and once I tell the arson investigators where to look, they're going to know it, too. Duvall burned this building on purpose, to collect on the insurance for someone else. He didn't care who died in the fire, and he was willing to blame you. Do you want your mom to be with someone like that? How safe is she going to be?"

Fresh tears brimmed in Robby's eyes and leaked out over his icy cheeks. He folded his arms over his knees and hugged himself. "I don't know what to do."

"Start with the truth," Download said. "I can help you with that."

"No, you won't," a man's harsh voice stated.

Turning, Download saw a squared-off man with a heavy build enter the room, following the harsh angles of the big pistol in his fist. "You're Duvall," he said.

"No shit, Sherlock." Duvall was dressed in a silver fireproof suit complete with mask. There was no way to tell what he looked like. The pistol never wavered. "And now you're both gonna have to die."

6

Chicago, Illinois | *10:49 a.m. CST*
Great Lakes Authority (GLA) | *1649 Greenwich Mean*
87.7 degrees W Longitude | *March 28, 2024*
41.8 degrees N Latitude | *Friday*

Assignment: Electra, cont.
Tactical Ops: Apprehension, Use Necessary Force
Status: Code Red, Contact Made

Even before the accident that had revealed him as a metable, Refit had never been interested in finesse. The guy with the baseball bat on his right made the first move. Without taking the Detonics .45 from his trench coat pocket, the patchwork giant shot the Cybered Shadow in the face.

The Para-bullet slammed into the youth's forehead just above the left eye with enough force to split the skin and throw him backward. He was unconscious before he hit the ground.

By the time the first knife-user was within reaching distance, Refit already had the spray can of OC out. He gave the girl a shot in the face. The pepper spray was ruthless, bringing instant, debilitating pain without injury.

The girl dropped her knife and fell to her knees, screaming

and clawing at her burning eyes.

Refit stepped around her, bringing the Detonics up. He fired two shots into the other bat-wielder's chest, knocking him back and putting him down.

"Damn ugly freak!" the boy with the chain snarled as he whipped the vicious weapon at Refit.

Standing his ground, the FREELancers agent lifted his left arm and let the tow chain snake around his forearm. Surprise stained the Cybered Shadows member's face. The other end of the chain was wrapped around the ganger's own wrist.

"Bad move, punk," Refit said with an evil, twisted grin. He set himself and yanked on the chain. Along with the ability to incorporate the flesh and organs of others as his own, Refit also had the ability to use that muscle mass to his utmost. His strength and speed were far greater than a normal human's.

The Cybered Shadow came off his feet. The impromptu game of crack-the-whip ended with the ganger slamming into the hallway wall. Plaster dust showered down over him. He didn't get back up.

The remaining gang member tried to bolt and run past Refit. Sticking a boot out, he caught the guy at the ankles and tripped him. As the ganger flew through the air, the patchwork giant shot him three times. The Para-bullets had already invaded his system and rendered him unconscious by the time he sprawled the length of the hallway.

"Skeet," Refit said. He shook the length of chain from his arm, then advanced on the door bearing the Cybered Shadows' chop marks. He wore a Kevlar vest that protected his groin and half of his thighs. Everything but his head was meat, just a tool he had to do the job with.

He kicked the door open and went through, struck in the chest almost immediately by four bullets. The sound of autofire rolled in his ears.

The room had been expanded in recent times, but it hadn't been done neatly. The walls were filled with gaping holes large enough to walk through. More graffiti covered what was left of the walls. Black sheets covered the windows, blotting out the sun.

Rocking back from the bruising force of the bullets, Refit fired at two targets in front of him—not even taking the time to ascertain sex—and was in motion as they went down. He scanned the surroundings, looking for Jeannine Hartley.

Out of his peripheral vision, he spotted a guy bringing up a rifle and pointing it in his direction. He spun, bringing the Detonics around, knowing it was going to be too damn late. He fired just after the .308 Netmaster coughed to life.

The shooter went down, but the four rockets on the expanding nylon weave rushed toward the FREELancers agent, spinning the net out behind them. In the enclosed space, the net wasn't able to get a large spread.

The nylon strands coiled tightly around Refit's shoulders, trapping his arms. He cursed and tried to slide it over his head. The net didn't move. Taking a deep breath, he flexed his muscles, drawing on everything he had. Black spots clouded his vision from the effort. The strands parted with a rip.

"ChipMother!" the ganger with the Netmaster rifle shouted.

Refit put a round into the young man's thigh, then emptied it into the girl diving over one of the mismatched sofas sitting in the center of the room. When the slide blew back dry, he pressed the magazine release and spilled the empty from the butt of the pistol. He took another clip from inside the trench coat and slammed it home.

He wheeled, in motion now and leaving the ruined net on the torn carpet. Jeannine Hartley was nowhere to be seen. To his left, the first room ended bluntly against the corner of the apartment building, its two windows overlooking the streets.

On the right, holes chopped through the plaster walls led into two other apartments. One of them seemed to be filled with all kinds of beds, including roll-aways and sofa beds. Pornographic posters hung on the wall. The surroundings held no personality or warmth. It was just a warm, dry place that housed predators. Their stink—of unwashed bodies, colognes, spoiling food, and sex—hung over everything.

He raked the two rooms with his gaze. The apartment filled with beds wasn't a likely option. Another round impacted against his Kevlar vest from the back. Spinning, he fired two rounds into the shooter who had taken cover in a closet.

Choosing the other door, Refit ran toward it. There was movement on the other side of the hole in the wall. The door was closed.

"He's coming! He's coming!" someone shouted.

Refit read the movements and knew he was headed into a trap. They were shifting together in a pattern, expecting him to come through the hole.

Instead, he threw himself at the door, putting all of his weight into it, a human battering ram. Pain flooded him, but he ignored it. The feelings were just a warning system. There wasn't anything he could tear up that couldn't be replaced.

The door jumped off of its hinges as if it had been bombed. The extra muscle power he was able to derive from the borrowed meat was an awesome force even without the weight of his body. He landed on the door, his gun out before him and firing.

Two rounds hit a boy standing behind a pantry and spread him out over the stove at his back. Luckily, none of the burners were on, though pots and pans crudded over with debris days and possibly weeks old went flying.

He fired another round at a black girl taking cover behind an overturned table. The round caught her on the side of the neck and knocked her down like a paper target.

The door didn't land flat. Someone was underneath, spewing forth a wealth of curses.

With the kitchen area clear of gangers, Refit stayed on top of the door and peered under it.

A chunky guy with kinky hair and a prosthetic ear that had been torn loose and was leaking down the side of his face was trapped under the door. A buzzbuster was trapped under him, the gnarled head of the shock stick poking into the Cybered Shadow's chin. "Get off me, you ugly son of a bitch!" He howled in pain.

"Kid, you got a mouth like a public toilet. And obviously poor eyesight." Refit bounced up and down on the door, scanning the area. No more gangers were in his immediate vicinity. "Tell me where Jeannine Hartley is."

"Piss up a rope!" the ganger yelled, but the weight of the

door was squeezing the breath out of him.

Refit worked not to let it back in.

"I can't breathe! I can't—"

"Your choice," the patchwork giant said. "I don't find Hartley, I got no reason to leave you."

"Damn—*ugh!*"

"And it's hard to sound threatening when you sound like a cartoon duck with a head cold."

"Back room," the ganger wheezed. "Back room. Window. Out . . . onto . . . the rooftop."

"The cops come to pick you up," Refit said, "you don't want to forget your ear." He leaned in and doused the ganger with the OC, then sprang up and raced toward the other room.

The back rooms had been used for storage. Piles of boxes and packages, shot through with empty purses and personal effects, testified to the fact that the Cybered Shadows had been busy on the streets.

"You getting this?" Refit asked, using the Burris transceiver.

It was a moment before Matrix answered, letting him know she was working more than one com-link at the moment. "Turn in a circle. Get everything. Underhill was adamant about that. The signal's coming in good."

Refit swung around once, keeping the pistol up.

"The gun's in the way," Matrix said.

"Fix it in the vid later," the agent growled. "I'm up to my ass in alligators here." He ran for the only window and glanced outside. A fire escape created a steel latticework that ran down the side of the building.

Staring down through the fire escape, Refit looked for his target. Traffic had come to a stop in front of the building, blocked in both directions by Chicago PD uniforms out on foot. Two unmarked sedans with flashing lights were parked against the curb. The FREELancers agent thought he recognized Detective Amos Haddonfield, broad-shouldered and short-legged, with unruly auburn hair poking out from under his snap-brim hat.

Jeannine Hartley wouldn't have gone down if she'd hoped to escape.

Refit pushed through the window and out onto the fire escape landing. A few feet away, a ladder mounted onto the building wall ran to the rooftop. He threw a leg over the landing's railing, put away the OC, and grabbed the ladder. He went up awkwardly, one-handed.

He paused at the top, letting his gun hand lead him. The rooftop was hot tar speckled with rock. The rusted hulls of a half-dozen street droids, cannibalized for their chipsets and on-board energy-grid uplinks, lay scattered over its surface. Until a street droid had been ruled officially dead or unproductive, the city power management kept the sat-links clear and allowed them to boot into maintenance power sites. Droid cannibalism wasn't new, but it was hard to catch. Often, power was stolen for anywhere from a month to six months. A lot of drug labs used the droids, and their coded sec-passes, to transport drugs through the city's underground sewer tunnels.

On the other side of the rooftop, Jeannine Hartley was making a leap out into space.

"Damn!" Refit growled. He hauled himself up the ladder. Keeping the Detonics in his fist, he ran to the spot where she'd disappeared. He stopped when he got there, pausing at the side of the low wall.

Almost seven feet down and over a dozen feet away, Jeannine Hartley was pushing herself up from the pebbled tar roof. A male ganger was helping her to her feet.

"Bastard followed us!" a third ganger yelled. He was lean and wore a black duster, his face as pale as an August moon, tinted by collagen cosmetics. Black tattooing created diamond-shaped shadows over his hard, narrow eyes and at the corners of his black-lipped mouth. His hair was as white as frost and stuck out like the baby chicken down Refit remembered from his grandfather's farm.

The patchwork giant fired the Detonics from the point, not taking time to aim. A bullet whispered by his cheek, sizzling against his skin. He fired eight or ten shots and missed maybe three or four times, creating craters in the pebbled tar.

The rest of the bullets smashed into the white-faced gunner and knocked him down.

Jeannine Hartley and the remaining youth scrambled for the other side of the roof.

Stepping up onto the low wall, Refit threw himself across the distance, afraid for a moment that he'd misjudged the jump. Hartley and her cohorts must have hit the edge of the roof running. He landed hard enough to jar his breath out.

At the other side of the building, Jeannine Hartley and her companion had run out of places to go. Even from twenty feet away, having closed the distance with his longer strides, Refit could see the next building was across a street, not a narrow service alley.

The girl spun around, bringing up her pistol in both hands. She pointed it at Refit's face.

The FREELancers agent returned the favor, hoping his increased reflexes would allow him to move too quickly for her to track him if she decided to pull the trigger. "I don't want to shoot you," he said.

She showed him a nasty smile that was full of fear and anger. "Sorry. I don't have that problem."

Refit shrugged, keeping his face devoid of emotion. "Suit yourself. But I'm betting I'll stay alive long enough to take out you and your friend."

"You figure you're that damn tough?"

Refit pulled his scarred lips and grinned at her coldly. "I look like I been spending my life doing flower shows and ice cream socials?"

"Are you a bounty hunter?" Hartley asked. Her partner was nervously holding his pistol in both hands, moving his attention from one of them to the other.

"No." Refit pulled the trench coat back slowly, revealing the FREELancers logo on the left side of his jumpsuit.

"Same thing," Hartley said.

"Ask the police in this town," Refit said. "According to them, we operate on the side of the angels."

Hartley laughed bitterly. "Thugs with rights, that's all you are. You pay off the right people, you get licensed for busting heads instead of jailed for it."

"Depends," Refit said. "After you get the license, you gotta be careful whose head you bust."

"Who sent you after me?" Hartley demanded. "My father?"

"Yeah." The patchwork giant didn't bother lying to her and telling her that Harris Hartley was worried about his daughter.

"I'm not going back to him! No way in hell! You might as well kill me now!" The girl's voice rose, becoming shrill. Her finger whitened on the trigger.

Refit threw himself to one side, passing on her for the instant and hoping he lived through it. Catching the other ganger looking at the girl, the agent fired two bullets into the boy's thighs, keeping them intentionally low so the blunt trauma wouldn't push him over the edge of the building.

Hartley's shots dug into the pebbled tar roof, zipping through the tails of his trench coat.

Aiming deliberately, ignoring the fact that the girl was coming around on him, Refit shot her in the shoulder. The drug entered her system and deadened her arm immediately, causing her to drop the gun without firing again.

Jeannine Hartley screamed in inarticulate rage, cursing fiercely as she fought the effects of the Para-bullet. She turned as quick as a cat and, before Refit knew what she planned, threw herself over the side of the building.

"No, dammit!" The big man pushed off like a starter coming out of the blocks. He hadn't expected her to have that kind of reaction. He dropped the Detonics, locking eyes on the girl as gravity claimed her and she dropped.

Refit slammed into the wall with his hip just as his outstretched fingers found purchase in the girl's leather jacket. He prayed it would hold, then prayed he could, then he said to hell with it and held on out of sheer meanness.

He roared with pain and the adrenaline rush as she hit the end of his arm. Off-balance as he was, the dead weight almost pulled him over the side of the roof. He held on with everything he had, his face grinding against the concrete parapet. He felt the friction lessen when the blood flowed.

Then, everything stopped: his slide across the rooftop and the girl's fall. He looked down, not believing he still had her.

She dangled inside her jacket, unconscious from the effects

of the Para-bullet. Below her, traffic whizzed along the busy street. Even if she'd somehow survived the drop, she'd have been killed by a car.

"I've got a heligyro on the way," Matrix said. "Underhill wants you to join Download."

Refit said sure. As he pulled the unconscious girl back onto the rooftop, he hoped Underhill was getting a fat fee for the agency. After seeing the girl's reaction to being taken in, and having listened to the tape of her father saying how much he cared and how worried he was about her, the patchwork giant didn't see either one of them getting much out of the deal.

The only thing that kept the whole rescue operation from being a total zero was the money. He tried to tell himself that he didn't care as he draped Jeannine Hartley's limp body over his shoulder, but it rang as hollow as his victory.

* * * * *

Chicago, Illinois	*10:58 a.m. CST*
Great Lakes Authority (GLA)	*1658 Greenwich Mean*
87.7 degrees W Longitude	*March 28, 2024*
41.8 degrees N Latitude	*Friday*

Assignment: Charon's Crossing, cont.
Tactical Ops: Protection & Transportation of VIP
Status: Code Yellow, Postponed

"You hadn't decided to come up here after the kid," Curtis Duvall said over the muzzle of his pistol, "I figure I'd have gotten away clean. He wasn't trying to save himself, even with those freaky powers. Now you're both going to have to go the hard way, and I'll just set it up where it looks like the kid capped you, then did himself."

Download looked at Robby. "You see this guy? This is what you were protecting. This is what you're afraid you don't measure up to." He slipped the Lesley Wright disk from the Octopus and shoved home the Henriksen one. The smoke in the room was thick enough that Duvall didn't notice the exchange. The familiar blue electricity rocketed through Download's mind and dumped the new skills into his brain.

"Hey, Bullet-head," Henriksen said in his heavy smoker's rasp. In corporeal flesh, the stuntman stood six-feet-five, weighed two hundred thirty pounds, and was deeply tanned. His long dark hair fell to his shoulders in the back and was razored on the sides. He always wore dark sunglasses and a Hollywood smirk. "That guy's got a gun pointed at us."

"You need a scene setup," Download asked, "or do you think you can go with the flow on this one?"

"*And* we're in a burning building?"

"They told me you were the best, Lou," Download said.

"Don't tell me we're supposed to rescue the sugar-frosted kid, too."

"Yep."

"Did I ever tell you that when they did the skill download on me, I had a hangover I lied about?"

"Every time I use this disk." Download could already feel the pain of the hangover slamming into his head.

Henriksen laughed inside Download's skull, making the pain more severe. "I'm still the best stuntman in the biz, guy. Spielberg, Cameron, Tarrantino, all those guys knew it."

"What have you got for me here?"

"You like Chuck Norris?"

"Always preferred the Bruce Lee movies," Download said truthfully. "Bruce had the snarl down."

"Him and Elvis," Henriksen said. "But I got the chance to do some one-on-one with Norris. Despite the goody-two-shoes image he had in the cinema, the guy was totally rad in the martial arts department."

"Lou."

"Yeah, yeah. Don't get your panties in a wad. Give me something to work with here, and I'll take care of you."

Download locked eyes with the lenses of Duvall's suit. "You won't get away with this."

"How do you figure, wise guy?"

"I'm wired for video and audio," the FREELancers agent said. "Everything you just told me has been recorded. And I can tie you directly to the Hastings Family. How long do you think they're going to let you live to testify against them? Inside *or* outside of jail?"

The statement froze Duvall for just an instant. The barrel of the pistol wavered. "I don't believe you."

Download took the miniature speaker out of his ear canal and held it between thumb and forefinger. Robby was almost catatonic against the wall. "Matrix," he said over the vocal pickup, loud enough that Duvall could hear, "give him a playback that's a convincer."

Accessing another function of the speaker, Matrix put an audio-feed through. The video part *had* been a lie, but it gave Duvall something else to think about. The broadcasted words were Duvall's, captured over the roar of the fire: ". . . both going to have to go the hard way, and I'll just set it up where it looks like the kid capped you, then . . ."

Matrix had evidently programmed the receiver for maximum audio level. The words blasted into the room, drowning out everything else.

Duvall was visibly shaken.

Acting on that moment of indecision and surprise, Download tapped into Henriksen's reflexes and erupted from the floor. Duvall fired the gun, but the FREELancers agent was no longer where he'd been. Keeping his fists doubled in front of him, Download set himself, then came around in a spinning kick that crashed into the arsonist's stomach.

Duvall's mask exploded off him in a rush of escaping breath. He went backward and slammed into the side of the doorway.

"Go with it, man!" Henriksen shouted into Download's mind. "Don't let this bastard have a shot at you! Man, that's movies, not real life!"

Before Duvall could recover, Download followed up with two more kicks: one to the abdomen, and one a snap-kick to the man's face that broke teeth and stretched him out into the hallway. The gun was lost in the debris.

The FREELancers agent stopped in the doorway, breathing harshly. Duvall wasn't moving.

"He's out," Henriksen said.

"He'll die if I leave him there." Download scanned the hallway. Most of the ceiling was down now, lying in broken, flaming heaps. There was no way back to the door or the elevator.

"Damn," the stuntman said. "I could, I'd shed a tear for the son of a bitch. Truly, I would. You got maybe one damn slim chance to save the kid and yourself, and you feel guilty about not taking this guy out with you. You want my vote?"

"No."

"Good. Get your ass in gear."

Download abandoned his position and went back to Robby Hatch. "Time to go."

The icy sheath that had covered the boy's body had melted, leaving fat water droplets behind. He reached up for Download without a word.

The boy was an unwieldy size, and Download knew he was already pushing exhaustion, but he had no choice. He lifted the boy up in both arms as if he were a baby and held him tight against his chest. "You hang on there, Robby. I'm going to get us out of here." He stared into the sheet of flame in the hallway, partially obscuring the floor.

"What does the front of the building look like?" Henriksen demanded.

Even before he'd received the Download device, Jefferson Scott had possessed an almost eidetic memory and a talent for mimicry. He described the front of the apartment building, including the air impact bag the firemen had been putting up as he'd entered the building.

"Seven stories up," Henriksen said incredulously, "and the air bag's in the wrong place. Damn, you guys are getting your money's worth out of the time I gave you."

"We don't have a lot of time here," Download reminded him. Robby Hatch was holding on around his neck tightly.

"Okay, but oh, man, you aren't going to like this at all."

"Let's just do it." Download saw the images in his head and felt his reflexes gearing up for it. "Robby isn't going to manage it without help."

"So we're down to one arm," Henriksen said, laughing. "You think you're going to live forever?" It was the stuntman's favorite saying.

Download didn't give himself time to get any more afraid of what was coming. He shifted Robby's weight around, then dashed through the flames. The heat scorched his jumpsuit, burning the hair from his arms and filling his nose with a new stink.

He didn't pause at the broken windows. He put one foot on the sill, and then he was through, the sucking arms of the fire twisting after the vacuum he left behind.

The street waited below them seven stories down in a twisting panorama of lights and emergency vehicles and onlookers.

Robby tucked in close beneath Download's chin and squeezed his eyes shut.

The FREELancers agent wanted to shut his eyes, too. But he couldn't.

"C'mon, dammit!" Henriksen yelled. "You're falling. Gravity's your friend, but you're going to have to be aggressive with it."

Following the reflexes, Download roped a hand back over the sill they'd just left long enough to partially brake their fall and correct the angle. Possibly, if he'd had Henriksen's strength and body mass, he'd have been able to catch them. But he didn't. When he hit the end of his arm, it felt as if the shoulder joint were going to be torn apart.

"It's still together," Henriksen said. "It's just pain. Ignore it."

Together, Download and the boy dropped down the side of the building. He made contact with his tennis shoes, slowing the fall by aligning his body with his back against the wall. The rough surface of the bricks bit into the Kevlar vest, ripping away the jumpsuit at first kiss.

A parapet ran around the building at the fifth floor. It stuck out almost eighteen inches and looked tempting as a landing point. They needed to hit that in order to correct the fall and give them the shot they needed for the air bag. He could see it now, tall and tight and almost ten feet too far to the right.

"Don't even think about it," Henriksen said. "You try to do more than bump and run there like we've planned, you're going to blow out a knee, maybe both. Then you and the kid go splat."

At the parapet, Download caught his weight on his bent legs just long enough to lose some more of the speed they'd built up by stepping into the gravity well. He didn't have the strength to stop completely. Keeping his arm tight around Robby Hatch, he heard the boy's labored breathing and felt the wetness from the boy's skin soaking into the jumpsuit.

He left the parapet in an angular dive, falling forward and twisting his body, losing distance to the street level without totally committing to gravity.

"Flagpole's coming up," Henriksen stated.

"I've got it," Download replied. He reached out with his one free arm. There was no time to wonder if it would handle the combined weight of the boy and him. He curled his fingers around it and worked the centrifugal force. Not only did he have to break the speed he'd gained, but he had to get some outward momentum to manage the distance to the air bag.

As he rounded the flagpole, he brought his knees in as far as he could with the boy there. Using the reflexes and knowledge he'd borrowed from the stuntman, he pushed out with his feet and caught the side of the building. When he released the flagpole, he was still falling, but he'd changed the path toward the air bag.

Download turned his body in the air, putting himself under the boy to take the brunt of the impact. He was aware of the firemen and EMTs running away from where they thought the impact would occur.

Robby Hatch was as tense as a bowstring.

"Go limp," Download said. "Loosen up and—" Then he impacted against the air bag, hitting one of the outside corners. Black spots swam in his vision, and it felt as if he'd been hit in the ribs with a sledgehammer. Robby groaned in his ear.

Out of wind and not really believing what he'd just done, Download remained on his back and held the boy tight. When he blinked his eyes open again, they were ringed with firemen, police, and ambulance workers who were scrambling across the air bag to reach them.

"*All right!*" the Hollywood stuntman yelled. "Damn, did anyone have any film in the camera? I don't want to have to do that again."

Neither did Download. He held the boy tight and stared through the crowd at the BirdSong JK91 heligyro hovering above the building. FREELancers was emblazoned in gray and silver on its metal hide. For the moment, he ignored it and closed his eyes, already regretting the promise he'd made to the boy clinging so desperately to him. What was he going to do when Robby found out what he was really like? That he was holding on to another false dream?

7

Outside Melaka City, Melaka — ***12:07 a.m. Local Mean***
Indonesia — ***1707 Greenwich Mean***
102.3 degrees E Longitude — ***March 29, 2024***
2.4 degrees N Latitude — ***Friday***

Gunfire followed the screams. Then another man was yelling for help.

Tabor went left, following the narrow corridor. His shoulders nearly touched the stone on both sides, and if he straightened out of his crouch he figured his head would scrape along the low ceiling. He radioed Wallsey and told the man to bring a team inside on the double.

The tunnel took two more vicious lefts. In design and layout, it was exactly like one of the other catacombs they'd investigated. Some of the maze areas were dictated by the need to provide support for the buildings overhead and to avoid problem areas in the ground itself, especially underground water supplies and tree roots. If the builders had simply hacked their way through any root systems that had been in their way and killed out the jungle areas overhead, the dead areas would have marked the locations of the catacombs. Secrecy had been part of the overall design.

The hallway widened at the end and filled with the glare of electric torches. The flagstones were stained with age, and the crevices between them were irregular from shifting substrata. Shadows jerked across the walls.

Tabor's hair stood on end from the electricity filling the chamber. Tiny, crackling blue arcs jumped along his arms and chest.

"My god," Fook said in a voice that was barely audible.

An apparition stood at the other end of the room, bent over despite the seven foot ceiling. Electricity ran from it in bolts that narrowed to spidery veins before seeming to disappear altogether.

The thing must have been nine or ten feet in height and easily four feet across at the shoulders. The face belonged on a mandrill, its pointed snout a mix of red, blue, and white pigmentation. The brow sloped to a point over close-set eyes that looked as inviting as cold, black grease. The legs were too short for the barreled chest and long midsection. The arms were almost half again as long. The creature held the second merc up in three metal appendages more than twice its height. The appendages hooked into a harness on its body, disappearing under the crimson robe it wore.

The merc hung several inches off the floor, struggling weakly in the deadl'y grip. His hands pried at the metal fingers that sank into his flesh.

The other merc lay in a bloody heap at the thing's feet. He'd been gutted quickly and efficiently, his insides spilled across the flagstones.

Seemingly without effort, the fourth metal arm shot forward. It crunched through the front of the man's skull with an audible, wet smack, continued on through the brain, and exited the back of the man's head, scattering blood and matter behind it.

The merc quivered out his life, losing all control over his responses.

The bloody metal appendage sucked back through the wound, then spun quickly with a whirring sound, throwing splatters of blood in all directions. The misshapen, gargantuan head turned to focus its malevolent gaze on Tabor. Without a thought, it flung the dead man away. The thick black lips pulled back to reveal yellow tusks. A growl rolled out and filled the chamber.

The torches didn't penetrate very far inside the opening behind the creature because the angle was wrong. The smooth side of the doorway indicated it had been carefully contrived to be almost invisible when closed.

"Shoot it!" Fook exclaimed. "Quickly!" The Melakan politico cowered in the corridor.

Tabor waited, gazing down the open sights of the Nova. If he destroyed the beast, there would be no chance to study it. But he was no fool. He reached inside himself and gathered the power he'd first discovered when he was twelve.

"Do you understand English?" he asked.

The creature turned, still hunched over, its head only a couple of inches from hitting the ceiling. The mandrill face hardened, then cocked to one side.

"That's right, you bloody bastard," Tabor said. "Fook! Talk to this bleeding thing."

"What would you have me say?"

Tabor kept his sights over the creature's face. "Tell it we mean no harm, that we come in peace. The usual drivel you tell a bloke before you reach into his chest and yank his heart out."

"We come in peace," Fook said. "We mean you—"

"In Malay, you cretinous fool."

The creature's eyes shifted to Fook, and it stopped growling. The four metal appendages around it moved restlessly, clicking together and scraping against the floor and ceiling as it kept in touch with its environment.

Without warning, it launched one of the metal arms at Tabor, moving with the speed of a harpoon.

The merc colonel took one step sideways, into the Void. It was the only thing he'd ever been able to think of the place as. The Void was cold and dark and black, and seemed to put the real world just out of his reach.

The metal arm shot through the area where he'd just been

standing. The sharp knuckles of the skeletal fingers slammed into the wall, gouging chips from it as they sank into the stone. The sound of the grinding impact rang throughout the chamber.

Inside the Void, where the physical world no longer existed on a tactile level, a chill gale-force wind blew at Tabor, shoving him back toward the physical world. He strained for a moment, holding back the wind, then chose his spot. He came back into corporeal being seven feet to his left, having never crossed any of the space between. He brought the Nova up and flamed a low intensity laser blast at the creature's head.

The harsh green pulse of light slapped into the mandrill face and knocked the creature back. Its two real hands clapped to its head as it roared in pain and rage. The sickening odor of burnt flesh and hair filled the air. Fighting for self-preservation now, the creature lashed out with all its artificial appendages. The metal hands pounded the walls, ceiling, and floor.

Rock dust and chips fell across Tabor's back from the ceiling as he dodged. He had to step into the Void twice more to keep from being hit. With his metability engaged, his senses worked faster than a normal person's would even on panic mode. But the speed of the ape-thing put it only a heartbeat behind. For a moment, he thought the initial laser burst wasn't going to be enough to put the creature down.

The flailing arms grew weaker. Another few tries and its legs buckled from underneath it.

Tabor stopped moving, but kept the Nova pointed at the thing's head. He was breathing hard. Using the metability always took a lot out of him.

As a metable, Tabor wouldn't have been accepted as commander of the mercenary unit. There were still too many prejudices against metables. However, he'd managed to put together a small cadre of soldiers like himself, who had metabilities they used to further their own ends, yet managed to keep secret. One of the manifestations of his own gift included an ability to know as soon as he touched someone if they were metable. He'd used that to his own advantage in putting together a core group.

Besides his own ability to perform line-of-sight teleportation, Tabor had also discovered an ability to render himself insubstantial for short periods. He still needed air to breathe, but nothing else could touch him.

Tabor moved forward, keeping the laser pistol on the creature as it jerked spasmodically. The metal arms rang against the flagstone floor. Several of the stones had been broken by its efforts to find him. The electrical discharge that had filled the room was also gone.

"Is it dead?" Fook asked.

"As dead as it's going to get," Tabor replied. He'd glanced at the man after teleporting, only to find that Fook had been in full retreat back into the corridor. The Malaysian hadn't seen him use his metability.

Three mercs, bristling with automatic weapons, pushed their way past Fook into the center of the impromptu battlefield. Sergeant Wallsey headed them up, his walrus mustaches twisted out into fine points.

"Colonel?" Wallsey asked.

"At ease, soldier," Tabor said. "We're done here."

"Jeez, that's a big son of a bitch," the sergeant said.

Tabor kicked one of the mechanical arms, causing it to slide out away from the body of the ape-thing. Blood covered the floor. "I want this area policed as quickly as possible and scrubbed down. Hot, soapy water. And lots of it. Then I want a generator brought down so we can properly inspect the premises."

"Yes, sir." Wallsey turned and barked orders to the two men with him.

"Set up a security perimeter," Tabor said. "No one in or out unless it's on my say."

"Done."

Tabor squatted beside the dead thing. As he looked at it, the hackles along the back of his neck rose.

A metal corset connected the mechanical appendages to the beast-man. Tabor was sure that's what it was. Too much intelligence had been exhibited for him to simply write it off as an animal.

Tabor rolled the beast-man over and looked at the head. The

laser beam had hit it flush. The hair on the face had burned off, leaving crooked stubble. The multipigmented skin stretched tight over the thrusting snout held dozens of blisters. Some had burst. The eyes were glazed white as if they'd been parboiled, rolling hollowly in sockets that had been rendered dry.

The metal corset held a few more surprises. Not only was the craftsmanship of excellent quality, with every joint uniquely fitted on each arm, but it also had an independent power source. Silver wires, as thin as thread and still shiny, were wrapped around a dark gemstone that looked like a garnet, then led to all four arms without touching other metal surfaces. The gemstone, hardly bigger than a thumb, was mounted in a recessed socket over the beast-man's left breast.

Taking his broad-bladed combat knife from a boot sheath, Tabor knelt and quickly sliced through the thin wires leading to the metal arms. Sparks flashed, but the contacts went dead in nanoseconds. Leaning back, he shoved the point of the knife under the gem and worked to pry it out of its place. It sparked again and continued sparking, the electricity eating into the big blade while the colonel worked.

The gem popped free without warning, landed on the flagstones, and went skittering across the rough rock to fetch up against the wall. A dull luster seemed to coil and move under its carved facets.

"Is that a ruby?" Fook asked, getting closer.

Tabor threw the ruined combat knife away and closed on the gem. "I don't know. Pete, let me borrow your penflash. I lost mine somewhere in all the excitement."

The sergeant handed over the penflash, then kicked absently at the corpse. "Wonder if he's got any kith and kin, sir?"

"Get a team organized," Tabor said, gazing at the darkened opening of the doorway in the wall across from him. "We're going to have to find out. I'll want net guns down here, a couple of flame throwers. And some wrist rockets."

"Yes, sir."

"I'm going to need that body out of here too, Sergeant."

"Yes, sir. I suppose you want the damn thing of a piece as well?"

"Peele's going to need to take a look at it." Tabor answered the question automatically, trying not to show the excitement that was about to consume him. The catacombs hadn't been opened in centuries. For the beast-man to still be alive meant a righteous bit of tech had been invented to either put the thing on storage or somehow extend its life. Either promised a fortune if he recovered the tech that made it possible.

"Peele's ready to take a look at it now," a feminine voice declared.

Tabor glanced over his shoulder.

Margo Peele was a tall, striking woman. Her ancestry was Norwegian, and it showed in the volcanic blue of her eyes, the platinum blond of her hair, and in the generous build. She wore dark jodhpurs tucked into thigh-high jungle boots and a crimson blouse. A SIG-Sauer P226 rested in a cross-draw belly holster at the front of her belt. With one hand she carried a black leather backpack by its straps.

Tabor watched the fatigue in her face melt away as she studied the dead beast-man. Without apparently noticing its presence, she stepped over the corpse of the soldier in front of her and knelt beside the beast-man.

"It was alive?" she asked.

"For a while," Tabor said.

With a snap, she pulled on a pair of elbow-length hygienic gloves. "Would have been nice if it had stayed that way a bit longer."

"Came down to me or it bloody well quick," Tabor said. He prodded the dark red jewel with the penflash. Nothing happened. Getting a little more daring, holding the power in him ready to phase his whole arm out of the physical world if he had to, he touched the gem with a fingertip.

Nothing happened.

"Did it talk?" Peele drew her hands across the beast-man's face. Her background was archeology, but her business was dealing in black-market antiquities. She was a Savant, able to touch a piece and know if it was the genuine article. As such, she was paid quite handsomely.

Tabor knew she had a burning need to see places and things

that hadn't been seen before. She'd been a sharp negotiator when, to help pay for his convalescence, he'd hired her to move some of the museum pieces he'd confiscated during the Sand Wars. When he'd decided how he was going to handle the post in Melaka, he'd gotten in touch with her. The colonel knew she wouldn't turn him down.

"We didn't exactly sit down to tea," Tabor growled. "These men scattered in bloody flinders about you are the work of this thing. There didn't seem to appear time for proper introductions."

"The voice box seems well developed." Peele pressed her gloved hands into the folds of the dead thing's neck. "I'll know more once I get it on the table and open it up. Did these men attack it?"

"I don't know. By the time I got here, they were pretty much as you find them now."

"These metal appendages work?"

"Yes. There's writing on the breastplate." The gem Tabor held felt cool to his touch, not hot at all. He closed his hand over it, absorbing the angular points and trapping it. Without warning, the jewel pulsed, and a ruby glow slid out from between his fingers. There was still no burning. The gem held power, but it was untapped at the moment. He dropped it into a shirt pocket.

Peele ran a gloved hand over the surface of the breastplate. "I'll know more when I can actually touch it for myself. After I clean it up."

Tabor joined the woman, holding the Beretta/Douglas Nova in his fist. Congealing blood covered the breastplate and smeared her gloves.

"I get a feeling of security," Peele said, looking at the inscription. Her voice was distant, letting him know she'd slid into her Savant state. "This man was a guard. Connected with religion. There's a sense of station and devotion."

"He was a follower, not a leader?" Tabor asked.

The woman nodded. "I'm almost positive."

The skin between Tabor's shoulder blades prickled. "Doesn't make much sense for a guard to be hanging around here for a couple thousand years, maybe more, without something to guard."

The hidden door still gaped open, but only darkness showed within.

Tabor turned to face the opening, leveling the Nova. "Pete, let me borrow your hand torch." He pocketed the penflash and caught the light when the sergeant tossed it to him.

Margo Peele stood and drew her pistol.

"Ladies first?" Tabor asked.

"I don't think so," the archeologist responded. Fook stood against the wall behind her, not looking at all inclined to enter the door.

"I've got your back, sir," Wallsey said. An Ingram M-11 Stuttershot was in the sergeant's capable hands.

Tabor went through the door with the Beretta ahead of him.

* * * * *

O'Hare International Airport	***11:13 a.m. CST***
Great Lakes Authority (GLA)	***1713 Greenwich Mean***
87.7 degrees W Longitude	***March 28, 2024***
41.8 degrees N Latitude	***Friday***

Assignment: Oracle, cont.
Tactical Ops: Information Compilation
Status: Code Green

"Who's picking up the tab for ousting Colonel Tabor and his bully boys?"

"I can't answer that," Underhill said. "There remain some details that have to be dealt with first."

Dr. Gideon Gregory smiled, and the FREELancers administrator could see how he must have looked as a small boy. He definitely had to have been mischievous.

"You play your cards awfully close."

"It could be a big pot," Underhill said.

"There are some in the media who decry you as a larcenous wench with an eye always focused on the dollar."

"On the bottom line," Underhill replied without rancor. "Never on the up-front money. That can all too often be deceiving. I am a professional. Your point being?"

"I don't see your proposed action in Melaka as being very financially rewarding. Yet I know from my past experiences in dealing with others that you're committed to this."

"You haven't talked with the client; I have." Underhill shifted in her chair. Normally she wouldn't have let anyone challenge her or her principles so directly, but there was something about the archeologist that intrigued her. Still, she wasn't about to respond to his baiting. "Tell me about the excavation in Melaka. How advanced do you think the culture was?"

"They had a number of farming tools and a written language. Obviously they felt threatened by the other people living in the area at that time, otherwise why build catacombs and live there?"

Underhill nodded. "Henshaw feels the Guardians of the Scarab was a secret society that was anchored for some reason to that area. As cities and civilizations fell around them, they maintained their location. For centuries."

"I don't know that I agree with that," the archeologist said. "We can't safely assume that the so-called Guardians of the Scarab were a separate entity for that long. It's possible that other cultures that lived in that area simply used the preexisting catacombs for their own needs."

"Did you feel that only one people lived there?"

"Ms. Underhill, from what I saw, whoever lived in those catacombs was a violent race. There were pictographs, with untranslated accompanying text, that definitely showed acts of aggression and possibly some human sacrifices as well. I find it troubling to think that in all those years, that society or people didn't grow past that point."

"Maybe they did," the FREELancers administrator replied. "But perhaps it was important that they remain as they were, too."

"That's Henshaw talking." Gregory shook his head. "I'm not one to throw stones at a peer's conjectures—"

"You've been known to," Underhill stated. "Claude Deeson's work with the Mayans. Jeremy Vogel's thoughts on the Chaldeans."

"Okay. There are a few instances, and you're obviously aware of them." Gregory held up a hand. "If anything, I think the Guardians of the Scarab society is an offshoot like the Thuggee society in India. It's a bastardized concept that was kept around for the amusement of the depraved in the civilizations built over the catacombs to use as an excuse to whet their own sick appetites."

"Some say digging around in the bones of people who've been lovingly laid to rest by their families is a sick appetite."

"Touché, Ms. Underhill."

"Did you get a chance to look at any of the scrolls?"

"A few."

"And what are your thoughts?"

"They had a really complicated alphabet." Gregory regarded her. "Look, I really don't know what you want from me."

"Henshaw believes several of those documents have plans for technology that was beyond the scope of the sciences at that time."

"You're referring to the drawings of airplanes and boats and spacesuits?"

"Yes." Underhill studied the man's face.

"They'd have to be carbon-dated," the archeologist said. "Myself, I didn't see any of those. Henshaw insists that he did at another site, but that one of his employees made off with them. Maybe it was his way of trying to leverage money from the UFO-chasers. At the time, he'd just learned his benefactor had died, leaving him broke. He was desperate."

"From the material I've read on Lord Castlereigh, he was interested in digging through the catacombs as well as rebuilding Melaka."

"He and his people found the first tunnels while putting up new buildings and tearing down some of the older parts of the city," Gregory said. "That's only natural. Curiosity keeps us moving. There was no mention of the Guardians of the Scarab by him or his group."

"I see that I wasn't the only one who checked," Underhill said.

"No. I like Frank. I'd like to see him succeed. But I'd need more convincing before I bought into something like this."

Gregory sighed. "People of every culture have dreamt about flying, just as they dream about getting around without walking or about exploring the bottom of the ocean. Most of the concepts are the same simply because there aren't that many ways to do those kinds of things. It's also possible that those scrolls are a hoax, or that they were done after those things were getting into public knowledge. It's impossible to tell without getting your hands on one of them."

Underhill glanced at her watch. Two minutes of her allotted time remained. "Castlereigh maintained a close surveillance over those excavation sites until his death."

"Presenting—again—the possibility for a hoax. Why didn't he publish his findings? Why didn't someone else? Paul Derembang was busy in those days consolidating United Nations support for Melakan independence. There'd been such a rash of it, especially in the eastern European countries and Mideast, that it took some persuasive arguments on his part to pull favor in that direction. Derembang could have used that find as a trump card."

"Unless it was being used in another way," Underhill pointed out. "After Lord Castlereigh put Melaka together and organized his resources, domestic companies started coming out with one patent after another regarding scientific breakthroughs."

"In medicines and computer programming areas, sure. But look at the people Castlereigh brought in from Hong Kong. Those people lived and breathed those fields. That was no big surprise."

"Do you believe in coincidence?" Underhill asked.

"Sure. Sometimes." Gregory shrugged.

"Only when everything else has been ruled out?"

The archeologist leaned back in his chair and grinned. "You're a hard woman to figure out. Every time I think I have you pegged, you switch. If you'd wanted support on your theories, you'd have had Frank Henshaw in here. You didn't. Why? To convince me?"

"Maybe it was to convince myself," Underhill answered truthfully. "I've got a couple of things for you." She reached into her purse and brought out a manilla business envelope. She passed it across.

"I've already been paid."

"I know. You'll find a plane ticket in there, a line of credit that's short of extravagant, and some documentation letting you know your excavation site in the Ukraine has been cleared for immediate use. Your plane leaves in just a few minutes. I've already talked with the university. They've released you from the schedule till you get back."

A look of disbelief filled Gregory's features. He slit the letter open with a thumbnail and glanced inside. "How'd you do this?"

"People tend to think that my owing them a favor is worth something. I have a history of making sure it is." Underhill stood up from the table and gathered her things.

"And what do I owe you?"

"I'll let you know."

Gregory's eyes met hers. "So is this to pay me off or to get me out of the way so I won't be able to talk to anyone about this meeting?"

"Maybe both. Don't worry about owing me," she said. "It won't be anything you can't handle."

The professor put away the envelope. "That's pretty oblique."

Underhill smiled, knowing the archeologist was aware of the chemistry between them. It had risen to an undeniable pitch, and Gregory had been around enough to know. "Whatever it is, it'll be purely professional." She turned and walked away, then turned back around, catching him looking at her figure just as she'd known he would.

He didn't look at all repentant as he raised his eyes to meet her gaze.

"One other thing, Dr. Gregory," she said. "There's a small piece of metal in there you might be interested in. I've had metallurgists look it over. Henshaw gave it to me and told me it's from one of the sites. According to the people I paid to check it out, that piece of metal has an atomic structure like none they've ever seen before."

Gregory looked back at the shiny disk he held, then back at

her, questions already on his lips.

"They're doing final boarding on your flight," Underhill said. "Have a nice trip, and good luck." She left him, heading in the opposite direction than the one in which he had to go. She felt his eyes on her and allowed herself a few seconds of self-satisfied pleasure, then she surreptitiously adjusted the .380 Beretta in the jackass holster under her jacket.

The sun slanted in through the glass windows facing out onto the runways, warming her, but it didn't go quite all the way through. She had an assassination attempt to attend, and even knowing Agent Prime and Scratchbuilt were backing the play didn't completely take away the chill.

8

Outside Melaka City, Melaka
Indonesia
102.3 degrees E Longitude
2.4 degrees N Latitude

12:19 a.m. Local Mean
1719 Greenwich Mean
March 29, 2024
Saturday

Colonel Will Tabor halted at the side of the door and panned the hand torch around the room. It was larger than the chamber outside and was filled with a multitude of shapes. He felt excited and wary at the same time. The gem in his pocket had started to glow a violent red, staining the front of his khaki shirt.

Tables lined the walls and occupied much of the floor space. Objects, made of blown glass and pottery and metal, covered the tables.

Tabor walked into the room, holding the metability inside him within easy reach. He could phase and become intangible long enough to spot a safe place to teleport to if another of the beast-men was inside.

Wallsey flanked him, coming out around the side to cover everything with the machine pistol. The flash taped to the top of it swept into the darkness along with Tabor's.

"Empty," Margo Peele said. Her voice was still tight, but the relief was evident.

Tabor kept the pistol out. "Fook, it's safe in here. Fetch a lantern and bring it in."

"At once," the elderly man called from outside.

"Place has been shut up a long bloody time," Wallsey commented. He swept the Ingram around, playing the beam over the room. "Smell the air, mate. Like death in here."

Tabor had to agree. The sickly sweet odor was at once reminiscent and repulsive. It reminded him of battlefields days after the fact when the dead hadn't yet been collected.

Besides the tables, the walls also were filled with heavy stone cabinets.

"That's Italian marble," Peele said, staring at the cabinet Tabor was investigating.

The merc colonel reached out and touched the marble surface. It was cool and smooth. The doors were neatly artificed into place, making for a tight fit. Lengths of bone, yellow with age and engraved with cuneiform writing highlighted in black, secured the doors from the outside.

"How do you know it's Italian?" Reaching out to the cabinet door, Tabor tried to get his fingers around it to find some kind of purchase.

"Pink-veined marble like that," Peele said, "Italian is the only kind it could be."

"Italy's a hell of a long way from here." His knife blade, surprisingly, wasn't thin enough to slide between the space between the cabinet door and frame.

"Melaka was the center of the spice trade for a long time," Peele said. "They did a lot of trading with Venice over the years."

"Evidently part of it was for marble."

"Those are Greek-style locks," the woman archeologist stated, touching the lip of a bored hole. "The key that fits it is going to be curved, about a meter long." She showed the measurement with her hands. "It'll probably have three pegs on the end of it. They'll be of different lengths."

"It'd be kind of conspicuous to carry around, wouldn't it?" Wallsey asked. He turned and started moving the flash across more of the tables. "Hey, I found the crate monkey-boy must have climbed out of."

Tabor left the cabinet and went to join his sergeant. The cubicle Wallsey had found was coffin-shaped, only taller than any coffin Tabor had ever seen. The sides were almost a foot thick all the way around. A huge lid, probably weighing three or four hundred pounds, lay on the floor beside it. Clear glass tubes stuck out from the right side of the cubicle, and a thin, greasy-looking fluid seeped from them, adding to the small pool against the silk pillows lining the bottom of the crate.

"Look here, mate," Wallsey said, dragging a finger around the lips of the glass tubes. Crimson stained his skin. "That's blood."

Curious now, Tabor walked back through the door to the outer chamber, almost running over Fook in the process.

"I have a light," the little Malaysian said, holding up an electric-powered bulls-eye lantern.

Tabor took it from him, making adjustments to the beam so he could play it against the ceiling and illuminate most of the chamber. The com-link buzzed, but it was for Wallsey. The sergeant stepped away to handle the posting questions.

"What do you think?" Tabor asked Peele.

"Definitely not cryogenics," the archeologist replied. "But that isn't my field."

Tabor rolled the beast-man's head to the side. There, like two purple mouths formed in the flesh, were openings in the flesh that matched up with the tubes in the cubicle. Traces of blood were around them.

Peele stuck a finger in one of the neck holes. It made sucking sounds. She moved it back and forth. "A lot of scarring has built up in there, so it wasn't a new addition to the guy. The tubes must have provided some type of nutrient/byproduct exchange. You can feed a body, but you've got to figure in the elimination process as well. And muscle atrophy." She took her finger out of the neck hole. "I can't wait to get this thing on the table for an autopsy."

Tabor nodded, then took the lantern and returned to the secret room.

"After everything we've seen so far," Peele said as she joined him, "you've got to admit we've no real idea what these people were capable of."

It was the truth, and the merc colonel knew it. In fact, after two months of pulling bodyguard duty in the country, that truth was why he'd decided to usurp control of Melaka and take charge of the excavations going on. There were billions of dollars yet to make on new discoveries.

Tabor worked quickly and efficiently, the way the military had taught him, arranging objects that fit together in order of largest to smallest. He kept a loose mental catalogue of everything he touched.

Peele reached into a long drawer under one of the tables and cried out enthusiastically, "Found it!"

Tabor glanced at her, noting the yard-long wooden dowel in her hand.

"It was hidden up under the counter," Peele said. "I didn't figure it would be far from this room after it was sealed up the way it was. Whoever had this laboratory wouldn't have wanted to go looking for it."

"Okay," Tabor said, "let's get some of these cabinets opened up and take a look."

Peele started with the cabinet behind her and worked to the right. She opened five cabinets while Tabor stood behind her with the Beretta/Douglas Nova in his hand.

The cabinets contained vials and containers of pellets, powders, and pastes. Neat cuneiform script covered papyrus glued onto them. Each had a seal of wax on the lid, the impression of a beetle, probably from a signature ring, to document authenticity and that it hadn't been opened. Peele told Tabor that she thought they were medicines of some kind, but she'd need more time and better light to better discern the contents.

The sixth cabinet was off to itself at the back of the room. A band of cuneiform, printed larger and bolder than any they'd seen before, ran across the front of it.

Peele ran her fingers across it. "Put your light on it more directly."

Tabor moved the flash, chasing the shadows away from the

inscription. Small blue lightnings followed the archeologist's touch. The eerie feeling he'd experienced earlier had returned. "This is personalized," Peele said. "It says this belongs to Saikalen. I'm not sure about the pronunciation. There appears to be a title here, too, but I don't know what it is. I want to say king, but I know that's not right. More like teacher, only stronger."

Tabor stared at the cabinet. It was built like a grandfather clock, almost as tall as he was, and not even half as wide. "Let's be getting it open. Time's running against us."

Peele nodded and inserted the long key. There was a series of clicks when she forced the pegs up inside the locking mechanism. "The inscription goes on to warn of death, quite colorfully, I might add. That part of the language is easy to understand. They labeled everything with threats and curses. There. It's open." She pulled the key out. She swung the door open, stepping back involuntarily.

Inside, a perfectly preserved head, the skin a little tighter over the cheekbones than had probably been the case in the beginning, sat on a small shelf. The skin tone was almost devoid of color, making the dark features even more prominent. Though thinned down to skin over bone so that it was little more than a barely clad skull, it was larger than most human heads Tabor had seen. The features were Slavic, thick and blunt despite the emaciation. Dark hair was slicked back and twisted into a heavy braid that coiled behind the head. Long wisps of mustache and beard hung down a foot or more.

Tubes, like the ones found in the cubicle holding the beast-man, fed into the back of the head through purple woundlike apertures. The sight sent a tingle of trepidation through Tabor. He raised the Beretta again involuntarily.

"The head has been expertly truncated," Peele said. She stripped off her bloody gloves and put on a fresh pair. Reaching out, she lightly traced the tubes at the base of the skull. They disappeared through the shelf, oozing through holes that had been drilled for them. "But why preserve it?"

"Maybe it's a trophy," Tabor said.

"Or maybe someone thought it had mystical properties," the

archeologist said. "A number of cultures keep objects made from the bones of the dead." She knelt down and examined the lower part of the cabinet.

Tabor studied the bronze collar around the head's throat. It was inlaid with red gems much like the one in his pocket. "Mysticism and the apparent devotion to the sciences don't seem to go together."

"Back when this thing was first created," Peele said, "the dividing line between science and magic was thinner than the separation between a multiple-personality disorder." She stuck out a hand. "Let me borrow your light. This hand torch is too awkward to move around inside here."

Switching off with her, the merc colonel played the torch over the disembodied head. He found himself mesmerized by it. There was an old scar just below the right cheekbone that pulled at the lips. Tabor recognized it as coming from a blade. The length and breadth of it indicated that it was a long and heavy blade, possibly a sword. Upon closer inspection, there were other, lighter nicks and slashes, almost invisible with the way the skin was stretched so tight.

"Look at this," Peele requested.

Tabor slid in beside her, aware of the brush of feminine flesh against his. As conqueror of Melaka, there'd been no shortage of women for his bed. He and his men had taken what they'd wanted and killed those who'd tried to stop them. They'd been selective, though, and none of the media had definite proof of it.

Margo Peele had been placed off-limits, first by Tabor, and secondly by the lady herself.

Still, the merc colonel found himself drawn to her, especially with fear maxing out all his senses. He breathed in her perfume and woman-smell.

"Look," Peele said, apparently unaware her breast was resting against his shoulder.

With difficulty, Tabor stared into the depths of the cabinet. Below the head was a skeleton made of hammered iron. The metal gleamed dully. At its center, no bigger than a bowling ball, was a metal canister. The tubes led from the skull down to the container.

"What the bloody hell?" Tabor asked, taking the penflash from her and moving it around. The arms and legs had been broken down and folded in on themselves. The feet were monstrosities, at least eighteen inches in length, with three forward toes and one reversed toe like a hawk's talons. The nails were cruel blades. Big enough to crush a normal man's head, the hands were similarly made.

"My guess is that this man was the victim of some accident," Peele said. "Obviously he was someone who was revered. Whatever they believed of the afterlife, they must have felt he'd need a body there."

"So someone made this one for him?"

"That's what I'm guessing."

Without warning, the blue electricity began whirling inside the cabinet. In a heartbeat, it became a spinning maelstrom that crackled and spat audibly.

Instinctively, Tabor grabbed Peele by the arm and yanked her back. He stepped partially in front of her, not to protect her, but to get her clear of his field of fire.

Around the collar of the truncated head, the red gemstones began to glow the color of fresh-spilled blood. Silvery lines shot free at the base of the skull, coming from somewhere inside. They were supple, as thin as thread as they stabbed down inside the mechanical skeleton, flowing into pores made in the metal spine and extremities.

With a jerk, the skeleton pushed itself into a standing position and began to come out of the cabinet.

Tabor kept his finger on the laser's trigger. The sweat had gone cold on his body. He started Peele backing away, keeping the pistol pointed at the metal body.

The shine of the silver threads against the iron was a sharp contrast. The joints clanked as they moved around, the sound of gears falling into place. Blue sparks kept moving inside the skeleton, filling in the chest as well as the bones of the arms and legs. The fingers ratcheted as they flexed. Then they reached back for the head.

Tabor resisted shooting the metal being. There was all that wealth waiting on him to think of. And iron wasn't going to stand up against the laser.

"It's not dead," Peele said in a voice filled with fear and wonderment. "The head's alive."

The skeleton settled the head onto its shoulders and turned it slightly. Tongue-and-groove locks clicked into place. With whispering slithers, the wires tightened up like silver snakes flexing. Blue sparks slid along their lengths.

The feet struck the stone floor heavily as the incredible being shifted around. At least eight feet tall, the apparition focused on Peele and Tabor. The eyes opened, revealing black hollows even darker than the shadows surrounding it.

Tabor felt and heard the voice inside his head.

Behold, the awesome might and power of Saikalen, word-speaker for the Star Scarab. I have returned from a voyage of years.

* * * * *

O'Hare International Airport — ***11:27 a.m. CST***
Great Lakes Authority (GLA) — ***1727 Greenwich Mean***
87.7 degrees W Longitude — ***March 28, 2024***
41.8 degrees N Latitude — ***Friday***

Assignment: Steel Wall
Tactical Ops: Protection, FREELancers 02
Status: Code Yellow

"I see a familiar face, kid."

John-Michael DeChanza hated being called a kid, but Agent Prime wasn't someone he particularly wanted to take umbrage with. Inside the thirty-five foot tall MAPS unit, he rested in total comfort with the computer-controlled environment. He was also totally fruit bat nuts with boredom. Stakeouts reminded a guy of everything else out in the world he was missing.

"So you're going to take off and chat with a chum while I'm stuck up in this warehouse?" DeChanza didn't want too much of his annoyance to show, but he was way past the point of taking a pat on the head and remaining calm.

In order for the Scratchbuilt armor to be discreetly on hand for the morning arrival, DeChanza had been delivered in the dead of night by semi, then hoisted up to the third floor storage area Underhill had rented for the week. He and Prime had spent three hours uncrating the MAPS. Given the strength of the man-amplifying power suit, DeChanza had suggested simply creating a hole in the crate big enough for him to crawl through, so he could get inside the Scratchbuilt armor and bust free.

Agent Prime, stickler for detail that he was, hadn't seen it that way. To top it off, DeChanza had been forced to spend the night in the suit, and despite the controlled environment, he still felt the need for a bath.

"He's not exactly a chum, kid," Prime replied. "I move on this guy, things could pop loose damn quick."

"Ahh, action," DeChanza said, though not over the comlink. He was fourteen years old and gangly, a sharp contrast to the MAPS unit. His unruly black hair fell beyond the nape of his neck and hung long on the sides, framing the high cheekbones bequeathed him by his Mesquite Indian and Central American heritage. He wore black jeans and a Big Johnson tee shirt that his mother absolutely hated. He, on the other hand, had found it at a garage sale and fell in love with it at once.

Before joining the FREELancers, DeChanza had lived in Somotillo. His father had died there, caught between the warring factions of the Contras, Sandinistas, Mesquite Indian revolutionaries, Cuban mercenaries, US advisors, and Israeli security teams. With their homeland no longer safe, DeChanza, his mother, and his three younger sisters had disappeared into the underground railroad that moved them into FREEAmerica, despite the walls across the southern border.

His metability for mechanics had helped him get a job and support the family. His mother worked as well, while the oldest sister cared for the two little ones. Times had been hard, and DeChanza had never forgotten the hungry days and nights when there wasn't enough to eat. He'd given his portions over to his younger sisters despite his mother's admonitions.

That was why, even though he'd been afraid of showing people how good he really was at mechanics, he'd gone out and started working on assembly-line robotics for different corporations at thirteen. The forged papers furnished by the underground railroad had falsified his date of birth. Management hadn't cared, except to provide him with better forgeries when they'd seen the kind of work he could turn out. They had an investment to protect.

Summer Davison had heard about him and made a recruitment pitch on behalf of the FREELancers. For a while, the corporation matched the agency's offer, but eventually was outbid. John-Michael had already mentally stepped into the shoes as the family's major breadwinner and was terribly efficient at renegotiating yearly contracts. But he was also good at what he did.

When he'd gone with the FREELancers agency, the corporate execs had made threatening noises about the forged papers. At that point, Underhill stepped into the discussions herself. The threats, and the corporate people and lawyers, went away overnight.

At first, DeChanza had been a mechanic for the agency. Then they'd realized his metability regarding mechanics. It was a strictly controlled Savant ability, allowing him to focus on something without being absorbed by it. During his free time in the mechanics pit in the FREELancers building, he'd started designing weapons suits. He'd been through a number of overall concepts and systems designs, and even some prototypes before creating the Scratchbuilt system he had at present.

The war in Somotillo had left its scars on him. He still heard the din of machine-gun fire and the whistle of incoming rockets and missiles in his dreams, and some nights he wasn't able to sleep. He'd sworn his family would never again know an existence like that. His two younger sisters, at least, had a chance to forget most of what had happened.

Life with the FREELancers for John-Michael DeChanza was violent. He lived with that. Some of his nightmares had new images and death screams, but he'd become the buffer between that way of life and his family. At least with the FREELancers, he was able to make a difference.

"System on," he called out.

A robot arm extended down from the hull overhead. A retina-imager was attached to it.

DeChanza fitted his eye to it. He'd been keeping the Scratchbuilt unit's systems down on low impulse, barely enough to keep it revved, while giving out an almost nonexistent electromagnetic signature.

<ID confirmed> printed out on the heads-up display. <Welcome back, John-Michael.>

"I wasn't gone. Trust me." DeChanza shifted in the seat. "Boot me into the system."

<Affirmative. Systems on-line?>

"Bring 'em up." DeChanza held his arms and legs still as sensor-cuffs shot out of the chair and locked onto his feet and hands. A cybernetic veil dropped over his head, exchanging his personal senses for those of the MAPS. At once, he was no longer a boy inside a thirty-five foot metal shell, he was a steely giant.

<Weapons systems?>

"Them too," DeChanza said.

<Bringing weapons systems on-line.>

DeChanza *felt* the weapons come alive. There were four firmpoints on the armor, on both shoulders and both forearms. His right shoulder held a .50-caliber machine gun, while his right had a 40mm grenade launcher. The Wallaby wrist rocket on his right forearm was specially modified, holding a half-dozen rockets. A laser was locked onto his left wrist.

"Access the FREELancers satellite," DeChanza ordered, locking into the heads-up display.

<Accessing.>

The cybernetic link formed in DeChanza's vision. He cycled through the various outlets and located the vid portions. He magnified the optic resolutions, vectoring in on O'Hare International Airport. In seconds, he found the door Underhill would be using when she quit the building.

He also spotted Prime making his way toward a UPS delivery van parked in a yellow-striped no parking area. He stayed with the agent, marveling at how bold as brass Prime could be.

If Prime recognized a familiar face, the guy—or woman,

DeChanza amended—it was attached to would be a certified death dealer. Those were the circles Prime traveled in.

Other movement became apparent to DeChanza as he watched, realizing the doorway had become the eye of a deadly storm. He tagged the Burris frequency, intending to voice a warning.

Instead, his HUD went red, bathing the inside of the MAPS with ruby light.

<Attention> the on-board computer advised. <This unit has been successfully targeted. Lock is inevitable.>

DeChanza's mind spun. "Backtrack the lock."

<Tracking.>

On-screen through the sat-link, DeChanza saw Underhill emerge from the building, saw the vehicles and people converge on her, saw the overall pattern of the assassination attempt take form. He tagged the com-link and tried to yell a warning to Matrix to give to Underhill or Prime.

<Target lock successful. Warning, this unit has been fired on.>

There was no time. The world went to pieces around DeChanza, devoured by an explosion that knocked thirty-five feet of weapons suit away like a child's toy.

9

Chicago, Illinois | *11:31 a.m. CST*
Great Lakes Authority (GLA) | *1731 Greenwich Mean*
87.7 degrees W Longitude | *March 28, 2024*
41.8 degrees N Latitude | *Friday*

Assignment: Gutenberg
Tactical Ops: Record and Evaluate
Status: Code Red

Locked into a video feed from the FREELancers satellite, Matrix watched the building where John-Michael DeChanza had been hiding. The signature she'd picked up indicated the strike had been from an overnight delivery service truck. A fiery halo wreathed the top of the warehouse, sending twisting black plumes scrambling into the sky. From her vantage point in the FREELancers building, she was privy to five different perspective points. Lee Won Underhill had made sure the assassination attempt was going to be well photographed even if there wasn't much she could do about the choreography.

Matrix, leaned down to sinew over bone, was almost six feet tall and weighed only one hundred and ten pounds. She kept her dark hair chopped off in a crew cut. Ruby tinted goggles covered her upper face, lending only a hint of roundness to the angular features, and made her look insectoid. Normal light hurt her eyes these days, another concession she'd had to make to the Savant side of herself.

She worked the keyboard in front of her with grim authority, pounding out commands in a syncopation of tapping. The sat-link was the main relay, picking up four other broadcasted signals from the airport and combining them with the view afforded from the geosynchronous orbit.

The first monitor held the view from space, looking down onto O'Hare. Security at the airport was only now starting to react to the violence that had broken out. Fire trucks and ambulances stationed on-site erupted from warehouses out near the runways where problems normally occurred.

Matrix brought up another audio feed, tapping directly into O'Hare's sec-frequencies, and started taping it as well. Some of the sound bytes overlaid with the pictures she was getting would provide the drama Underhill wanted.

The other four monitors showed a variety of angles taken by sec-cameras at the airport, which Matrix had cannibalized by hacking through the computer programming at O'Hare. When she was finished, she would activate the embedded command to erase everything on tape from the start of the explosion till things were wrapped.

The cybernetics systems Savant wished Underhill had been wrong about the attack, but there was something very reassuring about the FREELancers administrator calling everything precisely. Underhill would be more than satisfied, provided she lived long enough to see the results.

* * * * *

O'Hare International Airport	*11:32 a.m. CST*
Great Lakes Authority (GLA)	*1732 Greenwich Mean*
87.7 degrees W Longitude	*March 28, 2024*
41.8 degrees N Latitude	*Friday*

Assignment: Steel Wall, cont.
Tactical Ops: Protection: FREELancers 02
Status: Code Red

The first concussive waves were still moving across Agent Prime as he slid the Ingram monocle into place over his right eye. The eye-tracking scanner had on-board computer chips that linked it to the M-11 Stuttershot he had sheathed under his jacket along his left side. When he activated the monocle, the denseness of the optical device went away, leaving him with normal vision—except for the bright blue cross hairs that insinuated itself into his vision.

Underhill had emerged on his right, coming through the double doors from the airport. Prime felt certain that at least two rounds had hit the FREELancers administrator, but he knew her jacket was top-shelf designer bulletproof.

Underhill seemed slow out of the blocks, almost making herself a perfect target before throwing herself over the sid[illegible] Bullets tore fresh pockmarks in the cement, chipping the WELCOME sign engraved in Perma-kolor. The greeting droid at the doors caught at least a half-dozen rounds and flew back through the glass, its thin, articulated arms waving wildly as it screamed a perfunctory warning in a shrill voice. "Danger!"

More vehicles were in motion out on the pavement. There were at least four cars, not counting the delivery van. Autofire raked the wall next to Prime, chewing through the glass and brick and chopping down the manicured brush.

Prime took a step back, the cross hairs lining up on the sedan as it sped for him. He leveled the Stuttershot and triggered a burst that took out the windshield and the driver.

The car slewed wildly, coming around to broadside a line of parked cars.

Prime stood six feet tall, with a broad-chested build that allowed him to carry his extra muscle mass with ease. Bleached blond hair was echoed by thick brows over piercing blue eyes that always kept the world at arm's length with glacial cold. A diamond-shaped scar on the right side of his chin kept his features just short of perfect.

He moved into action at once, holding the Stuttershot in one hand while reaching around to flip the Burris mouthpiece from hiding so he could speak into it. "Scratchbuilt, report," he ordered. A man struggled to get free of the passenger side of the wrecked sedan. Prime dropped the merc with a hip-to-shoulder burst that threw his body back.

The FREELancers agent's background was military. The beginning he'd hidden from everyone except himself. It lay somewhere in Australia, in a younger man who'd lived and breathed idealism until he'd been betrayed. He'd ended up working for the CIA before the states formed the alliances, doing contract work that was supposed to forge a better world. After a bitter falling-out with the CIA, he went into international bounty hunting, racking up kills among criminals and political despots who'd put themselves beyond the reach of the law. Vengeance had been for hire, and he'd never taken on an assignment that he felt didn't deserve his deadly attention. The red-fletched crossbow bolts he'd used as a signature on several of the contracts still put fear into the hearts of men and women who considered themselves above the law.

George Anthony Underhill had recruited Prime on a contractual basis. In return, the FREE founder had helped Prime shake the name he'd been born with, erasing all links to his past. He became Thaddeus Johnson, an almost invisible man in the current society because he was strictly cash-and-carry. After Underhill senior had succumbed to his cancer, Prime had signed on with Lee Won Underhill. The lady was definitely a class act all the way.

She also tended to push the envelope on ops when she wanted to.

Prime muttered a curse as he flamed down another man who was moving in on Underhill's position. The effort drew return fire that sent him scrambling for cover behind the ridge of a sculptured hill near the side of the airport terminal.

Bullets slammed into the landscaped hill and tore loose fist-sized clods that whizzed over his head. Flowers burst into colorful explosions as the petals suddenly shot free in all directions. Behind him, the glass in the multipaned windows shattered and spun inward.

Prime squeezed off another three-round burst that caught a man in the face in midrun toward Underhill's position, almost decapitating him.

Not receiving any answer from Scratchbuilt, Prime glanced toward the building. The structure was almost engulfed in flames. Whatever it had been hit with had contained incendiaries. A fresh round of explosions started, smaller than the initial one, but gaining intensity.

Prime tagged the transmit button on the Burris. "Matrix, get me a scan on Scratchbuilt." He reached inside his jacket and palmed a miniature grenade. He set it for impact and threw it overhand, lobbing it onto the hood of a four-wheel-drive utility wagon.

The grenade detonated, throwing a wave of flames over the windshield and tearing gouge marks in the sheet metal. The driver panicked for just a moment, but quickly recovered. Little actual damage had been done.

"I can't read him," Matrix said. "The fire is making it impossible to get a thermal signature, and his suit's stealth systems are keeping me from picking him up on spectro."

"What about Download, Refit, and the heligyro?" Prime asked. He slipped a fresh magazine into the Stuttershot. The blue cross hairs locked on a target and glowed. He brought the machine pistol up smoothly and fired a quick burst that destroyed the hand of a gunner who was shooting from the four-wheel-drive.

"They'll be arriving any minute."

He pushed himself up. Keeping the Stuttershot in his left hand, he filled his right with his SIG-Sauer P226 9mm. Without pause, he aimed himself at the UPS delivery van.

The woman merc in the doorway saw him coming and moved out onto the steps, a UK Silver Spector backpack laser coming up in her hands. She had a headset on and was calling out orders, moving her team around even as she unleashed a burst in Prime's direction.

The FREELancers agent let his reflexes and combat skills take over. He went to her left, knowing she would have a harder time making the sweep to pick him up.

The bright red laser beam slapped into his backtrail, setting the landscaped area on fire and turning the pavement into pools of bubbling tar and scorched rock.

At the back of the UPS delivery van, he shoved the pistol under his armpit long enough to fish another grenade from inside his jacket. He clicked on the grenade's electromagnetic field, then stuck it to the back doors of the van. He tripped the timer and threw himself around the side of the truck.

The explosion sounded a heartbeat later. There was enough force to rip one of the doors completely off and send it spinning away. The van rocked.

Both weapons in his hands, Prime went forward along the driver's side. The man must have spotted him in the rearview mirror, because he thrust his gun through the window.

Prime triggered a half-dozen rounds from the Ingram machine pistol that caught the gunner in the chest and knocked him through the shattered windshield, stretching him out over the vehicle's blunt nose. He scanned the area, but there was no sign of the woman merc.

Moving back to the rear of the van, he looked inside. The smoke was already dissipating. Computer hardware lined both sides of the van, relaying signals for the attack team. He unleashed the full thunder of the Stuttershot, letting the ripping blast follow the line of destruction his eye traced through the monocle link.

Sparks started jumping at once, cybernetic equivalents of arterial leaks. More smoke followed. The two human operators inside had already been knocked down by the grenade explosion. Prime fired into them without mercy. The only enemies he wanted to leave behind him were ones he was sure wouldn't be getting back up.

When he sprinted away from the van, he was certain all the com-links between the assassins had been destroyed except for their man-to-man frequencies. It improved their chances of survival, but they were still slim. He lifted the SIG-Sauer and put a bullet through the head of a man who'd come up behind him. He stepped across the falling corpse, making his way toward Underhill.

The FREELancers administrator had kept her position beside the raised concrete dais in front of the doors, which were only empty frames now except for a few jagged shards of glass.

She was drawing heavy fire.

"Stay back, Prime!" Underhill ordered over the Burris.

Prime knew from experience that the steely edge in her voice would brook no trouble from him. He broke his approach and took up a position in another doorway twenty yards from her. "All right, you contrary little sheila," he muttered, making sure it wasn't broadcasted over the Burris. "But damn your eyes for making this so bloody hard."

He fired the Stuttershot dry, then reloaded. The terminal had turned into a battlefield. Fifty-caliber bullets tore fist-sized holes in the concrete walls around him, reducing the plate glass doors behind him to flying shards. Focusing on the wreckage of the car he'd shot up, he spotted a Beretta/Douglas F-3000 laser rifle canted against the shattered front windshield.

Pushing himself out of the recessed doorway, he pumped his legs hard and sprinted for the car. Bullets chased him and tore the wind in front of his face. He leathered the pistol only an instant before throwing himself into a home-stealing slide across the hood of the wrecked car. He grabbed the barrel of the laser rifle and yanked it through the shattered windshield.He ducked below the line of the car as bullets caromed from it. Getting his bearings, he realized the top of the orange maintenance pickup that had been abandoned near the side of the terminal would put him within reach of the roof of the second story.

Flipping the Ingram's Whipit sling over his shoulder so it would keep the weapon within reach while leaving his hands free, Prime slung the Beretta/Douglas laser rifle across his back. He broke at a dead run from the battered car.

By the time the gunners had corrected their aim, Prime was almost at the pickup. He didn't break his stride as he rushed toward the truck. Putting his hands out in front of him, he rolled in a flip that put him forward and up. He came down exactly as he'd planned on top of the cab and used its reinforced surface as a springboard to take him even higher.

The fingertips of his left hand brushed against the ledge and missed. He barely maintained a hold with his right, knowing if he lost it, he was too off-balance to recover properly and would be a sitting duck for the assassins.

Flailing, putting his feet against the concrete, he brought his left hand back and managed the hold. He hauled himself up and over the ledge, rolling onto the top of the terminal. More rounds knocked large chips from the edge.

Staying low, he moved to the left, unlimbering the laser rifle. A swift check let him know it held twenty-three of the thirty-charge capacity. As he took up a position, he envisioned a mental map of the area, planning his shots. Underhill was already in danger of being overrun again. He settled in behind the laser rifle's sights and took up the trigger slack, wondering what the hell the FREELancers administrator had on her mind.

Prime was sure Underhill had known about the assassination attempt and decided to walk right into it. He just didn't know why. Given that they survived, the big warrior fully intended to ask her about that.

* * * * *

O'Hare International Airport — *11:36 a.m. CST*
Great Lakes Authority (GLA) — *1736 Greenwich Mean*
87.7 degrees W Longitude — *March 28, 2024*
41.8 degrees N Latitude — *Friday*

Assignment: Gutenberg, cont.
Tactical Ops: Dissemination
Status: Code Red

Lee Won Underhill put the last full clip she had into the .380 and snapped the slide to chamber the first round. She had her back to the raised concrete slab and was bleeding from at least a dozen scratches caused by flying glass and stone.

She broke from her position reluctantly, knowing she was chancing the camera shots. She wore fitted body armor under her clothes that didn't break the lines of her generous curves. A bullet caught her in the side with enough force to knock her from her feet. The FREELancers administrator went down, her breath torn from her lungs from the impact.

Underhill sipped her breath in, gradually working out the pain. She pushed herself up from the ground, wincing from the effort. She made her way toward the line of cabs and limousines that had been abandoned as soon as the violence broke out. Movement alerted her a moment before a man stepped out from behind a small tour bus.

The guy was big and burly, his skin the color of anthracite, his head as bald as an egg, and his ears sporting a pair of long gold earrings. "Got you, bitch," he snarled.

Without hesitation, Underhill shoved the snubby snout of the .380 against the man's forehead. His pink-filmed eyes widened in surprise. She took away the suspense and the mystery by pulling the trigger. The dead man's head flew back from her and his grip fell away.

Stooping, Underhill recovered the man's weapon. It was a Glock Model 26, a weapon she was familiar with, cycling caseless 10mm ammunition from twenty-five round magazines. A three-round burst modification had been added. She shoved the .380 back into the shoulder holster, then frisked the dead man, turning up four unused magazines. She dropped them in her jacket pockets.

"Talk to me," Underhill said to Matrix over their private frequency.

"Martha Trimble of *21st Century Rolling Stone* has just contacted HQ through e-mail. She wants video and audio footage if we can release it, and an interview with you."

"Give her the prelim stuff we agreed on," Underhill said. She kept moving down the line of cars, holding the Glock in both hands. "Give her a maybe on the interview." It depended on how things went with Congressman Hartley.

"Including Cornell's identity?"

"Yes. Let them guess at why he's wanting to contract FREE-Lancers, though." Underhill stood up beside a bulletproof limousine long enough to fire a three-round burst that chased a female assassin back into hiding among parked cars in the garage area across from the entrance. "What about CNN?"

"They're connected."

"Straight-line feed?" Underhill asked.

"Distant shots only. Details are blurred, as you requested, but it's easy to see the violence. The burning warehouse sets the tone. I'm making sure it stays in all the perspectives. I'm also keeping them at a sixty-second lag time before I let them have the vid in case there's any editing we need to do."

"Do they know?"

"They're still scrambling to put it all on the air. We'll have a few minutes yet before local news has a vid-link that will show the lag."

"And when the local media is on-site?"

"Before they go on, I explain to CNN that we suddenly lost the camera. The self-destruct switches we have in them will insure that."

Underhill felt satisfied. The assassination was an important linchpin in the series of events she'd orchestrated. The assassins weren't there by chance. She'd known Colonel Will Tabor would be sending them. Manipulating information was a practiced art form for her, and she'd deliberately let the information of her arrival at the airport leak out. She just hadn't counted on John-Michael DeChanza getting blown up.

"Have you identified one of the shooters?" Underhill asked. She stayed with the limousine for the moment, taking advantage of the cover it provided.

"Nine so far," Matrix answered.

"Do they trace back to Tabor?"

"At least two of them have worked with him before, as mercenaries during the Sand Wars."

Underhill turned that over in her mind; it would fit in neatly with what she planned. During the Sand Wars, Tabor had hired on in an unpopular war with the most unpopular side. "Release the identities of those two to the media. Full splashes. Arrange the pictures through one of our independents. Close-ups. Backgrounds. The tie to Tabor during the Sand Wars. The first release is going to make the most impact. See if you can find some stills or vid footage of them with Tabor on-site during the war. If you can't, digitize some. Locate someone who'll take credit for them. As I recall, there were eight, perhaps ten reporters who were killed over there. Maybe one of them could use some posthumous exposure."

"Understood. I'll work with documented pictures first."

"Get everything over to Kent so he can set it up in my office.

When I finish with Cornell and Fiscal Development, I'll want to put the finished media package together myself."

Underhill cut out of the com-link. Everything was falling into place. All she had to do to administer the coup de grace was stay alive.

Without warning, a rocket slammed into the limousine with enough force to almost overturn it. Swirling fire wrapped around the vehicle, reaching for her. She turned away, partially covering her face with her jacket.

An eighteen-wheeler raced at her, the diesel motor revving loudly.

Abandoning her position, Underhill was only inches away when the big truck slammed into the burning limousine and shoved it over the curb. Whatever flex she'd had on the play was drastically cut.

* * * * *

O'Hare International Airport *11:39 a.m. CST*
Great Lakes Authority (GLA) *1739 Greenwich Mean*
87.7 degrees W Longitude *March 28, 2024*
41.8 degrees N Latitude *Friday*

Assignment: Steel Wall, cont.
Tactical Ops: Protection; FREELancers 02
Status: Code Red

"Damage report."

<Systems still registering.>

"Give me your best guess," John-Michael DeChanza ordered.

<Compliance, though demand made upon this system may not be in human operator's best interests. Biofeedback systems are sorely stressed. As per programming instructions, in the event of traumatic experience beyond this unit's ability to counteract, systems shut down to negate shock to operator. It may be in your best interests to remain as you are.> Numbers spun across the monitor.

"Let me figure that out for myself," DeChanza said. He could tell by the way the pressure was on him that he was lying on his back. The cyberveil clung to his face, but the senses connecting him to the MAPS's simware was off-line.

<Systems on-line at sixty-three percent.>

"What about weapons?" As soon as the biofeedback systems reconnected with his own senses, DeChanza felt the weight of the building on him. And the heat was enough to roast him alive. It registered as pain, but a controllable pain that he'd been conditioned to, like an athlete pushing his own threshold. He'd researched for weeks until he'd found a template for it in psychological systems, then had to ask Dr. Rhand to explain the framework of the human nervous system to him. At the end of another few weeks, he'd designed the system he used now. It was a system Dr. Rhand said should not work, and wouldn't if not for DeChanza's metability. Some days, that really got John-Michael down. If even one of his really radical designs for MAPS units could be produced for commercial use, he could patent it and make millions of dollars. It would be all the security his mother and sisters would ever need.

<Weapons systems on-line, except for 40mm grenade launcher on right shoulder.>

"Status?" DeChanza shifted under the flaming tonnage. His visor opaqued, dimming the light till he could see the leaping fire spreading throughout the wreckage of the warehouse. Timbers and chunks of concrete spilled all around him, shifting into the empty areas left by his movements.

<Inoperable. That sector absorbed the greatest damage during the explosion. Circuitry is gone. Response is gone. Visual inspection suggests replacement at earliest convenience.>

"Yeah, well, looking around suggests that earliest convenience is going to be some time in coming." Finding a leverage point, DeChanza set himself. His arms and legs worked inside the cuffs, and he felt as if he were the one shrugging through the burning debris. "Give me some resistance figures. Straight up. We're going airborne."

<Warning: Systems suggest such a maneuver is risky. Calibrating forty-two percent probability of failure. Eighteen percent chance of terminating this unit and human operator.>

"I built this machine," DeChanza said, "I figure I ought to

know best what it'll take." He moved his limbs in the sensor-cuffs and locked the Scratchbuilt unit's arms at its sides.

DeChanza readied the compressed-air jets in the arms and legs, giving the unit a limited jump capacity. "Link me to the satellite feed."

<Compliance.>

"Stand ready to alter course as necessary."

<Compliance.>

The sat-link filled the monitor. The view took in most of the parking area in front of the door Underhill had used. With all the movement scattered around, it was hard to find his teammates. "Highlight Prime and Underhill."

<Compliance.>

Immediately, neon-green circles materialized around Prime's position on top of the second-story roof and Underhill, who was running from the big eighteen-wheeler crashing through the limousine, rolling the luxury car ahead of it. The FREE-Lancers administrator was almost boxed in between the threat of rolling steel and gunfire.

DeChanza hit the compressed-air jets. The MAPS shuddered like a wild thing caught in a trap. He felt as if he'd been caught in the eye of an earthquake. On the monitor linked with the sat-feed, he watched as flames suddenly flared out from the building in all directions, spread by the air jets.

<Systems pushing into critical zones> the on-board computer warned.

DeChanza watched the indicators on the heads-up display rush toward the red zones. Then, he felt the weight begin to shift around him, lightening the load. It was slow at first; then the debris slipped around him like water off a duck. Nearly exhausted, the compressed air still maintained enough power to send him shooting skyward. Watching himself from space, he hoped someone had a camera, because the vid footage of the Scratchbuilt suit breaking through the roof of the burning building was totally rad.

He went up almost three hundred fifty feet before the jets emptied, then began the fall back toward the ground. He flailed for balance when he unlocked the suit's joints. Through the sat-link, he saw himself falling. "Where's the gyro stabilization?"

<Stabilization on-line.>

DeChanza felt the gyros spin into orbit around him. Suddenly he knew how fast he was falling, to what degree, and most importantly, what he needed to do about it.

<One point eight-six seconds remaining before impact.>

Rolling the Scratchbuilt suit over, DeChanza managed to land on both feet and turned in the direction of the eighteen-wheeler running Underhill down. It was only a few yards behind her. Sweating heavily inside the suit, knowing the environmental controls were reflecting the amount of damage that had been done, DeChanza ran in an interception course, zeroing in on the semi.

DeChanza knew there was no way he could use any of the weapons pods. Neither the laser, the .50-cal machine gun, or the rocket launcher would guarantee that Underhill would be unharmed. The suit's feet made two-foot depressions in the parking area as he ran. He stepped onto the wrecked remains of vehicles that had already been damaged in the firefight and explosions, flattening and crushing them.

DeChanza locked on to his target, then lunged in a body block, sacrificing the shoulder that had the dysfunctional grenade launcher. He connected with the truck in a scream of hammered metal, then dug the huge feet in and kept pushing, curling around to keep the vehicle in front of him.

The truck buckled between the cab and the trailer, losing its momentum. The tires shrieked against the pavement, leaving black skid marks, then cutting through the grass before slamming up against a reinforced wall. With a stuttering cough, the diesel engine died.

DeChanza brought the Scratchbuilt unit back up on its feet. "Oh, yeah!" he shouted. "WWF, eat your hearts out!"

<Damage report upgrade: Systems now at fifty-seven percent.>

Wheeling, DeChanza brought up the wrist-rocket pod. There were two vehicles out in the parking lot that were making for Underhill's position. He fired two rockets at each, destroying both sedans in fiery explosions.

A rocket crashed against one of his legs, but he held his balance. Shifting again, he brought the .50-cal machine gun on-line and fired at the ground crew that had manned the rocket launcher. They went down immediately. Flames still clung to the Scratch-built's steel hide, but he ignored them and waded through the debris scattered across the parking lot to take up the front line.

"Glad to have you back with us, kid," Prime called over the Burris.

As suddenly as it came, the attack broke off. In seconds, emergency rescue vehicles and police cruisers covered the scene. DeChanza stood his ground, towering above them all. A wasp shape formed in the air in front of him, streaking closer.

"ID that craft for me," DeChanza told the on-board computer.

<Assessing threat.>

Not waiting, DeChanza locked the laser and the remaining wrist rockets on it.

<Target confirmed: Aircraft number N1151961, registered to FREELancers, licensed by city of Chicago, Great Lakes—>

"Cancel," DeChanza said. He lowered his weapons. Using the suit's systems, he focused on Underhill and made sure she remained protected.

Incredibly, the FREELancers administrator walked through the battlefield straight into the waiting line of police officers without apparent fear. Besides his mother, Underhill was the strongest woman DeChanza knew.

"Stand easy, kid," Prime said. "Let Underhill iron out the details with the cops."

DeChanza was more than happy to. He watched as the Bird-Song JK91 was waved down to an open area in the parking lot. "Are we involved in something here?" he asked Prime over the Burris. "I mean, I can't see something this major happening unless we've got an active assignment."

"The lady's always juggling a lot of balls," Prime said. In the distance, he stood up on the rooftop, the taller sections of the terminal behind him. "But this one must have a hell of a butcher's bill attached to it."

Looking at the bodies and the wreckage strewn about him, DeChanza figured a big down payment had already been made.

10

Chicago, Illinois — *12:43 p.m. CST*
Great Lakes Authority (GLA) — *1843 Greenwich Mean*
87.7 degrees W Longitude — *March 28, 2024*
41.8 degrees N Latitude — *Friday*

Assignment: Janus Gate
Tactical Ops: Negotiation, PR Dissemination
Status: Code Red

The office held the flavor of the Pacific Rim, rendered in antique vases that sat on specially designed shelves inset in lacquered teak walls. Behind the desk in a place of honor was a set of samurai swords displayed between a pair of banners that hung almost to the floor. Pale yellow-and-teal dragons stood out against the unblemished white silk.

Books in four different languages lined the floor-to-ceiling shelves that filled another wall. Delicate figurines in ivory and jade and polished woods were inset with various gems that boosted their intrinsic value almost to the level of their uniqueness. The subject matter ranged from war to philosophy, from theology to economics, and more. The volumes weren't there just for show. Lee Won Underhill had read them all.

She leaned back against the desk, part of her weight on her hips and part of it on her hands. She was tired, riding the nervous edge of exhaustion. She'd managed a quick shower and a change of clothes, but the results were purely cosmetic.

A huge monitor screen was revealed behind another hidden section of wall. Five windows were open on it, three of them playing the footage from the assassination attempt at the airport, another the footage that Underhill was cutting and resplicing through her PR department on the tenth floor of the building, and the final one cycling through the media channels that were doing breakdowns on the story.

"You've given them the two men connected with Tabor during the Sand Wars?" Underhill asked. She pointed the remote control at the monitor and punched up window three, backing up the footage till she found the sequence of events when she'd been shot. None of the news channels had any of this footage.

"Three actually," Matrix said. "I verified another man while you were unavailable. I took the liberty of pushing that into the media as well."

"That's fine. Kent?" Underhill marked the tape, running it through the sequence again, watching herself be hit by the bullet and go down. It wasn't flattering, but it was memorable.

"Yes?" Philip Kent was her personal aide-de-camp, and responsible for her daily agenda.

"Who do we know in the marketing division at I-Shield Body-Armor?" At the end of the sequence, Underhill placed another marker, then downloaded into a temporary directory Matrix had set up for her. There was a pause, and the FREELancers administrator turned her attention to Matrix. "I've got another piece of vid for you. Ship it off to the stations carrying live transmissions first, starting with CNN and *Headline News*, down from there, staying with the A-list we designed. Dump local Channel 43. Management there has decided to be adversarial and put Victor Ellam on. Every chance he gets, he tries to spew negative publicity on FREELancers. If we keep feeding the new stuff to the other stations, the viewers will stay the hell away from him."

"How do you want the vid tagged?" Matrix asked.

"Have we used Cooper yet?"

"Not yet."

"Is he up to date on this?"

"As per your instructions, yes."

"Give it to him. Let him know he's going to be fronting at least three more vid bytes to the networks. Two of those he can negotiate for and see what he can bring in for himself in addition to what I'm paying. The other they get for free. I'll mark them." Underhill studied the images, holding them frozen on three of the screens.

The first was of a Chicago police officer being shot and killed by the assassins. She tapped commands in to Matrix to soften the view and reduce the graphics. The family didn't need to see everything, nor did anyone else. The footage as it was made the point well enough. The other two were shots of Agent Prime as he took up a defensive position, and Scratchbuilt as he rammed the eighteen-wheeler. Both showed the professionalism of the team, and neither invited memory of bloodshed.

"I've got them," Matrix said. "Cooper will have the download in seconds."

"Lee," Kent said. "I've got the name of the guy at I-Shield. Cecil Baxter. Only been at his present position for nine days."

"Good," Underhill said. "He'll be hungry to make a big splash and generous with the corporate purse strings. Call him and set up a deal. He gets the footage of me taking the bullet. I was wearing their armor at the time."

"That footage is public domain," Kent said. "Why should he pay for it?"

"He won't be." Underhill picked up a computer pad that turned her fingerprint impressions into writing. She made notes to herself as she spoke. "Tell him that what his company will be paying for is an endorsement from me regarding their body armor, and the right to franchise a torso protector with the FREELancers logo on it for a limited run that we'll agree on later."

"*That*," Kent said, "he'll jump at."

"As an added bonus," Underhill said, "I'll throw in the body armor I was wearing at the time. Maybe we can cut a deal with the police to keep the bullet embedded in it instead of having it removed for evidence."

"Done. I'll get right on this."

"In a minute. First I want you to get hold of the Chicago Fraternal Order of Police. Find out the name of the police officer who was killed at the scene. There was only one. Make a donation to the FOP in his name, and a donation to the widow and family, if he has either. Tomorrow morning. See if you can get it covered quietly at first, then get a bigger release during the actual presentation by Tuesday of next week. The assassination attempt should have died down a little by then, and we can recoup some positive feedback." As well as doing someone some good, Underhill hoped.

On the media screen, the footage of the FREELancers administrator getting shot was just starting to go out. Underhill floated through the channels, seeing the same shot over and over in various stages. Except on Channel 43, where Victor Ellam was voicing another diatribe against the FREELancers, who—he insisted—brought more problems into Chicago than they supposedly resolved.

"Matrix," Underhill said, "get me Harris Hartley." The FREELancers administrator kept picking and choosing from the video footage, tagging some of it for use now, some for the evening, and making notations of people who would be good to interview by pro-FREELancers reporters the following day.

As she worked, a headache was starting to form, coming from the tension between her shoulders. Despite the armor she'd been wearing, there were a number of impact areas from the blunt trauma that promised spectacular bruises. Many were already starting to form.

Static electricity crackled to her left. Without looking, she knew her father had taken shape beside her. She glanced in that direction in time to see the final few pixels slide into place to create the holo of him.

When alive, he'd been a tall man, with thick shoulders and sandy hair. He'd had a warm laugh but a permanent chill in his pale gray eyes. He wore his hair swept back, regulation length, and sported a salt-and-pepper mustache beneath his blade of a nose. His black slacks were pressed and neat, the creases looking sharp enough to cut paper. The sleeves on his white shirt were rolled to midforearm, and the collar was left open.

"You're pushing too hard, Lee," the elder Underhill said.

Underhill glared at her father. Even when he'd been alive, they'd argued over how things should be handled. Her way was more aggressive in his eyes, but she felt he didn't take into consideration how much respect he'd already earned in the intelligence community. It had accounted for a lot of the ease he'd found putting operations together.

In 2013, George Anthony Underhill had been diagnosed with inoperable cancer. The only chance he had at a future was in being cryogenically frozen. However, the technology was radical and legally unsupported, so Underhill had been declared dead. Only a handful knew that his body was kept on ice down in the bowels of the FREELancers Base, and that he could make contact with the outside world through a device Dr. Rhand had developed.

In the first few years after that, Underhill had struggled to maintain the client base. With news of her father's death, many of those clients had gone to other security agencies, including Hammer Associates and Independent Operators International down in Texas and fronts for WEBONE and WEBTWO, spy families who moved in the crime circles as well. She'd had to use every trick she'd ever learned or created to keep the company solvent. Now, that same energy was required to stay on top.

"It's going to come together," her father said. "You've invested wisely."

"Have I? There was a bloodbath down at the airport. I wasn't expecting that kind of reaction from Tabor."

"How could you not? After you let it leak to his people that Fiscal Development, Incorporated was going to hire you to get Tabor out of there?"

"That may have been a mistake."

"The mistake was that you came so close to being killed," her father said. Concern was etched deeply into his face.

Underhill saw it and looked away. When her father had had a physical body, they'd both avoided emotional issues except for anger over professional differences. "I knew it was going to be close," she replied.

"You stared death in the face today," her father said softly.

"I've done it before."

Her father nodded. "Yes, you have, but you allowed yourself some recovery room the other times. Also, you were riding out an adrenaline high before, not walking into a situation cold. Only a few minutes before the assassination attempt, you were getting cozy with that archeologist."

Underhill looked up at the holo of her father. Though the device allowed him to interact with her in the office and in some of the other rooms of the building, and he didn't necessarily see her only from the perspective of the holo form he took, she wasn't sure she knew the extent of his capabilities.

"Surprised?" Her father thrust his hands into his pants pockets. He shrugged and turned partly away from her. "So am I. It appears that even Doc Random doesn't know the full extent of his device."

"You followed me."

"I was unable to converse with you, though, I'm afraid. It made me feel old and ineffectual. Scared the hell out of me to think that I was about to lose you."

Underhill stood there, not knowing what to say.

"My advice to you is this," her father said. "Let the situation ride. Pull the strings that you've got open to you. You've set it up well." He looked at her. "And if you're as interested in this archeologist as I think you are, give yourself a chance to live a little just for yourself. FREELancers isn't a house of cards. We built it strong, you and I. Lean on it for a while."

Before she could say anything, her father's holo disappeared in a whirl of winking static bursts. Then Matrix beeped the headset to let her know Harris Hartley was on the line and Patrick Cornell was at the door. She took a deep breath and set her mind. The play in Melaka was intricate and rife with disaster. However, there remained a few more dominoes she had to kick over before she'd know how it was going to shake out.

She picked up the phone and buzzed Cornell through the door.

11

Melaka City, Melaka	*1:46 a.m. Local Mean*
Indonesia	*1846 Greenwich Mean*
102.3 degrees E Longitude	*March 29, 2024*
2.4 degrees N Latitude	*Saturday*

"You've made a prisoner of me," Saikalen said.

Colonel Will Tabor sat across from the mockery of human anatomy and stared into the scarred visage. "For all practical purposes, yes." The truth was a harsh weapon when wielded expertly, almost as damaging as lies and deceptions.

Saikalen returned his gaze full measure, dark fires burning in the hollows of the too-tight flesh spread so thinly over the skull. Upon closer inspection, Margo Peele had quietly hazarded a guess that Saikalen was even older than they had at first thought. The bone structure in his face and head possibly dated back a couple thousand years more than they presumed.

"Why?"

Tabor shifted in his seat. They were in a room of the new government building Castlereigh and his people had built and filled with their political puppets. "I don't know you, and I don't know what you're capable of. For the moment, I'm in charge here."

After reanimating in the catacombs, Saikalen had been angry that no slaves were standing by to take care of his needs. He'd become belligerent and refused to accompany them out of the chamber. Then Tabor had shown him the business end of the Beretta/Douglas laser pistol and what it could do. There hadn't been any further arguments.

Tabor was growing irritated. The man, whatever remained of him, undoubtedly held answers to many of the questions they had. Margo Peele was still in the catacombs, cataloguing and cross-referencing everything she found. More scrolls were turning up, with enigmatic diagrams and written in a language even harder to read than the ones they'd found before. Castlereigh's people had been sitting quietly on a number of the scrolls as well, which so far had proved undecipherable.

"Who was this bloody Star Scarab you keep referring to?"

Saikalen shrugged, the effort looking disjointed with the metal skeleton. "We never knew. He came to our people one day, talking of things that would come to pass."

"Fortune-telling?" Tabor asked.

"No." Creases formed at the sides of Saikalen's mouth. "He talked of the rise and fall of nations and of the wondrous things that would be invented. Several among us copied down his teachings without him knowing about it, because he was afraid of what might happen if we possessed the knowledge."

"Why?"

"He never said. Other than to say there are some things common man should never know until the time is right."

Tabor figured that was a sure sign of divinity. The thought was a sarcastic one, but there was no denying the technological advances written about in the scrolls.

"I studied with him for a while. He'd been among our people for many years then and had gotten quite old and somewhat addled, but there were still moments of clarity. We were very covetous about them, and wrote down his every word. The world he described to us was amazing."

"When was this?"

Saikalen paused theatrically for a moment as if to think back. Tabor was growing bored with his behavior, but how the hell could he torture the truth from a *thing* like Saikalen? Peele had already said that whatever nerves were left inside the head were probably useless. She'd tried to get closer to the man to inspect the head joining the metal skeleton, but a few of the silvery wires had uncoiled and menaced her with their barbed tips. She also ventured a guess that the wires were how Saikalen got the air and moisture he needed to survive, through some type of chemical exchange.

"A few hundred years before the arrival of the man known as Christ. I would have to do the arithmetic to be exact. Calendars were changed upon his death, but we marked ours from our first meeting with the Scarab."

"Did he call himself Scarab?"

"No. That was our name for him. I think its origins lie with the Egyptians; our scholars were studying them before he came among us. They used drawings of scarabs to represent the soul. For us, he became our soul."

"What happened to him?" Despite his own doubts about the story, Tabor was engrossed. Saikalen's words were all too certain, too fluent for him to be making the tale up as he went along. The inattention to detail, his not trying to explain everything, made it even more believable.

"He grew old. His heart gave out. He'd already been talking about leaving, so it was not a surprise. In his teachings, he mentioned ways of cutting the heart from one man and replacing it with the heart of another, thus preserving the life of the first man. Any among us would have gladly given his heart to keep our teacher one more day with us."

Tabor had his doubts about Saikalen's volunteering. The man was a walking poster child to man's fight against the inevitable. "But you're alive."

Saikalen turned his mechanical hands up in a humble gesture. The sharp talons gleamed. "I," he said, "am not as other men."

"Why?"

"Because I chose not to be." Saikalen smoothed his whiskers. "It caused a rift within my people. When the Star Scarab found out we were taking down his words, he made the elders promise that the scrolls would be used only when man was ready to use them. He insisted there was a time for everything, and that they would know when that time was. Until then, they were to be kept locked away. I used the knowledge contained in some of the scrolls to save myself."

"What happened when the others found out what you'd done?"

"They hunted me. For years. The ones who tracked me were not gentle. I was tortured, every bone in my body broken, some several times. Once I was back in Malacca, I was forced to suffer the indignity of a beheading."

"But you lived through it."

"As you so plainly see. Knowing that I was being stalked as I was, I took precautions."

"Such as those wires in your head."

"Yes. And the building of this metal body." Saikalen whacked the iron skeleton. "Now, I see that many advances have been made in metallurgy. I would not have to remain with this bulky apparatus."

Tabor filed the comment away. If there was something Saikalen wanted, it was something the colonel could use to blackmail the creature with. "You knew you were going to be beheaded."

"Of course. It was decreed by the council. My captors could harm my body, and did most grievously, but they could not take my life, else theirs would be forfeit in its place. After I was executed, people who were loyal to me arrived too late to save me, but managed to take my head. Usually, the heads of inner circle members were saved."

"Why?" Tabor asked.

"Eventually, autopsies were going to be performed. One of my peers wondered if the Scarab had somehow changed our minds as he taught us. The things he described, not everyone could grasp. There was a great gap between many of us, and others could understand only some of the mathematics he talked of, or another branch of science or music."

Tabor kept silent, but he knew he was listening to proof of the theory that Savantism had been around for hundreds and perhaps thousands of years.

"When our medical skills grew great enough, and we knew they would from the Scarab's teachings," Saikalen said, "it was believed an answer could be found for why we were different."

"If you had the metal body ready and your comrades were able to spirit you away before your head ended up in a collection, how did you come to be in the catacombs?"

"The inner council of the Guardians knew I lived. Their pursuit was unflagging. For most of a year, I hid out. However, my condition"—he waved to indicate his body—"ensured I would be remembered if noticed. I returned here quietly, on my own. My only choice was to put myself into suspended animation and let time pass. It pleased me that I was successful in hiding myself under their very noses."

"For how long?"

"The last time I saw a calendar, it was 1873."

"And you survived?"

"In my present condition, I can survive most anything. As long as I have access to a small amount of nutrients like those in the vial, I can live for extended periods. While in suspended animation, my needs are greatly reduced."

Tabor struggled to get everything he was being told in focus. It was more than he'd ever thought he'd be confronted with. When he'd first phased through a wall at twelve while dodging a bullet fired by one of the gangs inhabiting the West End, he'd thought he'd never be more surprised. But that was before he'd teleported the first time at nineteen, when a mate in the British army dropped a live grenade into the foxhole during maneuvers. Saikalen's story topped even those, but was so strange that he felt distanced from it in spite of his belief and the proof that stood so eloquently before him.

"How long were you planning to sleep?" Tabor asked.

"Fifty years or so. Evidently something went wrong. If you hadn't opened the casket, perhaps I would not have wakened at all. I find that possibility most distressing."

"What was the ape-thing?"

"My bodyguard. Grosz. I created him with the help of the doctor acquaintance who helped me put the wiring into my own head. The doctor, I'm sorry to say, ended up quite mad by the time we finished our experiments. The document we were working from wasn't complete. There were certain things we didn't have access to because they hadn't yet been invented, but we made do surprisingly well. We robbed graves for materials to work with, then had to use a certain amount of live matter. Unfortunately, we had access only to a carnival, where we bought the ape that we used to cobble everything else together. It's a shame you killed him. I found him quite useful."

Tabor pushed himself up.

Saikalen folded his metal hands before him, his iron fingers interlacing. "You came to me to make a deal."

Remaining quiet, the colonel just looked at the thing standing in front of him.

"It was evident in your manner," Saikalen said. "I've been reading people for a very long time now. The talk about the Scarab was only allowing you time to make up your mind and remind me that I am at your mercy. I, also, would like to make a deal."

Tabor turned to face the creature, not trusting Saikalen. Disembodied or not, he knew the man was far from helpless. "What do you want?"

"The obvious things," Saikalen replied. "My freedom for one."

"When it's time."

"Of course. I'd also like some clothes. I am not as hardened to the way I look as you might think. At least, clothed, I would feel more like myself."

"I'll have an orderly bring something up."

Saikalen smiled. "Something like what you're wearing will do nicely."

Tabor nodded.

"And a beret like the ones I saw on some of your men."

"No," Tabor said. "Those hats mean something. They have to be earned."

"Forgive me if I've offended you."

"None taken." Tabor waited a beat. "And what do I get in return?"

"It's evident that you and your people are here to plunder the catacombs," Saikalen said. "And I'm convinced you're certain there are a great many things you've not found yet. I know where the main vaults are. They may still be intact."

"I do want to know where those vaults are. I just don't know how much I can trust you."

"You have me at your mercy."

"That's what the guys who chopped off your head thought."

Saikalen laughed, and the sound was dry and brittle. Peele had hypothesized that instead of air, the wires vibrated inside the man's head and gave him a voice. At times, like now, it sounded like something that had been digitally created.

"Which brings up another question," Tabor said. "Where are the Guardians of the Scarab now?"

"All dead, I'm afraid." Saikalen's eyes blazed. "You see, there was an unfortunate epidemic, an illness no one had ever seen before that swept through them after they executed me. In many cases it proved deadly, and so thinned their numbers. But the main thrust of its effects were hereditary. A virus was introduced into their systems that permanently scarred their reproductive capabilities. Within a generation or two, three at the most, all the children born to them would have been short-lived monsters with no higher reasoning power and precious little in the way of autonomous systems. The Guardians were very xenophobic. No one ever came to them from outside their ranks."

The cold spot in the center of Tabor's belly that had been there ever since they'd discovered Saikalen spread a little more. He let himself out and pulled the door closed behind him. The two men he'd posted as guards stood on either side of the entrance. He looked at them. "If that son of a bitch even tries to get out of that room, you burn him down where he stands. Do you read me?"

"Yes, sir," they responded.

"Sir, if you don't mind my saying so, that's one creepy bastard we've got bivouacked here," Corporal Lewis said.

"I don't mind you saying so, solider. Hell, I couldn't agree more." Tabor walked down the hall, shifting his gear to get it more comfortable. Castlereigh had built the new government building to last, and he'd designed it for show as well as comfort. The hallways were wide and covered in plush carpet.

His thoughts turned to the liquor selections in the room he'd claimed as his own after kicking out the prime minister who'd replaced Paul Derembang. He wanted a stiff drink and a woman, a hot bath, anything to get the stink of the catacombs out of his mouth, off his skin, and out of his mind.

Once he had the scrolls, though, that wouldn't be just a pleasant diversion. It would be a way of life. He wasn't going to let anyone or any*thing* stand in the way of that.

He was nearly to his rooms on the fourth floor when his radio beeped for attention. "Tabor."

"Colonel, it's Wallsey."

"Go, sergeant. You have my attention."

"The attack on Underhill went south."

Tabor halted. Since he'd learned of the FREELancers' probable involvement on behalf of FDI, breaking that threat had consumed a lot of time and manpower. Knowledge of Underhill's arrival at O'Hare hadn't come easily or inexpensively. "Explain."

"The strike went down, sir, but it didn't come off. Underhill managed to break the attack and escape. It's all over the news. So are we."

"How bad is it, sergeant?"

"Plenty bad, sir. The situation here in Melaka is drawing a lot of attention again."

"Meet me in my ready room in five minutes."

"Yes, sir."

Tabor clicked out of the frequency and went back to the nearest elevator. The ready room was down in the basement. Castlereigh's people had put in a bomb shelter and enough supplies to last for years, fearing attacks from the other Malaysian countries for their succession. It had been a logical choice for mission control once Tabor had located it.

As he dropped downward in the elevator, he considered his options. There weren't many. So far, international attention had been avoided to a large degree. There were the bleeding-heart journalists pumping emotional garbage out on vid and in electronic print, but no nation or the UN had stepped forward to take part in the rebellion that had quickly swept the Melakan government from power. He wanted it kept that way. Once the operation in Melaka was over, he and his men had other names, other faces they could wear for the rest of their lives. Anyone who came after them would be searching for ghosts.

But with Underhill making waves, disappearing was going to prove much harder. The FREELancers generated a lot of attention in their own right. He didn't want Melaka turned into an international hot spot, or face the possibility of a UN peace-keeping effort being brought in. He was working out the damage control possibilities when the elevator doors opened and a man shoved a gun to his face.

12

Chicago, Illinois — *12:52 p.m. CST*
Great Lakes Authority (GLA) — *1852 Greenwich Mean*
87.7 degrees W Longitude — *March 28, 2024*
41.8 degrees N Latitude — *Friday*

Assignment: Janus Gate, cont.
Tactical Ops: Negotiation, PR Dissemination
Status: Code Green

"If you'll have a seat, Mr. Cornell, I'll be with you in just a moment." Lee Won Underhill waved the Fiscal Development, Incorporated representative to one of the plush chairs in front of the desk.

Cornell still looked a little pale as he took his seat and checked his tie. His attention was drawn by the footage playing across the big monitor.

Underhill had intentionally reduced it to only one screen that filled the entire monitor area. The broadcast was from the footage the FREELancers administrator had just released.

On-screen, the Chicago police officer was killed again. Following their policy of getting the news out as quickly as possible, CNN didn't edit out the gore. Blood splashed over the white exterior of the police cruiser behind the man, creating patterns of violence.

Cornell flinched.

"Yes," Underhill said into the phone. She punched in a query to Kent, then read the computer printout across the screen.

THREE DRINKS. ALL DOUBLES. NOTHING SOLID. CONSUMED SOME TABLETS WHILE IN HIS ROOM. NOTHING IN HIS FILES TO INDICATE A MEDICAL REASON.

Underhill switched the prompter off.

"Hello," a man's voice at the other end of the phone connection said.

"This is Lee Won Underhill." The FREELancers administrator surveyed Cornell as she spoke. The man was pointedly ignoring her conversation, but she knew he was soaking up every word.

"Yes, I know," Harris Hartley said. "That was the only reason I took this call. As you're aware, things around here have suddenly gone crazy, what with the terrorist attack in GLA territory. So if we could make this quick—"

"I'm well aware of the current situation," Underhill stated.

"Damn," the congressman said. "I forgot. You were there! Jeez, there you are on the news! They just shot you! Are you all right?"

"I'm fine. How are things going there?"

"Chaos at the moment. With the appointment hanging fire, the party is somewhat reluctant to jump either way on this issue. It couldn't have come at a worse time. As you know, the alliances have been pushing to start up talks with other countries, independent of the federal government."

On CNN, the anchor was promising an interview with the GLA ambassadorial steering committee regarding the act of terrorism on their soil. Harris Hartley's name was one of those mentioned.

"Which way does it look like things will bounce?" Underhill asked.

"Isabella and Danner are all for shoving their heads in the sand for a few hours and seeing how this thing shakes out."

"Leaves them open for an ass-kicking," Underhill said.

"Exactly what I told them. If you choose right or wrong, people know you stood for something, but if you pull that neutral bullshit, people are going to remember that too. If they don't, you can bet your ass the opposition will when it's time to go to the polls. If we weren't in the lead at the moment, we'd hang back till they committed; then, if we weren't sure, we'd go along with them. That way it looks as if one politician's just as stupid as the next, and the competition isn't so quick to point out when you screw up."

Underhill knew that, and it was that party resistance to making a mistake by themselves that she was counting on. "If you make a decision now, you're going to force the others to go along. At the moment, they're earning interest on the time you spend trying to decide."

"Believe me, I know. I've been pushing for a decision."

"What decision?"

"I want to wash our hands of it. Let the police handle it and push it off on the feds. It's a joke to think they're going to deal with it, but at least we'd have put on a good face."

"That's a mistake," Underhill said flatly.

"What would you have me do? Go out there in a few minutes and promise the citizens of the GLA swift retribution against the people who did this?"

"That's exactly what I'd do," the FREELancers administrator said.

"Do you realize we don't have a standing army capable of backing up something like that?"

"I do." Underhill watched Cornell fidget in his chair. She deliberately kept her comments cryptic. Listening to only her side of the conversation, the FDI man wouldn't be able to guess what she was talking about.

"You're trying to tell me you'd involve your people in this?"

"One way or another," Underhill said, "they will be. It would be better if they were operating under some kind of blessing."

"An umbrella I can put up through the steering committee?"

"That's exactly what I was thinking," Underhill replied. "I'll call you later and work out the details."

"There's no way I'm going to agree to that," the congressman said. "Even if I could convince the steering committee to back me."

"You can get it done." The line went dead for a short while. Underhill waited.

"I've really got to be going," Hartley said. "My aide is signaling me now."

"I was also calling you to let you know we picked up your package."

Hartley hesitated. "You've got my daughter?"

"Yes."

"Where was she?"

"With a faction of a West Side gang called the Cybered Shadows. Maybe you've heard of them." Underhill knew the congressman had. The gang had been in the news a lot lately.

"Yes. She'd joined them?"

"She was heading up the outfit," Underhill said. "Quite the little leader from what I've been told. It must be hereditary. There's vid footage of the *rescue* if you want to see it."

"This is blackmail."

"I like to think of it as extremely effective political lobbying," Underhill said. "It's a business arrangement. You're getting what you want, and I'm getting what I want. In the end this is going to be the best thing for you. Trust me."

"Damn you if this works out wrong."

"To put it as eloquently as I can," Underhill said without rancor, "you already had your pecker in a wringer when you came to me. No matter what else happens, I've managed to uncrank it a few notches."

"I'll do it."

Underhill cradled the phone and looked at Cornell. "Sorry. Now what can I do for you, Mr. Cornell?"

"I'm with Fiscal Development, Incorporated—"

"A major credit collection agency out of the Mid-Atlantic Alliance."

Cornell gave her a weak smile. "We prefer lending agency."

"That," Underhill said, "would be a misnomer. By my recollection—and I just looked at the research today—FDI has never made a loan to anyone. Your company specializes in taking over high-risk loans other companies have made and seizing the collateral for a finder's fee and a percentage. The original investor rarely sees more than forty percent back on the return."

"Most of our clients feel that beats the hell out of nothing, Ms. Underhill."

"It does. That's why this agency's fees are as high as they are."

"We are aware of that," Cornell said. "Our executives talked for a long time before they decided to make this offer to you."

"There was some question?" Underhill raised her eyebrows as if offended.

"Not for professional reasons," Cornell said. "But there are only so many pieces of the pie."

"And FDI was worried about getting a thin one."

"To be frank, yes."

"But it beats no pie at all."

Cornell looked uncomfortable. He burped quietly and almost covered it with a hand. "I apologize. My stomach hasn't quite settled down from the earlier experiences."

"What have you got, Mr. Cornell?" Underhill asked. "As you can see, I'm rather pressed today."

"Yes, well." The man shifted in his seat and reached for the briefcase at his side. "I'm afraid that after the events today, things are going to be somewhat confused."

Underhill waited. The trap was set, all that remained was to snap it closed.

"You're aware of the current situation in Melaka?" Cornell asked.

The FREELancers administrator gave him a blank stare.

"I thought you might be." Cornell shuffled through papers, then put them on her desk. "What you see before you are loan agreements between the Melakan government and Burleson National Bank of New York. Do you know of Burleson?"

"They're the biggest banking industry on the East Coast," Underhill said. "They fund businesses, manage huge tracts of real estate and, at last count, had four space stations in various stages of development."

"Yes. You do know them."

"I've done business with Hayden Burleson myself." Underhill flipped through the papers. She'd already seen electronic copy of them. Matrix was able to get into nearly everything on cybernetic systems. FDI maintained a number of websites they used to keep tabs on business and industry.

"Melaka had been having trouble the last few years," Cornell said. "Since the death of Lord Castlereigh and the advent of a new cabinet that ousted Paul Derembang—he was the prime minister there and linked closely to Castlereigh at the end, which was not a good thing in light of the crises that started when it became apparent Castlereigh was not a well man—Melaka found itself under renewed attack from a number of directions."

"In business and political circles, as well as from assassination teams being turned loose in-country."

"Exactly. Prime Minister Derembang turned to Burleson and asked for a large loan to hire an army to keep them operational. With the amount of technological advances suddenly coming out of the country, it seemed like a wise investment. The Melakan leaders would have had the money themselves, except they'd put all their cash flow into development."

"No one had counted on Tabor deciding to take over himself."

"No."

"What is it you want me to do?" Underhill asked.

"My company would like to hire FREELancers," Cornell said, "to remove Tabor and his men."

Underhill pinned the man with her unflinching gaze. Events at the airport might have gotten out of hand, but she sensed she had Cornell exactly where she wanted him. "You came here to hire me to go up against Tabor."

Cornell nodded.

"And it appears that the assassination attempt on me was made by people in the employ of Tabor."

The big screen was cycling through footage again, including

the still Matrix had digitized showing two of the three identified mercenaries standing beside Tabor in front of a tent. The proof was undeniable.

"Looking at things the way they've unraveled, I'd say so," Cornell ventured.

"It's no leap of faith to think Tabor knew you were going to offer this job to me even before I did."

"No, I guess not," Cornell said weakly.

"You should have told me there might be danger."

"It wasn't my decision."

"It was sure as hell someone's," Underhill accused. "You and your company endangered my life today by playing games. I'm not sure, but I think my attorneys could make a case for a civil suit regarding willful negligence."

Cornell was silent, fidgeting in his chair.

Sensing that it was time to give the man a reprieve, Underhill said, "If I undertake this assignment, and if this agency is successful in removing Tabor from the country, how is that going to help FDI or Burleson? If Melaka doesn't have any money, it doesn't have any money."

"It has assets," Cornell said.

"And how do you propose to leverage those?" Underhill asked. "Have you ever heard of nationalization, Mr. Cornell? It happened to America during the 1970s. American companies went into the Middle East and set up oil wells. A change in government occurred in some of those countries; then the new leaders simply made it law that the oil wells belonged to the new government. Outside of war, there was nothing the American businesses could do except take their losses."

"The Melakan government put the country itself up as collateral."

Underhill sat back in her chair and brought her hands together in front of her. Even though she'd already read through the specifics of the financial agreement, it was still astounding to hear it voiced. "FDI plans on taking the country?"

"As soon as you can turn it over to us," Cornell said. "There's a lot of profit potential involved with this deal, Ms. Underhill.

We've already got a list of prospective buyers."

"What does Burleson say about this?"

"As of this morning," Cornell replied, "he's out of the loop. FDI paid him off at eighty percent of the loan."

"Twice what he would normally get."

"Yes. We feel the potential for profit in Melaka is fantastic. The collateral was vastly underleveraged."

Underhill knew exactly what the man was talking about. If the loans had been greater, it would have been in the best interests of the lender to find a way to keep the borrower solvent till the debts could be paid off. But if FDI could walk into the country and start piecing it off at immediate profit, there was little hope for the borrower. "That's what happened with *McCartney's Star*. Simon McCartney fell behind in his payments on the space station, and FDI repossessed it."

"Yes. I was part of that." Cornell rubbed his hands together, obviously feeling more confident about his work.

"I'd heard he was trying to make a deal regarding his companies down in Texas."

"Yes, but it would have taken an additional ten months for him to pay off what he already owed with interest, plus catch up. We didn't want that much exposure involved where our money was concerned."

"As I recall, the space station was still under construction."

"True. And if we'd have waited a few more weeks, more of the major sections would have been put together and it could have cost more to parcel it off. Time was of the essence."

Underhill locked eyes with the man. "I also recall that you hired Hammer Associates to do the repo work for you."

"They are not as expensive as the FREELancers," Cornell explained. "Nor was seizure of the space station expected to be all that challenging."

"Not at all like taking a whole country back from a man like Colonel Will Tabor."

Cornell froze for a moment, knowing where Underhill had so easily led him. The FREELancers administrator could see the dollar signs in the man's eyes. "No," he admitted. "For that, we wanted the very best."

"I just hope you're prepared to pay for it."

"I've been given negotiating windows. There are several ways we can—"

"Good," Underhill interrupted, "it's always nice to have a starting point. Let me tell you what I want: Ten million dollars a day for every day my team and I are in-country until you're satisfied with the results. Fifteen percent of the monies you make after recovery of your initial outlay of investment capital. And a full medical package for every member of my team."

Cornell turned white. "There's no way—"

The intercom buzzed.

"That's the minimum I'll consider," Underhill said. "If you want to change the mix a little, move the cash per day in exchange for points on the profits, I'm willing to entertain that. Underhill." She spoke into the handset.

"CNN is about to go to a live interview with Harris Hartley," Matrix said. "You left orders that you didn't want that aired in your office until you were ready."

"Thank you," Underhill said. "I'll let you know when I want it." She cradled the handset and looked expectantly at Cornell. Out of the corner of her eye, she noticed the slightest flicker in the monitor as Matrix's recording equipment took over, spinning a taped loop of the earlier broadcast.

"Ms. Underhill, FDI was thinking more along the lines of perhaps two million a day plus a five percent finder's fee."

"Then FDI should be thinking Hammer Associates," Underhill said, "and not FREELancers. I don't do charity work here, Mr. Cornell, and I don't set out to do a half-assed job. Colonel Tabor has a lot of experience, a lot of men at his disposal, and he's had time to settle into Melaka. Getting him out of there is going to be hard work. I'll need working capital to field a fully equipped unit capable of getting the job done."

Cornell didn't say anything.

"Furthermore, I want to add this: If FDI hires a group that goes into Melaka and can't do the job, that money will have been wasted. If you can't recover your investment soon, the company loses all the interest it could have been making, as well as the investment potential that may come and go during this time. And if the indigenous peoples in that country are harmed during the exchange, your company won't be earning any brownie points with them or with the United Nations. In fact, FDI may be inviting even more legal repercussions. You're paying me for a one-strike, one-kill mission. I'm telling you now that's how I'm going to handle it. If you can do better, you should. But I don't think you're going to do it for any less." She tapped the intercom button to Matrix's office.

"I'll call the company," Cornell said. "Maybe something can be worked out. Let me get back to you in a day or two."

"You may not have time," Underhill said, pointing at the monitor.

On-screen, Harris Hartley, looking resplendent in a blue pin-striped suit, was speaking at a podium in front of a packed room of reporters. He was a big man with fair hair and glasses that gave him a philosophical, serious look.

"You're all aware of what happened today," the congressman was saying. "The attack at O'Hare Airport is unconscionable. From the leads developed by the crime units and alliance task forces, we are certain the assassins were sponsored by Colonel Will Tabor, the mercenary leader who has forcibly taken over Melaka in Indonesia."

The picture cut to a photograph of Tabor in full uniform standing with a group of his men in front of the Melakan government building. They looked professional and polished.

"We are not sure at this point," Hartley said, "why the attack happened here, but rest assured that this alliance is not going to take this lying down. Even now, negotiations are underway regarding possible involvement on behalf of the Great Lakes Authority through the FREELancers. A victim of the attack herself, I'm certain Lee Won Underhill, head of the agency, would be predisposed in our favor should such an offer be extended."

Cornell was grabbing the sides of his chair in consternation. "They can't do that." He looked at Underhill. "*You* can't do that."

"Not," the FREELancers administrator agreed, "if I've already got a client. And rest assured, if the GLA comes to me with an offer, predisposed or not, I'll give them the same quotes."

"We are also opening communications with the United Nations Security Task Force," Hartley continued, "regarding possible intervention on their behalf."

"If that happens," Underhill said, "I'm out of it no matter what. When you get the military in on an operation, covert ops like you're asking for are out of the question. Everything gets bogged down, and the only safe place is behind armor."

"Could you excuse me while I go make a phone call?" Cornell asked.

"You know how to find your room from here?"

"I won't have to go that far." Cornell held up a cel phone with a scrambler hookup built in.

"Fine. I'll be here when you get finished."

Cornell left the room.

A rapid series of electric snaps filled the room in front of Underhill's desk. George Anthony Underhill took shape, standing at rigid attention with his arms folded over his chest. "He's going to deal."

"He has no choice," Underhill agreed. "However there is one more thing I want out of him."

Her father raised his eyebrows. "The money, the percentage points, a medical package, I don't see that there's anything else."

"Then I'm one ahead of you." She smiled, feeling good. "You've read over the documentation regarding FDI?"

"Of course. As far as Matrix has been able to find out, FDI is an independent entity."

"An entity that seems to have sprung out of nowhere fourteen years ago and has been a prime mover in quick corporate kills."

"They don't enjoy a good PR stance, do they?" her father asked.

"Not at all. But the company has deep, deep pockets. I'd feel better if I knew for sure who we're dealing with on this."

Her father paced the room. It was something he'd done when he'd been alive, and he'd hung on to the habit even after being reduced to a pixel representation of himself. It still appeared to help him think. "Are you sure about those catacombs, Lee?"

"How else can you explain the technological advances Castlereigh and his people developed?"

"I can't, other than to say that when he imported all those people from Hong Kong, he got his hands on some real talent."

"The answers lie in those catacombs," Underhill stated. "I'm sure of it. Why else would Tabor seize control of the country and continue digging into the catacombs?"

"He could have seized the country because it was ripe for the taking," her father pointed out. "Divided as it was politically, struggling against forces from without, he had no trouble at all once he started."

"Too much trouble to hang on to it, and there aren't enough liquid assets to risk freedom and his life for." Underhill shook her head. "No, it all scans toward something bigger. He's looking for a mega-score, something he can move easily and sell off whenever he wants."

"So what of Melaka?" her father asked.

Before she could answer, the door buzzed. Her father vanished in a cyclone of electrons. Underhill scanned the sec-monitor built into her desk and saw Cornell standing there, then pushed the release button unlocking the door.

The man looked even paler than before, and his mouth had compressed to a thin, hard line. "I was told to offer you eight million a day," he said as he dropped back into the chair, "and twenty points against profits after expenses."

"The medical packages?"

Cornell nodded. "They're yours."

"I also want death benefits for my people," Underhill said. "A million a person."

The FDI man blinked. "How many people are you taking over there?"

"Sixty-three."

Cornell shifted in the chair. "That's a lot of money to be responsible for."

"It all is." Underhill returned his gaze full measure. "Don't balk on me now, Patrick. I'm not taking those people over there to get them all killed. I'm not planning on losing any of them, but I want their families covered if it does happen."

"Done," Cornell said reluctantly. "We'll need to draw up a contract."

Underhill leaned forward and thumbed the intercom button. The monitor was showing more footage from the live press conference with Harris Hartley. "Kent," she said.

"Yes," her aide responded.

"Contracts department, joint legal council, and yourself."

There was a brief pause. "They're all on-line."

"Good," Underhill said, leaning back in the chair. The movement almost took her breath away as the pain from the bruised ribs claimed her. "The contract is to be an agreement between Fiscal Development, Incorporated—known from now on as the first party—and FREELancers—known from now on as the second party, date-marked today and now. As to the particulars, the first party hereby agrees to hire and support in the endeavor described below as second party's obligation. The first party agrees to pay the sum of eight million dollars per twenty-four hour cycle beginning at the execution of this agreement, plus twenty percent of all profits made from properties later described as Melaka after costs shall be deducted, plus a medical package—insert the standard international hazard pay quotes here, including death benefits of one million dollars per operative, to be paid to the next of kin within three days after such operative is legally declared dead." She paused to look at Cornell.

The FDI representative nodded but didn't look happy about it.

The phone rang, and Underhill picked it up.

"Matrix," the cybernetics specialist said. "I locked on to Cornell's signal carrier from the cel phone, but I haven't managed a trace-back yet. Just as you expected, there are a number of cut-outs along the way. I checked the phones listed at Fiscal Development, but none of them was the one he called. I'll let you know."

Underhill hung up and continued with the contract. "As to

the second party, this agreement is binding in all respects toward these objectives: the removal of one Colonel Will Aaron Tabor, the force he maintains as his army located within the property known as Melaka, and the return of the property known as Melaka. Failure to do any of these three will result in a broken contract, and all monies except agreed-upon expenses shall be returned to the first party within five working days."

Cornell nodded again.

Underhill continued. "The property designated such in this agreement is the country known as Melaka—insert geographical coordinates and particulars—which the first party has legal right to per court order regarding liens. Signed, Lee Won Underhill, FREELancers. Signed, Patrick Bernard Cornell, Fiscal Development, Incorporated." She looked at the man. "Satisfactory?"

"I'd like our lawyers to look it over it first."

"No problem. I'll have copies e-mailed at once. They can look at it and get back to you. Just give me the destinations." Printouts spewed up from the slot in Underhill's desk, putting the sheets neatly in front of her. She passed copies over.

Cornell gave her the e-mail addresses without hesitation, then started looking over the neatly printed sheets.

"Kent," Underhill said. "Get the teams ready. I want them boarded and ready for takeoff within one hour."

"They'll be there."

Standing behind the desk, Underhill offered Cornell three signed copies of the contract, affixed with her notary stamp.

He took them, looking at her questioningly.

"A show of good faith," the FREELancers administrator said. "I'm going to be on that plane with my team. If your attorneys agree to it, sign them and leave two copies with my aide, Philip Kent. He'll know where to find you. I'll expect them signed before we go in-country, so that leaves you between twelve and fourteen hours for your decision. If they're not signed by that time, I'll simply turn the plane around, chalk up the expenses, and come home."

"I understand," Cornell replied.

"There is one other thing I'll need."

Cornell pulled the copies of the contracts in protectively. "What?"

"The spy code access to the equipment you have emplaced in Melaka."

For a moment, the FDI rep was taken aback. "I'm afraid I don't know what you're talking about."

"Then find someone who does," Underhill said. "If I were going to invest as heavily in that country as your company has, I'd have made sure I had a way to monitor the situation."

"And if there isn't one?"

"Then there'd damn well better not be one there when I arrive." Underhill offered her hand.

"How will I get back to you?"

"Call Kent. He'll know how to reach me."

Cornell showed himself out.

Underhill returned to the chair and let out a sigh. It was almost impossible to find a comfortable position. She closed her eyes for one blissful moment, then heard her father's chuckle. When she opened her eyes, he was standing there.

"I'm impressed," he said. "I hadn't thought of a guerilla corporate action inside Melaka, or of our getting access to it."

"It's nice to know that I can be one up on you," Underhill said. "You're the undisputed master of scheming and double-dealing. However, now it remains to be seen if I've been clever enough to keep us all alive."

13

Melaka City, Melaka
Indonesia
102.3 degrees E Longitude
2.4 degrees N Latitude

2:03 a.m. Local Mean
1903 Greenwich Mean
March 29, 2024
Saturday

Looking beyond the pistol thrust into his face, Will Tabor studied the eyes of the man holding the weapon. They were black, framed by yellowed and bloodshot whites. Fear struggled with the sudden realization of power within their muddy depths.

"You really going to pull that trigger?" Tabor asked in a soft voice. "Or are you just modeling for a picture?"

"Surrender yourself to my custody," the man demanded. He was thin and bronzed by the sun so dark he was almost black. There were signs of mixed races in his features, including the Oriental folded eyelids. He was in his early twenties, if that, and wore the uniform of the building's housekeeping staff. "I don't want to kill you if I don't have to."

Tabor smiled cruelly, reaching deep inside himself for the power he needed. "Don't you?" he asked softly.

Perspiration dripped down the younger man's face. He blinked rapidly, as if afraid the pistol might go off by itself.

"I've always found it better to send a man into battle who had to show some restraint than to have to send a boy in to kill who had to force himself to take a life."

"Shut up," the young man said.

Tabor kept his hands well away from his body. The metability thrummed within him. "Are you the only one they sent?"

"No," a feminine voice declared. "He isn't."

Tabor stared down the hall, past the imitation trees and plants in ceramic pots and the still life pics on the wall. He saw the woman standing in the shadows, a full-blown Uzi cradled in her arms. He recognized her and smiled. "I know you, but I don't recall your name."

She spat on the carpet and shifted nervously, keeping watch over both ends of the hallway. Her black hair ended abruptly at her shoulders, and bruises still mottled her face and arms.

"Seems to me, chickie," Tabor said derisively, "that you were invited to a private party with some of my men earlier this week. I believe they even mentioned what a good time they had."

She cursed at him. "Shoot him, Kasturi, and be done with it. He is an animal and deserves no better fate."

"That may be, darling," Tabor said, "but it'll take more than the likes of you to put me down." He phased and became intangible, then swung an arm at Kasturi.

The young Malay's fingers whitened on the pistol. "For my country, may god forgive my trespass." He pulled the trigger, and a foot-long snarling belch of flame came from the barrel and dug deeply into Tabor's face.

Somewhere, in a part far off from himself, the colonel thought he might have felt the heat of the muzzle blast. But it could have been his imagination. The muzzle flash nearly blinded him. Strangely, there was no pain, no sharpened spikes of light being driven deep into his eyeball. The bionic one reacted automatically to close the light-amplifying aperture and protect the optic nerve it was grafted into. Blinded in one eye, he could see perfectly out the other.

An instant before his arm moved into contact with Kasturi's, he phased again, coming into the physical world. His hand cracked against the younger man's forcefully enough to shatter his wrist and send the pistol tumbling from numbed fingers.

Kasturi screamed in pain, and the bullet ricocheted from the elevator interior. Before he could recover, the mercenary colonel backhanded him with enough force to knock him from his feet.

Phasing back out again, Tabor wheeled on the woman as she fired a burst at him. The tracer rounds winked purple in the hallway and were gone in an eyeblink. They passed through him as if he were a ghost.

"Bloodthirsty little bitch, aren't you?" Tabor asked. He made his hand solid again, then reached out for the woman's blouse. Gripping it, he twisted and threw her back toward the Malay youth. Weighing less than a hundred pounds, the woman was easily moved.

Tabor went back after them both. Alarms were sounding in the hallway now, and he heard the clatter of armed men coming up behind him. He glanced over his shoulder and saw Wallsey in the lead.

"Keep those men back, sergeant," Tabor commanded.

Wallsey threw up his hand, and the half-dozen mercenaries behind him came to a dead stop like parts of a well-oiled machine.

"Get them out of here," Tabor said, freezing in his tracks. "You and I can handle this."

"Yes sir." Wallsey issued the orders and the group peeled away.

The woman was painfully trying to drag herself to the Uzi she'd dropped. Her leg was bent awkwardly behind her. Tabor knew from experience that it was broken.

Kasturi struggled dazedly to get up from the floor. Blood trickled down his chin from the corner of his mouth.

Tabor stepped on the Israeli machine pistol just as the woman's hand clutched the folding wire-stock. She spat at him, and he phased in time to let it pass through.

"You can't stop me," Tabor said. "You're pathetic."

"Someone nearly did," the woman said. "Unless you were just born with that ugly eye. And if it happened once, it'll happen again." Her voice was pitched low and hard in an effort to cover over the fear that filled her.

"You won't be here to see it, bitch," Tabor promised. He phased his hand, then slowly reached for her face.

The woman tried not to flinch, but she couldn't help recoiling in terror. The floor stopped her, and a prayer started from her lips, picking up tempo and passion as Tabor reached behind her face into her head.

Making a fist inside the woman's head, captivated by the way his flesh seemed to disappear within her, Tabor shifted the metability and made his hand suddenly solid again. By whatever physics ruled his ability, he was able to take precedence over the preexisting molecular structure and maintain his own integrity.

The inner pressure blew the woman's head apart. Bone fragments rattled off the walls and thudded across the carpet.

Howling in fear, Kasturi threw himself at Tabor.

The mercenary colonel drew his blood-drenched hand from the remains of the woman's head. Her body continued to quiver spasmodically at his feet. Before the young Malay could reach him, he spun, bringing his left foot up in a perfect roundhouse kick that caught the man's jaw and knocked him back, unconscious.

Tabor looked at Wallsey. "Grab that and come with me."

Wallsey nodded and went over to pick Kasturi up.

After kicking the woman's corpse over with his foot, Tabor fisted the back of her blouse and lifted her with one hand. He carried her into the elevator. Wallsey joined him a moment later. Tabor punched the button for the main lobby floor.

"You think Underhill will come?" Wallsey asked.

"If somebody's paying her way," Tabor said, "she'll be here. Bank on it."

"Kind of figured she'd want a pound of flesh after that botched job at the airport."

"That's not what's going to bring her here, Pete," Tabor said. "She gets her nose opened by money. Vengeance doesn't float her boat, unless somebody's picking up the tab. Even if that attack didn't kill her, it did make sure Underhill's asking price to FDI was raised. Those people may balk at what she'll demand."

"And if they don't?" the sergeant asked.

Tabor watched as the floor indicator binged and lit up on 1. "Then she'll be here. We're going to plan on it anyway."

"We've got a lot of those scrolls. Could be it's time we thought about getting the hell out of here."

"We can't even be sure if a tenth of what we have is worth anything." Tabor walked out of the elevator dragging the body after him. At this time in the morning, there was no one in the halls except the cleaning staff.

Four women working carts and vacuum cleaners stopped what they were doing and watched as the mercenary colonel made his way to the posthumously-erected statue of Lord Castlereigh. The statue was thirty feet tall, made of white stone, and showed the industrialist characteristically holding his briarwood as he talked. The smile the statue wore had been copied from hundreds of photos the man had appeared in over the years.

Two of the cleaning ladies started to cry, covering their mouths with their hands in an effort to quiet the involuntary noise.

Tabor ignored them. He faced the pristine white of the stone and in two hands lifted the woman's corpse. He phased her and slipped most of her body into the statue's left leg. When he had her positioned so that her body fit squarely into the leg, with her arms and legs sticking out to the sides, her feet inches above the floor, he unphased her.

There was a liquid hiss as the molecules of the two separate objects bonded. The stone bulged, making room for the flesh and blood as they fused and became one. Blood streamed along the outside of the stone, and threaded through the veins of the rock as it was pressurized from inside, creating a handful of miniature geysers that lasted only seconds. When he was finished, the dead woman's body looked like an alien, breached birth.

Wallsey's face had paled a little when the colonel turned to take the Malay youth.

"Comments, sergeant?" Tabor asked.

"Never was one to know much about art, sir."

Tabor grinned, warming to his work. What he was about to attempt, he'd never done with living matter before. He held Kasturi's head in his hand and pushed the man down to his knees in front of the statue's other leg. Unconscious, the Malay's arms hung straight down from his shoulders. The colonel phased the man's head, then shoved it into the statue. Concentrating, feeling the headache coming on from overuse of his metabilities, he stroked the side of the statue's leg, phasing it partly too.

Kasturi's head slid easily into the phased stone. Tabor stroked the rock, altering it, letting the Malay's head remain in one piece. When he was finished, the stone had reformed around the youth's head and part of his shoulders, creating a stony outer layer that mirrored the human features.

Tabor partially unphased the stone.

Kasturi started jerking at once, the pain of the joining obviously too much for his system to ignore. He pushed against the stone, trying to free his head. But it didn't work. Screams echoed from out of the rock, muffled by the exterior. The rock lay over the Malay's face, still malleable enough to capture the screaming features. A dimple formed over the open mouth as the stone sloughed down the man's throat.

Capturing one of his victim's flailing hands, Tabor phased it into the stone as well, maintaining the integrity of both. Then he did the other one. It looked as if Kasturi were holding his head inside the stone.

The man kicked for a long time, suffocating slowly, his skin turning blue under the dark tan. Then, with a final prolonged shuddering that grew steadily weaker, he died and went limp.

"There's going to be some people who notice that," Wallsey said.

"Let them," Tabor replied. "That'll give the rest of them something to think about before they try anything." The man's body could be recovered by taking a jackhammer to the statue, but the woman's body would never be separated from it.

"Yes, sir."

Tabor walked back toward the elevator. "Let's go take a look at the vid and see how bad things really are."

"I figure if the UN does get a bee in their bonnet about this," Wallsey said, "it's going to take them weeks to mobilize. As desolate as this place is, we'd bloody well notice. We could be gone by then."

"If we get the cooperation from that thing we recovered in the catacombs beneath the mosque," Tabor said as he punched the elevator keypad for the basement level, "we should be able to hit the mother lode within a few hours. A day or two at the most."

In minutes they were inside the nerve center of the bunker, surrounded by walls filled with monitors that showed a dozen different television channels, as well as security points around the city. A digitized map of Melaka City, including a five-mile DMZ out from the city limits, covered one full wall. The time and temperature were in the lower left corner legend box, as well as a computer readout listing what all the various colored blips on the map were. The elongated sequence of blue blips chugging toward the city was the mag-lev train coming in from the tin mines. Castlereigh had upgraded the system, and Tabor had allowed it to continue running to appease the companies dependent on the shipments. Of course, there had been a small fee posted per load to guarantee safe passage. But it wasn't much more than the Melakan government had been charging.

"The UN will make a lot of noise," Tabor said as he watched the monitors over the shoulders of the men operating the network. "But they're not going to act unless they can gain something by it and the whole situation becomes cost-effective for them. Jezierski knows me and knows I won't leave unless I'm ready."

"There are the various constituents in the UN who will lobby for intervention, sir," Wallsey said. "If you don't mind my playing the devil's advocate for a moment."

"That's fine. But the ones who'd most heavily lobby against us—the British, the Portuguese, and the Japanese, because they're interested in getting part of Melaka for themselves—are divided about who would get what. Plus, they don't want to have to share the spoils with anyone else. No, sergeant, as far as the UN is concerned, we're in good standing for months."

"That leaves Underhill, sir."

"Yes." Tabor viewed the monitors again. He was tired, but feeling confident. "Given that she would take on an assignment like this, what would your first move be if you were her?"

Wallsey shrugged. "If possible, I'd link up with the underground resistance movement. They've been watching us, and they're likely to have the most information about our troop movements, as well as knowledge of the terrain."

"A war of inches, then."

The sergeant nodded. "If they could establish some kind of beachhead, Underhill could direct flurries against us that would prove damaging and disruptive, while holding on to a relatively safe position herself."

"She has a military bent, doesn't she?" Tabor thought back, remembering everything he'd read about the woman after hearing that FREELancers might take part in the occupation of Melaka.

"She can, sir. Agent Prime is one of her operatives. If she gives control of the campaign over to him, or relies heavily on him for advice, I feel certain that's what he'd suggest. The bloke is bloody good at what he does."

"Let's change the scenario a little, sergeant." Tabor glanced at the monitors filled with satellite shots of the jungles outside Melaka. "Let's assume that Fiscal Development, Incorporated has some inkling of the scrolls and the catacombs. And that they've hired Underhill to recover those."

"You think she might try to get into the catacombs, then?"

Tabor nodded. "She'll have to get into the city to do that. Using the underground resistance movement as cannon fodder would be a means to accomplish that."

"Come in behind them, then split off. I agree, sir."

"We've got satellite coverage on the resistance groups?"

"Yes, sir."

Tabor glanced at the monitors again. "Double the number of the teams out in the field, and let's keep the physical intel on a level with the electronic."

Wallsey agreed.

Tabor went over to another monitor and regarded it. There were three hidden cameras in Saikalen's room, and the various views kept flip-flopping in regular beats. He watched quietly as the man pulled a uniform on over his metal body. The fabric looked awkward hanging on the angular iron parts. When he was finished, Saikalen walked to the balcony and looked out over the city.

"Doesn't appear to like being kept locked up, does he?" Wallsey asked.

"No." Tabor looked at another man farther down the line of cybernetics operators. "Petersen."

"Sir?"

"You're radiating this man?"

"Yes, sir. Gamma waves in safe doses as you ordered." The round-faced cyber ops man glanced at the dials in front of him. "Another two hours, and he'll glow like a firefly when we put an electromagnetic detector on him."

"Good. We don't want him slipping away now that we've found him." Tabor turned to Wallsey. "Be about your orders, sergeant, and let's see if we can find out what Underhill's up to."

* * * * *

Chicago, Illinois — *2:08 p.m. CST*
Great Lakes Authority (GLA) — *2008 Greenwich Mean*
87.7 degrees W Longitude — *March 28, 2024*
41.8 degrees N Latitude — *Friday*

Assignment: Gate-Crasher
Tactical Ops: Organization, Information Retrieval
Status: Code Green

"Lee, we need to talk." Download shoved his way through the press of uniformed men on board the AC-130-H Spectre troop transport and gunship. Designed for military maneuvers, the plane normally had plenty of room, but Underhill had filled every cubic inch with supplies and personnel.

"I'm busy," Underhill said. She pushed her way through the crowd and crates and vehicles, punching off inventory on a

PDA no larger than her hand. She wore a crimson-and-white jumpsuit, with matching .45 automatics, one in a shoulder holster under her left arm and one snugged at the top of her right boot. Her hair had been pulled back and piled on top of her head.

"That's what you told me earlier."

"Hasn't changed." Underhill punched more information into the PDA, and the thin chirps of acceptance echoed along the airship over the steady stream of conversation.

Feeling pissed and knowing he was about to step in it, Download said, "Maybe we can talk when you get back."

Underhill stopped short and turned around. Over her shoulder, Captain Ares was pontificating on moral standards and telling the mercenary crew the FREELancers administrator had added into the mix to keep their chins up.

"You're coming," Underhill said flatly.

"Not if we can't talk." Download stood his ground. Once they'd been lovers. It was hard to remember those times now, with all that he'd been through and everything she'd become under her father's tutelage and the weight of managing the FREELancers agency. Normally he wouldn't have been able to weather the cold stare she gave him.

Evidently she saw something in him that convinced her force wasn't the answer. She called out Prime's name, then flipped the PDA to him.

Prime caught it deftly as he slid a laser rifle over his shoulder. The Aussie didn't ask any questions, just took a quick look at what she'd done, then started moving on through the list.

Underhill led the way to the short flight of stairs leading up to the HQ and ready room she'd had built inside the AC-130-H.

As he followed her up, Download couldn't help noticing the way her hips moved under the jumpsuit. Memory of what they'd had together and how she'd walked away from it, of how she'd come to him while he'd been in a rehab center recovering from a nearly fatal alcohol and drug inspired bender and offered him a job at the agency, rocked his confidence. He had to jog to keep up with her forceful stride.

Without a word, she palm-printed the ready room door,

which slid sideways with a *shush* of motion. She entered, then whirled about, her arms across her breasts as she glared balefully at him. "I've got a planeload of people depending on me to know what the hell I'm doing when we hit Melaka City twenty-six hours from now."

"Five minutes," Download said. Images of Robby Hatch's tears wouldn't leave his mind. No matter how bad a screw-up he was with his own life, he couldn't just walk away from the boy.

"The clock's ticking."

"A couple hours earlier, when I saved that boy on the call from the police department," Download said, "I made a promise to him."

"What kind of promise?"

"He's going to have a lot of problems adjusting to everything that's happened in his life. His metability. His mom. The media. A lot of things."

Underhill waited.

Download took a deep breath and let her have it. "I told him I'd be there for him."

"Did you promise any commitment from the FREELancers?" Underhill asked.

Download couldn't believe she'd asked that, but at the same time he could. This Lee was so different than the Lee he'd known back in college. Or maybe it was only his perspective that had changed. "No."

"Good." The FREELancers administrator headed back for the door.

"Lee."

"What?" Underhill looked at him. "Look, you didn't make any promises on behalf of the agency. That's good. I've got lawyers, and I'd have found a way out of it for you if you had. You'd just climbed out of a burning building with that kid; you can't be held accountable for your excesses. I'll talk to my attorneys, arrange a discount for you through the agency. It's not a problem."

"Dammit, Lee, you're not listening!" Download felt angry and scared all at the same time.

"I am. You told me you promised the kid something. I told you it could be taken care of. It's not a big deal."

"He believed me when I told him."

"Told him what?" Underhill asked. Her gaze was frank and square.

"I told him I'd be there for him."

"For what? His birthday? His bar mitzvah? His graduation?"

"I don't even know." Download turned away, wishing he'd never even brought the subject up, but knowing he couldn't have let it weigh on his mind either. He gazed through the bulletproof windows set into the wall overlooking the AC-130-H's cargo bay. Refit was on top of one of the three armored MAPS units, inspecting the weapons systems with John-Michael DeChanza.

"Then what does he think you're going to be there for?" Underhill asked.

"To help him get it together," Download said in a quiet, hoarse voice.

"If you feel like you have to," Underhill said, "do it. Just make sure the time you use isn't on my clock."

"I can't do it, Lee." Download heard the rush of voices whispering through his mind, all of them giving him different feedback. He tried to ignore them, didn't bother even sorting them out. "How am I supposed to help a kid who's been as bulldozed by life as he has?"

"Then walk away from it."

Download looked at her. "I'm desperate. Robby Hatch needs someone. He really does. I was thinking you could get someone to help him. Hell, he thinks Captain Ares is the greatest thing since sliced bread."

The FREELancers administrator was silent for a moment. Then, when she spoke, her voice was softer. "I looked over Robby Hatch's file on the way here. He was sexually abused. The system failed him. His mother failed him. He has no friends. He's got a metability that's going to be very powerful. And to top it off, for the moment he's a media sensation. Do you really want Ares trying to tell him what to do with his life?"

Looking back outside, watching Captain Ares strike up one heroic pose after another as he worked his way through the mercenaries, patting them on the back, Download knew that wasn't an option. No one knew where the Captain had come from, but the guy sincerely enjoyed being a superhero. The Captain made a good media darling, but the world he lived in had never been tainted by the darkness that had almost swallowed Robby Hatch. "No."

"I didn't think so. Captain Ares has a rather limited view on a lot of issues. Robby's going to need more than that."

"Get him some help, Lee," Download said. "Take it out of my pay. Hell, it's just accumulating in some bank somewhere anyway. I never do anything with it."

"I can do that," Underhill said. "But do you think Robby is ready to take another round of strangers trying to fix his life?"

The words brought back all the times Jefferson Scott had sat in one counselor's room after another, as a part of one group or another, trying to consider his own problems. He'd grown a shell over himself, protected all those weak areas from view, and became practiced at throwing the questions back at the counselors instead of dealing with them himself. He'd never found any answers to his own problems. Not in whatever favorite methodology it was that the counselors had used, and not in himself.

"No."

"The only way he's going to help himself is to want to help himself," Underhill said. "And the best way he can do that is to believe in someone who wants to believe in him."

"That can't be me, Lee."

"Looks to me like that's your choice. He's already taken sides."

"It's not fair."

"To you or to him?" Underhill was unrelenting.

"To either of us. I'm not what he needs, and I damn sure don't need to go through something like this."

"Then don't," Underhill said.

"Lee, I'm asking for help here."

"You're looking for someone to shove the responsibility off on."

"I didn't ask for it."

"No. I'll agree that you didn't. Life can be a bitch sometimes."

"I'll screw it up if I try to help."

"Maybe," Underhill agreed. "But how are you going to screw it up more? By trying to help, or by walking away?"

Download couldn't answer.

"Your five minutes are up."

"Sure," Download said sourly. "Glad we could have this talk. It's helped a lot." He walked to the door and started to go out.

"Jefferson."

He looked back at her, hopeful.

"If you decide to try to be there for Robby Hatch, let me know. I'll work around it on your schedule. And I'll get you some professional help to advise on how you'll best be able to do it. I've already instructed Davison to help the boy and his mother financially out of the staff development slush fund we keep, and to manage things with the media, get them a quiet place to live till they figure out what to do next."

"I'll keep that in mind." Download closed the door behind him and went down the steps. His feet rang against the metal. All around him, men and women were preparing for battle. His mind was a seething cauldron of confusion and anger as he worked his way through the tight quarters. Somewhere in there, he knew Underhill had left some assignments with his name on them. He also knew she'd assigned someone else to them as well, to make sure they'd get done. So he blew off even checking. Underhill knew not to trust him on details, and it was a system that worked for both of them.

Why the hell couldn't she have stepped in where Robby Hatch was concerned? Not to protect him. To protect the kid.

Hammered by the press of people and needing some privacy, Download clambered up a stack of crates and sat on top. No one really paid any attention to him, and when he leaned back against the steel ribs of the big airplane, he could no longer see most of them. The burble of voices became a rush, like the spew of a waterfall, and he was able to ignore it.

He settled himself as comfortably as possible, then dug into his chest pouch for his chipset. Dr. Rhand had given him a new one just before they'd left FREELancers Base. He took it out of the container and gazed at it. *DR. GARRETT JERICHO* was written in Rhand's precise block lettering.

Download tagged the built-in PDA and punched in Jericho's name. Once he'd plugged in the earjack from the chipset, he hit the play button.

"Dr. Garrett Jericho," a man's deep voice said. "An archeologist. Specializing in underground explorations in caves and various jungle habitats. Intuition level indicates some degree of metability. Extremely facile in dead languages. Has spent time among peoples who have remained largely unchanged for hundreds of years, both in the Australian Outback and in South America. Warning: Dr. Jericho has exhibited strains of recklessness and has been cautioned by his peers and employers on numerous occasions."

Sitting with his back against the side of the airplane and his knees tucked up almost to his chest, Download studied the chip and wondered why the hell Underhill had chosen those skills. He had no idea, and he didn't really care, but it beat trying to figure out what he was going to do about Robby Hatch.

* * * * *

Chicago, Illinois	*2:16 p.m. CST*
Great Lakes Authority (GLA)	*2016 Greenwich Mean*
87.7 degrees W Longitude	*March 28, 2024*
41.8 degrees N Latitude	*Friday*

Assignment: Gate-Crasher
Tactical Ops: Organization, Information Retrieval
Status: Code Green

"It's not really anything too major," John-Michael DeChanza said around the small screwdriver in his mouth. "I can have a new circuit board in there in a matter of minutes."

"That's fine, kid," Refit said, shining his flash down inside the access panel of the MAPS. "Long as the time comes we need these puppies they're available."

"Trust me." DeChanza leaned in, fitting his fingers over a small bolt head. His flesh somehow locked on to the bolt as securely as any wrench, part of his metability. He turned it, and the bolt came out easily.

Refit was in a dark mood. The most that Underhill had let out of the bag so far was that the assignment was in Melaka. Personally, he didn't feel FREELancers belonged there, but he hadn't had a chance to voice his opinions. It wouldn't have mattered anyway because Underhill called the shots, but he was ready to vent a little steam.

"If you got this, kid," the patchwork giant said, "I'll go help Mulligan with the other one."

"Sure."

Refit slid down the hulking MAPS and came face to face with one of the people he least wanted to see again in his life.

She was barely five feet tall, but sported a lush figure that would have stopped turnpike traffic in a radar-free zone. Her black leather ensemble didn't do much to cover it. Her top consisted of a halter-bra affair with strings feeding through ebony hoops and wrapping around her biceps. The bikini bottom was cut to allow maximum viewing pleasure and only maintained a modicum of modesty. Leather armor encased her arms from wrist to lower biceps. More straps curled around her legs, from bikini briefs to her calf-high boots, overlaying black fishnet stockings.

She smiled at Refit, revealing perfect white teeth in a ruby-lipped mouth. If there was any warmth in the expression, it was lost behind the onyx-black sunglasses she wore. Her blue-silver hair was cut short and styled spiky, making her light complexion look even more pale. "Hello, monster."

Refit took a step back, getting his personal space in order. He noticed that none of the other troops Underhill had recruited were anywhere near the woman. "Cythe," he acknowledged.

"I'd heard you were still around," Cythe said, "letting Underhill pull your strings. I figured you'd have outgrown that by now."

"What are you doing here?" Refit demanded.

"I got invited."

"Underhill?"

Cythe nodded, then popped the gum she was chewing. A quick, covert glance let Refit know she was still carrying her throwing knives in some of the usual places. Of course, with Cythe, it was hard to say if he'd ever seen all the places. "You know, monster," she said, "you look different." She put a finger to her dimpled cheek. "What is it? New arms? New legs?" Her frown showed only as drawn eyebrows behind the sunglasses. "When was the last time you had a matching set of either?"

Refit didn't say anything.

She gave him a saucy smile, then approached and laid a delicate hand against his massive chest. "How about the *personal* equipment? Is it still yours? Or is that new too?"

"Breeze, Cythe," Refit growled. "I've got things to do."

"Ah, a busy man." The woman withdrew her hand. "Who's the boy?"

Refit knew she intended for DeChanza to overhear the comment and take offense. She was barely ten years older. "If you're supposed to get to know him, you will."

She looked up at DeChanza. "I look forward to it. I love mysteries." She snapped her teeth together, then laughed when DeChanza's face grew red. Without another word, she turned and walked away.

"Who was that?" DeChanza asked.

"Cythe," Refit answered. "She used to be part of the FREELancers a few years ago. Before your time."

"What happened?"

"She quit," the patchwork giant replied. "She's a psychopathic little bitch who really gets into maiming and killing. Even Underhill couldn't control her. These days she sells herself out as an assassin overseas. The last I heard, she had a castle of some sort in one of the Russian satellite countries and had set herself up as some kind of ruler."

"You mean, like a queen?"

"More like a goddess," Refit said. "Some kind of religious sect that thinks she's the second coming of Death itself."

"Really?"

Refit glanced at DeChanza. "Look, kid, your hormones are all in a roar. She looks good and she smells pretty, but if you ripped that female open, only mayhem would fall out."

DeChanza gave the appearance of only halfway listening. "If she's so bad, then what's she doing here?"

"Just means that whatever Underhill is cooking up, all the stops have been yanked. It's gonna be a rough ride in Melaka City."

* * * * *

Chicago, Illinois	*2:19 p.m. CST*
Great Lakes Authority (GLA)	*2019 Greenwich Mean*
87.7 degrees W Longitude	*March 28, 2024*
41.8 degrees N Latitude	*Friday*

Assignment: Gate-Crasher, cont.
Tactical Ops: Organization, Information Retrieval
Status: Code Green

"Have you gotten any closer to finding out who FDI belongs to?" Lee Won Underhill stood behind the one-way glass and watched Download sitting on top of the crates staring at the open chipset. On one hand, she wanted to go confront him because he wasn't paying attention to the assignment sheet. On the other, she knew he probably would have ignored it even if he didn't have Robby Hatch on his mind. The Burris frequency she was using connected her to Matrix via satellite, and was kept scrambled even from the rest of the team.

"I'm still crossreferencing the cut-outs," the cybernetics expert said. "Using the phone call as well as the e-mail was a good idea."

"I know," Underhill said. "I'm counting on you to make good on it, though."

"I will," Matrix replied. "It's just going to take some time."

"What about the satellite network Tabor's using to run security over Melaka City?"

"I've already gotten access. I went in through the weather feeds, found a number of safeties that had been designed into the system, and got by them without alerting anyone. No matter what else, the weather and the news get beamed to every part of the world, and most people take it. I played with the CNN feed for a little while, just to let them know someone was interested, and let some of my snooper programs go bust against their defenses to make sure their egos were properly stroked."

"Can you shut them down?"

"Thirty to forty seconds after you give the word," Matrix said, "their satellites will be off-line for hours, possibly days with the structured virus I'm prepared to hit them with. I can fix them in the same amount of time."

"Good enough."

There was a burst of static from the intercom mounted on the wall. "Attention, people. This is the pilot. We'll be taking off in five minutes. All gear is to be stowed, and you're to be belted into your places."

Red warning lights flashed on around the cargo areas.

Gazing at Download, who wasn't moving in response to the declaration, Underhill said, "I also want you to check in with Family Hastings concerning Curtis Duvall and Robby Hatch. I want to make sure they keep their hands off the boy and let them know that I'm taking a personal interest in his welfare."

"Understood. Do you want a communications with Serle Hastings?"

"Look him up, but hold it. We'll see how things go. In the meantime, have Summer Davison put her personal attention on Robby Hatch. I want a psychologist assigned to him as soon as possible, not for one-on-one, but ready to act as an advisor."

"I'll put a message through now."

"What about the underground resistance movement in Melaka?"

"I've still got them on satellite recon," Matrix replied.

"What about the security access codes Cornell gave us to the cameras and audio pickups in the government building?"

"I'm in the process of bringing them on-line. Some of them have obviously been found and destroyed, but a few of them are still in place. I should have them within the next few hours."

"Let me know as soon as you do." Underhill broke off the com-link and looked at Download. "Okay, Jefferson, evidently this boy has reached out and touched a piece of you that you've managed to keep hidden away from everyone else all your life. Let's see if it's enough to save both of you."

There was a knock at the door.

"Enter," Underhill said, turning away from the glass.

Agent Prime entered the room and dropped into a chair facing the small metal desk that was bolted to the floor in front of a blank computer monitor. He tossed the PDA onto the desktop. "Inventory's done. Everything's there."

"Thank you."

Prime showed no signs of leaving. He steepled his fingers in front of him, his elbows resting on the arms of the chair. "Cythe made the plane."

"I know."

"You sent for her?"

"Yes."

"Why?"

Underhill looked squarely at the man. She'd chosen him to be her number two in the field on this campaign, but even with that, she didn't intend to tell him everything. "We're going to need her talents."

Prime cocked his head with interest. "Care to elaborate on that?"

"We're going to have to make an impression as soon as we get in-country," the FREELancers administrator said. "I'm not going in hoping for some kind of holding action, or to make a long-term stand against Tabor and his people. They don't care about Melaka. If keeping that country together at the moment didn't suit his purposes, Tabor would raze it and sow salt in the ground. Cythe's going to help make the impression I want."

With a forefinger, Prime stroked the diamond-shaped scar on the side of his chin. "You set us up at the airport."

Underhill didn't bother trying to deny it. Maybe no one else had put it together, but she'd guessed that Agent Prime would. "Yes."

"Why?"

"To get what I needed."

Prime was silent for a moment, then realized she wasn't going any further. "And what was it exactly that you needed?"

"One of the things was interest from the UN to put pressure on Cornell and FDI to make a deal, and to put pressure on Tabor. Put him on notice."

"Okay, I had that figured, but there were easier ways to do that."

Underhill shook her head. "Nothing that would have worked as fast or as effectively."

"Matrix knew, too."

"Yes."

"Why didn't you tell John-Michael or me?"

Knowing Prime as she did, Underhill knew the question stemmed from professionalism more than personal feelings. "You and Scratchbuilt were going to be in the public eye no matter how I played it," she answered. "The only way to demonstrate the attack was a surprise was by letting it be a surprise. If you'd known, you'd have reacted differently."

Prime was silent for a moment. "You could have been killed."

"But I wasn't. I was counting on you and Scratchbuilt to do exactly as you did."

"It could have gone the other way."

Underhill shrugged. "It was a premeditated gamble. Trust me when I say I felt I had no choice."

Prime nodded. "In all the years I've known you, I've never seen you do something on a whim. This contract with Cornell and FDI . . ."

"I've known it was going to be tendered for days. It should have been; I'd been working on it for weeks."

"There's more here than just a contract and a few bonuses."

Underhill retreated to her briefcase lying on the desktop. She opened it and took out one of the shiny pieces of metal that had come back from Henshaw's dig in Melaka. Each one had been extremely expensive at the time. Flipping it at Prime, she said, "Take a look at this."

Prime snagged it easily out of the air, then studied it.

"Something special about this?"

"It's not supposed to exist," Underhill replied. "Rhand studied it for a couple of weeks. From what he told me, that chunk of metal is processed and smelted differently than anything that's being done right now, or it's not from this planet at all."

"Which is it?"

"He couldn't say."

"Not like Rhand to get completely stumped."

"No," Underhill agreed, "it's not. That's only one of the reasons I thought FREELancers should take a look at what's going on in Melaka."

"Okay, I'll bite. How are we going to handle the insertion in Melaka?" Prime flipped the metal disk back to her.

Underhill caught the disk and stored it back in her briefcase. "What would you suggest?"

"Linking up with the underground. They'll have the most information together regarding troop movements, weak areas, and already have a base of operations set up."

"If we were going in with the intention of setting up a protracted engagement," Underhill said, "that's probably what I'd do."

"The downside being that Tabor would probably guess you'd do that and double up on whatever spying he's doing on those people."

"Actually," Underhill replied. "I'm counting on him to do just that." Then she told him why.

14

New York, New York | *8:37 p.m. EST*
Middle Atlantic Alliance (MAA) | *0137 Greenwich Mean*
74.1 degrees W Longitude | *March 29, 2024*
40.0 degrees N Latitude | *Saturday*

Theodore Herbst stood behind the one-way bulletproof window lining his apartment suite on the East Side and looked down over Broadway some twenty-odd stories below. "God," he said with real feeling, "you've got to love the nights in this town." He put his hands to the glass and felt the chill whipping by the skyscraper outside. "The money's still out there on the street. You listen really hard, you can hear it moving around, saying, 'Come and get me, come and get me.' " He turned to face his visitor. "Do you know what I'm talking about, Cornell?"

"Yes, sir." Patrick Cornell looked as if he were painfully constipated.

Theodore Herbst adjusted the diamond and gold pinky ring that carried his initials, catching the light in a practiced move that he used to intimidate people who were invited into his home. That was assuming they hadn't already been intimidated by the four armed guards he kept around him constantly, and the Olin/H&K CAWS assault shotgun with the cut-down barrel lying across the top of the ebony desk only one quick jump away.

Tall and lean, the billionaire was the epitome of the urbane male lion of Wall Street. His dark hair was carefully styled in tight curls that lay against his head. He was fresh-shaven by a female barber he had on staff, who serviced him twice a day, and still smelled of talc. It was after five, so he wore a black suit and a silver-and-blue tie.

He hadn't always been the richest man in the world. He'd started out middle class, had gone on to become an average student at the University of Michigan. There'd been some luck involved in his getting a job with a broker in a large Wall Street firm, but he was good with stocks, and luck ceased having to do with anything. Within a few years of wheeling and dealing, he'd made a sizable fortune. He had an uncanny ability to know the rise and fall of stocks, and many people whispered about a sixth sense, or metability, or even a deal made with the devil himself.

Once he'd gotten enough money, Herbst invested it in himself, buying a seat on the stock exchange. No longer having to deal with clients or brokerage-firm bosses, he turned the financial world on its collective ear, mowing through leveraged takeovers and shady operations like a dervish.

When the dust had settled, Theodore Herbst was the reigning king of Wall Street, despite the number of enemies he'd made. The forty-story skyscraper he lived in now was part of a shrewd acquisition from Boswell MacArthur that had earned him the eternal enmity of the man. He'd had two floors converted for his personal use and kicked out all the other tenants, creating a stone and steel and glass castle for himself in the heart of the financial kingdom.

"I've reviewed the contract you negotiated with FREE-Lancers," Herbst said. "You exceeded the parameters I set for you."

"I thought I had your approval, Mr. Herbst." Perspiration popped out on Cornell's forehead. "I was told by—"

Herbst held up a palm, quieting the man at once. "You were

told correctly. Underhill is a very capable opponent at a business deal. I knew that going in. Actually, she went only a little beyond what I'd planned to spend."

Cornell nodded but didn't look relieved.

Sitting in the plush chair behind the big desk, Herbst scooted the Olin/H&K CAWS assault shotgun over slightly, then put his feet on the desktop. Flaunting wealth was a good perk to having wealth. "Did she ask you any questions about FDI?"

"No."

Herbst sipped his drink, puzzled. "I figured she'd be more curious." He'd purchased the company some time ago, after getting involved with investments in Melaka. Lord Castlereigh and his group began hitting the technology fields with more patents than seemed possible, even given the amount of immigrants taken in by that country. Interested, Herbst had figured the odds personally and came up considerably short of the actual figure. That had never happened before, so he'd been intrigued.

As a result of his inquiries, he'd discovered Professor Frank Henshaw's work into the Guardians of the Scarab, which was another unaccounted-for denominator. Then he'd helped create an opening. A lot of Castlereigh's bad luck in the markets was directly due to Herbst's meddling. Deals that should have gone through and turned enough profit to keep the industry in Melaka afloat, even with its increased need for security and a proper military, suddenly went south, barely breaking even, and often cost a sizable chunk of Castlereigh's investment capital. By the end, Herbst was being so heavy-handed he figured Castlereigh would ferret him out.

But the man had died first, and the government split, shoving Paul Derembang out as Castlereigh's chief opponents came to power. Herbst had been thinking he was going to have to play another angle to buy himself some leverage; then Melaka floated the loan from Burleson and hired Tabor, who'd promptly taken over the country and given the billionaire even more to think about—and a way in when Melaka defaulted on the loans and FDI was able to step in.

"Have we returned the signed contracts to her people yet?" Herbst asked.

"They went by courier almost an hour ago," Cornell said, glancing at his watch. "They should be there within another couple hours. I left orders that I was to be notified immediately."

Herbst nodded. "And you did verify that Underhill sent her team on to Melaka?"

"Yes, sir. She went with them herself."

One of the subconscious balances that kept careful measure of debits and credits in Herbst's mind went off. "Normally, she never goes on assignments herself."

Cornell raised his shoulders and dropped them.

"I find that interesting." Herbst looked at his chief bodyguard, a hulking German mercenary who'd been cyborged and chromed over after a near-fatal rescue of his employer nine years ago. "Vlad."

"Sir." The bodyguard's hair was cottony gray and clipped almost to his misshapen skull on the parts that weren't covered by steel and ceramic. His nose was tilted up and angular, too short and too sharp to be considered human. With the burning he'd gone through, plastic surgery—no matter how gifted the surgeon—would have proven ineffectual.

"Underhill doesn't go out into the field much, does she?"

"No, sir."

"I thought not." Herbst pushed himself up out of the chair and started pacing. He called for the map, and one of the walls behind the desk opaqued suddenly and revealed itself as a computer monitor. A map of the world spread out in glowing electric blue. "With that as an operating given, why would she do so now?"

No one had an answer.

"Even if Underhill is successful—" Cornell began.

"*When* Underhill is successful," Herbst corrected him.

"Yes. When she's successful, what are you going to do with the people living there? They may not see FDI's presence as any better than that of the mercenary colonel."

"Ah, but there's where you're wrong," Herbst said. "Tabor

went in there and screwed everybody over. I'll find the people I need to make deals with, and I'll make them. Just as I did with Underhill, though she doesn't know I'm involved. I'll spread the profit around to whomever I need to as long as I take the lion's share." He studied the map more closely, zooming in on Melaka. "As for the rest of them, I'll drop earth-moving equipment into that country if I have to, and bulldoze them all right into the ocean."

* * * * *

Outside Melaka City, Melaka
Indonesia
102.3 degrees E Longitude
2.4 degrees N Latitude

8:16 p.m. Local Mean
1316 Greenwich Mean
March 30, 2024
Sunday

Paul Derembang was drenched with perspiration from walking through the jungle for the past three hours, and he stank of the insect repellent they'd purchased in Singapore. His right arm ached from the short time he'd insisted on taking a turn using the machete to cut a path through the dense vegetation, and his eyes burned from trying to stare holes through the darkness of the night that surrounded them.

The man who called himself Mat Kilau seemed unstoppable. Once they'd hit Singapore, he'd had no problem getting in touch with smugglers who worked the Strait of Malacca. None of them had been especially excited by the prospect of taking two passengers into the country. A vast amount of diamonds had changed hands, and the doubts and fears of the smugglers had gone away.

Derembang never found out where the gems had come from. There was much he didn't know about the man he was following into the hidden camp of the underground resistance movement. Anytime he was away from Mat Kilau, his head filled with questions. However, when he was with the man, the questions no longer seemed important. Everything just felt right somehow.

Melaka's ex-prime minister leaned heavily against a boulder that cast long shadows on the ground. He was breathing like a bellows, and he was afraid it was a sound that could be heard for miles. The *whack-whack-whack* of the machete was unrelenting.

To hew through so much foliage so tirelessly, the man had to be more than human. But less than the god he insinuated he was.

Fifteen yards away, Mat Kilau stopped and turned back. The lantern beam strapped in a harness on his chest flared through the jungle and turned the perspiration dripping down the length of the machete into drops of cobalt blue.

"How're you doing, Mr. Prime Minister?" Mat Kilau asked. In Singapore, he'd arranged to buy clothing and the necessary supplies they'd need for their trek in-country. He wore khaki trousers and matching shirt, with calf-high hiking boots that were stylish as well as serviceable, and an Australian hat that had caught his fancy. He'd pinned it up on one side and left the chin strap loose.

"I've been better," Derembang said. Another disturbing habit the other man had begun demonstrating was calling him by his official title. Or, at least the one he'd held up until a few months ago.

"Do you need a breather?"

"A short one, perhaps."

"Good." Mat Kilau shoved the blunt tip of the machete into the ground, then squatted down beside it. "I, too, have been needing one, but I hesitated to ask."

"I feel that you could have continued on many miles before needing to stop," Derembang said.

Mat Kilau laughed, the sound of it as pure and honest as a stream coming down from the Titi Wangsa Mountains. "You overestimate me, Mr. Prime Minister."

Derembang took his first deep and comfortable breath in a long time. "If I do, then we're both lost."

Taking the flat lantern from his chest, Mat Kilau hung it across the haft of the machete but left the beam on. "No, my friend, we are not lost, and neither is Melaka. She shall be ours again, and we shall be hers." He reached down into the thick loam and brought up a handful. "We are of her flesh, after all. She cannot turn her back on us."

At first, the mystical way Mat Kilau spoke had been offensive to Derembang. The words had sounded hollow and empty. Now it was accepted. The old man clung to the words, feeling a strength grow in him as he listened. He felt young again, at least in heart. "How much farther, do you think?"

"To the rebel base?" Mat Kilau shrugged. "Three, perhaps as many as four more miles."

"I'm surprised," Derembang said, "that they've not scouted us. Tabor has hunting parties out after them on a regular basis."

Mat Kilau showed him that dazzling white smile. "But they have scouted us, Mr. Prime Minister. They've been trailing along with us for the last two miles."

Derembang glanced around. "You're sure."

"Yes."

"Why didn't you say anything?"

"At the time, it didn't seem important."

"Not important?" Derembang turned his lantern on the man.

"Please, my friend. That is most blinding." Mat Kilau put up a hand to protect his eyes.

Derembang turned the lantern away. His confidence was shaken again. An eternal warrior, a man who had the power to walk from myth, wouldn't need to shield his eyes. Would he? "You should have told me."

"I'm telling you now." Mat Kilau blinked at him, not bothering to rise from his position beside the machete.

Derembang craned his neck in all directions, seeking to spot the men who'd been following them. Both he and Kilau were armed with pistols, but neither of them was outfitted to go up against the rebel forces if it came to that.

"Do you know who these men are?" the old man asked.

Mat Kilau leaned down and smoothed a patch of dirt with his hand. Slowly, he traced intricate designs into the surface, interconnecting them all. "Three men I know," he said. "Gilad Ahmad, Herman Zong, and Muzaffar Riayet. There are nearly twenty others."

All of the men were known to Derembang. Herman Zong, under different circumstances, had been a friend.

"How can you know this?" Derembang asked.

Mat Kilau smiled up at him. "How can you not?"

Derembang listened to the soft lilt in the man's voice, remembering how, on the flight to Singapore, he'd listened to it only to fall asleep each time within minutes without his questions being answered. He'd known he was near exhaustion back in Chicago, but that was almost twenty-four hours ago. Never had he slept so much or so long or so deeply. For a while, he'd thought he'd been drugged. But each time they had to make a flight change or had taken time to eat, he'd been sound of mind and not feeling any ill effects. It had been as though he felt as secure as a babe in its mother's arms. The man had never hesitated about talking to him on any subject he cared to discuss.

"Do not fear them," Mat Kilau said softly. "They will be yours again. They are hurt and confused, looking for a place to vent their anger. Most of all, they are beginning to realize they need a real leader."

"You?" Derembang asked. For a moment, he felt the hot flush of envy, then felt just as quickly ashamed.

"Not me," Mat Kilau answered. "I am a warrior. You are a leader."

"They will not follow me. Their trust in me is broken."

"Then it must be restored."

Derembang felt his heart hammering inside his chest as he gazed at the shadows. Many of the people had sworn death threats against him and the cabinet that had served to bring Tabor to Melaka.

"They're coming," Mat Kilau said.

Peering toward the dark jungle, Derembang said, "Where?"

There was no answer.

When Derembang turned back to look at Mat Kilau, the man was no longer there. He'd vanished like a ghost. Before he could shout out the man's name, shadows separated from the jungle and made their way toward him. He dropped his hand onto the butt of the side arm holstered at his hip. Then, remembering how events had gone in Chicago and how he'd come close to shooting at Lee Won Underhill, he reached instead for the buckle to his gunbelt. He stripped it and tossed it to one side, then waited for the arrival of the rebel forces.

Herman Zong, clad in black camou and carrying an AK-47 assault rifle, led the pack of men that descended on him as silently as wraiths. He was flanked by Ahmad and Riayet. There were eighteen other men.

Zong was a short and blunt man, with a bald head that sat on his shoulders like a round-nosed bullet. He wore black-framed glasses that gave him a scholarly look in spite of his battledress.

"Hello, Paul," he said. "What are you doing out here in the jungle?"

Derembang eased off the boulder. He wanted to be standing on his own two feet. "Looking for you."

"That was a mistake," Riayet stated in his thin voice. He was lean and dark, with a thick mustache that had been made fun of by most of the secretaries in the government building. "We've sworn death to oppressors and traitors."

"Where is your friend?" Ahmad asked. Of them all, he looked the most military, which was in keeping with his background. Before turning to politics, he'd been a decorated captain in the Melakan coast guard. He'd stood against corruption, taking down segments of the drug-trafficking organizations and white-slavery rings that had operated through the Straits with near impunity when he'd filled the office.

"I don't know," Derembang replied honestly.

Zong waved the men behind him in two directions, sending them into the jungle around the area. "What did you want with us, Paul?" he asked in a gentle voice.

For a moment, Derembang was hesitant, wondering how his answer would be taken. "To offer my services to your cause."

Riayet laughed out loud; joined by several of the men standing behind him. "You gave up your gun at our approach, old man. How can we trust you to hold the line against those trained mercenaries of Tabor's?"

Pride stiffened Derembang's spine. He'd found some of it

again while talking to Mat Kilau. "There is more to war than the fire and strength of youth, Ahmad. There's also negotiations and planning and rebuilding to do."

"But it's fire and youth that pave the way for what is to come."

"Even if you're successful in standing against Tabor," Derembang asked, "what then? If you are able to retake Melaka, what are you going to do with it?"

"We'll rebuild," Zong said.

"The city? The businesses? The spirit of these people?" Derembang challenged. "International ties, which you're going to need to survive against other nations that may take advantage of the situation here?"

"We can handle ourselves, old man," Riayet said.

"This is more than yourself, you insolent pup," Derembang snarled. He took a step forward, causing them to back away even though they were armed and he was not. "This is a country full of frightened people who are going to be looking for the right answers."

Zong met his gaze levelly. "You sound different, Paul. Are you sure you're all right?"

Derembang looked at the man who'd been his friend. "Herman, I'm better than I've been in a long, long time. Lord Castlereigh's death, in the middle of so many changes in this country, came too soon. It left me bereft of my own sense of direction. I knew the way of politics, but he worked in economics. The changes in Melaka sprang from those things, which I knew little about. But this I know: for Melaka to stand again, with all her problems, she is going to have to find friends to lean on for a time, till the internal strength is ours again."

"How do we know you won't sell us out to these new friends of yours?" Riayet demanded.

Derembang tapped his chest. "Because this heart beats with the existence of Melaka as an independent nation. Take that away, and you have killed me."

"Then why aren't you dead now, because the mad colonel has surely taken away our independence?"

"It's not gone forever," Derembang answered. "I thought it was, and I almost made the biggest mistake of my career. But a friend has convinced me otherwise."

Ahmad shifted his long flashlight around. "You're referring to the one who has so obviously taken a powder?"

For a moment, Derembang's newfound certainty wavered. "The convictions lie within me, Gilad. Remember back when you were going to clean up the coast guard, get rid of all the graft the smugglers and white slave traders inspired? Remember how many people told you it could never happen, because every man on the coast guard was corrupt?"

"Yes," Ahmad replied. "I insisted that this was not true. That many of these men were good men, needing only a leader to bring forth strong hearts again."

"A lot of people laughed in your face when you told them that," Derembang said. "You remember?"

The man nodded, his jawline hard.

"You were that leader then, Gilad," Derembang said softly. "And you knew it within your very soul."

"I had hoped."

"As strongly as I do now." Derembang locked eyes with the man. "Do you understand?"

Slowly, Ahmad put down his rifle, then waved to the rest of his men to do the same. "I only pray that you are right, my friend."

Herman Zong lowered his gun as well.

"What is this?" Riayet demanded, looking at his companions.

"He's right," Zong said, taking his glasses off long enough to clean them with his shirt. "Even if we did somehow succeed in getting Tabor out of Melaka, we don't know the people in international circles that we're going to need to ask for help. Paul does."

Riayet moved away from the other two men, keeping a fierce grip on his rifle. "I don't believe in him so easily." Over half the men sided with Riayet, moving in concert with him as the schism grew.

Derembang watched with a heavy heart. A division within

the rebel forces would weaken them further. To be successful, they needed to be a cohesive group.

"Then believe in me," a strong voice said. The words rolled over the jungle.

Derembang swiveled his head around to the right. The terrain had a definite incline there; he could remember coming up the other side, hoping that the descent would be easier. It hadn't been.

A shadow moved across the landscape, and it was a moment before the moonlight lanced through the trees and provided illumination. The stranger stood there, a mocking smile on his face as he held his arms out to his sides. The Aussie hat was thrown back and hung by the chin strap against his neck. "Believe in me, and I'll believe in Paul Derembang for you, because you're going to be vulture meat without him."

Riayet leveled the AK-47 in front of him. "Who are you?"

"I am called Mat Kilau."

The name had an instant effect on the men, and a torrent of whispering started up.

"That is the name of a hero," Riayet said.

"It is the name of a man."

"What are you doing here?"

"I've come to offer my services in your time of need," Mat Kilau said, "as the legends have said I would."

"Who is this man?" Herman Zong demanded. "He's going to get himself killed toying with Riayet that way."

"For all I know," Derembang replied, "he *is* Mat Kilau." There was no denying the man. The others had already seen them together. But the man's claim was going to seriously damage Derembang's chances at being heard by the rebel forces.

Riayet moved toward Mat Kilau, his rifle held at the ready. "Are you supposed to be some kind of ghost?"

That perfect smile twisted Mat Kilau's lips, and Derembang just knew the expression had damned the man.

"No," Mat Kilau said quietly, but loudly enough that everyone hung on his words. "I am much more than that." He held his hands aloft and spread apart.

Without warning, heated lightning sizzled from his hands and streaked over the heads of the rebel group, throwing off heat and leaving a sonic boom in its wake. The supercharged veins of light went on for a time until they vanished in the distance. Riayet was bowled over by the concussion, while Mat Kilau remained unmoved.

Lowering his hands, Mat Kilau walked forward and placed his hand on Derembang's shoulder. "Do you feel like going on, Mr. Prime Minister?"

Derembang had to struggle to find his voice. But looking in those smoky gray eyes, he found more strength in himself than he'd expected after walking so far. "Yes."

"Good. Then let's be about our business. Tabor and his people will know of your arrival soon enough." Somehow Mat Kilau took the lead, yet managed to have Derembang at the forefront.

The prime minister allowed himself to be guided, finding his strength growing with every footstep. He felt the man's reassuring touch on his shoulder.

"Well, come on, Riayet," Mat Kilau said with joy in his voice, "get up. We don't have all night. There's a country to take back. Don't you want to be a hero?"

Awkwardly, the man forced himself up and onto his feet. He stuck his fingers in his ears, trying to ease the ringing from the explosion Mat Kilau had triggered. He looked around for his rifle for a moment, recovered it, then stood his ground. Hesitantly, he started walking behind Derembang, but each step grew more sure.

Derembang glanced around and noticed the rest of the group falling in behind them.

"I told you these men were looking for a leader," Mat Kilau said in a voice pitched low enough that only the two of them heard it.

"You could be that leader."

The man shook his head. "As I've said, I'm a warrior, not a politician. They're going to need someone to protect their interests internationally. You can do that where I can't."

"It doesn't seem as if there's anything you can't do."

Mat Kilau laughed. "My friend, I can't let it appear any other way."

* * * * *

Off the Coast of Thailand — *2:47 a.m. Zulu Time*
23,000 Feet — *1947 Greenwich Mean*
101.1 degrees E Longitude — *March 30, 2024*
11.9 degrees N Latitude — *Sunday*

Assignment: Gate-Crasher, cont.
Final Briefing

"In less than two hours," Lee Won Underhill said, "we're going to enter the outer envelope of the drop area cited for the insertion into Melaka City." She stood at the head of the table and pressed a button. Despite the cramped confines aboard the AC-130-H Spectre, she'd managed to have a holo built into the table. As she pressed the button, a glowing nimbus of light popped into existence less than a foot above the tabletop.

"What are we doing in Melaka City?" Refit asked. The patchwork giant had pointedly sat as far away from Cythe as he could.

"We've been contracted to neutralize the mercenary force occupying the city and return it to FDI," the FREELancers administrator said. She used the remote control to activate the holo, unveiling satellite shots of the city. There was a series of them, showing troop movements through the streets as well as the heligyro patrols. The holo made it seem as if a small world had taken form inches above the tabletop.

"Who is FDI?" John-Michael DeChanza asked. He looked bleary-eyed and held his head up with one hand. Underhill knew he'd been pulling long hours with Refit working over the MAPS units.

"Fiscal Development, Incorporated," Underhill said. "They took over a loan that Melaka defaulted on."

"So they want us to rob the Melakan federal reserve while we're there?" Cythe asked with a pleasant smile. "If we're going to do that, why not just keep it for ourselves and divvy?" She sat in her chair in a manner to best show off her body. The black leather gripped tightly, but seemed about to explode in places.

"No, we're not going to rob anyone," Underhill said. "We're going to take possession of the country from Tabor and his people and give Melaka to FDI."

"What are they going to do with it?" Download asked. He sat apart from the group, arms folded over his chest. He was wearing the helmet, further sealing out contact with the others.

"Try to recoup their losses."

"How?" Download's tone was challenging.

"Why, by helping those people up," Captain Ares stated, as if it should be obvious to anyone. "By getting their country working again so they can pay off their debts. If you give people a chance to pull themselves up by their bootstraps, they can make a success of whatever they wish to do. My aunt always told me that."

Underhill glanced at the Captain. No matter how immune she thought she'd become to him, the man never ceased to amaze her with his simplistic, apple-pie view of life.

In his stylized suit, with that big crimson A on his chest and his Malibu good looks, he was certainly the most striking-looking individual of the group. The Captain looked the part of a hero. The problem that Underhill had with him was that he too often took that role too seriously. His strength was beyond measure and, aided by the Kevlar mesh of his uniform, he was damn near invulnerable. Even after exhaustive background checks, Underhill hadn't been able to find out anything out about the Captain since before he was approximately sixteen years old. He'd dropped in one day, full-blown in a FREELancers uniform knockoff and announced his availability for the agency. When asked why he'd decided to join up, he'd answered that after learning of his incredible powers, he'd known there was a responsibility that came with them, and he wasn't about to shirk it. His aunt would not have approved.

Underhill was thankful the Captain was also naive.

"I don't think it's going to go exactly like that," Download said.

"Why?" the Captain said, turning around and putting one

gloved fist on the table. "You don't think we'll simply go in there and ride roughshod over those people and take their country away from them, do you?"

Underhill interrupted. She didn't want to lose Captain Ares from the task force, because his presence would bring a lot of hope to the Melakan people. He was the most universally recognized of the FREELancers, and she'd spent considerable money making sure of that. "We're going to do the job we hired on to do," she said in a hard voice. "Anyone who doesn't want in can grab a parachute and leave the party at any time."

Download stood up without hesitation. "Be seeing you, Lee. I never figured civil insurrection for your game, especially when it looks like we're going to give the locals the shitty end of the stick."

Refit was showing signs of wavering as well, and DeChanza didn't look happy either. With his background of war in his own country, Underhill wasn't surprised.

"There's more to it than that," the FREELancers administrator said. She tossed one of the pieces of metal she'd brought onto the tabletop. The clink of the impact was audible even above the dulled drone of the big plane's engines.

Cythe reached out for it and turned it over in her fingers. "What's this?"

"The main reason I bought into this," Underhill said. She looked at Download pointedly. "It's a piece of metal found at an archeological dig a few months ago by a man named Henshaw. He's an archeologist. I found out he was looking for funding, showing pieces of this metal around to a select group of investors. One of them showed it to me, thinking I might be interested. Henshaw's previous financier had died, and the complications in Melaka had started. But he felt he was on the verge of the greatest discovery he would ever make."

"It has drawings on it," Cythe commented.

Agent Prime sat back in his chair, watchful. Underhill knew he was waiting to see if she could hold the group together. "Henshaw figures they were religious markings."

"Okay," DeChanza said, "what's so special about this piece of metal?"

"Other than the fact that it shouldn't exist?" Underhill asked. "Coupled with the fact that it was found on a dig relating to a secret sect in Malaysia that's been around thousands of years? A sect that has been known to intermingle with some of the greatest inventive minds of the ages, that possibly influenced radical thinking in all fields of science?"

The silence hung heavy in the room for a moment, but Underhill knew she had them hooked.

"This decision isn't a new one for you, is it?" Refit asked.

"I've been looking into it for weeks," Underhill admitted.

"With what end in mind?" Download asked. He leaned back against the door, his arms over his chest. His eyes were cold through the slits of the mask.

"For now, to learn about it."

"What do you mean this metal shouldn't exist?" DeChanza asked.

"The technology that allowed it to be smelted and processed hasn't been invented yet, and two of the elements are unidentifiable," Underhill said. "At least, not on this planet."

"You're thinking this came from space?" Refit asked.

"That's one of the possibilities."

"You're talking aliens visiting the Earth, that kind of crap?" The patchwork giant's lips turned up in a scarred snarl.

"Perhaps it came down with a meteor that struck the earth," Underhill said. "I don't know, and I don't care. What I do know and do care about is that that piece of metal represents a possible threat to us and everyone else on this planet."

"How do you figure that?" Download asked.

"What if that metal was part of a container?" the FREE-Lancers administrator asked. "What if something more than a few pieces survived the arrival of whatever it was?"

"You're throwing out wild shots here, Lee."

Underhill fixed Download with her gaze. "Am I? Let me trot out some facts for you." She ticked them off on her fingers. "One: We have pieces of metal Rhand has examined and concluded cannot be produced by current technology. Two: Castlereigh, the man who pioneered much of Melaka's industry and independence, was intensely interested in dig sites throughout the country. Three: There was a secret sect in the area called the Guardians of the Scarab that were devoted to the sciences. Four: Castlereigh's companies suddenly started going ballistic with patents for more and more advanced technologies within a short time after increased digging through the country was sponsored. Five: A man like Will Tabor wouldn't do what he did on a chance at a pig in a poke. And six—" She punched the remote control, calling up the shot she wanted.

In the holo area, the colors whirled rapidly, then settled down into another scene.

"This is from one of the hallways in the government building," Underhill said. "FDI had their own little spy system set up that I managed to wrangle from them. The tall, red-haired man is Colonel Will Tabor. The woman is Margo Peele, an archeologist with ties to the black market in artifacts." She tapped the remote control again and got a close-up.

There was no doubt the iron skeleton was moving under its own power as she let the vid play, nor that there was a very human head sitting on the massive iron shoulders.

"This one," she said quietly, "we've not identified."

When the vid footage reached the end of its loop, it vanished with a static pop.

"You think they dug this guy up?" DeChanza asked.

"That's one of the questions I want answered," Underhill replied. "Neither Castlereigh nor Tabor have had time to completely go through the catacombs beneath that country. Someone professional, someone like Dr. Rhand, should be allowed to go through there first."

"What's likely to be down there?" Download asked.

Underhill looked at him. "I don't know. Rhand feels that's open to speculation. It's possible there's nothing more than what's been found so far, but it's just as possible there's something harmful. Henshaw's reports hint that there was a plague that wiped out the Guardians of the Scarab over a hundred years ago. In case there's something else like that waiting down there, I'd rather have Dr. Rhand and his associates handling things." She looked around the group. "Agreed?"

"With the fate of the world hanging in the balance," Captain

Ares said, "there can be no other place than at your side, Miss Underhill." He gave her a salute and a steadfast expression.

"I'm in," Agent Prime said.

"So am I," DeChanza said.

Refit gave her a tight nod.

"If I'd known this," Cythe said, "I'd have probably gouged you for more pay."

"That's what the bonus areas are for," Underhill said. She looked at Download.

"That covers the threat of what's in those catacombs," Download said, "but what about the people?"

"You'll have to trust me on this," Underhill said. "They're a very big part of the equation."

"What about FDI?"

"I'm working on it." Underhill turned her attention back to the holo. "The attack I've got planned is going to require some fast movement. We'll be going in by parachute drop just before dawn, coming in from the west. Download, you're going first. Henshaw's notes indicated he felt certain he was on to one of the main areas of the catacombs. We're going to put you down there right after Matrix blacks out all the satellites Tabor's been using to head up his intel supply. We'll be fully functional ourselves, but his teams are going to have to rely on standard radio communication."

"They might as well have two tin cans and a string," Prime said. "They'll be able to talk to each other, but without the benefit of computer-integrated movement against us, they'll be slow and uncoordinated."

"You'll have a two-man team with you," Underhill told Download. "If you can reach the area where Henshaw feels the metal scraps came from, do it. Hopefully it'll give us more information to work with."

Download nodded.

"Target Two belongs to Refit and Scratchbuilt." The holo changed, depicting an airfield. "Tabor has a small air force organized and running all day. You two, and the team I'm sending with you, are assigned to knocking out as many of those craft as you can before they get into the air. Without air coverage ourselves, we'd have a problem competing with them."

The holo shifted again, showing the main government building.

"Prime, the targets belonging to you and Cythe are inside. There's a communications platform in the basement that will need to be taken out, plus whoever you can among Tabor's staff to demoralize the grunts. I've got candidate profiles set up for your review later."

"How are we getting into the building?" Cythe asked.

"The old sewer lines under the city run below it. Matrix accessed the building schematics. Wear a transponder, and she'll mark your spot for you. Blow your way through directly into the basement area."

"What about the rest of you?" DeChanza asked.

"We're going to be in the streets," Underhill said, "trying to take out the tank force Tabor has set up."

"That's where he'll have most of his army stationed if he's expecting trouble," Refit said.

Underhill clicked the holo off. "If everything goes right, they'll be elsewhere."

15

Outside Melaka City, Melaka
Indonesia
102.3 degrees E Longitude
2.4 degrees N Latitude

4:33 a.m. Local Mean
2133 Greenwich Mean
March 30, 2024
Sunday

"Hold the men up here," Mat Kilau said. "I'll be back in just a few minutes."

Actually, Paul Derembang was ready for the rest. Since his arrival in Melaka, he'd made up for getting too much sleep on the airplane. But he didn't want to let the stranger out of his sight. He turned, wanting to speak with the man, but Mat Kilau was already gone.

The man came and went like a wraith, with no explanations of where he'd gone or why.

Derembang couldn't remember who'd first brought up the idea of moving the base camp. It might have been himself, or Mat Kilau, or Ahmad. In the beginning, none of the group had wanted to leave the base. It meant tearing everything down and starting over again. Then Mat Kilau had produced the American and British cigarette butts from areas where Tabor's roving guards had kept watch on them.

Derembang signaled a halt, calling to the man Ahmad had put in charge of communicating with the rest of the convoy. Gazing back along the way they'd come, he watched the men and women put their packs and bundles away and take up the children who were old enough to walk, but were stumbling along because they were so tired. It struck him then how vulnerable they were. Cold fear reached into his stomach with icy talons.

If Mat Kilau had been sent to set them up, the man could not have done a finer job of it.

"Mr. Prime Minister."

Derembang turned back around to see Herman Zong hurrying up to him. The man carried a sleeping child who couldn't have been over two in his short, massive arms. "Is something wrong, sir?" His shirt showed sweat stains and stuck to him.

"No. Mat Kilau has gone ahead to look things over. He thought we might take a short break." Derembang hoped that was the truth. He held out his arms. "Let me take the child."

"No," Zong said. "It's okay. I've got him."

"Do you not trust me to hold him?" Derembang accused.

Zong passed the child over, then worked his arms up and down to restore the circulation. "Thank you."

"You're welcome." Derembang stared down into the small boy's face, seeing the innocence in the calm features. And, he hoped, he saw the future.

"I'm glad you came back to us," Zong said.

"I don't know if that was wholly my choosing," Derembang said. "After the way I left things, I wasn't convinced there was anything I could do here."

"What happened here, with Tabor, wasn't your doing," Zong said. "I think most of us knew that. We were just seeking someone to blame for our misfortunes."

Derembang gazed back at the line of ragged men, women, and children. "I'd say these are worse than unfortunate times."

"But it wasn't your fault."

"People have a tendency to blame rough dealings with the unfamiliar on the familiar," Derembang said. "It's human nature. Every politician knows this. His or her face becomes a promise of something more, something better. And when it doesn't happen, people blame the person, not the events that caused the disappointment."

"If Tabor had been another kind of man, maybe it would have. We were wrong to blame you."

Derembang touched the child's cheek, finding it soft under his fingertips. "Truth to tell, my friend, you were not the first to blame me. I blamed myself, and selfishly set my feet on a course of destruction. If Mat Kilau had not found me when he did . . ." He left the rest unspoken.

Zong placed his hand on Derembang's shoulder and squeezed.

The *whop-whop-whop* of a heligyro's rotor blades crashed into the dark quiet covering the jungle. Derembang automatically moved into the shelter of the nearby tree line and gazed up into the dark sky.

The combat heligyro swung around and locked on to an approach pattern. Derembang knew the craft would be equipped with a FLIR, forward-looking infrared, and would also be downloading any information it picked up via satellite to the government building and Tabor's shock troops. Ahmad's hand-picked crew started running along the lines of the convoy, urging everyone into hiding.

Pandemonium threatened to break out as excited voices filled the jungle, interspersed by the whine and throb of the approaching heligyro. Without warning, the two chain guns mounted on the stubby wings opened fire, throwing 7.62mm rounds through the leafy canopy, which did nothing to blunt the attack.

Derembang turned toward the nearest tree, holding the struggling, squalling child close to his chest as he protected it with his own body. Hoarse screams of men and women ripped loose all around him. He knew it would take a miracle to save them.

* * * * *

Outside Melaka City, Melaka — *4:38 a.m. Zulu Time*
Indonesia — *2138 Greenwich Mean*
102.3 degrees E Longitude — *March 30, 2024*
2.4 degrees N Latitude — *Sunday*

Assignment: Gate-Crasher, cont.
Tactical Ops: Infiltration
Status: Code Green

"Open the tail section," Lee Won Underhill ordered over the Burris transceiver, standing at the back of the big troop transport.

"Tail section opening now," the copilot responded.

With a clank of gears and servos, the tail section dropped open. The air stream buffeted the slab of steel as it dropped, until it was horizontal with the rest of the plane.

Underhill looked over at Download.

The agent was dressed in his FREELancers jumpsuit and wearing the shiny helmet. A parachute pack was strapped across his back, and he held a rucksack with the tools he'd need in one hand. A safety line tied it to his waist. He carried two Glock 17s with laser sights on his hips. In the tunnels at the excavation site, rifles wouldn't have been much good.

"Are you ready, Ferret?" the pilot asked.

"Ferret's ready," Download said. The two members of his team stood behind him, dressed in FREELancers' crimson and silver. One of them was a woman, but she was from Vietnam and was used to tunnel war, having logged some time in the black market battles through the underground passages of Cu Chi.

The Burris chirped for Underhill's attention, letting her know to go to the frequency she was using for direct contact with Matrix. "Go."

"One of Tabor's heligyros is attacking the rebel forces," Matrix said. "I've got them on-screen now. I can knock it from the sky with one of the lasers."

"No," the FREELancers administrator said. "If you do, Tabor is going to know something is wrong and won't send his troops to intercept the rebel forces like we're planning."

"Those people are going to get massacred."

Underhill pushed away the spill of images that flooded her

mind. She knew what jungle trails could be like when a helo attacked. With all the trees and foliage around, it looked as if there were a million places to run, but nothing stopped the hammering bullets. "We save a few people now, we're going to lose a lot later on."

"I know."

"Thirty seconds," the pilot said, his voice echoing throughout the transport ship's telecom speakers.

"I need you to take out Tabor's satellites," Underhill said. "Do it now."

"I am."

"And stay with what is happening to Derembang and his people. Maybe once this is over, we can get a med-evac team in there."

Matrix's voice sounded more distant as she spoke, and Underhill knew the woman had retreated to her Savant state. "Satellite system is shutting down," Matrix said.

"Ferret, you're in your drop zone."

"Ferret's away." Download took three running steps and hurled himself into the dark sky spinning out behind the Spectre gunship. His team was only a half step behind.

Underhill watched Download's dwindling figure till it vanished. "Okay," she ordered, turning from the cargo area and threading her way through the three inert MAPS units secured to the floor, "button it up, and let's get the hell out of here." She tried hard not to think about Derembang's people caught out on the trail. Even with the satellite system down, the communications platform in the government building was still on-line. If Tabor had put a bird in the air, he was sure to have ground troops in the area as well who could call in reports of a laser attack.

They were on their own, god help them.

* * * * *

Melaka City, Melaka	*4:40 a.m. Local Mean*
Indonesia	*2140 Greenwich Mean*
102.3 degrees E Longitude	*March 30, 2024*
2.4 degrees N Latitude	*Sunday*

Colonel Will Tabor was in the communications area watching the video feed from the heligyro attacking the rebel forces. Actually, there were two video feeds: one from the nose of the attack chopper, and the other from a ground team set up less than a mile away on a promontory.

The first screen showed the heligyro's view as it finished up the first pass. Bright lavender blips of tracer-fire cut through the foliage after the fleeing rebels. The second screen showed a horizontal shot of the heligyro flying along with its nose pointed slightly down, spitting sparks ahead of it.

"Do you really think they're trying to get to the city?" Wallsey asked.

Tabor watched the screens with interest. He pointed to another computer monitor with a close-up of Paul Derembang holding a small child in his arms.

"At this point," Tabor said, "I'm not willing to chance it. After the way Derembang's fellow politicians rode him out of the country on a rail once we took over, I figured the bloody fool would never show his face in Melaka again. Yet, here he is, thick with the rebel forces."

"Yes, sir. Not one for hindsight myself, but maybe we should have killed Derembang."

"And made a bloody martyr of the man?" Tabor shook his head. "That wouldn't have been the answer. No, we stop him now, totally crush him and the rebel forces and drub the noses of the rest of the populace in it, we'll have a properly subservient bunch of cattle till we're able to get the hell out of here."

Abruptly, most of the screens in the communications room went dead, leaving only depthless ebony in their wake. The cybernetics ops people started yelling immediately.

"What the hell is going on?" Tabor demanded.

"I don't know, sir," Stuart, the head tech, responded. He was a beefy man with the patience of a saint when it came to his computers and electronic equipment. He ran from power station to power station, checking dials and digital readouts. "Everything's functioning. We've lost the satellite relay."

"How?"

Stuart yelled for the teams to go to back-up systems. Some of the screens flared to life, but Tabor knew they'd lost much of the visual and audio pickup points. The heligyro harrying the rebel forces was no longer on-screen. A minute later, though, and radio communications had been brought back on-line.

"I don't know, sir," Stuart replied.

Tabor crossed the room to the Plexiglas map of Melaka City and the outer environs. He found the coordinates the helo team and the ground patrol had agreed on, ran his finger across the smooth surface till he located the points of intersection. He used a black grease pencil from the tray underneath to mark the position. "Stuart."

The cybernetics ops chief hurried over. "Sir."

"Your main satellite relay on the ground, where is it?"

Stuart studied the topographical map printed across the clear Plexiglas for only a moment, then shoved a thick forefinger against it.

Tabor used a ruler to measure the distance between the two spots and did the conversion from the legend at the bottom of the Plexiglas. "Four miles, Sergeant Wallsey, from Derembang's current position."

"Do you think he could have launched a smaller band of rebels toward the satellite relay to take it out?"

"It's possible," Wallsey said, gnawing a thumb. "But why? Even with the satellite system off for a few minutes till we can get everything rerouted to the back-up systems, what can he hope to accomplish?"

"The first thing I would do if I were proposing to start an insurrection in occupied territory," Tabor said, "is show that the people in control weren't as omnipotent as they act. As you recall, we've done it ourselves. How soon can you bring the satellite feed back on-line, Mr. Stuart?"

"Thirty-two, thirty-five minutes, sir."

"Get it done. Have you had any communications with the satellite outpost?"

"No, sir. But their communications are chiefly through the satellite system. The cellular phones, the radios, all of it."

"What about a regular phone line?" Tabor asked. "These people laid bloody hard fiber-optic line throughout that jungle for years before Castlereigh and the others brought communications here into the twenty-first century."

"They've got a phone," Wallsey said. "I've inspected the outpost myself. I know."

"Find out," Tabor said to Stuart. He walked back to the first two screens he'd been watching. They were still black and empty, but regular radio communications had taken over. He listened to the men talking to each other, relaying information about the scattering rebel forces. It was uncertain how much damage they were actually doing.

"Sir," Stuart called from across the room, one hand covering the mouthpiece of a phone, "they're not answering."

Tabor nodded, not surprised. "Sergeant, mobilize the ground forces and get teams out there on the double."

"What about the aircraft?" Wallsey asked.

"Keep them here. If Derembang and his people are prepared to make a stand, they may be willing to sacrifice themselves to bring the aircraft down."

"Right, sir."

"Tell those men I want Derembang's bloody head brought back on a stick. We'll put it down in front of the building for all to see. Then we'll see how many more heroes this country can summon up." The monstrosity he'd made with the statue of Lord Castlereigh and the two young rebels was still having an impact.

"Yes, sir."

Tabor continued standing in the communications room, overseeing the efforts that were being made. He hadn't counted on losing the satellite relay station. Something like this would not happen again. He wouldn't allow it. Melaka and the secrets it held were his; there was going to be no mistake about that.

* * * * *

Outside Melaka City, Melaka	*4:43 a.m. Local Time*
Indonesia	*2143 Greenwich Mean*
102.3 degrees E Longitude	*March 30, 2024*
2.4 degrees N Latitude	*Sunday*

"Mat Kilau!"

"Mat Kilau!"

The warrior's name thundering through the haze of tracer-fire gray against the night and the booming peal of the big guns was undeniable.

Crouched against the tree, the screaming child trying to kick its way free of his arms, Paul Derembang looked over his shoulder and saw the man come from the jungle. His heart swelled with pride at the same time it chilled with fear. Mat Kilau was certainly going to his death. "*No!*" he yelled hoarsely.

But there was a smile on Mat Kilau's face as he raced up the jungle trail. His eyes were locked on his target: the heligyro gunship even now wheeling around in the sky to make another pass.

Derembang watched, unable to leave the child. To see the man die in front of them would crush the spirits of the rebel force. There would be only ashes left.

Incredibly, even when the heligyro unleashed the terrible rain of gunfire filled with rushing purple light, Mat Kilau stood his ground. Whether or not he was the man from legend, he was most certainly a fearless champion.

With the wind from the rotors rushing through the opening of the trail and plucking at his clothing, whipping the Aussie hat with its folded brim, Mat Kilau screamed, "For Melaka! For *freedom!*" He lifted the laser rifle he had at his side and fired as soon as it reached his shoulder.

The ruby beam spat out across the distance as the twin line of chain-gun bullets kicked dirt up over Mat Kilau's legs. Caressed only for a moment by the laser, the rotor motor burst into flame that quickly spread to envelop the aircraft. The explosion that followed a heartbeat later was blinding and deafening.

The heligyro went to pieces, turning into an ellipse of orange and black fury that spread across the night. Flaming pieces of debris arced over the jungle, then fell to the ground.

Mat Kilau stood like the hero he was supposed to be, brandishing the laser rifle defiantly over his head. Behind him, the sun was just cresting the earth, rendering the sky in pinks and purples that looked regal.

"Do you want to live to be free again?" he challenged.

A few voices roared back a resounding yes. Then other voices picked it up, repeating the affirmative answer until the noise was a swell that beat down the last ringing sounds of the exploding heligyro and gunfire.

Men and women spilled out of the jungle and created a ring around the champion, shouting his name more and more loudly.

Derembang couldn't believe it. He walked out to join them, passing the child off to his mother. Tears filled his eyes, both from fear and pride. There could be no turning back at this point and he knew it. The future, whatever it held, had been set.

He knew in his heart that they couldn't be following a god or a legend. Could they? But there was no denying the fire he saw in Mat Kilau's eyes, nor the white grin of triumph pasted on his face. The man lived for this moment, and it had set aflame every person there.

He only hoped they weren't following a madman.

Mat Kilau waved his arms, quieting the crowd. "These people have been forced to run and hide for their lives, Mr. Prime Minister. They've been made to leave their homes. Is it time for them to fight their oppressors? Is it time for them to take back what is theirs?"

Derembang knew the challenge wasn't meant just for him. It was meant for all of them, for every man, woman, and child who would live free. There could be only one answer. He walked up beside Mat Kilau and looked at Zong, Ahmad, and Riayet. None of them were kidding themselves. They all knew the cost. And as he looked around, the prime minister realized it was the same with every person there.

They waited on him, waited to hear his words. But Derembang knew he could tell them nothing they couldn't already tell themselves. He looked at them, making his voice fierce, shutting off the fear for these people and what they were about to do. "Is it time?" he asked them.

The roar went up at once, drowning out the doubts.

Mat Kilau waved them to silence. He faced Derembang and used an orator's voice that the prime minister knew could be heard by everyone. "We're going to face the enemy, Mr. Prime Minister. Perhaps the greatest enemy this country has ever known. We need a leader who has in him the heart of a lion and the faith of a chosen disciple." He locked eyes with Derembang and paused.

Derembang couldn't mistake the zealous lights in Mat Kilau's eyes.

"We ask you," Mat Kilau said, "to lead us." He threw up his arms, urging the crowd to voice their opinion.

The screaming became a physical force then as support was offered. It was fired from the combined infernos of near-death and sudden salvation, and by the courageous man who stood with the brandished laser rifle at Derembang's side.

The prime minister's throat ached with the emotions that ran through him. He waited to speak.

Mat Kilau went to one knee in front of Derembang, his head bowed, the gesture obvious. In seconds, it was mirrored by the rest of the rebel force.

Wishing he were more sure of his convictions, but knowing there was no other answer, Derembang said, "Yes. I will lead you. And death will be the only thing that stops me from giving you back your freedom and your country. This is my promise."

Mat Kilau stood and led the cheering.

Derembang remained before them, looking out at the faces of the people he was about to lead into battle. It was possible, he knew, that others would learn of their approach in Melaka City. In fact, he could send runners ahead to tell about the march against Tabor and his people. Perhaps it could even serve to have the mercenaries attacked from the rear as they sought to do battle with approaching forces. It was a window of hope.

Mat Kilau broke free of the crowd after suggesting to Ahmad to get his people to organize the groups and get them ready for travel. He approached Derembang and dropped a friendly arm over the man's shoulders.

"Are you prepared to take a new place in history, my friend?" Mat Kilau asked.

"If we should survive, you mean."

The man laughed. "Ah, there was a time when you were not such a doubter."

"Ages ago," Derembang said.

"Then it's time to be young again."

Derembang looked up at the other man, his voice catching in his throat so that he spoke only in a hoarse whisper. "There is one thing I must know."

"Anything."

"Are you really Mat Kilau?"

"What do you think?" The gray eyes were level, frank.

"I wish you were," Derembang said, then reached out to touch the side of the man's neck where it was almost covered by the shirt collar. "But I have reservations." He showed the man the blood on his fingertips. "Ghosts don't bleed."

Mat Kilau smiled. "I never said I was a ghost, did I? Only a legend come to life." He clapped Derembang on the back good-naturedly. "Paul, trust me. This is all going to work out. Look at what you've accomplished. In only a matter of hours, you've raised an army. Those people need to be strong to take back this country. They have to be a part of it, deserving, or they'll never believe in themselves again. Even with Tabor and his men gone, there could be others who try to take what this country has. You know that, don't you?"

Derembang nodded slowly.

"Just as you needed to believe in yourself back in Chicago. You needed to know you'd go the distance. So do they." Mat Kilau regarded him. "Whatever you do, I'll be there for you. What's it going to be?"

"There's no turning them back after this."

"No."

"Then we go, and may god keep us in his sight." Derembang prayed as the army formed around him, knowing things would forever be changed in the next few hours.

16

Outside Melaka City, Melaka *4:51 a.m. Zulu Time*
Indonesia *2151 Greenwich Mean*
102.3 degrees E Longitude *March 30, 2024*
2.4 degrees N Latitude *Sunday*

Assignment: Ferret's Run
Tactical Ops: Recovery, Unspecified Target
Status: Code Green

Download saw the ruins. The jungle had nearly reclaimed them, leaving only the skeletal framework of the oblong structure. According to Henshaw's notes, the archeologist believed the ruins to be from a Portuguese fort that had garrisoned a few dozen men to protect the trade routes during the 1500s, but had gotten wiped out during one of the border skirmishes with the sultans. During his partial excavation of the last site, Henshaw had found mention of a hidden door within the ruins that led down into the bowels of the earth.

Download adjusted the shroud lines, bringing the parachute's glide path more in line with the ruins and concentrated on the descent. He was crashing through the treetops almost before he knew it. Branches whipped at his face and filled his nostrils with the thick, pungent scent.

Twenty feet above the ground, already feeling the harness grow tight around his chest as the black silk wrapped tightly over the branches, Download hit the release buttons and dropped out of the chute. The rucksack tied to his leg threw his balance off, so he went into a loose-limbed sprawl.

Recovering almost immediately after the impact, the FREE-Lancers agent picked up the rucksack of tools, detached the line from his ankle, and started for the ruins. The other two members of the team drifted to the ground near him. As soon as they were free, they followed him.

The ruins were less than fifty yards away, but they were harder to see in the dim light filtering through the jungle. From the air, the general outlines had been easily decipherable. Trees and brush snarled around the exterior, climbing relentlessly over the stone.

The doorway was high, set beneath an arch between two columns that stretched to the high roof and served as decoration as well as support. The doors themselves were stone. One was shattered into thousands of pieces and strewn over the jungle floor as well as the steps leading up into the building, while the other was partially open. It was dark inside.

After making a brief adjustment to the Octopus on his shoulder, Download inserted the Jericho chip. The blue lightning splashed briefly through his head as the new personality and skills took root.

He dropped the rucksack on the vine-covered porch under the arch. Over two-thirds of the steps had sunk into the ground, leaving only a half-dozen exposed. The two guards Underhill had assigned to him joined him on the steps, their laser pistols at the ready.

The woman's name was Cai, and the man's was O'Grady. Underhill had included more information about them, but Download hadn't bothered to remember any more of it. He didn't need to know them, just what to call them.

"What do we have here?" Jericho asked inside Download's mind.

"What does it look like?" Download asked sarcastically.

"A Portuguese fort," the archeologist replied. "Circa sixteenth century. Looks like nobody's been home in a long, long time."

"That's about the size of it, ace," Download replied, taking a long-handled flashlight from the rucksack. He switched it on and peered into the remnants of the building. Dawn was bursting across the sky now, sending thick, ropy veins through the clouds, looking like a battered jellyfish.

"Wait," Jericho said. "There's writing on the wall. Let's have a look at it, shall we?" He took control of Download's arm without asking, grabbing the cuff of the jumpsuit and using it to scour a large stone set into the wall beside the doorway. "Do you see that?"

"I can't read it," Download said. He knew the two agents with him were waiting for him to enter, not privy to the conversation taking place in his head.

"I can. See this symbol?" Jericho used Download's arm to point out a drawing near the top of the writing.

To the FREELancers agent, it looked like a broken eyeball. A dozen or so arcane symbols chased themselves around it.

"Evidently," the archeologist said, "one of the Portuguese soldiers garrisoned here was a fisherman at one time." He scrubbed at the stone some more, then blew on it. The dust caused Download to sneeze, but he noticed it didn't bother Jericho at all. "This is to ward off the evil eye. Spirits, curses. The writing bears this out, making reference to the terrors and abominations that haunted the jungle."

"Terrific, doc," Download said, "but we're kind of up against the clock here." He took control over his body and went into the building, following the hard ellipse of the flashlight's beam.

The smell of rotting vegetation overlaid everything. Twisted roots had plunged up through the stone floor, causing some of the flagons to be canted almost on their sides. A broken chair occupied one corner near a bank of dead coals that had left a permanent black smear on the floor and walls. It didn't look as if it had been used in years. A roasting spit made out of branches hung over it, along with the skeleton of some fowl.

Download walked around the room. His feet crunched against the broken stone and dying roots. The walls were tall and gleamed of moisture, green where moss found stray bits of sunlight that poured through the broken ceiling long enough to encourage growth. A pair of human skeletons lay in the corner, their skulls bashed in with a blunt object.

"A rifle butt," Jericho said.

"You'd know?"

"I'm an archeologist. I don't dig up many live people, and a lot of the ones I've found over the years didn't die of natural causes. Those people were probably robbed and brought here."

Download ran the light over the skeletons, feeling the humidity inside the building gather and start streams of perspiration running down his neck and back. The Octopus on his shoulder seemed to intensify the heat. There was no identification in the bathing suit trunks and bikini that remained. A spider crawled out of the bikini-wearer's nose socket, then went scuttling across the broken skull.

"Amorous and adventurous," O'Grady said. "Probably got off from their group or ventured out here on their own and got waylaid."

"This building used to be two stories," Jericho said. "The lower offices were administrative, and the upper floors were defensive. Probably had cannon up there and sleeping quarters for the men."

Download tracked the flashlight across the open space of the first ceiling. The sky was turning pale through the holes in the roof.

"There's a cellar, too," the archeologist said, letting Download know the man had accessed the information he'd read through but hadn't remembered with his conscious mind. "Should be a door in the floor somewhere around here."

"Spread out," Download told the two people with him. "Look for some kind of hatch or door in the floor."

"The Portuguese would have wanted a root cellar, someplace to keep the wine," Jericho said, "and a place to hide if an enemy tried to burn the fort down around them."

Download ran a sleeve across his face, and it came away wet. The humidity inside the room was growing, becoming stifling. He played the flashlight across the floor, having to work not to stumble across the root growth. "Wouldn't it have filled with roots by now?"

"Maybe," the archeologist replied. "But they may have lined the structure with lime to discourage growth."

Two minutes later, Cai called out that she'd found it. Download and O'Grady joined her.

The hatch was little more than a two-foot square, almost covered by roots and debris. Download took a trenching tool from his rucksack and snapped it together. The keen edge sliced neatly through the roots, and Cai and O'Grady pulled the debris away.

Once the door was cleared, Download slipped the handle of the trenching tool through the heavy iron brackets mortared into the stone and got enough leverage to move it. Scars across the stones showed where it had been moved several times before.

Download slipped through the hole in the floor. Cai held her beam down for him, lighting up the floor barely six feet below. He reached the ground easily, then had to stoop so he wouldn't scrape the helmet across the low ceiling. He played his light around the room as Cai joined him. The woman held a pistol in her hand.

Wine racks covered one wall, but the only thing that remained of them were broken bottles across the stone floor. The perfume of decayed and rotted matter cloyed Download's nostrils, almost gagging him. He sipped his breath for a time till his senses got better acclimated.

A small desk was built into another wall. Two straight-backed chairs that looked worse for wear and some ragged bedding rounded out the furnishing. Cloth sacks covered with mold littered half the floor, and cheesecloth draped over vaguely wheel-shaped items had turned blue with age. A handful of candles burned to various lengths sat on the small desktop.

Download checked both the desk drawers, but they were empty.

O'Grady scrambled through the door with difficulty, having to remove his pack and his bulletproof vest to make it. He put the vest back on at once. The room wasn't big, but whatever secrets it held had been hidden for hundreds of years. "Spread out. Check the walls first." Download pulled a combat knife free of his boot and left the rucksack in the center of the room. He went to his left and started pounding the hilt of the knife against the stone wall. The echo coming back was solid.

"The stones here are thick," Jericho said. "If you were dealing with a brick or wooden wall, you might be able to find a disguised entrance with your method."

"You got a better way?" Download asked.

"Use the water in your canteen. Pour it along the wall. If there are any cracks and crevices that bear investigating, that should reveal them."

Download took his canteen from his hip. Fresh water wasn't going to be a problem for a while. He called the others over to him and directed them to put their lights on the wall he was standing in front of.

"With the humidity in the air," Jericho said, "the rock won't be so apt to soak up your water. If we were in an arid clime, we wouldn't be able to do this at all."

Even using the water sparingly, it took a lot to cover the entire wall. Download was halfway through O'Grady's canteen on the third wall before he found a crevice that drank the water down instead of spitting it back out someplace else. It was about knee-high, and he'd almost missed it.

Download knelt and pulled his knife free again. He dribbled more water against the crevice, watched it ooze into the space and never reappear.

"Now," Jericho said, "I think we're on to something. Look around. If the entrance is this hold, there should be a locking-release somewhere close by. Try pushing on the other stones."

It took fourteen tries. Then Download heard a click, and the section of wall in front of him started to move, releasing a salty tang into the air.

"The sea," Jericho said, sniffing with Download's nose. This must lead out into an underground tributary."

"Shouldn't that be fresh water?" Download asked. The mortared section of stone turned out to be not much bigger than the hidden door leading down into the cellar.

"Part of the day it probably is," Jericho said, "but when the tides reverse or during monsoon season, salt water probably gets shoved back up in the small caves the stream flows through."

Download got on his hands and knees and shoved himself into the hole. It was a tight fit and measured at least six feet in length, with a gradual decline. The bottom of the shaft was wet from the water he'd poured.

A snap was the only warning he got; then Jericho was yelling inside his head. "Move! Move! Back out the way you came! Now!"

Digging in with his elbows, Download shoved himself back out of the tunnel. Not trying for a gracious exit, he rolled to the side as quickly as he could, yelling at O'Grady and Cai to clear the tunnel entrance. He was unable to get completely out of the way, but only one of the sharpened iron spikes meant for his face grazed his jumpsuit and ripped through the material without breaking the skin.

With a harsh clang, the projectile smashed against the opposite wall with enough force to scar the stone and thoroughly shatter the rusted iron.

"Okay," Jericho said, breathing a sigh. "We missed a trip release."

"No shit," Download said, pulling at the rip in his jumpsuit.

"Tells us something, though," the archeologist stated.

"What?"

"Nobody's been down here since the guys who built that neat little booby trap."

"Terrific." Download picked himself up and went back to the shaft. He'd abandoned his flashlight in the tunnel. Miraculously, the beam was still shining forward, not quite breaking the darkness on the other side. "Means there'll probably be other nasty little surprises."

"Yeah," Jericho said, "but now we'll go a little more slowly."

Reluctantly, Download fitted himself into the shaft again. He went forward cautiously, letting Jericho's skills and experiences guide him, hoping it would be enough.

* * * * *

Melaka City, Melaka
Indonesia
102.3 degrees E Longitude
2.4 degrees N Latitude

4:54 a.m. Local Mean
2154 Greenwich Mean
March 30, 2024
Sunday

Reports from the recon team were conclusive. Paul Derembang and the band of rebels were headed toward the city.

Colonel Will Tabor paced the floor of the communications as he listened. At least one heligyro had been lost in the earlier battle, and the recon teams he'd assigned to the field were going down in quick order. He glanced at the Plexiglas map. One of Stuart's people was making revisions on it every five minutes. The rebel forces were still six miles out. There was still time to break them before they reached the city.

Margo Peele entered the room, a dirty pair of rubber gloves in one fist. Dark rings circled her eyes, and her hair was pulled back in a single braid that was purely functional. "What the hell is going on?" she demanded. "One of your men just pulled me out of my lab. I had some very important work going on."

"I understand," Tabor said placatingly. "I wouldn't have bothered you at all, but it seems we're under attack."

Blinking, Peele peered around at all the dormant equipment. "What happened?"

"The rebels." Tabor pointed at the monitors containing the vid from the MAPS. "It appears they've chosen today to die. I wanted you to be where we could protect you, in case some of the locals decide to go out in a blaze of glory as well."

"Dammit." Peele blew a lock of hair out of her face and slapped the gloves against her dirt-encrusted pants.

Tabor kept watch over the monitors and kept track of the communications bursts. "Was it something important?"

"I've managed to decipher some of the entries in the book we found in Saikalen's personal little vault of horrors," Peele said. "Evidently it was a hand-written copy of other volumes that were floating around at the time. The language is mostly artificial, put together from dozens of other languages in a weird kind of shorthand."

"Save me the archeological rhetoric," Tabor said. "It's truly falling on unappreciative ears at the moment."

"I'll bottom-line it for you this way," Peele said. "That book is called *Oracle of Evil*. It's all about Saikalen."

Tabor turned toward her, his attention full on her now. "Tell me."

"Saikalen is telling you the truth that he achieved an immortality of sorts by using some of what the Scarab taught the Guardians. And by the way, Scarab was actually a shorthand version for Soul of Knowledge. They believed he was the seed that started all real learning in the sciences. Sort of the way there was one inspiration point for all religions, just different interpretations of them after the fact. Saikalen has been around since the early days of the arrival of the Scarab."

"He told me that."

"Yeah, well what he didn't tell you was that he was mixing in with the Forbidden Learnings all along. His apparent immortality was only the first of his thefts. When the elders found out, they banned him from the group."

"When?"

"There's no way to be sure. But Saikalen took a number of copies of the scrolls with him. The Guardians sent teams after him, men who'd dedicated their lives to tracking him down and killing him once they'd discovered what he'd done. The work Saikalen was primarily involved in at the time had to do with biology and chemistry. He was able to extend his own life through cellular reconstruction through a chemical means, as well as create those animated wires in his head."

"He had those before they lopped off his head?"

"Well before." Peele took a small note pad out of her blouse pocket. "According to the journal entries, he killed the Scarab and took them."

Tabor considered that. "Then those wires have to be connected to some kind of device inside Saikalen."

"That's what I'm thinking." Peele took a deep breath. "The elders believed that those wires—that device—is where the Scarab carried all his information."

"An auxiliary brain," the mercenary colonel said.

"That's oversimplifying things, but pretty much sums it up."

"So everything we're digging for—"

"Is already inside Saikalen's head. At least, most of it."

"Damn!" Tabor raised his voice. "Mr. Stuart."

"Sir."

"You have the floor. Call me if you need me."

"Yes, sir."

"Come with me," Tabor told Peele. He slipped the laser off his hip and checked the charge. Out in the hallway he broke into a jog. Peele stayed close behind him, followed by Fook, who was obviously reluctant to let his current meal ticket out of sight. "Com-station, this is Colonel Tabor."

"Yes, Colonel."

"Patch me through to Sergeant Wallsey."

"Yes, sir."

Tabor punched the elevator door, then held it open for Peele to enter. Wallsey, out in the field searching for a missing recon team, came on the radio as soon as they started upward, the signal somewhat distorted by the building. "Pete," the colonel said, "grab that heligyro and get back here. Leave Dorsey in charge."

"Yes, sir."

The elevator doors opened, and Tabor jogged out into the hall, noticing Peele had lifted the flap over her SIG-Sauer pistol.

A dead man was out in the hallway in front of the room where Saikalen had been held. The door was open, with bloodstains tracking back inside.

Tabor lifted the laser in a two-handed grip. "If the bastard's in there, don't shoot him," he ordered the archeologist. "I can cut the legs out from under him with this."

"If he takes one step toward me," the woman replied in a tight voice, "all bets are off. I'll do a salvage job on his head."

Coming around the edge of the door, Tabor dropped the laser into target acquisition before him. Inside the room, another dead man hung from the ceiling, his head and shoulders driven deep into the tangle of support lattice for the acoustic tiles. An electrical cable was twisted around his neck. Blood dripped from his limp feet, and one of his arms was missing.

"Com-station, this is Tabor. Get out a security alert on that monstrosity we dug up from the catacombs."

"Yes, sir."

Going on into the room, Tabor kept the Beretta/Douglas before him. He felt an uncomfortable itch down his spine.

"Monstrosity?" Saikalen's curious dry voice repeated. "How unkind, Colonel. And here I thought we had the promise of being bosom comrades."

"He's above you!" Peele screamed, firing before she even had the words out.

Already on edge, it took Tabor only a second to phase. Still, he felt the pressure of the huge iron fist come crashing through the space his head had once occupied. He turned, bringing the laser pistol up, but didn't fire. With the energy generated by his metability, he didn't know what firing the laser—or any weapon for that matter—would do.

Fook wasn't so lucky. When the iron fist passed through Tabor, it connected with the politician's skull, pulping it instantly.

Saikalen hovered over the support lattice, gripping the I-beams to hold himself up. He looked like a spider in the post-dawn shadows. A smile formed on his pale face. "You're one of them!" he said in an excited hiss. "The Star Scarab said you'd come."

"Come down," Tabor ordered. "Come down now or I'll shoot."

"I don't think so, my colonel. If you wanted me dead, you'd have already shot."

Without a word, Margo Peele fired, aiming for its head.

A guttural cry ripped from Saikalen's lips, epithets from a forgotten language. He recoiled, then threw a big iron fist at the side of the wall. Bricks and mortar and plaster exploded outward and rained down over the balcony forcefield below. A few more blows, as rapid as a jackhammer, ripped the hole large enough for the metal skeleton to fit through.

Tabor watched in frustrated anger as his quarry threw himself through the hole and vanished. He punched the keypad beside the forcefield, cutting the power. It died away with a pop. As he peered over the balcony, he saw Saikalen streak for a jeep parked in front of the building, leaving a depression in the ground that he had to have climbed out of. The colonel phased back in and shouted, "Stop that man!"

Four soldiers rallied quickly and tried to block Saikalen's escape. The iron fists made short work of them, leaving broken and dying bodies in their wake.

Tabor got three blasts off before the creature made the jeep, but he couldn't tell if the laser was doing any real damage. Peele was at his side, banging away with her pistol.

Saikalen didn't appear confused as he pulled himself behind the jeep's wheel. Those impossibly large hands slipped around the steering column and stripped wires. The motor caught.

"The airfield!" Tabor roared over the radio. "The bloody bastard's heading for the airfield!"

The jeep screamed through the streets, running down two pedestrians who weren't quick enough to get out of the way.

"Wallsey," Tabor said over the radio, "meet me on the roof of the government building."

"I'm on my way," the sergeant responded.

"Look," Peele said, clutching at his sleeve. She pointed in the direction of the airfield.

Tabor had to shade his eyes against the rising sun, but he saw what had caught the archeologist's eye. Fully a dozen parachutes, striped in the crimson and silver colors of the FREE-Lancers, were dropping toward the airfield.

"And there," Peele said, pointing up.

Tabor looked. More were dropping toward the government building. He got on the radio. "Stuart, get those men back here on the double! We've been set up!" He took a last look at the jeep with Saikalen in it, then grabbed Peele by the arm and headed for the door. "Come on. That's our future trying to make his escape."

The rooftop and Wallsey were only two short stories up. He only hoped Saikalen could get away from the invasion force as well. But then, looking at the mangled bodies of his men scattered around the room, he didn't have much doubt of that.

17

Melaka City, Melaka | *5:00 a.m. Zulu Time*
Indonesia | *2200 Greenwich Mean*
102.3 degrees E Longitude | *March 30, 2024*
2.4 degrees N Latitude | *Sunday*

Assignment: Fly-Catcher
Tactical Ops: Neutralize Enemy Airstrip
Status: Code Red

<The path you're choosing to follow is extremely risky> the on-board computer reported.

"Yeah, well sue me," John-Michael DeChanza said, working his hands and legs in the sensor-cuffs. "Those people down there are organizing faster than Underhill gave them credit for. If they get those machine guns up, they'll cut Refit and the others to pieces before they can get down." He watched the movement below through the power suit's foot cameras.

Most of the planes were in hangars or sitting idle on the runways. They were a motley crew of Korean and Russian fighters easily twenty or thirty years old. Not cutting edge any more, but deadly enough to cover a country like Melaka.

The machine gun emplacement at the north side of the runways was the main concern. There were at least three .50-caliber weapons and a 20mm cannon.

Cutting from the downward perspective, DeChanza switched to the satellite view, tightening the magnification till he could see the Scratchbuilt armor easily. Refit was to his left, working the control lines on the rectangular black chute.

A huge cargo chute had been prepped for the MAPS. The shroud lines were attached to firmpoints along the Scratchbuilt armor and were adjusted from inside the power suit.

"Give me an estimate on the glide path," DeChanza called.

<Specify target zone.>

"The machine-gun nest," DeChanza said.

<Computing.>

"Do it more quickly." DeChanza took the time to check his weapons pods. Everything was on-line. He was going in fully loaded, with wrist rockets, machine gun, grenade launcher, and laser locked into his weapons firmpoints.

<Necessary drift being displayed.>

On the monitor, an image of the Scratchbuilt armor superimposed itself over the actual picture. The orange lines stood out against the deepening blue of the morning sky.

"Okay," DeChanza said. "I'm making the corrections. Mark me."

<Marking.>

Using the auxiliary waldos to control the shroud lines, DeChanza altered his course as much as he could with the chute. The rest would depend on wind resistance and distance. "How far to the ground?"

<Two thousand nine hundred four point seven feet. There is a thirteen-percent chance of failure. This unit might not survive the impact in its full capacity.>

"I know." DeChanza hit the waldos again, cutting the shroud lines loose. Freed of the drag, the Scratchbuilt armor dropped like a rock.

The Burris transceiver tweaked, then Refit's voice came over the frequency. "What the hell are you doing, kid?"

"Taking the fast way down," DeChanza replied, hoping the fear he felt didn't taint his words.

"That's a half-mile drop."

"Less now." DeChanza cut off the com as his HUD fired up crimson in warning.

<Danger. Impact imminent.>

"Bring the emergency stations on-line."

<Emergency stations on-line. Adjusting for null-G.>

The numbers clicked by on the digital readout, bleeding arterial information across the HUD. DeChanza concentrated on the satellite view of his fall. As big as the power suit was, it was still lost against the panorama of sky and ground.

From the satellite view, DeChanza could tell he was dead on target. He dropped to five hundred feet, then three hundred. At two hundred seventy-five feet, he keyed the compressed-air jets.

He was almost on top of the machine-gun emplacement. Uniformed men scattered in all directions. The concussive force of the compressed air hitting them knocked them flat.

Strapped in the seat, the compensatory circuitry stressed by the sudden demands, DeChanza almost blacked out from the heavy g-load. It felt like an avalanche hitting him, only from the bottom up.

<Warning> the on-board computer said over the roar of carnage. <Warning. This unit taking on damage. At eighty-eight percent efficiency.>

Feeling as if he'd been beaten with a baseball bat, DeChanza straightened in the seat. "Realign the sensor-cuffs. Let's go." He flipped through the menus, making sure everything was still on-line. The outline of the power suit in the upper left of his vision showed he'd taken most of the damage to his right leg. "Check the leg."

<Checking.>

Linking back to the exterior view from the Scratchbuilt armor's own perspective, DeChanza swept his gaze around him. The machine-gun nest was destroyed, driven seven feet below the surface of the runways.

<Unit is under attack.>

"Where?" DeChanza swiveled his head.

<Bearing one-five-two. A TOW-mounted jeep.>

The TOW was tank-buster artillery and could take out the Scratchbuilt armor. He watched as the jeep came to a screeching halt ninety yards distant and locked down. The TOW elevated as the gunner operated the aiming computer.

<They have target lock.>

Emergency beeps filled the interior of the Scratchbuilt armor. DeChanza brought up his left arm and fired the laser pod. The bright ruby beam stabbed the warhead and set it off. The explosion sent the jeep spinning across the tarmac to smash into a light observation plane. Flames enveloped both vehicles.

<Right leg is operable. Injury consists primarily of cosmetic nature and damage to compressed air jets. Those systems are closed. Maximum efficiency of movement with rerouted electronics at ninety percent peak. Corrective action is finished.>

"Then let's move." DeChanza stepped out of the huge crater his landing had caused. The other paratroopers were touching down now, creating pocket groups and taking cover wherever opportunity presented itself. They unlimbered the LAWs and plastic explosives they'd been assigned by Underhill.

Planes turned into debris. Flaming metal pinwheeled high in the air. If it hadn't been for the audio filters in the Scratchbuilt armor, DeChanza knew he'd have been nearly deaf with the thunder of it all.

Fifty-cal bullets pelted the power suit but didn't do any appreciable damage. Tracking a MiG-29 that was streaking for a takeoff nearly a hundred yards away, DeChanza brought the 40mm grenade launcher on his shoulder into play and unleashed a full salvo. The HE rounds smashed into the jet fighter and reduced it to fiery pieces of sheet metal that skidded across the tarmac like a lava wave coming into the beach.

DeChanza used his own .50-cal machine gun whenever he could, conserving the other three weapons pods, which were all limited from a protracted engagement. The heavy bullets smashed through the idle planes, dropping them on deflated tires and knocking fist-sized holes in the wings and fuselages.

The battle wasn't all one-sided, even though they'd gotten the drop on the mercenaries. There were a few scattered crimson-

and-silver uniforms down on the airfield. Two of them wouldn't be moving again. The cost of recovering the country for FDI was gaining.

Forty yards from his current position, DeChanza saw two FREELancers ops trying to drag a third to safety. A heligyro was just clearing the ground, strafing the tarmac.

Without hesitation, DeChanza threw himself in front of the three ops. The strafing lines stuttered into the Scratchbuilt armor, setting off emergency alarms. Locked on to his target, not expecting a thirty-five-foot giant to swell into his view, the helo pilot struggled in vain to bring his craft up.

DeChanza showed no mercy. He raised both giant hands above him, then brought them crashing down onto the helicopter.

The rotor blades turned into shrapnel, but the Scratchbuilt armor protected the men behind him. The forward bubble went to pieces as if it were made of soap instead of Plexiglas, and the helo smeared across the power suit's chest like a bug hitting a windshield.

"John-Michael!"

Recognizing the voice, DeChanza told the on-board computer to locate Refit.

<Present bearing two-four-three.>

DeChanza spun around, the fiery debris of the smashed aircraft still dripping from his armor. "Here," he said.

Refit had taken cover behind an overturned supply truck. "They've got a 30mm cannon in the control tower. Can you take it out?"

DeChanza located the control tower to his left. It rose in a single spire above the carnage of the airfield. The thump of the 30mm cannon became identifiable as he watched the impacts rock the vehicles behind which the FREELancers had taken refuge. "Got it."

He brought his right arm up and triggered two of the wrist rockets he had waiting there, making course corrections through the targeting computer. The projectiles took off with forceful *whooshes* that left clouds of blue-gray smoke in their wake.

In less than a second, the top half of the tower disappeared in a spray of mortar and glass and metal. Only smoking ruin survived in jagged lines.

"Thanks, kid," Refit growled.

"No prob." DeChanza wheeled around, already in search of more targets. As a big target himself, he was drawing them to him. He pulled up the targeting bracket and overlaid it onto his visuals, becoming a gunsight. He was ruthless. It was almost like going back home, to Somotillo. Only this time he wasn't a scared child. He was big enough to take the war to the people who'd brought it, and he did so with a vengeance.

* * * * *

Melaka City, Melaka	*5:06 a.m. Zulu Time*
Indonesia	*2206 Greenwich Mean*
102.3 degrees E Longitude	*March 30, 2024*
2.4 degrees N Latitude	*Sunday*

Assignment: Gate-Crasher, cont.
Tactical Ops: Direct Infiltration
Status: Code Red

As soon as she touched the street surface, Lee Won Underhill triggered the harness release on the parachute and let it blow free. An army jeep, piloted by Tabor's mercenary crew, came straight at her, guns blazing.

The FREELancers administrator threw herself to one side and rolled. The jeep's bumper passed within inches of her head. She got to her feet automatically and pulled the Ingram Stuttershot from the sheath across her shoulders.

The monocle was already operational. Even as the jeep careened sideways, the driver struggling to bring it back on track, Underhill raised the Stuttershot and used the machine pistol's accuracy to put three-round bursts into the driver and the man in the passenger seat.

Out of control, the vehicle slewed sideways and caught up against the curb. Badly balanced, the jeep flipped over on its side and skidded across the sidewalk to go crashing through the front of a shoe store.

Underhill followed it, running. Only one man tried to climb out of the jeep, reaching futilely for his sidearm as she cut him down. She reached up and swiveled the mouthpiece of the Burris into place. "Sector chiefs, you have your assignments. Carry them out. Report back to me as soon as you have the integrity of your site complete. Underhill out."

The street fighting was brief. Most of the ground troops were out in the jungle. Tabor had spared no effort to make sure the rebels were put down.

The Burris tweaked for Underhill's attention, letting her know Matrix wanted her on their private channel.

"Go," Underhill said when she switched over.

"The mercenary forces have broken off their push toward Derembang."

"How soon before they get here?" Underhill ran down the street, getting her bearings. She'd studied the maps of the downtown area for hours and knew where she and her people needed to be to break Tabor's grip on the city. Using the monocle, she found three targets in the alleys and put them down with short bursts.

"Estimated time of arrival, nine, maybe ten minutes. They're trying to get organized."

Underhill put Matrix on hold long enough to relay the information to her sector chiefs. Back on-line, she said, "Any news from Ferret?"

"He's inside the main tunnel area," the cybernetics expert answered. "He's having more trouble than he expected. There's a river like we'd guessed, and the way is big enough for him to walk through, but there are booby traps along the route."

Underhill stopped and surveyed the gentle grade that spilled down from her vantage point. This was the main artery leading back into Melaka City. To return, Tabor's forces would have to pass the FREELancers. She didn't intend for that to happen.

"I also found out who's behind FDI," Matrix said.

The screech of a MAPS unit pushing a car into the middle of the street drowned out Matrix's next words. Underhill asked her to repeat them.

"Theodore Herbst," Matrix said again.

"You're sure?"

"Yes. I nailed him through both cut-outs, the fax and the cel phone call. Trust me, his deniability is still in good shape, but there's no doubt in my mind."

"Then there's none in mine," Underhill said. And Herbst made sense. FDI had deep pockets, and none came any deeper than Herbst's.

Another MAPS unit joined the first, dragging over a decrepit-looking pickup to add to the growing barricade. Her plan was to seal off the street and hold it long enough to spring her final surprise.

Just then, a white-and-crimson flash streaked across the sky. Captain Ares's latest addition, courtesy of Dr. Rhand during one of his Rolling Savant Syndrome states where he temporarily became a genius in different fields of science, were unique antigravity bracelets that allowed him to fly. Dr. Rhand had invented them almost a month ago. The designs he'd made were still being studied, although no real headway had been made.

Clad in his brilliant suit, with the cape trailing out behind him and the mask covering his face, the Captain was a symbol of hope at first sight, of dreams that could come true. Already people in the apartment buildings in the area were leaning out their windows, cheering. He flew like an avenging angel, streaking for a dark green sedan that was bearing down on a team of FREELancers working to open another of the equipment crates.

He landed effortlessly on top of the sedan, then reached for the roof and peeled it back. The driver overcontrolled, his attention suddenly divided, and sent the sedan crashing into the side of a building. A heartbeat ahead of the impact, the Captain leaped into the air, twisting to view the sedan as it smashed. It went up in flames a second later, the fiery tongues licking at the Captain's boot soles.

A ragged cheer broke out from the apartment dwellers again, and the cry of "Captain Ares!" could be understood as a constant among the other dialects.

Underhill watched the boyish grin spread across the Captain's face, and she could see the slight flush of embarrassment color his skin. "Matrix, tell me you're getting this on the video link."

"I am."

"Good. Push some of it to CNN. Let Davison handle the particulars like the statement to the press about the agency's involvement. She and I talked about this. Everything's set up."

"I'm doing it right now."

"Four-second delay," Underhill ordered. "And put on the audio in his mask. Let him know. He likes to make speeches. If he says something good, tell Davison to pass that along as well."

"Done."

"And get Serle Hastings for me."

There was a pause. "The Hastings Family?"

"Yes."

"Do you know what time it is here?"

"One in the afternoon yesterday," Underhill said. "I can do the math. It's Saturday, not a business day, so try the home numbers first. Someone will know where he is."

"Affirmative."

"Get back to me as soon as you have him." Underhill glanced at her watch. Two of the minutes they had before Tabor's forces arrived back in Melaka City had already passed. She kept her eye on Captain Ares, waiting for the mask radio to kick in.

"Is it on?" the Captain asked, continuing to float three stories above the ground. He made a perfect target, but the ground ops had almost neutralized whatever resistance remained in the area. "Oh, okay." He spread his arms and cleared his throat.

Underhill waited, hoping for the best. The select few she'd chosen from the ground ops to contribute to the vid footage had already set up on the Captain as well, while the others continued building the barricade.

"Good people of—of—" The Captain came to a halt, obviously at a loss for words.

"Damn," Underhill said. "He doesn't even remember where he is."

Undaunted, the Captain tried it again. "Good people of Lemaka . . ."

"Patch that," Underhill said, "and bump the audio relay up to a ten-second delay. Give us room to work. And no close-ups of his face. I don't want the lip-readers out there getting it right."

" . . . come here today to force the vile oppressor who has you in his grip to release you," the Captain said. "We are here to lift the fearsome yoke of tyranny from your thin, bowed shoulders and make you once more free."

" 'Come here today to make you free,' " Underhill said, picking the words she wanted heard.

"No man should have to live in the shadow of another's greed or lust for power. We are the FREELancers, and we're here today to burn that shadow away."

Underhill was pleasantly surprised. It was dramatically overstated, exactly the Captain's style, but technically correct. "Let it stand."

"If you're able," the Captain said, "take your place with us, because this fight is not yet over. Your enemies are even now returning. But be stout of heart, and live with the knowledge that evil will cringe in the face of good. The only thing you have to fear is fear itself."

"Over the top," Underhill declared. "Strike it."

With a final wave to the cheering crowd, Captain Ares flew forward to land on top of the barricade that the MAPS units had built to withstand the return of the mercenary army. He looked good standing there, his hands on his hips and his cape fluttering behind him.

Men and women poured out of the buildings behind Underhill, quickly taking places along the street. Most of them had weapons, and the others scavenged some from the dead mercenaries. Underhill gave orders to her section chiefs to spread the civilian populace around, hoping to protect them while at the same time making them noticed as a psychological deterrent to any further action on behalf of the mercenaries.

She'd made sure the cargo had included distance weapons, lasers as well as grenade launchers and 20mm rocket pods that would take down the mercenary armor without problem. She also knew with the airfield behind the FREELancers' position, the mercenary troops would see the clouds of black smoke funneling up from the airfield.

"I have Serle Hastings on the line," Matrix said.

"Put him through." There was a click. "Mr. Hastings."

"Ah, Ms. Underhill. I didn't think it really would be you calling. I thought I was to be the butt of someone's malicious prank. However I do recognize your voice. You have a very distinctive sound."

"I don't have time for chitchat, Mr. Hastings." In the distance, Underhill could see the first few lumbering forms of the enemy MAPs units at the head of the returning mercenary force.

"My god," Hastings said, "you don't mean to say you're embroiled in that mess in Melaka personally?"

"I mean to say that exactly." Underhill glanced on both sides of the barricade, watching the way her people tightened up the perimeters. "It's actually your lucky day. I've got a deal for you."

"How intriguing. I didn't know we had any business together."

The crime boss's tone was light, but Underhill knew she had him hooked. Ever since Download had rescued Robby Hatch and revealed Curtis Duvall as the perpetrator of the fire at the apartment building, the Hastings Family had to have been waiting for the other shoe to drop.

"Curtis Duvall," Underhill said.

"I'm afraid," Hastings replied, "that I'm going to have to plead ignorance."

"Plead it all you want to, but this isn't court. I'm here trying to cut a deal. I've got Duvall on vid and on audio talking to one of my people, telling how he worked for you setting fires in buildings you and your family wanted the insurance money from." It was all a lie, but one that Hastings had every reason to believe. "Since Duvall died shortly thereafter, the confession will stand."

"I think that could be successfully fought in a court of law."

"Your choice, though I can assure you, either way the family holdings are going to take some major hits before I'm through," Underhill replied. "But you haven't heard the deal."

There was a pause. "I suppose it couldn't hurt. Even if you're recording this conversation—as I am—my interest is definitely not an admission of guilt."

"You don't have to admit it," Underhill said. "I can ladle it on you and make it stick. You didn't keep your hands clean on this one."

"What do you want?"

"I've entered into a deal with Theodore Herbst. Do you know him?"

"Not personally. My family has had some dealings with him that have been regretful. However, we've never gotten directly confrontational with him."

Underhill knew that. "Now's your opportunity to get back a pound of flesh. I'm about to renegotiate some latitude in the agreement I have with him, and also with a preexisting agreement for someone else. He's not going to like it."

"How does that affect me or my family?" Hastings asked.

"I want you to talk to Herbst at a time I specify. You're going to tell him that I've got you in a tight spot, a spot so tight that if he should take hostile action against me or my agency, or seek to renege on our deal, that you'll have to get involved because I'll use what I have against you. And make no mistake, I will."

Hastings didn't say anything.

A rocket screamed free at the other end of the street, shooting from one of the mercenary-run MAPS weapons pods. It exploded against the barricade, shifting the pile of vehicles.

"I don't have much time," Underhill said.

"Disconcerting as it is, I am forced to acquiesce to your demands. When and how should I inform Herbst?"

"I'll be in touch," Underhill said. "Stay at this number till I get back to you." She broke the connection, clicking back over to Matrix. "Get Prime for me, and follow it up with Harris Hartley."

The line of mercenaries fanned out along the streets, slowing now as the commanders realized what was really before them. They were professionals, Underhill knew, and as professionals they'd be able to judge the cost of continued fighting for themselves. The trouble was, they were also desperate, and desperation made people extremely difficult to deal with.

* * * * *

Melaka City, Melaka	*5:14 a.m. Zulu Time*
Indonesia	*2214 Greenwich Mean*
102.3 degrees E Longitude	*March 30, 2024*
2.4 degrees N Latitude	*Sunday*

Assignment: Rocker
Tactical Ops: Seizure of Enemy Communications
Status: Code Red

"Plastic explosives are in place."

Agent Prime, covered in slime from the bottom of the old sewer lines they'd used to get to the government building, nodded at the explosives expert of his group. Besides himself and Cythe, there were only three men in the tactical squad standing somewhere beneath the floor of the building.

"Blow it, Thompson," Prime directed. He placed his fingers over his ears, making sure the sound plugs were in properly. He took cover behind the portable blast shield they'd brought with them.

A heartbeat later, the concussive force battered the shield with flying debris. The pipe filled with dust and smoke, but a hole had opened up in the floor overhead.

"Let's go, mates!" Prime roared. He drew his SIG-Sauer P226 and rushed for the aperture the shaped charges had made. The lip of the opening was within easy reach, but he had to pull himself through with arm strength, made harder by holding onto the 9mm pistol.

Two uniformed mercenaries were rushing toward the hole in the hallway floor when they spotted him and tried to bring their weapons up.

Prime lifted the 9mm and put a double-tap of rounds into the faces of both men. A rifle bullet slammed into the Kevlar covering his chest as they dropped. Someone below grabbed his foot, providing support. Prime kicked against the hands, coming out onto the hallway in a roll that brought him to his feet.

Fluid and deadly, Cythe came through the opening after him. She carried razor-edged steel along her forearms, like swords only with the hilts on the sides. She whirled them, readying them in a sparking metal gleam, then nodded at Prime.

Matrix dropped into the com-link, requesting Prime's attention.

"Not now," the FREELancers agent said. "I'll contact you when we have the area secure." He ran down the hallway, knowing his destination now. The blueprints he'd studied had included the layout of the basement levels. He passed a side corridor and spotted movement out of the periphery of his vision. He turned, coming around as quickly as a cat.

Cythe was faster. Her moves were almost a dance, but faster than anything that was only human had a right to be. Her metability flowed out of her, giving a glowing sheen to the martial arts blades she handled with deft grace. She made a series of slashes before the merc could fire his weapon. When she stepped back, sections of the dead man fell away, including his gunhand and head.

"Slowing down?" she asked Prime with a smile.

The agent raised his pistol. "Letting you earn your keep, sheila."

Her eyes flickered, burning hot with the passion locked inside her. She hovered on the edge of the berserker rage that made her so dangerous to everyone, including those around her.

Prime went forward, racing for the communications platform. The steel door was locked. "Thompson."

"Sir."

"I've got a bloody door standing in my way. Take it down."

The demolitions man moved forward, his hands already busy inside his chestpack.

A gun port opened up along the wall, and the snout of an M-60 machine gun poked through.

"Cythe," Prime called bringing up the SIG-Sauer. Farther down the hall, a mini-chaingun had popped out of the wall and was moving with a servo hum to lock on to the FREELancers targets.

"Got it." Cythe whirled, bringing the deadly blades around. There was a flare of pink energy as one of them met the M-60. The metal sheared through the machine gun as if it were paper, the blade lopping off enough of the front section to render it useless.

Bringing the SIG-Sauer to bear, Prime shot through the power cables on the mini-chaingun before it could start spewing death. Sparks danced along the wall, then winked out before they reached the carpet. He checked his earplugs again as Thompson gave him a thumb's-up. The Burris had a button speaker that fitted inside the ear canal along with the plug, and the button mike had a filter that cleared the frequency signature of extraneous noise, making conversation possible.

"Do it," Prime said, stepping back around the corner from the steel door. He dropped the nearly empty magazine and shoved a fresh one into place.

"Fire in the hole!" Thompson warned. The last part of his words were erased as the explosion banged the radio communications into white noise.

"Masks," Prime ordered, pulling the Nomex and ceramic full-head mask from his belt. It was fireproof and practically bulletproof, and had a built-in gas filter. It also echoed the silver and crimson colors of the FREELancers. He didn't particularly like the mask because it restricted vision, but it definitely served its purpose. Once he had it on, he freed two CS gas grenades from his equipment pouches, popped the pins, and heaved them through the empty space where the steel door had been.

The red smoke hissed out at once, dropping a murky cloud into the communications platform and spilling out into the hallway. Men erupted from the room, coughing and gagging as the smoke took away their breath and made them violently ill.

Prime drew the other 9mm from his boot holster and led the charge into the communications room. He killed two men who struggled to bring their weapons up. Cythe took out three more who never saw her coming. Prime knew the berserker rage was full on her then. Against the crimson pall of the CS gas, her skin turned the vivid cerulean hue of an asphyxiation victim. She'd disdained the use of additional armor and wore only the brief leather garments she favored in battle.

Cythe took the right side of the room, her blades flashing, her sunglasses like two black holes burned into her face. In her present state, the gas didn't bother her. A guy with an H&K MP-5 fired a burst into her at point-blank range.

The bullets struck her in the midsection and left flattened, oblong disks that only darkened the skin beneath. Her metability was full-blown and affecting her molecular levels, giving her a steely-hard skin that was proof against most projectile weapons.

The guy with the machine pistol wore a look of shock as his target descended on him. Cythe carved it off him, leaving the gleaming white of the skull below, crosshatched in crimson threads.

Prime fired with mechanical precision, taking out targets and leaving the communications gear intact.

Resistance in the room died away as the men were overcome by the gas and the unrelenting force the FREELancers team represented. They dropped to the floor and put their hands over their heads.

Putting one of the pistols away, Prime strode into the center of the room while Thompson and his men spread out. "Who's in charge here?" Prime's voice, relayed as it was through the gas mask, sounded cold and alien.

"Stuart," someone yelled.

"Where's Stuart?"

Hands pointed, and Prime followed them to the man. He leveled the SIG-Sauer at the man, staying at a safe distance, and said, "Up."

Coughing and gagging, Stuart stood. He held his hands over his face, tears streaming down from his eyes, and tried to block the gas.

"Where's Tabor?" Prime asked.

"I don't know," Stuart answered.

Prime grabbed the man by the lapels and yanked him down face-to-skull with the man Cythe had just killed. "I'd think about that answer, mate. I truly would."

"Rooftop," Stuart gasped. With a convulsive heave, his stomach gave up its contents.

"McMasters," Prime said, leaving the gagging man where he was, "what about the computers?"

"I'm finishing up now, sir," McMasters replied. He'd taken the front off the Cray mainframes and was reconnecting circuitry to a board he'd brought with him. The battery-operated soldering gun he was using sparked repeatedly.

Prime tagged the Burris and clicked over to the frequency Matrix was using. "I'm here. What's up?"

"The computers?"

"Two shakes of a lamb's tail."

"Underhill wants to talk to you."

"Put her through," Prime said. He used the security vid system to search through the building. Pulling down the pop-up menu, he tagged the rooftop cameras and searched for Tabor.

"Sir," McMasters called in a strained voice, crawling out of the Cray, "the mainframe should be ready."

"Matrix," Prime said, "see if you receive an answer at your knock here." He flipped from perspective to perspective, getting a hit on his fourth time out. Tabor stood next to a rooftop exit, the bionic eyepiece marking him instantly. A disheveled-looking woman was at his side, looking skyward. "Mr. McMasters, open a line to Base Operations."

"Yes, sir." The operative pulled a keyboard in front of him and typed rapidly. "Done."

"Prime," Underhill said. "How are things there?"

"About to connect up. How are you?"

"Under attack."

"Holding?"

"Yes. Where are Tabor and the metal skeleton?"

"Tabor's on the rooftop. The skeleton man is MIA. Did Scratchbuilt and Refit manage to get all the birds knocked from the sky?"

"I haven't heard."

Matrix interrupted them. "I've got their computer systems on-line."

"Good," Underhill said. "Reopen the mercenaries' satellite communications and target their positions."

"Going to give them the bloody lights, eh?" Prime asked.

"Should be a showstopper," Underhill commented.

Prime glanced around the room, signaling Thompson to take command. The man flipped a salute as Prime raced out to the hallway, working the schematics of the building around in his head. A bank of elevators was at the end of the hall. It looked operational. Prime hit the button, knowing the elevator would be faster than the stairs.

Cythe was at his side when he stepped into the cage. Blood dripped onto the floor from her blades and left splotches that looked purple against the blue of her skin. "Have you got anything to say about that man I killed back there?"

Prime met her level gaze, then reached up and stripped the Nomex gas mask off. "You might have saved the lives of the other men in that room by taking the one. Of course, at the time I don't believe you were thinking about it that way."

She laughed. "I'm surprised Underhill didn't have Charm in on this end of the operation. It would have been easy to slip him into Tabor's organization."

"Yeah, well we moved kind of quick on this one," Prime said. He knew that was a lie after everything the FREELancers administrator had told him.

Charm was the code name for Simon Drake. He was a metable, an empathic vampire whose powers of persuasion were unmatched. He'd also been an actor for a time and had achieved critical acclaim under another name in other countries before taking part in an assassination attempt that left him an international fugitive with a price on his head. With his metabilities and talent for acting and disguise, he made an excellent undercover op.

"Where is he these days?" Cythe asked.

Prime shrugged. "Who knows?"

Charm also had extremely weak willpower if left on his own.

After the *Rinji 8* operation, Prime and Refit had had to track the man down and bring him in. On his way back from infiltrating a WEBTWO unit, he'd managed to get himself appointed manager of a band. It had taken two weeks to recover him.

The elevator cage bobbed to a halt at the rooftop level. Prime took a fresh grip on the SIG-Sauer and brought it up beside his face as he stepped out onto the rough surface.

The thunder of beating rotors drowned out all other sound.

Prime broke into a run, turning the corner just in time to see the BirdSong JK91 heel over and fly away from the building. "Dammit!" he swore, spotting Tabor in the cockpit. He fired through the SIG-Sauer's clip, not stopping till the slide blew back and locked. He knew he'd hit the craft, but it was armored enough to shrug off the 9mm rounds.

It vanished, flying low over the rooftops.

Prime keyed the Burris transceiver. "Matrix, there's a helo that just took off from the government building. Can you track it?"

"I've got it on screen."

"Keep it that way. Tabor's aboard." Prime turned away from the path the BirdSong JK91 had taken and walked to the edge of the building. "Lee?"

"I copied. Refit."

"Go," the patchwork giant replied.

"Tell me there's a helo left at the airfield."

"I can find one."

"Get it done."

Standing at the ledge, Prime looked down into the street. Less than two hundred yards away, the battle lines had formed. The mercenaries had grouped automatically, getting set to assault the barricade Underhill and her group had established. The FREELancers were outnumbered almost four to one.

Prime reached over his shoulder and grabbed the buttstock of his CO_2-reload multishot crossbow. It held five bolts. The distance between his position and the mercenaries was well within the killing range. He targeted the first of the snipers he'd spotted on top of the buildings overlooking Underhill.

None of them were aware of his presence. He sighted down the barrel and took up trigger slack, backing the lady's play till the last card was dealt.

18

Melaka City, Melaka
Indonesia
102.3 degrees E Longitude
2.4 degrees N Latitude

5:19 a.m. Zulu Time
2219 Greenwich Mean
March 30, 2024
Sunday

Assignment: Fly-Catcher, cont.
Tactical Ops: Locate and Confiscate
Status: Code Red

Refit kicked the hangar's side door, shattering the lock. He followed the door inside. A shadow moved to his left, dawn light sparking on gunmetal. He swiveled the Ithaca shotgun around toward the mercenary's center and dropped the hammer. The shotgun banged back against his shoulder, but the double-ought buckshot cleared the threat.

The corpse stumbled backward and spread like a broken puppet on the oil-stained concrete floor.

Coming around the entrance, Refit stayed low. Bullets slammed into the cinder-block wall at his back and showered him with chips that stung the back of his neck. The hangar door in front of him had been hit with one of the rockets the FREELancers team had unloaded on the airfield. The wide door had been torn from its tracks and lay draped over the crumpled remains of a Canadair CL215 amphibian plane that was now missing a wing. A repair droid had been wrecked along with the craft, the top half of the unit lost somewhere in the debris.

"There's one of those bastards!" someone yelled.

Refit dove forward, sliding across the absorbent sand spread across the grease spot in front of him and fetching up against a large red toolbox screwed into the floor. From his vantage point, he saw the feet of a man who was taking cover behind the broken Canadair. He fired at the feet, keeping the shotgun's buttstock in close to his shoulder to regain his target as soon as possible.

The buckshot caught the feet with enough force to knock them from under the man. The merc fell, shouting in pain.

Refit's next blast put him out of his misery. Trying to get the other two men in focus, the patchwork giant barely heard the *tink* of metal striking the pavement near him. He looked down in time to see a grenade go sliding under the toolbox.

Muttering an oath, Refit didn't try for the grenade. He heaved to his feet and tried to put as much distance between the explosive and himself as he could. He turned his steps toward the buckled hangar door hanging over the badly listing seaplane. It was the one spot he knew for sure that none of the mercenary gunners lay in hiding.

He drove his feet hard, not hesitating when he started up the hangar door. It vibrated under his boots, rattling with enough noise to wake the dead. The incline was steep, but he drew on his metability, using it to suck every erg of performance possible out of his stitched-together body.

The grenade exploded just as he reached the top of the makeshift ramp. Something hammered into his back and left side, throwing him off-balance. He threw himself along the length of the plane, then rolled to his right, marking the mercenary who'd been making his way around the rear of the craft.

Refit came down from the plane off-balance, only registering then that he'd lost the Ithaca somewhere. Metal scraped along metal. Pressure just below his left arm brought sudden pain. He shut it down before it could escalate beyond a disruption. It was just meat, nothing to him, and he'd be damned if he'd let it distract him.

The mercenary came around swearing, the big-bore pistol coming up in his fist. "You're dead!" Muzzle flashes flamed.

One of the bullets smashed against the Kevlar covering Refit's heart. The other slammed into his left thigh. Refit knew at once the damage was going to be enough to necessitate amputation and replacement of the limb. Although his metability allowed him to take any transplant, it also kept transplanted organs and limbs and tissue groups from repairing even minor damage. An open wound was subject to gangrene, and he was extremely susceptible. The only meat he could wear was healthy meat.

Staggered, Refit went to his right, gathering his balance, then sprang at the mercenary. The pistol barked again, sending another bullet into his abdomen that was blocked by the armor. Then he was on the guy, his left hand closing over the merc's hand and gun. They crashed to the floor, Refit's other hand searching for the man's face. He got his palm under the merc's chin and shoved back with all his strength.

The guy's skull separated from his spinal column with a dry crack. Instantly, the body started quivering spasmodically.

Breathing hard, denying the pain buried deep inside and ignoring the warm spill of blood down his body, Refit forced himself to his feet. He glanced at the smoking ruin of the toolbox. The grenade had blown the drawers open and ripped through the sheet metal.

Looking down, Refit found the source of his injuries. Three wrenches were buried deep in his side, lodging between his ribs and making it difficult to breathe. A screwdriver pierced his biceps.

He left the tools where they were, blocking out the pain. It wasn't him. No matter how bad it looked, it wasn't him. A little more damage, but nothing a decently staffed and equipped med center couldn't handle—as long as it had a fresh supply of cadavers ready to have their organs, limbs, and tissues harvested.

"Two out of three," Refit growled loudly, locating the Ithaca and picking it up. "That ain't bad."

"Yeah, but they wasn't me."

Refit turned around to face the third man. He lifted the Ithaca and pointed it at the merc. "You must be awfully damn sure of yourself. One blast from this will cut you in two."

The merc grinned and shook his head. He held a .45 automatic pointed at Refit. "Then I'll have you outnumbered." He had a military crewcut, a broad face that lacked a certain definition in the features, and tattoos covering both arms.

Without another word, Refit squeezed the trigger. There was no hesitation after he'd looked through the reports Underhill had offered concerning the way the mercenaries had treated the civilian populace. The shotgun *ba-loomed* in the confined space. The double-ought pattern caught the merc dead center in the chest.

He staggered back, arms jerking from the impact, the pistol flying away. He bounced off the hangar wall behind him. Miraculously, he remained standing.

The first thing Refit noticed was the lack of blood.

Bent over from the force of the pellets, the merc straightened, revealing a tattered shirt with no body armor underneath. His stomach and chest were pocked with deep holes centered in bunches of pulpy-looking flesh. The man stretched his arms at his sides and grunted. "Hurts like hell, but you can't kill me."

The puckers in his flesh suddenly spat out the double-ought buckshot. Still perfectly round, they went bouncing across the pavement.

Refit fired again, but the hammer fell on an empty chamber.

"My friends call me Flex," the merc said. "Beat the hell out of any India rubber man you ever saw." Only dark circular bruises showed where the pellets had hit him. He reached down to his boot and slid a Crain combat knife free. He held it tightly in his fist, point down and blade running sharp-edge-out along his inner forearm. "You can tell your friends about me when you get to hell."

Refit reversed the shotgun, gripping it in both hands. "Me? Hell, I'm gonna find out just how much bounce you got to the ounce, Flubber-Boy." He swung the shotgun off his shoulder like a home-run hitter going for the Green Monster in Boston.

Flex tried to move, but the shotgun came too quick, slamming into his head. His features warped around the buttstock, his mouth becoming an open, screaming C that wrapped partially around the blow. He pulled back immediately and blocked Refit's second swing with a forearm that stopped the motion like a shock absorber.

"Now, man," the merc promised, "you're going to get yours." He launched himself at the FREELancers agent.

Refit grabbed the knife wrist and held on to it. The man had enough power and leverage working for him to bowl the patchwork giant over. Refit fell onto the tools embedded in his side, driving them even deeper. He felt one of them lock two of his ribs together. The pain was incredible, but he shut off acknowledgment of it. A guy used meat, he had to expect to lose a little of it.

Flex head-butted him, splitting his lips. "How many pieces you come in, Mr. Potato Head? Can I get one just like you outta some box? Put you together anyway I want?"

"If I put my hand over your mouth and nose and my foot up your behind," Refit growled, "you gonna blow up like a balloon from all that hot air you're spewing?"

The merc spat into his face and tried to bite him. "All that hardware you're sporting," he said, forcing Refit over onto his injured side and grabbing the screwdriver embedded in his biceps, "you getting retooled?" He twisted the screwdriver.

Refit tried to push the man away, but the merc's joints bent all wrong. It was like wrestling with an octopus. Before he knew it, Flex had slithered around behind him.

"Oh, look," the merc said, "a wrenched back too." He grabbed one of the wrenches and pulled on it.

Getting his feet under him despite the other man's weight, Refit shoved himself up. Flex clung to his back, still working the tools.

The FREELancers agent stepped away from the pain. Spotting the wall of tools and metal hangers sticking out of it like spikes, he backed into it as hard as he could. He heard the explosive bleat of Flex's breath leaving his body. The rubbery arm around his throat loosened.

Breathing hard, Refit stepped away from the man, then turned and faced him. "How do you like getting needled, pal?"

"Told you, butthole, you can't hurt me." The merc pushed against the wallboard, sliding his body free of the spikes that had shoved into his flesh. "Punctures seal on me like they were never there. I get down off this board, I'm gonna twist that ugly head off."

Spotting the massive bulk of the battery charger near the tool board, Refit switched it on, pushing the levers up to full amp. He grabbed the clamps, holding them close enough to send blue sparks sizzling between the polarities.

He stepped forward as quickly as he could, slamming his good forearm into Flex's head hard enough to drive it back onto the spikes. The merc's eyeballs bulged from the internal pressure. The patchwork giant shoved the first clamp into the man's crotch and let it close.

Flex howled in pain.

"No more play for you," Refit said, "until you learn how to conduct yourself better." He slammed the other clamp onto the man's neck.

Electricity coursed through the merc's body, turning huge sections of it black before the battery charger gave out. The dead man was a smoking ruin hanging from the spikes. Refit figured it was a look of total shock.

He turned and made his way back to one of the three Bird-Song JK91 heligyros he saw farther back in the hangar. He didn't try to remove the tools piercing his flesh. It might have started bleeding that he couldn't stop.

There was movement in the middle heligyro, and the engine suddenly came to life.

Refit drew the Detonics .45 and advanced on the machine. He stopped outside the Plexiglas bubble with the pistol aimed at the man. "Get out," the patchwork giant growled.

"I can't," the man said. He looked frightened as he lifted his hands and put them on his head. "Don't shoot. I'm not armed."

Refit went closer, holding the Detonics steady. He stepped up on the wheeled landing skids, feeling the vibration of the forward rotor. He opened the door carefully, keeping the man covered. "You're not taking this vehicle."

"Oh, but I'm afraid he is," said a sibilant voice, barely audible over the throb of the engine. "I went to great pains to keep this one alive."

Refit turned his head toward the voice, bringing the Detonics with him. He had a brief impression of the man's head sitting on top of a lanky build, then noticed the metal skeleton through the open collar of the uniform blouse. Two corpses were draped over the seat and on the floor. Before the FREE-Lancers agent could act, a heavy iron fist crashed into his head.

He flew back out of the heligyro, dazed. Brain firing sporadically, he struggled to get to his feet as the BirdSong JK91 sailed past him. The hangar door opened in front of the aircraft.

"Refit!" DeChanza called over the Burris.

Trying to make his lungs work again and remember how to breathe, whether inhalation followed exhalation or it was the other way around, Refit wanted to answer but couldn't. He spat out a mouthful of blood and knew his med insurance was going to take a heavy hit in the dental department this time out. By the time he caught a breath, the heligyro had pinwheeled west, out of range of the Scratchbuilt armor's weapons.

"Me, kid," Refit said.

"Where?"

"The hangar. I'm out next." Refit stumbled toward the other BirdSong JK91.

"Who was that?" DeChanza asked.

"The metal guy Tabor and his boys dug up out of one of those crypts." Refit yanked open the heligyro's door and clambered aboard. The keys were in the ignition, and he kicked the engine over.

"He escaped Tabor," Agent Prime said.

"Yeah, well it remains to be seen if he can get away from me." Refit powered the forward prop up and sent the heligyro forward through the hangar. The fighting out on the airfield had been reduced to sporadic forays. Most of the mercenaries had already given up. Black smoke drifted across the tarmac, and many of the aircraft were still burning. Scratchbuilt stood like a monolith in the middle of it all, fresh scratches and craters showing across the metal body.

"Let him go," Underhill said.

"He's not that far away," Refit said, gazing into the blue sky. He powered up the top rotor and the helo leapt from the ground. "And this bird is armed."

"No," the FREELancers administrator said. "I need you to pick up Paul Derembang."

"The rebel leader?"

"Yes."

"Where?" Refit shifted in the seat, trying to find a comfortable position. The tools sticking out of his side made it almost impossible. He didn't bother arguing with Underhill about priorities. The lady set them.

"I'll guide you," Matrix said. "I have the homing beacon onscreen now."

"How are they going to know I'm coming?"

"I'll tell them."

"Yeah, well make sure they know I'm one of the good guys by the time I get there." Refit sent the craft screaming into the sky, circling around and taking the heading the cybernetics specialist gave him.

* * * * *

Outside Melaka City, Melaka
Indonesia
102.3 degrees E Longitude
2.4. degrees N Latitude

5:33 a.m. Zulu Time
2233 Greenwich Mean
March 30, 2024
Sunday

Assignment: Ferret's Run, cont.
Tactical Ops: Recovery, Unspecified Target
Status: Code Red

Download played his weakening flashlight beam over the pile of rubble that blocked the underground cavern system the stream flowed through. Rocks and earth mounded all the way to the top of the cavern and were visible well below the surface of the stream.

"So what now?" Cai asked. She held the tail of her uniform

blouse to her head to staunch the flow of blood. An avalanche of rock had come tumbling down on her when they'd taken one of the false tunnels a hundred yards back, before finding the one that actually went through and didn't just let the water seep up from the ground.

Download didn't know the answer to her question. He gazed at the water, playing the flash beam over it, turning it green where it was normally black.

"If the stream's moving, and it is," Jericho said inside his head, "that means the water's getting through."

"Maybe between the rocks," Download replied.

"Only one way to find out."

Download didn't like what the archeologist was suggesting at all. But he liked the idea of calling in to Underhill and telling her that the tunnel had led to a dead end even less. He sat down and began unlacing his boots.

"What are you doing?" O'Grady asked, readjusting the sling they'd fashioned to take care of the broken arm he'd gotten.

"Stay here," Download said, taking off his last sock and shoving it down into the boot. "I'll be back as soon as I can." He pushed himself to his feet and snapped his waterproof pistol holster closed.

"Here," Cai said. "My flash has stronger batteries than yours."

Download traded with her. "Thanks." Before he could talk himself or Jericho out of his chosen path, he took two quick steps forward and dove into the water.

The cold, almost painful in its intensity, chilled him instantly. The current was more of a steady drag than a strong push. He aimed the flashlight ahead of him, finding that the beam penetrated only two or three feet of the darkness that enveloped him. Glancing back over his shoulder, he thought he saw a bright, flickering dot that might have been Cai's flash. It seemed a long way off.

Moving the light, Download found an elongated shadow at the bottom of the pile of rock. He swam farther down and pushed his free hand into it. It was a hole, and the current coming out of it was running fast. It also appeared large enough for him to go through.

"That's it!" the archeologist exclaimed. "There's your entrance!"

Download wasn't convinced, but he had no choice about surfacing. He abandoned the hole and swam up. "I found a hole underneath. I'm going to check it out. If I run into trouble, I'll get you over the Burris." Neither of the two agents were in shape for the swim and both knew it. They didn't argue.

Taking a final breath, Download flipped around and shot back down through the water, letting his memory and Jericho's be his guide. He found the hole easily. Shoving the flash ahead of him, he followed it inside. It was hard swimming against the current, and the tunnel seemed longer than it should have been.

The flash revealed irregular gaps in the passage, and after a few seconds—when his lungs got tight and he desperately wanted to suck in a breath—he started to think that he was following a fault line in the pileup and not a tunnel at all. The pressure on his ears told him it was only getting deeper.

Without warning, the end of the tunnel caved in, creating a swirl of water that suddenly doubled back and pushed the FREELancers agent forward.

"No way out now," Jericho said, suddenly stopping the struggle. "Whoever built this tunnel must have booby-trapped it. Go dammit, I don't want to be down here with you when you die."

Download quelled the panic that threatened to overwhelm him. He clung to the anger and made himself stroke forward. Only blackness remained ahead, chill and washing over him. It was going to swallow him. The pain in his lungs felt as if someone were prying his chest apart.

Then the flash beam framed a hole in the blackness, giving sides to an opening through another mound of rock. Download grabbed the lip of it and hauled himself forward, awkwardly working his shoulders through the narrow space.

He shined the flash upward, letting buoyancy be his guide. He almost couldn't see the light through the black haze that was trying to claim his vision.

"Swim!" Jericho yelled.

The flash broke the surface first, and it seemed like a long time to Download before his face followed. He could feel the chill air dancing across his forearm as water dripped from it.

"Bank's to your left."

Download swam to the bank, finding the bottom of the stream in short order. He stood and sloshed his way out of the water. The flash revealed a hard rock shelf ahead of him, patterned in colors and craters from the drip of stalactites overhead. When he was on dry land again, he found he could no longer stand.

He collapsed to his knees and dropped the flash beside him. Sickness bubbled out of him, sour and thin, not really bringing up anything. The effort wore him out.

"Come on," Jericho urged.

Download blinked and tried to keep from shivering. It was colder in this cave area than in the last. He found the other end of the cavern with another sweep of the flash. It looked as if the stream definitely came from underground. There was no telling how far under it ran.

"You're not trapped yet," Jericho said. "There could be another way out. Look, there's some writing."

Letting the archeologist guide his hand, Download spotted the symbols on the wall. They'd been carved into the rock surface, but the passage of years, and the seasons when the stream was more swollen, had taken their toll. He didn't recognize any of the symbols.

"What is it?"

"Some kind of hybrid Egyptian language," Jericho answered. "More modernized than anything I've seen before."

Download let him have his hands.

The archeologist ripped off one of the arms of the jumpsuit and started scrubbing at the writing. Without warning, something gave a mechanical click, and the ground shifted beneath Download.

"Don't freaking move!" Jericho shouted, clamping down on the FREELancers agent's reflexes. "You do and you'll be dead!"

A bell-shaped iron cage, connected to a long chain and too

short for Download to stand in, had dropped from somewhere in the shadows gathered overhead. Wedge-shaped iron spikes had driven into slots in the rock, breaking through what Download could now see were false surfaces. He grabbed one of the bars of the cage, feeling the rough, jagged edges under his skin. The section of rock beneath him shifted again, letting him know it was none too stable.

"Don't move," Jericho whispered. "There's no telling what's under this section of rock. If we're dropped into the water, we'll be drowned like rats in this cage."

"Then what do you suggest?" Download asked sarcastically. "Staying here doesn't seem like a great idea either."

"Look." The archeologist pointed at the wall where the symbols were. A rectangular space as large as a pumpkin had opened up. Miniature statues, carved of different rock, stood inside the hollow space.

Download stayed still, disconcerted by the way Jericho moved his hands and the flashlight around even though he was supposed to remain motionless. The cage and platform shifted from side to side, as if it were on some type of ball bearings.

Ten figurines, none over three inches in height, were inside the hollow. All shared a common theme: men at work, with hammers and saws and axes, dressed in robes or bare-chested, with ancient-styled breeches or leather aprons. Some wore beards and some were clean shaven.

Three holes, approximately the size of the carved pedestals of the figurines, had been hewn inside the lip of the hollow. More writing was on the back wall.

Jericho crouched down and scanned the writing. "Damn, I wish I had a pencil and paper to work this out. The first writing we found seems to be some kind of warning about trespassing on forbidden ground, something about an Oracle of Evil."

"Nice to know that now," Download said dryly.

"The writing says there's a key to getting inside."

Download scanned the rocky wall in front of them. Looking at it with an idea of seeing something other than just a wall, he saw that the wall had an artificial shape as well. "We have to use three of those guys," he said. "Fit them in the holes."

"Yeah," Jericho said. "But they're going to have to be the right three."

Download looked at the figurines again through the borrowed knowledge from the chip. The Octopus tingled inside his head as it managed the interface. He recognized some of the stone now, knowing it was actually the borrowed archeological skills at work.

He listed them from left to right, keeping the order in mind in case it meant something: oily black obsidian, dark-red scoria, yellow felsite, rose quartz looking almost see-through in the flash beam, greenish mica crystal, brownish-gray limestone, orange sandstone, pink marble, brown-and-white feldspar, and mango-colored quartzite. There was a link between them. He could feel it nibbling at the edges of his conscious thought.

"Do you see the inscription?" Jericho asked.

"Yeah," Download said. Amazingly, in sync with the skill chip because his life depended on being able to borrow the skills, the symbols started to make sense. " 'Know me for the common laborer of the world and you will live.' " He licked his lips, finding them unbelievably dry with his clothes still dripping wet. "But I don't know what the hell it means."

"You read it wrong," Jericho said with raw excitement in his voice. "It isn't common laborer. It's common builder."

Download stared at the figurines. "Maybe we're supposed to know which three trades were first. Carpentry." He reached out and touched the rose quartz figurine of a carpenter. "Or a blacksmith." It was rendered fittingly in obsidian. "Or a sailmaker. Ships helped build the world." The bearded sail-cloth maker was made of limestone, a bundle of fabric in his lap.

"Not builder either. It has to be something that definitely ties the three figurines together. Geology."

The answer came to Download first, and he put it into words. "Granite," he said. "The most common igneous rock in the world. Even the first civilizations used granite for buildings and for roads. Some of the cities in Europe still have granite cobblestone streets that were laid hundred of years ago. And granite could be polished and used for decoration."

"Rose quartz," Jericho said, taking up the carpenter, "mica

crystals and feldspar. It takes all three of those to make granite." He plucked the cobbler and wheelwright from the midst of the figurines as well.

The platform bearing the heavy iron cage shifted, dipping lower.

Download shoved the three figurines into the holes and prayed he was right. He felt something grate against the base of each figurine. Counterweights inside the rock wall shifted with loud clunks.

Abruptly, the iron chain snapped taut, and the cage lifted upward. The platform steadied again and locked into place.

A flat boom of sound echoed through the cavern, bouncing back quickly from the placid surface of the underground stream.

Freed from the cage, Download pointed the flash toward the source of the noise. A dark rectangle had opened in the rock wall.

"You ready?" Jericho asked.

Filled with the skills the chip had given him, infused with the archeologist's curiosity, Download nodded. "Oh, yeah." He pointed the light ahead of him and followed it into the hidden room, wondering what kind of deadly secrets the Guardians of the Scarab had secreted away for so many years.

19

Melaka City, Melaka | *5:36 a.m. Zulu Time*
Indonesia | *2236 Greenwich Mean*
102.3 degrees E Longitude | *March 30, 2024*
2.4 degrees N Latitude | *Sunday*

Assignment: Gate-Crasher, cont.
Tactical Ops: Take-Down
Status: Code Red

"This is Lee Won Underhill, administrator of the FREE-Lancers Agency of the Great Lakes Alliance. I am here to negotiate your unconditional surrender and make arrangements regarding your immediate deportation from this country." Underhill listened to her voice roll away, pushed by the loud-hailers her teams had set up to cover the street. She stood in the palm of one of the MAPS units beside Captain Ares, who remained standing on the barricade of cars. She knew she was a highly visible target, and she felt a tightness in her stomach. A show of confidence at this point would undermine the mercenaries' own security.

"Deport this, bitch!" a man yelled. An anti-tank rocket streaked from one of the men at the forefront of the mercenary group.

The Captain stepped sideways quickly, becoming a shield for Underhill. The warhead exploded against the agent's Kevlar-covered chest and steel-tough skin. He staggered from the impact, but remained standing.

A cheer broke out from the crowd as the Captain launched himself into the air, apparently unhurt.

The man who'd fired the LAW dropped among the other mercenaries, a red-fletched crossbow quarrel through his head. Within the space of three seconds, two more men dropped from buildings on either side of the street, quarrels through one man's heart and the second man's neck, proof of Prime's marksmanship with his favorite weapon.

"Gentlemen," Underhill called over the loudhailer, "you're not leaving much room for negotiation." She gazed out over her opponents and knew it wasn't going to go down without bloodshed. She clicked over to the frequency Matrix had set aside for the two of them. "Matrix."

"Go," the cybernetics expert replied.

"The lasers?"

"On-line and ready."

Underhill looked at the advancing line of mercenaries. Autofire rattled off the barricade, and other rockets sailed into the buildings and the stacked autos, creating a string of fiery explosions. A sedan blew free and turned turtle, spinning upside down as it sent FREELancers agents fleeing from its approach. She waved at the MAPS team holding her up, signaling for them to put her down.

Underhill took up her ops helmet from where she'd left it and put it on. She pulled the faceshield down. "Give me video on my helmet." Capable of GPS linkup as well as linkup with other helmets possessing the necessary circuitry, the inside of the faceshield darkened, then pulsed once and showed her a birds-eye view of the street.

The mercenary power suits took the lead, weapons pods on their shoulders blazing away. If they'd had aerial backup the threat would have been even worse. Refit and DeChanza and their team had negated that threat, though.

Many of the civilians who'd joined the FREELancers broke and ran, falling back to their apartment buildings.

Underhill didn't blame them. Outnumbered four to one, the FREELancers wouldn't have been able to hold their position for more than a few minutes. Even at that, the cost in men and equipment would have been tremendous.

"Matrix, fire now!"

An instant later, the sky lit up with a new dawn as laser beams struck down from the heavens, shooting thin columns of iridescent pink and fiery red light into the forward ranks of the mercenaries. The main targets hit were the power suits, followed by three jeeps. The heavy-duty military lasers took out their targets in an eyeblink, exploding them into smoking, molten ruins. A heat wave smashed against the barricade and came boiling over, hot enough to take Underhill's breath away.

The laser station, a remnant of the old Star Wars program from the 1980s that the public had never quite learned about, had been part of a deal George Anthony Underhill had worked out with the federal government on a sensitive assignment ten years ago. It had been kept quiet after the orbiting laser platform had been turned over to the FREELancers agency. Many nations had nuclear bombs now, and Underhill had wanted a way to protect his people with first-strike capabilities.

Now that it had been revealed for what it truly was, Lee Won Underhill didn't expect it to last out in space another twenty-four hours before one of the large corps or other alliance governments had it quietly and anonymously destroyed. The best defense a warrior had were offensive weapons that weren't known about. This one was definitely out of the bag. If she were working only for the money FDI and Cornell had offered, she would never have used the laser.

Underhill studied the flaming carnage scattered across the street. She switched back to the loudhailers. "I offered you a chance to surrender less than a minute ago. You refused, and a lot of your people died needlessly. The offer remains on the table. No one else has to be hurt. There will be only deportation twelve miles off the coast in an ocean-worthy craft. I repeat, no one else has to get hurt."

Even before the echo of her words died away, the mercs were

throwing down their weapons and walking out into the street. They knelt en masse in the center of the street, their hands locked behind their heads.

Underhill switched to Matrix's frequency. "Cut the vid and audio off me. Get the camera crews to focus on the street."

"Done."

"Prime."

"Go," the warrior responded.

"You're in charge of the clean-up teams. Put those people under protective custody until we can get them out of the country. Switch everyone over to Para-bullets to handle the civilian personnel."

"If it were up to me, I'd let the blighters take whatever they got coming from the locals."

Underhill silently agreed. But letting the civilian population in at the mercenaries was likely to start a riot they might not be able to control.

Now that FREELancers had saved the country, she had to see if she could leverage Melaka's future free as well.

* * * * *

Outside Melaka City, Melaka — ***5:41 a.m. Zulu Time***
Indonesia — ***2241 Greenwich Mean***
102.3 degrees E Longitude — ***March 30, 2024***
2.4 degrees N Latitude — ***Sunday***

"Get back! Get back! There's a helo coming!"

Memories of the earlier attack galvanized Paul Derembang. He turned and spread his hands, shooing screaming children back into the brush. Over his shoulder, he could see the distinctive wasp-shape of the BirdSong JK91 heligyro as it descended. The chain guns and rocket pods depending from the sharply veed wings were clearly visible.

Rebel gunners scattered among the trees and rocks, taking up positions.

"Tell them not to fire."

Derembang glanced to his right, and found Mat Kilau suddenly standing there. The man watched the heligyro closely, a smile on his face.

"What?" Derembang asked.

"That isn't one of the mercenaries," Mat Kilau said. "It's a friend. C'mon, Paul, you're in charge of these people. They'll listen to you."

Looking into the smoky gray eyes, Derembang suddenly knew Mat Kilau was speaking the truth. He stepped out of hiding and raised his voice. "Hold your fire, my friends. This is not our enemy."

There was some uncertainty among the rebel forces, but they obeyed. Derembang knew Mat Kilau could just as easily have ordered the cease-fire, but had deferred to him on purpose. As a skilled and experienced politician, the prime minister knew the man was making sure there was no confusion about who was in charge, no chance of splinter groups forming. At the moment, with the potential of destruction all around them, the rebels were following Derembang's lead.

Mat Kilau raced ahead of him and waved a silver-and-crimson banner.

After a brief hesitation, the BirdSong JK91 settled down into a clearing ahead of them. Rebel troops jogged forward, still on edge from the way the mercenary forces that had suddenly descended on them had broken off their attack and sped back to Melaka City. Then there had been that unexplained series of flashing lights and the sounds of battle that reached them even this far out.

Derembang had rushed through the jungle, not able to keep up with the younger men. But Mat Kilau had paced him, holding on to his elbow and giving him support.

"It's over, my friend," Mat Kilau said.

The heligyro sat in the clearing, the main rotor still spinning and whipping the brush around. The pilot made no move to get outside his craft.

"What's over?" Derembang asked.

"The war," Mat Kilau said. "We've won. The mercenary forces have surrendered."

"To whom?"

"To Lee Won Underhill's teams."

Derembang stopped at the edge of the clearing, through sheer willpower not giving an outward appearance of being suddenly uncomfortable with Mat Kilau. "Underhill is working with Fiscal Development, Incorporated to take our country from us."

Mat Kilau lost some of his easy affability. He turned his gaze on Derembang full measure. "My friend, it's not as simple as that. I ask that you trust me."

Derembang felt the pull of that suggestion and fought to resist it. "You work for her."

A smile played at Mat Kilau's lips. "I never said that I didn't."

"You betrayed me," Derembang said with quiet, cold fury. "You betrayed all these people."

"I don't remember it that way," Mat Kilau said. "I recall taking on that heligyro almost single-handedly to save these people."

"You were gone for a long time before that," Derembang accused.

Mat Kilau nodded. "Just long enough to run to the phone cable connecting the satellite outpost to Tabor's communications platform and take it out so they'd be working blind." He stepped forward and put his hand on the older man's shoulder. "Please, my friend, together we've accomplished so much in such a short time, saved so many lives. Don't stop now, or I won't be able to help you."

"What about Fiscal Development, Incorporated?"

"That's what we need to take care of now," the man who called himself Mat Kilau said. "Underhill is waiting to talk to you. She has some ideas."

Derembang glanced through the open door of the heligyro and saw the big man in the FREELancers uniform all battered and bloody behind the controls. "There is very little choice," he said to Mat Kilau.

"No. I'm afraid not."

"Underhill's reputation isn't inspiring."

Mat Kilau regarded him solemnly. "Whose is, my friend?

Not so very long ago, you were driven from office in this country. Now, you find yourself in position to lead it again. I've helped you regain that position, and through me, so has Underhill." He paused for effect. "Only two days ago you were ready to be killed by her or someone protecting her to further the push for independence here in Melaka. Why not put that same courage into listening to her?"

"Why should I?"

"Because she believes in you," Mat Kilau replied. "It's going to take a strong man to lead Melaka out of its present difficulties, and she's putting her faith in you."

"In exchange for what?"

"You'll need to discuss that with her, but I don't think it will be anything you can't live with."

Derembang looked at the heligyro, but he was really watching the people ringing the clearing. All of them were looking to him to make a decision, and the time he was taking to make it was weighing on them all, undermining the trust they had that everything would be all right. "Go on ahead, and I'll join you."

Mat Kilau appeared hesitant.

"Belief works both ways," the Melakan prime minister reminded him.

"You're right." Mat Kilau flashed another smile that was full of confidence, then clapped the older man on the shoulder. "I'll be waiting on you." Without a backward look, he went to the heligyro.

Derembang returned to the crowd and found Herman Zong. "I have to go," he told the other man. "During my absence, it'll be up to you and the others to care for these people."

Zong's eyes were hard as he stared at the aircraft. "That pilot is one of the FREELancers."

"Yes."

"And Mat Kilau?" Zong put it to him, challenging.

"Is someone I'm choosing to trust," Derembang answered.

"Where are you going?"

"To Melaka City, to meet with Lee Won Underhill."

"To negotiate our surrender?" Zong asked. "She was supposed to be hired by Fiscal Development, Incorporated to repossess our country."

"Mat Kilau assures me that isn't the way it's going to be."

"Then how do you know—"

"Sometimes," Derembang said, cutting the other man off, "when you lead, you have to take the chance of being wrong, and can only hope you're proven right. At any time, Mat Kilau could have killed us, or arranged for us to be killed so he could take over the leadership of this group. You would have followed him yourself."

Zong nodded. "And what does your heart tell you about this meeting?"

Derembang answered without hesitation, knowing he could speak only the truth. "I have to go."

Zong grabbed the older man and hugged him fiercely. There were tears on his cheeks. "Then go and follow your heart, my friend. It is a strong heart, one that has guided the dreams and future of Melaka for a long time when eyes were blind to see and ears were deaf to hear. I shall await word of your triumph."

"Thank you. You'll know soon. Keep up the spirits of our people till I return." Derembang squared his shoulders and walked to the heligyro.

"Like to sit up front?" Mat Kilau asked, waving to the empty copilot's seat beside the jigsaw man.

"Normally, no," Derembang said. "But today I want to see what's been done." He sat and buckled himself in. The big man took the BirdSong JK91 up smoothly. "What is your name?" He looked at the man in the FREELancers uniform.

"Call me Refit." The heligyro scooted around and aimed at the city in the distance. Black plumes of smoke came up from the streets, breaking apart in the wind.

"Are you well?" Derembang could see the blood staining the seat.

The big man gave a wry grin. "I will be, soon as I get some fresh meat."

Derembang didn't even want to guess at what the man was talking about. There were many stories about the strange powers of the metables. He sincerely hoped not all of them were true. "What about the city? How bad is the damage?"

"You lost the airfield." Refit kicked in the heligyro's jet turbine into play.

The g-force shoved Derembang back in the seat.

"Everything else is pretty much intact. Underhill put together a surgical strike that crippled the mercs in as few minutes as possible. And you lost a street downtown. Lasers tore the hell out of it, they tell me."

That explained the lights. "And the mercenary leader? Colonel Tabor?"

"That," Refit said, "is one of the angles we're still working on."

Derembang turned his thoughts to the coming meeting with the FREELancers administrator. But there was one thing more he needed to know. He turned to look at the man he'd known as Mat Kilau. "What is your real name?"

"Simon Drake," he replied with that same easy grin. "Sorry about the deception, Mr. Prime Minister, but it was felt necessary to achieve our ends."

"Let's hope so," Derembang said. "But why Mat Kilau?"

The smile's wattage dimmed slightly. "I don't know. I read about him somewhere, but I didn't know I was going to take that name until you asked me. I was just going to play myself off as one of the rebels." He shrugged. "Once I'd said it, the role seemed to fit somehow."

"Then maybe you weren't the sole reason Mat Kilau came back to my country." Derembang smiled and sat back in his seat. "You won't mind if I take some small comfort in that."

* * * * *

Outside Melaka City, Melaka — *5:44 a.m. Zulu Time*
Indonesia — *2244 Greenwich Mean*
102.3 degrees E Longitude — *March 30, 2024*
2.4 degrees N Latitude — *Sunday*

Assignment: Ferret's Run
Tactical Ops: Recovery, Unspecified Target
Status: Code Red

"Abandon hope all ye who enter these premises," Download said.

"It isn't quite that bad," Garrett Jericho said inside his head. He used Download's free hand to wipe away the accumulated buildup of centuries from the plaque on the wall beside them, while holding the flash with the other one.

They stood in an alcove in front of a stone slab door that they hadn't been able to move. Jericho had spotted the writing.

"Can you get this?" the archeologist asked.

"Some of it," Download admitted. The occasional symbol brought forth a concept or an idea.

"It's more intricate than the writing in the other area where we found the door release. Probably used for affairs of state."

Download pushed the chill of his clothes out of his mind and tried to ignore the way the shadows shifted and slithered around him due to the movement of the flash. He concentrated on the skills available through the Octopus. For the moment, they were trapped inside the alcove. When he'd tried the stone door in front of them, the one behind had shut with a deafening thump. He could reach the ceiling over his head, and at least the floor seemed to be steady.

Satisfied with the cleaning job he'd done, Jericho pulled Download's hand back.

"I'm going to paraphrase here," the archeologist said.

"It's okay," Download said. "I think I've got most of it." Letting the skills fill him helped distract him from the thought that he was trapped in the alcove, waiting for starvation or sudden death in some other form to reach out for him.

Know you, men of learning, that you are about to enter a place held sacred. This is the tomb and final resting place of the being we have known only as Soul of Knowledge. He has been a teacher to us, banishing thoughts of mysticism and superstition, enlightening us as to the true nature of this world and the next.

At the request of our teacher, we have not preserved his body. But we have taken care to place it within the tomb, though not in the fashion of the pyramid-builders and cat-worshipers. He did not want to be revered, but his remains are left for study by true seekers of knowledge, with the mark of Time laid upon them as he wished.

The sum knowledge of his teachings are contained within the scrolls inside. Some we have seen come true, others we have seen will be true in future years. From him, and from us, much has been shared with the world. If there had been more time, perhaps even more could have been passed on.

The world has lost with his passing, taken too soon from us by the spiteful hand of the Oracle of Evil, Saikalen, one of our best and brightest who was a special pupil to Soul of Knowledge before his betrayal of us and of our beliefs.

In these rooms, too, you will find some of the devices built by the Oracle of Evil. Our people have tracked him down over the centuries, finding him in many places, before we were finally able to put him to death. With the immortality he bestowed upon himself, execution was the only way to accomplish an end to the malicious being he had become, though it is not our way.

These devices were built by the Oracle of Evil and have dangerous potential in the wrong hands. We were unable to destroy them because they contain knowledge that he wrested from Soul of Knowledge that we had not yet had access to. We hope that the learning we can have from them outweighs the risk of keeping them intact.

With this in mind, forgive us this, our last test of you. We feel only men who have chosen knowledge over war will benefit from the legacy inside this building.

Download stomped the floor tentatively, feeling painful vibrations shoot up through his bare feet. The inside of the alcove lacked the humidity present in the outer chamber, and much of the water from his clothes had dried. What hadn't dried up remained in puddles along one of the walls, showing that the floor wasn't entirely level. But it was airtight.

"Look around," Jericho said. "There's got to be a release lever somewhere."

The lights in the flash were starting to grow dim. Download had no extra batteries. Being trapped and in the dark at the same time held no appeal at all.

"Here," he said, kneeling. "There's a stone down here that sticks out farther than any of the others."

"Try it."

Download curbed the archeologist's borrowed enthusiasm

and tried to keep it at confinable levels. He traced the stone with his fingertips, hand quivering as he fought to keep Jericho from pushing it, and found that it felt springy in its setting. It was no bigger than his fist, and stuck out no farther than a quarter-inch, barely visible at all against the smooth symmetry of the wall.

Perspiration trickled down Download's face, incongruous with the wet clothing. Having no other way to proceed, he put his palm against the stone and pressed. He felt the click, then heard a series of them over his head.

Sand, as fine as powder and the color of straw, came pouring into the alcove. In the space of a couple of heartbeats, it had already covered Download's feet. He cursed and stood up, protecting his nose and eyes with one hand while trying to stanch the flow of sand into the cubicle with the other. Neither door had budged.

"Sand trap," Jericho said. "You're not going to be able to stop it."

Download found that was true. Even if he'd had four hands and could reach all the entry points at the same time, the tubes had wire baskets that thrust out and prevented blockage. The sand, up to his shins now, continued spilling into the enclosed space.

He dug in it, trying desperately to find the flashlight he'd dropped. Once he had it, he tucked it inside his belt, then ripped a sleeve from his jumpsuit and tied it around his lower face. There was nothing he could do about his eyes except keep them squinted. He pounded on the doors, but both were immovable. The sand had risen to his knees.

On one of the walls, a stone had popped open on hidden hinges, revealing a flat surface with small, round holes drilled into the inner wall. A red silk bag sat on the ledge in front of them.

"Get the bag," Jericho said.

Download already had it, slipping its leather thongs to open it. Multiple clicks sounding like glass echoed from within, almost drowned out by the *shush* of rising sand. He shone the flash inside the bag, seeing the round, translucent shapes and taking a moment to recognize them. "Marbles." The FREE-Lancers agent couldn't believe it.

"It's another puzzle," Jericho said. "Look, the marbles are different colors. You're going to need them separated."

Download glanced at the writing on the inner wall above the holes. "Balance me, for I am the scales of your judgment." He counted the holes. There were nine, three sets of three, set up like tic-tac-toe.

"Count the marbles as you separate them," Jericho said. "That's going to give us some clue about what we're supposed to do. Dammit, this is some kind of mathematical problem. I got to tell you, buddy, math was never my favorite subject."

The sand had risen to Download's waist. The open panel with the nine holes was almost at eye level. He had time if he hurried. "I know what this is," he said. In college, he'd been a fantastic student, gifted with an eidetic memory. Mathematics had been simple because they were contained sets, always aiming toward a single answer—until imaginary numbers were brought in. It was in the real world, when his potential didn't meet his expectations, that he'd stumbled and lost everything.

"What?" Jericho asked, backing off the pressure to take over Download's body.

"It's a magic square," Download answered. He used the extra pockets in the jumpsuit to store the colored marbles, keeping track of their number as he worked. He took as much time as he dared; if he dropped a marble into the sand it was certain to be lost. "Invented by the Chinese at least five hundred B.C. You've got nine numbers, one through nine, and they've got to fit on the square so that no matter how you add them, sideways, top to bottom, or diagonally, they add up to fifteen."

By the time he finished sorting, he had nine brown marbles, eight black ones, seven white ones, six red ones, five blue ones, four green ones, three yellow ones, two orange ones, and a single purple one.

Download took out the nine brown ones first, making sure he had them all. The sand was almost up to his chest and it was getting harder to breathe. Grit cracked against his teeth and made it difficult to swallow. "The even numbers go in the corners, and the odd ones go between. Five goes in the middle."

He slid the first marble into the top middle hole and found it fit easily, then followed with the remainder. They clicked as they went down. He put the two orange ones on the top right and four green ones in the top left. The five blue ones went into the center, followed by the three yellow ones on the middle left, and seven white ones in the middle right hole. He put the eight black marbles in the bottom left hole, followed by the six red ones in the bottom right hole. The sand was already spilling over into the opening with the marbles when he fit the single purple one into place in the bottom middle. He was so choked he couldn't take a complete breath. He flipped the remaining marble forward from his fingers, sending it on its way.

When the marble clicked into place inside the stone wall, a series of racheting noises came from inside. The sand continued to fill the cubicle. Download tried to push it away from his face as it started sliding into him.

Then the door slid free, spilling him and the sand into the next chamber.

Hacking his guts up in an effort to get all the foreign debris from his respiratory system, Download floundered in the powdery sand and pushed himself to his feet. He ripped the torn sleeve from around his face and sucked in cool breaths of air.

The chamber inside the rock wall was much larger than he'd ever thought it would be. The flash beam didn't quite reach across it.

"Jeez," Jericho said quietly.

Download stood on a wide dais coming out from the door, which, along with the first one he'd come through, was now open. A long flight of steps descended to the lowest level of the chamber in front of him. The flash beam was too weak to reveal what was at the center of the chamber below. When he tried to focus the beam, the batteries gave up altogether.

"Over by the wall," Jericho said. "There are some torches."

Using his lighter flame, Download made his way back to the door and found the basket of torches inside a niche in the wall. They were a combination of pitch and oils, which Download was able to identify through the archeologist's skills.

"They should still be good," Jericho said, "but they may not last long. Take three or four of them."

Holding the lighter to the torch, Download was gratified to see it catch nicely, then settle down to a steady burn. He took three more torches and stuck them in his belt.

He walked down the steps, watching as the shadows retreated before him. The chamber was at least seventy yards across. All along the circular wall that surrounded the interior of the room were niches devoted to science and lab equipment. Microscopes and telescopes that were hundreds of years old occupied spaces similar to those taken up by pestles and mortars, test tubes and incubator jars, mounted skeletons of fish and fowl and mammal and lizard. Some of the species, Jericho told him, had been extinct for hundreds of years.

In the center of the area at the bottom of the chamber was a glass coffin. Inside the coffin were the remains of a man dressed in plain black robes. The skeletal arms, covered still yet with sloughing flesh gleaming a waxy yellow in the torchlight, held a thick book.

Download played the torch over the glass coffin, ignoring Jericho's demands to shove the lid off and look at the book. By careful examination, he found the top to the coffin to be hinged on one side. It had a simple lock on the other. He passed it up for the moment, not wanting to dive into another near-death experience if he could help it.

He held the torch up high, peering at the rounded ceiling dome and wondering at the amount of work that had gone into building such an area under the ground. Now, looking back up the steps and at the niches, he saw the ledges that had been carved so meticulously into the solid rock.

"An amphitheater," Jericho said. "Must have been here where they came to speak and study."

There were dark hollows along the walls framing the chamber at the bottom. Upon closer inspection, Download found they were doors.

"The book," Jericho pressured.

Download stepped forward to the coffin and worked the latch. The top came up easily. Nothing else happened. A stench still remained with the body, but it wasn't bad, having worn off decades and perhaps even hundreds of years before. He gripped the edge of the leather-bound book and pulled.

The dead man's arms slid free of it, twisting and turning as they gave up their prize. Something metallic flickered along one of the limbs.

Wondering if he were imagining things, Download set the book aside and grabbed the suspect arm. He turned it, watching closely as the torchlight caught on metal again.

A pin was implanted in the ulna, where the bone showed signs of stress and damage that had received expert orthopedic care. It was a technique that hadn't existed back when the man had died. Download was sure of that.

Curious and wary at the same time, the FREELancers agent reached for the dead man's skull. Part of the face remained, shrunk tight to the underlying bone. It cracked and split and fell away at his touch. Forcing the jaws open took more strength than he'd expected, but the joints gave way with sharp cracks, leaving the lower mandible hanging loosely by one side.

Several of the teeth had been capped and filled.

"There's no way that was done when this man was supposed to have died," Jericho said. "No one had the technology or expertise."

Download nodded. Feeling an oddity about the back of the skull, he turned it over. A gaping hole was revealed that was large enough to shove a tennis ball through. None of the missing skull fragments were there.

"Guess we know how this Saikalen guy killed him," the archeologist said.

Quietly, Download put the skull down. He opened the book and began to read with difficulty, distracted by having to hold the torch. Finally he gave up and shoved the torch through the dead man's ribs, lodging it so it stayed upright. He hunkered down beside the coffin and began to flip through the pages.

An inscription at the beginning was written in a different style of cuneiform than the other sections of the book. It was easier to decipher.

This is the last testament of our people, who were known as the

Guardians of the Soul of Knowledge. I say this because I know there will be no other. I am the last, and I will not be long for this world. Even now, I can feel myself dying.

We were betrayed by one of our own even after we thought we had killed him. When the sickness first came among us and nothing we could do would stop it, we checked his tomb. His body was still there, but his head was missing. We knew then that he had found yet a new way to live on.

If you have found this book, perhaps we have triumphed over him even in death. At least, maybe you have heard of us in legend, because there was some talk of us while we yet lived, though we tried hard to remain in the shadows as our teacher taught us, so we would not disrupt the flow of Time itself. We have many good things to pass on to you. Our only hope is that you will know what to do with them.

If you have not heard of us, this book will explain to you who we were and what we thought, and perhaps much of how we lived. About our teacher, the man we knew only as Soul of Knowledge, we wish we could tell you more. There is another book, one which was stolen from us by the one among us who betrayed our ideals and our teachings. With luck, you will be able to find it. This book is called the Oracle of Evil, *and it is about the Great Betrayer and the madness that consumes him.*

Read on, then, as my body has very nearly failed me and my mind blurs with pain and confusion. And may your wisdom guide you in your path to the enlightenment we offer.

"Download," Jericho said.

"What?" The FREELancers agent stared at the page, thinking about all the years that separated him from the man who'd written the passages, yet the pain could still be felt.

"I need you to look at that skull again."

"Why?"

"Something about it doesn't fit."

Curious, Download put the book aside and stood up. He took up the skull and looked at it, feeling bad for the way he'd interrupted the man's sleep.

"Look at the hole in the back of the skull again," Jericho directed.

Download turned the skull over.

"Feel the edges," the archeologist said.

"I think I'll pass," Download said. "It was bad enough prying his mouth open. I don't feel like sticking my fingers inside his head."

"Just do it, dammit!" Jericho shoved Download's fingers inside the hole and felt around the edges. "See, the sharper edges are on the inside, not the outside. The slope is outward, not inward."

"Yeah? So what?" Download managed to get his fingers out of the skull.

"It means that this guy didn't die from someone bashing his head in," the archeologist said. "Something inside his head exploded out."

Download put the skull back in the coffin, uncomfortably aware of the weight of the Octopus on his shoulder and the steel-sheathed fiber-optic cables tapped into his brain. He had to force himself to pick up the book again and resume reading.

20

Melaka City, Melaka
Indonesia
102.3 degrees E Longitude
2.4 degrees N Latitude

5:49 a.m. Zulu Time
2249 Greenwich Mean
March 30, 2024
Sunday

Assignment: Broker
Tactical Ops: Strategic Negotiations (Blackmail)
Status: Code Green

"Mr. Prime Minister." Lee Won Underhill stood in the office area of the AC-130-H Spectre gunship and offered her hand to Derembang.

To his credit, Paul Derembang looked as if he had been expecting to be invited aboard the military ship and greeted by the head of a mercenary operations group. He took Underhill's hand warmly, then bowed slightly. "So pleasant to finally meet you, Ms. Underhill. I've heard several things about you."

"Not all of the bad ones are true." Underhill waved him to a chair at the table in the center of the room. Then she tagged the Burris transceiver. "Get us into the air and follow the route Matrix has set up for you." She took a chair as well. "You might want to buckle up. The airfield isn't in the most optimum shape."

Scratchbuilt and a dozer-droid crew had worked the last few minutes clearing a place for the Spectre gunship to land.

"It appears we almost met in Chicago."

"I would expect," the prime minister said, "looking back on things, that you would admit to some culpability in the matter of my being in Chicago, prepared to do what I was about to do."

"Completely," Underhill said. "I made sure Tabor and his people knew I would be arriving at the airport that day, as well as what time, although not necessarily which flight." She glanced at her chron. "I've got only a few minutes, and in those few minutes, you and I need to cover a lot of ground.

"I know about the Guardians of the Scarab, and I know about the scrolls you and Castlereigh's people were using to leap into the high-tech market. Tabor and his people located a being that was buried in one of the catacombs."

Derembang's eyes widened. "I'd not heard. We'd not expected anything like that."

"Nor did I. However, that creature is making for an area where Dr. Henshaw believed a number of scrolls were buried."

"The Star Scarab's tomb," Derembang said. "We'd been searching for it and hoped Dr. Henshaw would be more charitable with his findings. He wasn't without pressure, we discovered. Then, when Tabor took over, Henshaw and his people were kicked out of the country."

"I have an agent in there looking for it now. Tabor is also en route, tracking the catacomb creature. I hope to intercept them before they can get any of the scrolls and leave the country."

"I see."

"Not yet you don't," Underhill said. "Your country has a number of problems facing it, not in the least of which is the matter of FDI wanting to collect their collateral, which they're legally entitled to do."

"We would fight to keep that from happening," Derembang said.

Underhill nodded, proud of the aggressive spirit she saw in the older man. His experiences hadn't broken him, and that was good, because he was going to need everything he had in him over the next few months to set things right. "That's noble, but stupid."

"You'll pardon me if I object to such crassness." Derembang's face darkened with anger.

"Pardon my brusqueness," Underhill said, "but it's necessary. You've seen only the tip of the iceberg where your problems are concerned. You've heard of Theodore Herbst?"

"The media is fond of calling him Teddy-Boy because they know he doesn't like it. Yes. Lord Castlereigh had several dealings with him, none of them pleasurable."

"Right. Herbst owns FDI." Underhill waited a moment for the man to digest the information. "My guess is that he won't turn loose of his hold on Melaka unless he's forced. To put it bluntly, your country is in no shape to try to stand against him."

"Against you, you mean?"

"I was hired to return Melaka to him," Underhill agreed, "and I plan on doing that."

"Then why are we talking?" Derembang demanded. "You should know that I won't agree to that. You're only wasting your time and mine." He locked eyes with her. "Unless I'm to be used as a hostage."

"Paul," Underhill said in a gentler voice, "your country has something that a lot of people want. No matter what you do, you can't change that. The only options are to try to hang on to it, which you're not able to do at this point; give it up, which means you'd be managing a country that's had its future stripped from it in a matter of months; or take on a partner who can help you."

"Herbst?" Derembang shook his head. "That man—"

"*Me*," Underhill said. "FREELancers. I can provide you with security while your people go about their business. Your companies have already got a system together where they're developing the technology in those scrolls, and I'd be a fool to try to take that on. But security I can manage. If you'll let me."

Derembang was quiet for a time, considering. "And what would you get out of it?"

"After you get your feet up and under you again," Underhill

said, "I want five percent of the net."

"It's hard to believe that you would want so little. Have you seen the figures on the companies' profits?"

"Yes. I'll admit, when I first heard about Tabor taking over Melaka, there was some sympathy in me for you and your people. But I'm a businesswoman, Mr. Prime Minister, and that's what I have to take care of first. I see a way, though, to overlap our business interests and manage a blow for democracy at the same time." Underhill paused. "It was those figures that assured me I could provide the services I'm willing to provide for five percent. Nothing less, though, I'll warn you about that. I'm trying to feed an agency, and you're trying to feed a nation. For five percent, it'll be worth my while."

"What if we find there are no more scrolls we can decipher?" Derembang asked. "They have been getting harder to understand and implement as we've searched through them. On some of them, our people understand the processes being discussed, but we still lack the means to carry them out."

"Then we'll both cut our losses," Underhill replied.

"Assuming I enter into this agreement with you, what are we going to do about Herbst and the claim FDI has on Melaka?"

Underhill checked her chron and found the time getting short quickly. "For starters, you surrender to me."

The Melakan prime minister looked at her as if to see whether she were joking. "I fail to understand how that—"

"Sir," Underhill said as politely as she could, "if I had more time, I'd gladly explain everything to you. But we're going to be at that drop site in just a few minutes. I don't know what that thing from the catacombs hopes to do by traveling to that tomb, but I'm certain it's not good. I have Herbst waiting on a satellite up-link"—she waved at the blank monitor built into the wall—"as well as other people who I feel will be able to help us. If you'll just follow my lead, I think we'll be able to resolve the FDI matter fairly soon."

"And if I don't?"

"Then I stop Tabor and the other man, collect my money from FDI, and bag the trip. You'll be left to your own devices."

"I thought you wanted to help Melaka."

"Yes, but you and your people are going to have to accept that help first. I can't do it in spite of you." Underhill leaned forward. "I've gotten the mercenaries out of Melaka City, and when I'm through Tabor will never be a threat again. Please trust me on this."

Derembang sighed. "This is so sudden. I wish I had more time to think."

"Paul," Charm said softly, leaning forward to put his hand on the man's shoulder, "take the chance. You've got nothing to lose. Even if we tried to yank you around, how much worse off could you be? You told me this morning that maybe I didn't really decide to become Mat Kilau for you on my own. If you believe there's something else at work here, don't you have to go with that belief?"

Underhill waited, realizing the enormous weight that had been put on the old man's shoulders in the past few minutes. He was putting his pride on the line, and whatever confidence had been restored in the last two days. And he had nothing better to show for it than a gamble.

"Surrender, you say?" he repeated, looking at Underhill.

The FREELancers administrator nodded.

"Let's do it." Derembang straightened in his seat. "Where do I face for the camera?"

"The monitor," Underhill answered. "There's a vid and audio feed in the upper right corner that will broadcast us back to the other people we're going to be talking to."

The prime minister turned in his chair. Charm took that moment to go stand in the corner of the office, out of the camera's view.

Underhill swung the small mike on the Burris forward. "Matrix, bring up Harris Hartley first. I'll signal you when to cut in the others."

"I'll be ready."

An instant later, the GLA congressman's image formed in a window in the upper left corner of the monitor. He looked perfectly attired, but not at all pleased to see Underhill.

"Ms. Underhill," Hartley began.

The FREELancers administrator cut him off. "I assume

you're apprised of the current situation, Congressman."

"Hell, yes," Hartley said. "What you people are doing over there in Melaka is making every major news agency and format there is."

Underhill smiled, and she knew the effect in this instance was like a cat baring its claws. She'd worked at it. "There's nothing like a high public-quotient, is there?"

The congressman hesitated, the tic in his left eye giving him away. Underhill had studied him thoroughly, paying a professional card player Hartley sometimes sat in with for the information about the tic. Hartley had a jones for hot cards and big pots, though luck seldom ran with him. In the card player's business, the tic—or whatever it was that gave away another player's bluff—was called a tell. "What do you want?"

"I'm offering you a seat at the table of a high stakes game. I'd like you to meet Mr. Paul Derembang, Prime Minister of Melaka."

"You'll excuse me," Hartley said, "but I thought he was ousted from office."

"Returned by an avalanche of support first thing this morning," Underhill said.

"So now that you've got Tabor out of the way," Hartley said, "your boy Derembang is in charge of things."

"I'm not anyone's boy," Derembang said coldly.

"No," Underhill agreed, "he's not."

A slight flush colored Hartley's face. "Pardon me. I seem to have stepped on some toes. What do you want from me?"

"A promise of your interest as chair of the international affairs council in the GLA in what happens in Melaka," Underhill said.

"And why should I do that?"

"I thought there might be some way I could convince you," Underhill said. She still had the vid and audio of the capture of the congressman's daughter.

"What do you want me to do?" Hartley asked in a less than enthusiastic voice.

"I'm about to bring Theodore Herbst on-line to chat with us," Underhill said. "As the real owner of Fiscal Development,

Incorporated, he holds the note on the country of Melaka. I know he's going to want to seize the country. In fact, he hired me to clear the way."

"The Melakan people entered into that deal willingly," Hartley pointed out. "If they try to nationalize the debt, Herbst may be well within his rights to send another mercenary crew into the country." He paused, staring straight at Underhill. "If he hasn't already."

"That's what I want to take care of. What I'd like you to know is that I've entered into a deal with Mr. Derembang this morning that will net me five percent of everything Melaka exports in its industries."

"Sounds like you've cut yourself another winning deal," Hartley said sarcastically. "I suppose I should offer congratulations, but somehow I don't feel so inclined."

Underhill didn't respond to the thinly veiled contempt. "What you fail to realize is that even with the protective concessions the FREELancers agency has within the GLA, we're still in the thirty-five-percent income tax bracket. That means out of every five percent my agency receives from this country, one-point-seven-five percent of Melaka's profit is going to find its way into the GLA coffers in the form of income tax. You know yourself how much this country has been making in the past few years thanks to Castlereigh and his people. How would you like to be the person who helped negotiate the deal? Personally, I think that would make you out to be an instant hero in the eyes of your constituency. Not only that, with the international chair up for grabs, you can make a lot of points by getting the chance to do some patriotic flag waving. And I can promise you'll be more accessible to the public than I will be." But not much, Underhill thought to herself, because it was a chance to get more exposure for FREELancers.

"What do I need to do?" Hartley asked.

"You'll find the script easy enough to follow. Hold on while I bring Herbst on-line."

"Coming now," Matrix said.

Another window opened up on the monitor. Herbst sat in a plush chair, wearing a dark suit and a happy smile. "I must say,

Miss Underhill, I'm not too terribly shocked that you found out my little secret. In fact, I guess I'm pretty damn pleased that it lasted this long. I've been watching the footage from Melaka City, and everything seems to be progressing nicely. Truthfully, I didn't expect results so quickly."

Underhill nodded. "There is a problem, Mr. Herbst."

Some of the smile died away. "What?"

"Do you know Mr. Paul Derembang sitting here beside me? He's the Melakan prime minister."

"I thought he'd been ousted."

"Dismissed," Underhill said. "But he was reinstated this morning." It was stretching the truth, but after everything Derembang and Charm had done with the rebel forces, there was no other way it was going to end.

"I don't see a problem. I'm happy for you, Derembang. It's good for a man to have a job."

"Mr. Derembang would like to officially surrender to you, Mr. Herbst," Underhill said.

"That's fine by me. Didn't know I was holding a gun to his head."

"FREELancers, in its present capacity," Underhill said, "can be construed as that."

"Is that a fact?" Herbst said. "So you're surrendering, Mr. Derembang?"

"Yes," Derembang said with quiet dignity.

"That's okay," Herbst said. "I can hire another prime minister to run the country till I get things squared away."

"It's not that simple." Underhill had more edge in her voice than she'd intended. She curbed the irritation she felt for the billionaire. A lot of people considered her coldhearted, but she could never think of depriving a whole nation of people of their homes. "There's the matter of reparations."

"Reparations?" Herbst repeated.

"It can be interpreted that, technically, we invaded Melaka on your behalf. And that is an act of war. At least, it could be according to the Geneva Convention, of which FREEAmerica is a part, at least it was the last time I looked." And the last time the FREELancers administrator had looked had been right before she started the chain of events that had brought her to Melaka.

"I'm not a country," Herbst protested.

"No, but as Mr. Derembang also pointed out, you have assets and holdings that are in excess of the holdings of several countries in existence. Also, you are moving against the nation of Melaka as a whole, not against a company or an individual."

"Whoa! Wait a minute! They entered into that agreement with Burleson as a group, put up the nation and its holdings as collateral. I didn't make them do that."

"No, and that's why they're not trying to nationalize the debt and simply declare it null and void."

"I'd sue them within an inch of their lives. I'd have attorneys stacked on attorneys in international court in a matter of minutes." Herbst glared at Underhill and Derembang.

"You can still go to court if you want, but Mr. Derembang has already surrendered on behalf of his country. He just wants reparations for his people so they can rebuild."

"What kind of figures are we talking about?" Herbst asked. "Just for yuks, because I have no intention of submitting to highway robbery like this."

"They're asking sixty-two billion point three for a quick settlement, and you can take possession of the country as soon as it's paid."

"That's insane! That's over forty times what I've got invested in that country!"

"I wasn't aware of how much you had invested," Underhill said, though she was. "I can't refuse his surrender. I've already talked with my attorneys and his and—"

"His attorneys?"

Underhill pretended to check a note on the tabletop. "Actually, I guess they'd be the country's. A firm called Paulson, Madden & Philips. They're out of Chicago and specialize in international law." She knew because she'd filed a retainer with the law office in Derembang's name less than an hour ago, along with the brief she'd written herself regarding the claim. "I found out I'm just as culpable as you, but the damage in my case will be limited to my fee for coming over here. If you want to work out the reparations, I'm going to ask that you pay them my fee as well. At least the balance of it. I'll pay the amount I've already collected from you up front."

"You're part of this, aren't you?" Herbst asked, growing cold and hard. His eyes focused on Underhill. "You set me up on this deal."

"I'll remind you," Underhill said in a voice like silk over steel, "you were part of this, then invited me in."

"Well to hell with both of you," Herbst said. "You can't make this stick."

"I've got a Great Lakes Authority congressman on the line who thinks Melaka has every chance," Underhill replied. "His name is Harris Hartley; he's on the council for international affairs in the GLA. He also told me that the GLA will back Mr. Derembang's and Melaka's claims as part of a treaty they are entering into."

"How the hell is the GLA going to enter into a diplomatic treaty with these people when I rightfully own the goddamn country?" Herbst demanded.

"The default on the loan entitles you to the land and its assets," Underhill said. "Not the populace. Even as a disenfranchised people, without a physical nation possessing geographical boundaries, they can enter into treaties. Just look back to the Palestinian Liberation Organization of the last century. There are precedents. Doesn't that pretty much sum it up, Congressman Hartley?"

"I could extemporize on the issues you've covered so succinctly, Ms. Underhill, but you've covered all the bases. Unless you'd like me to, Mr. Herbst?"

"No," the billionaire said in a heavy voice. "The bottom line is I'm getting screwed here. A blind man could see that."

Underhill settled back in her chair slightly, relaxing somewhat. She knew Herbst would spend time trying to find a way out of the box she'd built for him, but time was on her side. One thing Hartley was good at was beating the drum, and there were several government heads who owed her and the agency. She still had access to an arsenal she hadn't used up yet. And Serle Hastings was waiting on another line. She rested her elbows on the arms of her chair and touched her fingers together in front of her.

"You aren't exactly walking away from the table empty-handed. Mr. Derembang is willing to renegotiate the terms of the original loan. You'll get the face value of your loan agreement, plus a fifteen percent increase, and twenty-four million dollars up front as a signing bonus. So to speak."

"When would I get the twenty-four million?" Herbst asked.

"Keep the money you owe me," Underhill said, "minus the death benefits, medical, and expenses. I'll take it out of the advance I received, get a summary to you within the next few days, and send you the check for the remainder by the end of the week."

"Twenty-four million is three days' work," Herbst said. "You've only worked two."

"It may be Saturday there," Underhill said, "but it's Sunday here. You hired me on a Friday. That's three days."

"You bitch!" Herbst said, erupting from his chair. "Do you know who you're screwing with here? You'll be dead before I settle for a deal like this."

"Matrix," Underhill said, "drop the congressman and pick up Serle Hastings."

"Executing," the cybernetics expert replied.

On-screen, the window showing Hartley disappeared, replaced almost immediately by the suave good looks of the Hastings Family member. "Ms. Underhill," he said politely.

"You know Herbst," Underhill said.

"Ah, Teddy-Boy Herbst," Hastings said.

"What the hell are you doing in this?" Herbst asked, calming somewhat.

"I was about to explain to you," Underhill said, "that you hadn't met all my partners yet. Mr. Hastings has a vested interest in my well-being these days. I thought he might share that with you."

"Gangsters! Damn street punks! You're going to side with her against me?"

"I don't think you've quite entered into the spirit of things," Serle Hastings said, eyes narrowing. "You know us, Teddy-Boy, and you know our organization. We don't always play boardroom games the way you do. I just want to make one thing clear to you: While you may be the lion of Wall Street, and good at the art of a deal, none of that is going to save you against us. The people you usually piss off come at you through the market, through a series of credit and debit columns. Not us. If you value your life at all, value Underhill's just as much."

"Is that supposed to be some kind of threat?" Herbst exploded.

"That's a promise," Hastings replied. "Ms. Underhill, will there be anything else?"

"No," Underhill said. "That'll be all."

Hastings's window snapped shut and vanished.

Underhill locked eyes with the billionaire through the monitor. "You're still going to make good money out of this deal, Herbst. And I'll be here to make sure the checks come through on time."

"Enjoy your victory, Underhill," Herbst said. "You won't *ever* get the better of me again. And those checks had better come on time. Otherwise I'll be hiring someone else to come after those people *and* you." The window closed abruptly.

Underhill pushed herself out of her seat, no longer able to simply sit still. There was no other way events could have ended up. She'd planned too carefully and had studied her opponents too well. The Hastings Family had been a nice bonus to add to the pot.

"Reparations for a war," Derembang said in a soft voice. "The rights of a disenfranchised people. The Geneva Convention. A treaty with the GLA. A restructuring of the loan we needed to get this country up to speed." The prime minister chuckled. "And all this credit you've given to me. I'll admit, Ms. Underhill, I should perhaps give some thought to being around you more often. People would think I'm brilliant."

Underhill smiled and massaged the back of her neck, trying to work out the tension. "I'm just getting you back on your game, Mr. Prime Minister. I studied what you did with this country in the past, and I was impressed."

A hulking shadow formed at the door, then rapped on the glass.

Underhill waved Refit in, and he took a chair. "Are you going to be up for this?"

"No prob," the patchwork giant answered. "You ever seen me start something I couldn't finish?" He was still dressed in his jumpsuit, blood staining it in many places.

"Three minutes," the pilot called over the intercom in the room, "and you're going to be at your jump site."

"Matrix," Underhill said, grabbing her gear and getting ready. "Give Download another call."

"I did," the cybernetics expert said. "I've got him on the line now."

"Put him through." Underhill faced Derembang again and offered her hand. "Mr. Prime Minister, I look forward to working with you."

"As I look forward to working with you," Derembang said, getting to his feet.

"Please make yourself comfortable here. The plane will be returning to the airfield."

"How will you get back?"

"Agent Prime will send someone when the time is right." Underhill led the way out of the office. Charm and Refit fell in behind her. "Download, this is Underhill. Where the hell have you been?"

"That's a long story," Download said. "We'll get to it another time. I just got the damn Burris dried out enough to work." He paused, excitement in his voice. "It's all down here, Lee. The corpse of the Star Scarab. The ship that brought him here. The scrolls. The things the Guardians took from Saikalen."

"Saikalen?" Underhill seized a parachute from the rack on the wall near the back of the plane while Refit, Charm, and Cythe did the same. The tail section was open. Below was the green, verdant jungle.

"That's the name of the metal man," Download said. In a few terse sentences, he gave her an overview. He halted in midsentence. Then, "What the hell?"

There was a gunshot; then the frequency filled up with white noise from an open mike transmitting nothing.

Underhill touched the side of her helmet and pulled down

the faceplate, juicing it to accept the GPS feed Matrix had arranged of the jump site. It was just over one minute away.

Looking down from space, the view spread across the inside of her faceplate, the FREELancers administrator saw the two BirdSong heligyros lying abandoned on the mountainside below, partially hidden by the trees and brush. She tapped the controls, bringing the view in closer, targeting the second craft where men were still moving around. There must have been between fifteen and two dozen mercenaries.

Underhill recognized Tabor at once, as well as Margo Peele. She watched them, feeling the airplane vibrate around her and the wind come whipping through the open tail section.

Tabor was in the lead, his pistol drawn, moving as if he had a definite target in mind.

"Okay, jump team, you have your drop zone," the pilot called.

Underhill blanked the satellite feed but kept the faceshield down. She walked out onto the tail section, then launched herself into freefall. It was all coming down to a final roll of the dice, winner take all.

21

Outside Melaka City, Melaka
Indonesia
102.3 degrees E Longitude
2.4 degrees N Latitude

6:13 a.m. Local Mean
2313 Greenwich Mean
March 30, 2024
Sunday

Colonel Will Tabor held the Beretta/Douglas Nova in his fist and surveyed the opening in the side of the mountain thirty yards away. The edges of the entrance were squared off, proof the structure was man-made, not an accident of nature.

"Your thoughts, sergeant?" Tabor asked. He used the magnification properties of the bionic eye to enlarge his view of the opening and amplify the light inside. All he could see was worn rock. The passageway appeared to lead down into the mountain.

"Could be he was overconfident and left the door open," Wallsey said. "Could be he just forgot, in a hurry to get to whatever he's after."

"And it could be a trap."

"Yes, sir. Not one of his, though; he hasn't had time. But it could be whoever built it left some nasties behind."

Tabor agreed. Saikalen had been in a hurry. The pilot of the downed heligyro had been killed, his head nearly ripped from his shoulders. "Then we'll go smartly about it, sergeant. You and I will enter the cave. Leave fifteen men out here with the hostages so they can cover our retreat in case that becomes necessary. The rest we'll take with us."

Wallsey agreed, then turned from cover behind the tree line and yelled to the mercs he'd brought with him. He'd also taken four women prisoners from the government building's cleaning staff on Tabor's orders, with the intention of using them against Paul Derembang. If threatening to kill the maids would have brought the rebel leaders forward, Derembang and the others would have been killed instantly. Then the merc armor would have rolled over the rest of the rebels.

With the FREELancers on the scene, Tabor had decided to keep the women until he'd gotten Saikalen's head and made his escape out of the country. The merc colonel waved his point man into position.

Corporal Darrel LeBeau hailed from the Florida Everglades. He'd spent eight years in special forces, but went into the mercenary business after a car-bombing he'd taken part in had blown up in his face. His metability had saved his life.

Always quick, and possessing senses outside the ken of most people, the regeneration LeBeau's body had undergone after the explosion was fitting. His features were still vaguely human, but his eyes held a feline coldness to them, and his nose was almost flat against his face. A bandanna covered his sharply tapered ears most of the time. Now they were loose, pricked up and twitching as he held his M-16 and walked toward the cave entrance. He'd taken off his shirt, revealing the gray-blue fur that covered most of his upper body where he'd once had third-degree burns.

LeBeau was one of Tabor's elite ops and had been for years. The others were equally as bizarre and had powerful metabilities. Matches Murray was a dark-haired Bostonian who had a power over flames. He followed LeBeau into the cave.

Tabor went next, holstering the laser pistol to take the Ingram Stuttershot Wallsey handed him. He had a machete slung over his back. Once he found Saikalen, he intended to make short work of the man and get the hell out of the country. From the reports he'd heard over the radio, he knew Underhill and her team had already taken the city.

"This is the place," Margo Peele said, trailing close behind Tabor. She ran her flash beam over the writing on the walls.

"The tomb of the Star Scarab?" Tabor asked.

"Yes." The woman ran a hand over the writing. "I'd need days in here to decipher everything."

"You don't have them," Tabor said, continuing down the narrow passageway. He could smell water up ahead, and the dankness of damp earth.

Reluctantly, the archeologist left the wall and continued after him.

The steps continued down, winding around until the light from the entrance stopped penetrating the gloom. The only sound was the slight scuff of boot leather on stone.

Tabor used the light-amplifying mode on the bionic eye, reaching inside himself to stroke his metability and keep it on edge. Another door loomed before them.

LeBeau paused and scented the air in a reflex that was totally inhuman. He twisted his head, pricking his ears forward and back. His cat's eyes gleamed in the dark. He looked back at Tabor. "Getting close. I can smell him now. Dead things always smell stronger."

Tabor nodded.

After a final test of the air, LeBeau went forward. He had his M-16 canted up now, ready to drop it into target acquisition.

Saikalen didn't know they were coming. They'd tracked him and stayed out of sight. Tabor reached up and touched the worn handle of the machete, then smiled to himself. Things were going to work out after all.

Then he heard the gunshot coming from somewhere up ahead, and one of his men broke into the radio frequency to let him know the FREELancers Spectre gunship had just deployed eight parachutes.

"Don't wait until they get on the ground," Tabor ordered. "Kill them now." He went forward toward his prize, knowing there was someone in the cave besides Saikalen, but reflecting that it didn't matter. Whoever it was, they were dead too. Just as soon as he could reach them.

* * * * *

Outside Melaka City, Melaka	*6:16 a.m. Zulu Time*
Indonesia	*2316 Greenwich Mean*
102.3 degrees E Longitude	*March 30, 2024*
2.4 degrees N Latitude	*Sunday*

Assignment: Ferret's Run, cont.
Tactical Ops: Recovery, Unspecified Target
Status: Code Red

"Don't try for your weapon. I'm much better than my first attempt may indicate."

Download believed the thing standing before him. His ears still rang from the shot. A piece of flying stone from the wall had hit him in the ear with enough force to draw blood. Another piece had squashed the Burris transceiver against his Kevlar vest. He recognized the creature from the description and drawings he'd found in the book he'd gotten from the Star Scarab. "Okay if I put my hands up?" He silently damned himself. He'd gotten so deep into Jericho's examination of the object they'd found that he hadn't heard anyone behind him.

"Slowly," Saikalen agreed. The iron body was barely visible in the dim light put out by the dying torch stuck in a sconce on the wall. It looked as if the head were floating in the air, a pistol stuck out in front of it. "Who are you?"

"My name is Jefferson Scott."

"What are you doing here?"

"Looking around."

Saikalen regarded him with hooded eyes.

The room was thirty feet across, round like all the others Download had gone through. Shelves built into the wall were interrupted only by the two doorways on opposite sides of the room. Stone tablets and papyrus rolls filled the shelves. The FREELancers agent hadn't had time to go through any of them. His attention, and Jericho's, had been seized immediately by the object in the center of the room.

It was a pyramid of a shiny metal that Download knew he'd seen only one other time, during the briefing with Underhill.

For some reason, it stood on point, balanced carefully in a hammered iron ring that had been set into the stone floor. Fully ten feet tall, it almost scraped the ceiling in the room. Download had touched it once and had immediately yanked his hand back. The tingling that had filled his body hadn't been painful, but it had carried with it an alien discomfiture that he didn't want to repeat. It appeared to be formed of a piece, with no doors.

The plaque mounted on a stone pedestal in front of it announced that it was the craft of Soul of Knowledge.

"Did you find anything of interest?" Saikalen asked. He came forward, the iron skeletal body picking up dulled firepoints from the torchlight.

"Plenty." Download, conscious of the weight of the pistol at his belt, kept his hands raised.

"You can take him," Jericho said. "If you don't want to try it, let me."

Download squelched the archeologist's zealousness and shoved it back in his mind. The stone felt cold against his bare feet. He placed the door behind Saikalen, knowing he was directly in front of the room's other exit. He didn't know what lay on the other side, but it would give him running room to work from. Judging from the creature's appearance, killing it was going to take some time and considerable effort.

"Who sent you here?" Saikalen demanded. He stopped nearly ten feet away.

A quick side-step, and Download knew he could put the pyramid between them. But the pistol in the iron hand was unwavering. "Lee Won Underhill."

"The name means nothing to me."

Download shrugged. "Truth to tell, she found out about you not long ago."

"Such insolence," Saikalen said, with a cruel smile, "I find unbecoming."

"It's a character flaw," Download replied, keeping his gaze

on the creature's eyes. He wondered if he'd be able to tell when the thing was going to pull the trigger, hoping he was just fast enough to shave some inches off in the right way. His body was armored, but his face—where it wasn't covered by the helmet—was open. The pistol muzzle stayed focused on his mouth and neck where he was vulnerable.

"Fatal?"

"I've always hoped not. But one never knows with these things."

"You're an amusing little man," Saikalen said. "Why do you wear the mask?" He reached back and touched the upside-down pyramid, showing none of the discomfort Download had experienced.

"To disguise myself."

"Yet you gave me your name."

For the first time, Download noticed the silvery wires twisted among the iron skeleton's parts. Several of them were writhing in wicked animation. "I'm still new at this."

A section of the pyramid popped open, revealing an interior lit by a pale blue light. Other lights danced around inside.

"Must have a hell of a battery," Download said, still wearing the archeologist's curiosity.

"Do you know what this is?"

"The craft the Guardians found Soul of Knowledge in."

"Soul of Knowledge," Saikalen repeated. "You've read some of the old books."

"In this place, there aren't many other kinds."

"You know who I am?"

"You couldn't be anyone else," Download said, "looking like that." A symbol inside the pyramid caught his attention, but he couldn't quite make it out.

"What do you know about me?"

"They say you killed Soul of Knowledge."

"And you believe that?"

"Yes," Download answered without flinching at the harsh gaze.

Saikalen approached. "Take off your mask." His voice no longer sounded harsh. There was an undertone of curiosity.

"Why?"

"Because I wish to see your full resemblance."

Knowing it was on the line now, Download acted as if he were reaching for the helmet; then he dropped his hand, going for the pistol at his hip.

Barely seeming to move, the skeleton's free hand whipped out and caught Download's right forearm. The bones snapped with a ragged *crunch*.

Pain exploded, sucking the FREELancers agent's senses away. He dropped to his knees, trying to cradle his injured arm, but the metal man kept hold of it.

"I said, take off your mask," Saikalen said.

Download looked up at the creature through pain-blurred vision. "Go to hell!"

Towering over him, Saikalen released the broken arm long enough to take off the helmet, leaving the fiber-optic cables open for inspection. A sigh of surprise escaped the man as he studied them. The silvery wires within the skeleton frame moved excitedly. "What is this?"

"A hookup for cable television," Download gritted, trying to push away the pain.

"We're kindred spirits of a sort," Saikalen said, "though you're probably not aware of it. Do you know where Soul of Knowledge came from?"

On his knees, trying to find some leverage to work with, feeling the broken bones in his arms grate against each other, Download made no reply. He was hypnotized by the way the silvery wires inside the metal man were uncoiling from the iron skeleton and reaching for his face.

"He came from the future," Saikalen said. "That was his secret. He was a scientist, the first to attempt to use a time machine built by his government. Something went wrong. Instead of merely taking him back in time, his travel created a split-time continuum. His trip back had destroyed his future. That knowledge drove him insane."

Despite his pain, Download hung on every word, knowing it had to be true. Nothing else added up. All the knowledge in the scrolls had to have come from somewhere.

"He was a weak man," Saikalen said. "He decided not to use the time machine again for fear of destroying another future."

"He didn't come alone either, did he?" Download asked. "I saw his skull. Everybody seems to think it was bashed in. But in actuality, something came out of it."

Saikalen laughed, and the sound was dry and humorless. "You of all people would know." He fingered the fiber-optic cables leading to the FREELancers agent's head. "You, too, have a Traveler, though obviously a very ancient one. Are there many more like you in this time?"

"No," Download replied.

"Well then, you'll have to be enough." The silvery wires hovered in front of Download's face like silvery snakes.

"You're not Saikalen at all, are you?" Download asked. He had to work to keep from throwing up as the silvery wires caressed his skin.

"Once. Now we are what you see in front of you." The voice changed, became automated. "My original vessel was weak. Knowledge of what he'd done crumbled his mind, leaving me trapped inside his head as he withered and died over a period of years. They would have buried him had he died, and me with him. My programming wouldn't allow that."

"Who are you?" Download asked. One of the silvery wires rubbed across his lower lip slowly. He kept his teeth clenched together, fearing that it might suddenly try to stab down inside his throat.

"Once I was Traveler. Now I am more. We are Saikalen. I prolonged my original vessel's life as long as I was able, but I knew he could not last, and he would not use the knowledge I imparted to him to change that."

"But Saikalen did."

"I was very ambitious," the creature said in its original voice. "There was much I had to learn and do before I could take Traveler into myself."

"The scientist warned the others," Download said.

"Not about Traveler, but about the information he gave them. He was afraid that so many of the things that had been invented would never be discovered, and it would be his fault.

There was much he knew, and even everyday life from his time was a marvel to the Guardians. He spoke of everything, telling them to hide the secrets away and monitor society, especially science and mathematics. If a field of research started drying up and not progressing to the point where it should, he asked that they provide someone enough information to get them going again. It was what he felt he had to do to rebuild his future. At first, he figured that if he were successful, they would send someone back for him."

"Only that never happened."

"No. He assumed that even with everything he'd done after a few years, it wouldn't balance the time stream enough. He wanted to give up, but he couldn't. He was a teacher, a man of science. He knew so much, and there were so many willing to learn, willing to guard his secrets. So he kept trying, thinking maybe what he taught would one day be enough."

"It never was."

"Obviously not. That was thousands of years ago. Yet here we are."

Download looked into the glassy eyes of the slack face in front of him. "What is Traveler?" The silvery wires slid around both sides of his face.

"Originally, a military AI device. The scientist thought it was only a recording instrument, but it was much, much more."

"What was it programmed for?"

"Survival. Those parameters have expanded. There are still changes to be made in the time line. Traveler/Saikalen can make them. Before, there was not enough knowledge. Events in history had to be mapped out, a better perspective gotten. Time had to pass so that time could be measured. We believe we know where to make these changes now."

"And if you do that," Download said, "you'll destroy this time line."

"So be it. This time line would not have existed had the earlier mistake not been made. That's why no one could come back. You see, time still flows forward, even when someone goes back. The previous time line just dies, and the new one starts from that point."

Revulsion filled Download. He pushed the pain as far away from himself as he could.

"We shall create the new world," Saikalen said. "And it shall bow down to us." The wires slid lightly over Download's face. "And we choose you to come with us."

The FREELancers agent felt the wires skate along the fiber-optic cables, sliding inside his head like mercury. He tried to fight the invasion, but found he suddenly couldn't move.

"We shall take you," Saikalen said, "and mold you in our image."

Over the creature's shoulder, Download saw Tabor and members of his mercenary force spread out around Saikalen. The creature was unaware, and the FREELancers agent couldn't speak. He knew Tabor would have no hesitation about killing both of them if it came down to it.

* * * * *

Outside Melaka City, Melaka ***6:19 a.m. Zulu Time***
Indonesia ***2319 Greenwich Mean***
102.3 degrees E Longitude ***March 30, 2024***
2.4 degrees N Latitude ***Sunday***

Assignment: Falconstrike
Tactical Ops: Terminate With Extreme Prejudice
Status: Code Red

Refit fell from the sky. He'd pulled his chute open after Underhill, giving him the lead on reaching the ground. He handled the Ithaca shotgun in one big, scarred hand, pointing it at one of the mercenaries taking a position behind a tree trunk. He pulled the trigger.

On target, the double-ought buckshot load caught the man and slammed him to the ground. The assault rifle briefly raked the tree canopy with autofire.

"Spectre, this is Underhill."

"Go," the pilot called back.

"You can lay down your field of fire."

Refit didn't bother looking. He knew Underhill had already set up a strafing run to take out the mercenaries.

The gunship's 20mm cannon and chain guns lashed out against the jungle, shredding it. The on-board targeting systems were augmented by the satellite views provided by Matrix and her computers. The result was spectacular and devastating.

Most of the mercs left behind forgot all about being aggressive. Two of them were taken out by a 20mm cannon round that left a gaping crater in the ground where they'd been only moments before. The tricky part had been in figuring the hostages into the mix, but Matrix had spotted them.

Refit's chute caught in a tree as the last echoes of the cannon and chain guns died away. Swinging nine feet off the ground at the end of the shroud lines, the patchwork giant slid his combat knife free of the boot sheath and raked it across the strands. The nylon parted easily, and he dropped to the ground. The impact jarred the wounds he'd received from earlier, but he pushed the pain away.

"Refit," Cythe called over the Burris.

"Go," the big man said, racking the slide and pumping another round into the chamber.

"I've spotted the hostages."

"Where?" Refit watched as Underhill kicked free of her parachute and dove for concealment while hostile guns targeted her position. He covered her, firing into the trees and brush and scattering the gunners.

"One o'clock," Cythe said. "There are four of them, and two guys with them."

Refit peered through the jungle in the direction Cythe had indicated. He thumbed fresh cartridges into the shotgun by feel.

Sixty yards away, the four women, still in their cleaning uniforms, were pressed down onto the ground by one of the mercs while the other one stood guard. The mercenaries were yelling for their comrades, trying to ascertain who was still alive.

"You ready?" Refit asked.

"Yes." Cythe sounded totally together.

The patchwork giant spared her a quick glance, getting an impression of black-leather-clad feminine curves in action. She drew fire as she went into an attack, her skin hardened and bulletproof from her berserker state.

Refit whirled, holding the .12-gauge high in front of him as he cut through the brush and pumped his legs hard, trying to circle around behind the two mercenaries holding the hostages. He got a glimpse of Cythe using her blades, cutting a man to pieces in a heartbeat while the others tried to target her. She was a pale wraith, the sunglasses like onyx eyes as she swept the combat zone with her gaze. Bullets bounced from her skin, leaving dark bruises in their wake.

A heavy rifle shot cracked through the battle zone, and a mercenary suddenly pitched backward. Simon Drake had found his position and the range to lend backup to the play as sniper.

Leaping over a boulder, Refit suddenly found himself in the sights of another mercenary. He watched as the Stuttershot came around automatically, channeling in on the guy's reflexes and eyesight. If the guy got off a shot, it would warn the pair he was trying to sneak up on.

Refit landed in a coil, going down to deliberately throw off the computer-assisted aim of the Stuttershot, counting on it not to fire unless it had a confirmed lock. Coming out of the dip, he put all the muscle and weight of the meat he was wearing into a butt-stroke with the shotgun that caught the man in the face.

Bone crunched as blood exploded outward. The merc flew backward and landed in an unconscious heap almost ten feet away, still out of sight of the men holding the housekeeping staff.

Out in the clearing, Cythe was still in motion. She'd picked up a 40mm grenade launcher with a ten-round clip and was harrying other positions. The smile on her face wasn't anywhere near sane as the string of explosions went off as if they'd been timed by a metronome.

The women were crying and scared, holding each other as

they kept their faces pressed into the earth.

"Look out!" the man standing to the side yelled to his partner as he tried to bring his AK-47 around.

Refit fired the shotgun twice while he ran, hitting the man in the chest and face. The second man was too close to the women to risk firing. The FREELancers agent threw himself at the man, dropping the shotgun. Catching the merc in a full body block, Refit drove him to the ground yards away from the hostages.

The guy struggled to recover, coming up with a derringer that popped from a wrist holster. He shoved it into Refit's face and pulled the trigger.

Using every bit of reflex he had available, the FREELancers agent grabbed the man's gunhand, then slammed a forearm shiver into the merc's neck that crushed the windpipe. His opponent still managed to get off two rounds that slammed into Refit's arm. He held on to the man until death took him, the women screaming hysterically in the background.

Seeing the guy die at such close range, taking in the guy's last breaths himself, left Refit feeling cold and empty. Even though he was saving lives, he wasn't totally callous. He made himself move, stripping the derringer from the guy's hand and retreating back to recover the shotgun.

He scanned the jungle; for the moment they held the high ground. He tagged the Burris. "We started with fifteen. Cannon fire took two that I counted. I took out four more."

"Two," Underhill said.

Refit spotted the FREELancers administrator near the entrance in the mountainside. He headed in her direction, jogging quickly but taking advantage of the available cover.

"I got three of them," Cythe said. "You're one ahead of me, monster." Her laugh over the frequency was cold and brittle.

"Two," Charm said, "but I think I winged a third one."

Refit fell into position beside Underhill, breathing hard, only noticing then that he'd picked up a bullet in his chest. It had a familiar feel. The only thing he could figure was that the derringer held .22 rounds that penetrated the flesh, then bounced around and followed the bone, sliding under the meat.

He felt warmth on his chin. Wiping his mouth with the back of his hand, it came away stained red. Evidently the bullet had managed to puncture a lung before it was entirely spent.

He muttered a curse. The meat was taking a hell of a beating this time out. "Okay," he said. "There's two of them left; they've either had enough of us or they retreated to Tabor's side." He took ordnance tape from his hip kit and affixed a flash to the underside of the shotgun.

Underhill nodded, looking at the entrance into the mountain. She pulled a mini-Maglite from her chest pack and slid it into the grooves set up on her Government Model .45. She switched it on, then took up the pistol in a two-handed grip. "We go inside."

"I've got point," Refit said. "Give me some room before you come after." Charm and Cythe were running up behind them.

"I've got your back," Underhill said.

Without another word, Refit turned and plunged into the darkness. He switched on the flash and followed the bright white cone down the steps leading inside the mountain.

The rattle of autofire drew him on. In the black light of the flash, he saw his breath blow out ahead of him, small blood drops going with it. He felt a tightness in his right lung and knew the organ was in danger of filling up.

The tunnel twisted and turned, dropping away into a lightless abyss. Refit kept the derringer in his left hand and gripped the shotgun's barrel, keeping his finger on the trigger.

The autofire sounded again, coming from the right. Another turn, and he came out onto a larger entrance cut into the solid rock. Shining the flash mounted on the shotgun ahead of him, he got the impression of a round room filled with scientific apparatus and tables and benches, with another door on the opposite side. Light from another room framed the doorway, and flashes from gunfire broke up the symmetry.

Combat reflex had him already in motion when he saw and felt the shadow shift at his side. Then he was face-to-face with a two hundred pound cat-man.

* * * * *

Outside Melaka City, Melaka — *6:22 a.m. Zulu Time*
Indonesia — *2322 Greenwich Mean*
102.3 degrees E Longitude — *March 30, 2024*
2.4 degrees N Latitude — *Sunday*

Assignment: Ferret's Run, cont.
Tactical Ops: Recovery, Unspecified Target
Status: Code Red

Download felt the cold probes stabbing into his brain, following the leads from the Octopus. Garrett Jericho went offline. So did all the other voices he normally heard. For the first time in years, there was actually silence in his brain.

Then a *wrongness* settled into his mind, disrupting his thinking and his senses. He screamed inside his own head but wasn't able to hear himself. Half-blind, he saw Colonel Will Tabor approach from behind and slash with the machete.

One eye closed and the other only half-open, and unable to tell which, Download watched the events spin out in slow motion as if from a long way off. He was more terrified than he'd ever been in his life. Worse than the times when he'd woken up after alcohol or drug binges and not known where he was. Worse than when he'd been beaten by police in a town he hadn't even known he was in, for a reason or reasons he didn't know.

The keen edge of the machete bit through Saikalen's neck, flashing through to the other side and capturing the gleam of the flashlights in the mercenaries' hands.

The silvery wires coming from the truncated neck were also severed. Download felt them short-circuit in his head, burning like dry ice. Then he snapped back inside himself as the head dropped from the metal skeleton's shoulders.

Forcing the frozen breath out of his lungs, Download threw himself to his uninjured side, taking cover behind the pyramid craft. The jar sent blazing pain through his broken arm and almost caused him to black out.

"Get that head," Tabor told one of his men, pointing with the machete, "and somebody kill that son of a bitch."

Struggling to keep his eyes open and not scream with the pain, Download pushed off the pyramid ship and ran through the door on the opposite side of the room. Two rounds slammed into the back of his Kevlar vest, bruising his kidneys. He felt the slashed ends of the silvery wire plucking at his jumpsuit sleeve.

The tunnel outside the room ran for twenty paces, then took a sharp right. Download took up a position at the corner, unable to run any farther. There was no way he could leave the area until he was certain the threat Saikalen and Traveler posed was truly over.

He could see back into the room he'd just left, watching as one of the mercs reached down for the severed head. Before the man could grab a fistful of hair, a dozen strands of the silvery wire shot out of the head's tear ducts, nose, mouth, ears, and neck. They flicked like a live thing, wrapping with the speed of quicksilver around the man's wrist, amputating the hand in an eyeblink, then sending a twisted coil of wire driving through the merc's forehead, killing him instantly.

The sight chilled Download, thinking about the way the thing had crept into his mind. He reached into his jumpsuit and took out his chipset. He found Lou Henriksen's chip, took out the Jericho one, and slipped the stuntman's in. Fearful of what might happen, he juiced the Octopus.

The familiar blue lightning flashed, then Henriksen was with him.

In the other room, the silvery wires had curled around the head, elevating it on a dozen slender legs, then scuttling toward the pyramid craft like a gruesome spider.

Tabor drew his sidearm, and the pink pulse of the laser streaked across the room. It flared into a football-sized explosion against Saikalen's severed head.

When the dazzle evaporated, Download saw through the left-over spots that the laser blast had reduced Saikalen's head to charred ruin. The concussion from the exchange of energy had also blown the head against the wall, but the silvery wires hadn't stopped moving.

"What the hell is that?" Henriksen asked.

"Something we've got to stop," Download replied. "If it makes it into the pyramid, we're cooked." He reached up and gingerly pulled the silvery wires from his head. The sensation wasn't quite physical, but he could feel them sliding away from his brain. He dropped them to the floor, then managed to cross-draw the Glock 17 at his side.

"Busted wing?" Henriksen asked.

Download gazed at his forearm. The swelling and mismatch of bone were apparent even through the sleeve. "Yeah. You handle a pistol okay with your off-hand?"

"Like Johnny Ringo, buddy. But why don't you let those guys handle the spider-thing?"

"Because they want it," Download said, "and letting them have it is a close second to letting it get into the pyramid."

A mercenary came running into the corridor, an AK-47 in his hands.

Tapping into Henriksen's skills, Download stepped out of hiding with the Glock 17 at the ready. The merc tried to bring the Russian assault rifle up but was burned down with four rounds from the high-capacity automatic. He was in full motion before the corpse slapped in a loose jumble on the floor, taking advantage of the fact that Tabor and his people were concentrating on what remained of Saikalen/Traveler.

* * * * *

Outside Melaka City, Melaka — ***6:22 a.m. Zulu Time***
Indonesia — ***2322 Greenwich Mean***
102.3 degrees E Longitude — ***March 30, 2024***
2.4 degrees N Latitude — ***Sunday***

Assignment: Falconstrike, cont.
Tactical Ops: Terminate With Extreme Prejudice
Status: Code Red

The cat-man snarled when Refit blocked the reaching hand followed by the sharp panga. Eighteen inches of curved steel glided by the patchwork giant's throat.

"I don't think so, Tom," Refit gritted.

The cat-man flattened his ears against his head and stepped back, trying to gain more room.

Refit didn't give it to him. The gunfire in the other room

had intensified, and Underhill had passed him. Cythe was on the other side of the room, dealing with another one of the mercenaries.

Closing with the cat-man, Refit caught the panga in his left hand. He'd been trying to get the man's hand, but ended up clenching cold steel instead. He held on tight anyhow, feeling the bite of the blade as it sank to the bone, spilling hot blood around it.

Stepping in again, Refit head-butted the cat-man, listening to the sweet, sharp snap of breaking cartilage. The merc yowled in pain, sinking back. Refit yanked the panga out of the merc's grip and threw it away.

"C'mon, monster," Cythe taunted as she dodged a flaring fireball that went from the size of a grapefruit to a basketball as it streaked for her from the hands of the man she'd intercepted. The fireball smashed against the wall and spread a pool of flame that leaked down to the floor. "Time to put out the cat." Her blades whirled in her hands.

The cat-man sprang at Refit.

Never one for pretty fighting, the patchwork giant bulled ahead and met the deadly merc head-on. His greater weight and greater strength drove the cat-man back. Closing his slashed hand around the merc's throat, Refit held his opponent up against the wall and pounded him with his other hand.

The cat-man hissed and clawed and spat.

Refit kept hitting the man until the fight had gone out of him. He let the unconscious body drop and glanced over his shoulder at Cythe.

"Playtime's over, Sparky," the woman said. She whirled into him as he released another bubble of fire that barely missed her, then drove both of her blades into the man's stomach and stood up, lifting the dying man from his feet. A smile was on her lips and madness was in her eyes.

The flashlight on the shotgun let Refit know where he'd dropped it. He recovered it and went after Underhill.

* * * * *

Outside Melaka City, Melaka | *6:23 a.m. Zulu Time*
Indonesia | *2323 Greenwich Mean*
102.3 degrees E Longitude | *March 30, 2024*
2.4 degrees N Latitude | *Sunday*

Assignment: Falconstrike, cont.
Tactical Ops: Terminate With Extreme Prejudice
Status: Code Red

Lee Won Underhill went through the door to the room with the inverted pyramid with both hands on the Government Model .45. The mini-Maglite threw out a cone of white, hot light. She recognized Sergeant Pete Wallsey at the same time she saw Download burst back into the room, firing his pistol repeatedly at the burnt head of the metal man.

Wallsey turned at once, bringing his Stuttershot around.

Without hesitation, Underhill caressed the .45's trigger and put a round through Wallsey's head. The sergeant jerked from the impact, stumbling into the still-erect iron skeleton and taking both of them down in a confused, clanging tangle.

Download's bullets hit the disembodied head several times, knocking it off balance and back toward the wall. Chunks of boiled and blackened flesh were knocked off, revealing a platinum multifaceted object no bigger than a tennis ball. The silvery wires jutted from it, apparently fitting seamlessly into it.

Underhill noticed the blood streaming down the side of Download's face from the brain taps, then scanned the rest of the room. Only Tabor and one other man remained alive. She dropped the .45 into target acquisition over Tabor's face, then squeezed the trigger. The balanced piece of machined precision bounced gently in her hands, and she knew she was on target.

Only her bullet didn't hit Tabor. The round passed through the air where the mercenary colonel had been before he'd vanished.

He reappeared five feet to the left of where he'd been. His pistol blazed a laser pulse that missed her head by inches before sizzling into the wall behind her and leaving a black smudge mark with a two-foot radius.

Underhill went to ground at once, throwing herself on her stomach and shoving the pistol straight out in her fist. She fired two rounds, aiming for the center of the mercenary colonel's chest. Even if he was wearing bulletproof armor, the impacts might be distracting enough to keep him from using his power.

She hadn't known about the metability. Evidently Tabor had gone to great lengths to keep it secret. She'd known that others among his men had such powers, but in a mercenary band that was to be expected.

Tabor winked out of existence again, only a short time before the bullets reached him. "You can't touch me, bitch," he said in a voice that sounded far away, "but I can sure as hell touch you."

Underhill scrambled to her feet. Only the rush of air at her back warned her what was going on. Moving quickly, she hurled herself to one side.

A laser bolt cooked through the air where she'd been standing, splashing against the shiny exterior of the pyramid but leaving no damage.

The FREELancers administrator whirled, pushing off the wall with her free hand while bringing the .45 at full extension. She had him in her sights, but he just laughed at her.

She and Dr. Rhand had discussed the possibility of teleportation developing as a metability. Chained to the instinct for survival, it seemed natural. There'd been a number of cases reported over the years of people escaping the inescapable.

Refit came running through the door.

Stepping over, Tabor brought up a Beretta 9mm in his other hand, keeping the laser pistol covering Underhill.

"Refit!" the FREELancers administrator yelled. "Look out!"

The patchwork giant brought the shotgun up and fired.

The buckshot passed through Tabor without him vanishing. There was a minor rippling effect in the image; then it firmed, and the Beretta 9mm in Tabor's fist belched flame twice.

A hole opened up in Refit's forehead, like a dark, unblinking eye that wept blood. Staggered, he dropped the shotgun, then fell to his knees.

By the time he fell forward on his face, Underhill was firing. The .45 cycled dry, and the slide locked back empty.

"I can kill you at my leisure," Tabor said, "and there's nothing you can do about it." He kept both guns out.

Underhill didn't say anything. She slipped a fresh clip into the pistol and kept it trained on Tabor.

Cythe and Charm entered the room, stepping over and around Refit's body.

Underhill tagged the Burris. "Matrix."

"Go."

"I need a med-evac here now, and a full emergency med-team."

"It'll be there."

The pool of blood under Refit grew steadily larger.

"Keep your guns on him," Underhill instructed. "He's got a metability that allows him to slip into and out of the physical world. Spread out. The instant he fires at any one of us, he'll be vulnerable to the others."

Cythe and Charm spread out, forming the other legs of a triangle around Tabor. Behind them, Download succeeded in wrapping his bulletproof vest around the multifaceted object, then shoving it into the Kevlar-coated backpack he'd cut off Refit. The bag jerked as he zipped it closed.

"Good thinking," Tabor said sarcastically, "but it's not going to do you any good." He took a few steps to illustrate. "I can walk out of here, get to someplace where I can teleport myself farther."

"You can try," Underhill replied. "I've got a satellite blanketing this area. How far do you think you're going to get?" She returned the man's hard gaze.

"I could kill you all before I leave," the mercenary colonel said.

Underhill refused the bait, but quietly shoved a hand under her jacket, finding what she was looking for by touch.

Tabor looked at Download, who was holding the jumping bag by its straps. "Give me the bag, and I'll let you live."

"There's no way in hell," Download replied. He slipped the bag farther down his arm and pulled his Glock out of his waistband. The blood on the side of his face gleamed darkly, picking up light from all the flashes present in the room, as well as from inside the pyramid craft.

"I didn't come this far or fight this hard to give up now," Tabor said. He vanished.

Underhill felt the gust of wind at the back of her neck. Then Tabor roped an arm around her neck from the back and screwed the muzzle of the Beretta/Douglas laser into her temple.

"Don't shoot," Underhill ordered as the other three FREE-Lancers started trying to target Tabor. The mercenary colonel yanked her back to him, pressing his body against hers. She closed her fist around the object she'd taken from her gear and waited for the opportunity.

"Now," Tabor said, "I'll take that bloody bag."

Download slowly shook his head. He talked to Underhill. "I can't do it, Lee." The Glock in his hand didn't waver. "If you knew what it could do, you'd agree."

"Tell him," Tabor said, pressing on the pistol hard enough to make the front sight break skin.

Underhill kept her voice level. "He won't listen to me. He never has."

"Then one of the others will." Tabor moved the laser, shoving it at Download and firing. The bright ruby beam hit the agent in the shoulder and sent him spinning backward, the bag dropping to the ground.

Taking advantage of the heartbeat of time that she had, Underhill bucked against the mercenary colonel and shoved the object into a pocket of his combat harness. For Tabor to phase into insubstantiality, he had to take everything that was on him, stopping short of the ground and other items that he didn't directly manipulate. She was counting on that.

Twisting quickly and raising a heel to kick back against the man's shin, Underhill broke free and fell to the ground, unable to keep her balance. "Shoot him now!" she said. She was already counting down.

Cythe and Charm opened up at once, their bullets knocking chips from the stone walls as the deafening report of the shots being fired rolled over the room.

Tabor had already phased from the physical world, not even bothering to teleport. He pointed his pistol out before him, leveling it at Underhill. "I get the opening," he promised, "you're going to get dead real quick."

Underhill pushed herself to her feet. Just before time ran out, she said, "I don't think so," and showed him the grenade pin.

Tabor had only a split-second to realize what she'd done. His face went slack with surprise. Then the mercenary colonel became a swirl of mixed atoms as the grenade went off. Evidently, at the point of death, some of his powers waned and pushed a portion of the blast back into the physical world. A concussion of wind swept over Underhill, and a gallon or so of bloody, oozing glop dropped onto the stone floor.

Cythe was on her knees beside Refit, her face showing concern. The patchwork giant's eyes were open.

"Is he still alive?" Download asked weakly. He pushed himself up with his one good arm. The laser blast had spent itself primarily on his bodyarmor, but there were some flash burns under his chin and along the side of his face.

"I've got a pulse," Charm said, holding on to the big man's wrist. "Thready but steady." He peeled back an eyelid and shined his pocket flash into it. "Remains to be seen if anyone's home."

"The med-evac chopper is en route and will be there in three minutes," Matrix said.

Download picked up the bag and walked over to the pyramid vessel. Underhill followed him.

"Soul of Knowledge was from the future," Download said. "*A* future, anyhow." He encapsulated everything he'd been told by Saikalen/Traveler. "The Traveler unit itself was military, possibly covert ops of some sort. But I didn't figure on this." He pointed inside the pyramid.

There, in damning crimson and silver, was a FREELancers logo. But it was a bastardized one, slanted and twisted in a way that Underhill had never authorized. Still, the sight of it shook her, and she found she had to turn away.

Epilogue

Chicago, Illinois — *9:43 a.m. CST*
Great Lakes Authority (GLA) — *1543 Greenwich Mean*
87.7 degrees W Longitude — *April 5, 2024*
41.8 degrees N Latitude — *Saturday*
FREELancers Base

Even though the vid was hours old and rooms removed, watching it still gave Lee Won Underhill an unaccustomed sour twist in her stomach. She sat behind her desk in her office, an untouched cup of tea at her elbow. A yellow legal pad of neatly written notes was in front of her, but she wasn't nearly as far along on them as she'd planned to be.

On the screen of the monitor across the room, the Traveler unit crawled like a fat, metallic spider with a dozen silvery metal legs or more at any one time, exploring the confines of the special armored-glass cage Dr. Rhand had designed for it. Cameras were kept on it twenty-four hours a day. She knew it never stopped moving.

"Brooding doesn't become you, Lee."

She glanced over at her father. His holo had taken shape in the office without her knowledge. That, too, was unusual.

"Sorry, I was distracted."

George Anthony Underhill nodded. "You have been since you returned from Melaka three days ago."

"It's been a busy three days." Reluctantly, Underhill switched off the monitor. Watching the Traveler was hypnotic. If she observed it long enough, she couldn't help feeling she could puzzle out some of the hidden truths about it.

Rhand still ran tests on it, trying to figure out a way to tap all the data recorded inside. In Melaka, Derembang had the industrial arm of the country rolling again, and people were working on the scrolls they'd found in the main tombs.

"Contracts and legal are still hammering out all the points of the agreements between the Melakan government, FREE-Lancers, the GLA, and Herbst's people," her father said, "but there aren't going to be any stumbling blocks."

"No," Underhill agreed. "They should be tying those up by the end of next week."

"Yet you remain petulant."

She looked at her father, feeling the irritation she'd had itching around for days suddenly turn into a full-blown mad. She squelched a scathing retort with difficulty. "Not petulant. Disturbed."

"From where I stand," her father continued, "the only downsides are the people we lost over there and the fact that Refit hasn't come out of his coma."

"He will," Underhill said. But that was stated in the face of discouraging reports from the med center. They'd replaced his limbs, organs, and massive amounts of damaged tissue, and even reworked the area over his forehead. The bullet had lodged too deeply in his brain to be taken out and, though all the pressure had been removed, the coma showed all the signs of continuing.

"Lee, look. I know this Traveler unit bothers you and—"

She cut him off before he could say anything to further piss her off. "It should bother you, too. If everything Download says about it is true . . ."

"If what Download says he was *told* is true." Her father let out an angry snort. "Hell, we can't even confirm that."

"Yeah, well the FREELancers logo in the pyramid ship was an impressive touch."

Her father, walking across the room to lean on the desk, regarded her. Though he couldn't actually touch it in his current state, he certainly gave the illusion of leaning on it. "What are you afraid of?"

Underhill made herself speak. "All that technology coming out of Melaka from those scrolls is going to change a lot of things."

"That was coming out even without us."

"I need to know about the Traveler," the FREELancers administrator said. "I need to know where it came from, who was responsible. If it really was us."

"You may never know that," her father said. "There are things in life that you just never get to figure out. Lee," his voice grew softer, "that's what makes it life."

"I don't accept that. Not where this thing is concerned."

"Then you're going to have to shelve it for a time and get on with your other work." Her father straightened and folded his arms across his chest. "I know for a fact that there are eight files Matrix sent up to your office for review that you haven't even looked at."

"I've been busy."

"You've always made time to keep current before."

She glared at her father. "I'll get current again. Getting everybody together on this deal took a lot out of me. Give me some space."

"You're at your best when you're working, Lee." George Anthony Underhill looked down at her, a tenderness in his eyes.

"I know." She leaned forward and picked up the pencil beside the yellow legal pad. "Do you realize how far we stepped over the operating parameters of this agency?"

"You mean the way you arranged the treaty and shored up the Melakan government when it was ripe for a takeover from outside forces? Yes, I'm aware of that. You gave those people a new lease on life. And you're not that far out from the parameters of this agency. In the past, American agencies have toppled foreign governments."

"Still, I have to ask myself how far is too far. How far can I go without stepping over the line? How far can I go before *we* become *them*?"

Her father smiled at her. "From me to you, Daughter, and take this to your heart. As long as you care enough to ask yourself that question, you're not going to ever step over that line. All you have to worry about is forgetting that question. And if you ever do, I'll be here to remind you."

Underhill pushed up from her desk and walked to the window to look out at the world. The weekend had claimed Chicago, slowing down some of the daily grind. The sidewalks were filled with families today, and not just business and corporate workers filling out another week.

And somewhere, she knew—and would know exactly where if she checked the e-mail waiting for her—Download was meeting Robby Hatch, making good on his promise. He'd even decided against using the psychology chip Rhand had downloaded for him. Underhill didn't know exactly what had caused that decision, but she'd watched Scott make it during one of her peeks via closed-circuit in his room. She kept a constant monitor on him because he always walked so close to the edge. It remained to be seen who would benefit most from the outreach of emotion: Robby Hatch or Jefferson Scott.

Underhill had her hopes.

"You can't stop progress," her father said. "At best, you can direct it to some little degree. You and the agency saved the lives of a lot of people in Melaka. Concentrate on that."

"I will."

"Look at that billboard out there," her father said.

Summer Davison had arranged for it to be put up only a couple of days ago. It was a PR photograph of Captain Ares working with some of the Melakan children at a triage station shortly after the battle for the city. Smiling infectiously, he cradled a baby in his left arm, and a five-year old girl had her tiny palm placed trustingly in his right hand. A dozen children surrounded him, holding on to his cape and mugging for the camera. At the bottom of the picture were the words: NEED HELP?

CALL FREELANCERS.

"You see that caption at the bottom of that picture?" her father asked. "That's not a merchandising tool. That's the promise I made when I started this agency up as an independent arm. That's our promise to the world. What you need to remember is that it's also our promise to ourselves."

"I know," Underhill said. "It feels good to be reminded that it goes both ways."

And she knew it was true. She studied the smiles on the children's faces as they held on to the Captain's cape in the picture. There was hope in their eyes, and as long as FREELancers had that to offer, she knew the agency was everything she'd ever want it to be.

That was good enough.

For another exciting adventure, be sure to read

F.R.E.E.Lancers

When the *Rinji 8* space station is invaded by a deadly force, secret information is passed for safe-keeping into the hands of an unknowing twelve-year-old boy back on Earth. Aramis Tadashi will stop at nothing to find and gain the computer program that will allow him to control the world. Only the members of the F.R.E.E.Lancers, and their beautiful-but-deadly leader Lee Won Underhill, are capable of stopping him.

It's a race against tyranny as the agents of the F.R.E.E.Lancers pit their skills and metabilities against those of Tadashi and his hired killers. The life of one small boy—and the fate of the planet—hang in the balance.

(ISBN 0-7869-0113-6)